Run
Away

ALSO BY HARLAN COBEN

Harlan Coben

Run Away

CENTURY

1 3 5 7 9 10 8 6 4 2

Century
20 Vauxhall Bridge Road
London SW1V 2SA

Century is part of the Penguin Random House group of companies
whose addresses can be found at global.penguinrandomhouse.com.

Penguin
Random House
UK

First published in Great Britain by Century in 2019

www.penguin.co.uk

A CIP catalogue record for this book is available from
the British Library.

HB ISBN 9781780894256
TPB ISBN 9781780894263

Printed and bound in Great Britain by Clays Ltd, Elcograf S.p.A.

Penguin Random House is committed to a sustainable future for
our business, our readers and our planet. This book is made
from Forest Stewardship Council® certified paper.

To Lisa Erbach Vance,
agent extraordinaire,
with love and gratitude

Run
Away

CHAPTER
ONE

S imon sat on a bench in Central Park—in Strawberry Fields, to be more precise—and felt his heart shatter. No one could tell, of course, at least not at first, not until the punches started flying and two tourists from Finland of all places started screaming while nine other park visitors from a wide variety of countries caught the whole horrible incident on smartphone video.

But that was still an hour away.

There were no strawberries in Strawberry Fields and you'd be hard-pressed to call the two-and-a-half-acre landscaped grounds a field (singular), let alone more than one, but the name was derived not from anything literal but from the eponymous Beatles track. Strawberry Fields is a triangular-shaped area off Seventy-Second Street and Central Park West dedicated to the memory of John Lennon, who was shot and killed across the street. The centerpiece of this memorial is a round mosaic of inlaid stones with a simple caption in the middle:

IMAGINE

Simon stared straight ahead, blinking, devastated. Tourists streamed in and snapped photos with the famed mosaic—group shots, solo selfies, some kneeling on the inlaid stone, some lying down on it. Today, as it is most days, someone had decorated the word IMAGINE with fresh flowers, forming a peace sign of red rose petals that somehow didn't blow away. The visitors—maybe because the place was a memorial—were patient with one another, waiting their turn to step toward the mosaic for that special photo that they'd post on their Snapchat or Instagram or whatever social media platform they favored with some John Lennon quote, maybe a Beatles lyric or something from the song about all the people living life in peace.

Simon wore a suit and tie. He hadn't bothered to loosen the tie after leaving his office on Vesey Street in the World Financial Center. Across from him, also sitting near the famed mosaic, a—what do you call them now? vagrant? transient? drug-addled? mentally ill? panhandler? what?—played Beatles songs for tips. The "street musician"—a kinder name perhaps—strummed an out-of-tune guitar and sang in a cracked voice through yellowing teeth about how Penny Lane was in her ears and in her eyes.

Odd or at least funny memory: Simon used to walk past this mosaic all the time when his children were young. When Paige was maybe nine, Sam six, Anya three, they would head from their apartment only five blocks south of here, on Sixty-Seventh Street between Columbus and Central Park West, and stroll across Strawberry Fields on their way to the Alice in Wonderland statue by the model-boat pond on the east side of the park. Unlike pretty much every other statue in the world, here children were allowed to climb and crawl all over the eleven-foot-tall bronze figures of Alice and the Mad Hatter and the White Rabbit and a bunch of seemingly inappropriate giant mushrooms. Sam and Anya loved to do just that, swarming the figures, though Sam at some point always stuck two fingers up Alice's bronze nostrils and screamed at Simon, "Dad! Dad, look! I'm picking Alice's nose!" to which Sam's mother, Ingrid, would inevitably sigh and mutter, "Boys," under her breath.

But Paige, their firstborn, had been quieter, even then. She would sit on a bench with a coloring book and intact crayons— she didn't like it when a crayon broke or the wrapper came off— and always, in an ironic metaphor, stayed within the lines. As she grew older—fifteen, sixteen, seventeen—Paige would sit on a bench, just as Simon was doing now, and write stories and song lyrics in a notebook her father had bought her at the Papyrus on Columbus Avenue. But Paige wouldn't sit on just any bench. Something like four thousand Central Park benches had been "adopted" via big-money donations. Personalized plaques were installed on the benches, most of them simple memorials like the one Simon now sat on, which read:

IN MEMORY OF CARL AND CORKY

Others, the ones Paige gravitated toward, told little stories:

For C & B—who survived the Holocaust and began a life in this city...

To my sweetie Anne—I love you, I adore you, I cherish you. Will you marry me?...

This spot is where our love story began on April 12, 1942...

The bench that Paige most preferred, the one she'd sit on for hours on end with her latest notebook—and maybe this was an early indicator?—memorialized a mysterious tragedy:

The beautiful Meryl, age 19. You deserved so much better & died so young. I would've done anything to save you.

Paige would move from bench to bench, read the inscriptions, find one to use as a story prompt. Simon, in an attempt to bond, tried to do that too, but he didn't have his daughter's imagination. Still, he sat with his newspaper or fiddled with his phone, checking the markets or reading the business news, as Paige's pen moved in a flurry.

What happened to those old notebooks? Where were they now?

Simon had no idea.

"Penny Lane" mercifully came to an end, and the singer/panhandler segued right into "All You Need Is Love." A young couple sat on the bench next to Simon. The young man stage-whispered, "Can I give her money to shut up?" to which his female companion snickered, "It's like John Lennon is being killed all over again." A few people dropped some coins into the woman's guitar case, but most people stayed clear or backed away making a face that indicated they had gotten a whiff of something of which they wanted no part.

But Simon listened and listened hard, hoping to find some semblance of beauty in the melody, in the song, in the lyrics, in the performance. He barely noticed the tourists or their tour guides or the man who wore no shirt (but should) selling water bottles for a dollar or the skinny guy with the soul patch who told a joke for a dollar ("Special: 6 Jokes for $5!") or the old Asian woman burning incense to honor John Lennon in some vague way or the joggers, the dog walkers, the sunbathers.

But there was no beauty in the music. None.

Simon's eyes stayed locked on the panhandling girl mangling John Lennon's legacy. Her hair was matted clumps. Her cheekbones were sunken. The girl was rail-thin, raggedy, dirty, damaged, homeless, lost.

She was also Simon's daughter Paige.

Simon had not seen Paige in six months—not since she had done the inexcusable.

It had been the final break for Ingrid.

"You leave her be this time," Ingrid had told him after Paige ran out.

"Meaning?"

And then Ingrid, a wonderful mother, a caring pediatrician who dedicated her life to helping children in need, said, "I don't want her back in this house."

"You don't mean that."

"I do, Simon. God help me, I do."

For months, without Ingrid's knowledge, he'd searched for Paige. Sometimes his attempts were well organized, like when he hired the private investigator. More often, his efforts were hit-and-miss, haphazard, consisting of walking through dangerous drug-infested areas, flashing her photograph to the stoned and unsavory.

He'd come up with nothing.

Simon had wondered whether Paige, who had recently celebrated her birthday (how, Simon wondered—a party, a cake, drugs? Did she even know what day it was?), had left Manhattan and gone back to that college town where it all began to go wrong. On two separate weekends, when Ingrid was on shift at the hospital and thus wouldn't be able to ask too many questions, Simon had driven up and stayed at the Craftboro Inn next to the campus. He walked the quad, remembering how enthusiastically all five of them—Simon, Ingrid, incoming freshman Paige, Sam, and Anya—had arrived and helped settle Paige in, how he and Ingrid had been so cockeyed optimistic that this place would be a great fit, all this wide-open green space and woodland for the daughter who had grown up in Manhattan, and how, of course, that optimism withered and died.

Part of Simon—a part he could never give voice to or even admit existed—had wanted to give up on finding her. Life had, if not improved, certainly calmed since Paige ran away. Sam, who had graduated from Horace Mann in the spring, barely mentioned his older sister. His focus had been on friends and graduation and parties—and now his sole obsession was preparing for his first year at Amherst College. Anya, well, Simon didn't know how she felt about things. She wouldn't talk to him about Paige—or pretty much anything else. Her answers to his attempts at conversation consisted of one word, and rarely more than one syllable. She was "fine" or "good" or "'k."

Then Simon got a strange lead.

His upstairs neighbor Charlie Crowley, an ophthalmologist downtown, got into the elevator with Simon one morning three weeks back. After exchanging the usual neighborly pleasantries, Charlie, facing the elevator door as everyone does, watching the floors tick down, shyly and with true regret, told Simon that he "thought" he had seen Paige.

Simon, also staring up at the floor numbers, asked as nonchalantly as possible for details.

"I might have seen her, uh, in the park," Charlie said.

"What, you mean like walking through?"

"No, not exactly." They reached the ground floor. The doors slid open. Charlie took a deep breath. "Paige...was playing music in Strawberry Fields."

Charlie must have seen the bewildered look on Simon's face. "You know, um, like for tips."

Simon felt something inside him rip. "Tips? Like a—"

"I was going to give her money, but..."

Simon nodded that it was okay, to please continue.

"...but Paige was so out of it, she didn't know who I was. I worried it would just go..."

Charlie didn't have to finish the thought.

"I'm sorry, Simon. Truly."

That was it.

Simon debated telling Ingrid about the encounter, but he

didn't want to deal with that particular fallout. Instead he started hanging around Strawberry Fields in his spare time.

He never saw Paige.

He asked a few of the vagrants who played if they recognized her, showing a photo off his phone right before he tossed a couple of bills into their guitar case. A few said yes and would offer more details if Simon made that contribution to the cause somewhat more substantial. He did so and got nothing in return. The majority admitted that they didn't recognize her, but now, seeing Paige in the flesh, Simon understood why. There was almost no physical overlap between his once-lovely daughter and this strung-out bag of bones.

But as Simon sat in Strawberry Fields—usually in front of an almost-humorously ignored sign that read:

A QUIET ZONE—NO AMPLIFIED SOUND

OR MUSICAL INSTRUMENTS

—he had noticed something odd. The musicians, all of whom leaned heavily on the grungy-transient-squalid side, never played at the same time or over one another. The transitions between one street guitarist and the next were remarkably smooth. The players changed on the hour pretty much every hour in an orderly fashion.

Like there was a schedule.

It took Simon fifty dollars to meet a man named Dave, one of the seedier street musicians with a huge helmet of gray hair, facial hair that had rubber bands in it, and a braided ponytail stretching down the middle of his back. Dave, who looked to be either a badly weathered midfifties or an easier-lived seventy, explained how it all worked.

"So in the old days, a guy named Gary dos Santos...you know him?"

"The name is familiar," Simon said.

7

"Yeah, if you walked through here back in the day, boy, you'd remember him. Gary was the self-appointed Mayor of Strawberry Fields. Big guy. Spent, what, twenty years here keeping the peace. And by keeping the peace, I mean scaring the shit out of people. Dude was crazy, you know what I'm saying?"

Simon nodded.

"Then in, what, 2013, Gary dies. Leukemia. Only forty-nine. This place"—Dave gestured with his fingerless gloves—"goes crazy. Total anarchy without our fascist. You read Machiavelli? Like that. Musicians start getting in fights every day. Territory, you know what I'm saying?"

"I know what you're saying."

"They'd try to police themselves, but come on—half these guys can barely dress themselves. See, one asshole would play too long, then another asshole would start playing over him, they'd start screaming, cursing, even in front of the little kids. Sometimes they'd throw punches, and then the cops would come, you get the deal, right?"

Simon nodded that he did.

"It was hurting our image, not to mention our wallets. So we all came up with a solution."

"What's that?"

"A schedule. An hour-to-hour rotation from ten a.m. to seven p.m."

"For real?"

"Yes."

"And that works?"

"It ain't perfect, but it's pretty close."

Economic self-interest, thought Simon the financial analyst. One of life's constants. "How do you sign up for a slot?"

"Via text. We got five regular guys. They get the prime times. Then other people can fill in."

"And you run the schedule?"

"I do." Dave puffed out his chest in pride. "See, I know how to make it work, you know what I'm saying? Like I never put Hal's slot next to Jules because those two hate each other more than my exes hate me. I also try to make it what you might call diverse."

"Diverse?"

"Black guys, chicks, spics, fairies, even a couple of Orientals." He spread his hands. "We don't want everyone thinking all bums are white guys. It's a bad stereotype, you know what I'm saying?"

Simon knew what he was saying. He also knew that if he gave Dave two one-hundred-dollar bills torn in half and promised to give him the other halves when Dave told him when his daughter signed up again, he would probably make progress.

This morning, Dave had texted him:

11AM today. I never told you. I ain't a snitch.

Then:

But bring my money at 10AM. I got yoga at 11.

So here he was.

Simon sat across from Paige and wondered whether she would spot him and what to do if she bolted. He wasn't sure. He'd figured that his best bet was to let her finish up, pack up her measly tips and guitar, make his approach.

He checked his watch. 11:58 a.m. Paige's hour was coming to an end.

Simon had rehearsed all kinds of lines in his head. He had already called the Solemani clinic upstate and booked Paige a room. That was his plan: Say whatever; promise whatever; cajole, beg, use whatever means necessary to get her to go with him.

Another street musician in faded jeans and ripped flannel shirt entered from the east and sat next to Paige. His guitar case was a black plastic garbage bag. He tapped Paige's knee and pointed to an imaginary watch on his wrist. Paige nodded as she finished "I Am the Walrus" with an extended "goo goo g'joob," lifted both arms in the air, and shouted, "Thank you!" to a crowd that was not even paying attention, let alone applauding. She scooped the few pathetic wrinkled singles and coins up and then lowered her guitar into the case with surprising care. That simple move—lowering that guitar into the case—hit him hard. Simon had bought that Takamine G-Series guitar for her at the Sam Ash on West Forty-Eighth Street for her sixteenth birthday. He tried to conjure up the feelings to go with the memory—Paige's smile when she plucked it off the wall, the way she closed her eyes as she tested it out, how she threw her arms around his neck and shouted, "Thank you, thank you, thank you!" when he told her it was hers.

But the feelings, if they were real, wouldn't come.

The awful truth: Simon couldn't even see the little girl anymore.

Oh, for the past hour he had tried. He tried again now to look at her and conjure up the angelic child he'd taken to swim classes at the 92nd Street Y, the one who sat on a hammock out in the Hamptons while he read her two full Harry Potter books over the three-day Labor Day weekend, the little girl who insisted on wearing her Statue-of-Liberty Halloween costume complete with green face two weeks early, but—and maybe it was a defense mechanism—none of those images would come to him.

Paige stumbled to a stand.

Time to make his move.

Across the mosaic, Simon stood too. His heart pounded hard against his rib cage. He could feel a headache coming on, like giant hands were pressing in against both his temples. He looked left, then right.

For the boyfriend.

Simon couldn't say exactly how it all started spiraling, but he blamed the boyfriend for the scourge brought on his daughter and by extension his entire family. Yes, Simon had read all about how an addict has to take responsibility for her own actions, that it was the addict's fault and the addict's fault alone, all of that. And most addicts (and by extension, their families) had a tale to tell. Maybe their addiction started with pain medication after an operation. Maybe they traced it back to peer pressure or claimed that one-time experimentation had somehow evolved into something darker.

There was always an excuse.

But in Paige's case—call it a weakness of character or bad parenting or whatever—it all seemed somewhat simpler:

There was Paige before she met Aaron. And Paige now.

Aaron Corval was scum—obvious, unsubtle scum—and when you blended scum and purity, the purity was forever sullied. Simon never got the appeal. Aaron was thirty-two years old, eleven years older than his daughter. In a more innocent time, this age difference had concerned Simon. Ingrid had shrugged it off, but she was used to such things from her modeling days. Now, of course, the age difference was the least of it.

There was no sign of Aaron.

A small bird of hope took flight. Could Aaron finally be out of the picture? Could this malignancy, this cancer, this parasite who fed off his daughter have finished his feast and moved on to a more robust host?

That would be good, no question about it.

Paige started east toward the path across the park, her gait a zombie-like shuffle. Simon started to make his move.

What, he wondered, would he do if she refused to go with him? That was not only a possibility but a likelihood. Simon had tried to get her help in the past, and it had backfired. He couldn't force her. He knew that. He'd even had Robert Previdi, his brother-in-law, try to get a court order to have her committed. That hadn't worked either.

Simon came up behind her now. Her worn sundress hung too

loosely off her shoulders. There were brown spots—sun? illness? abuse?—on her back, blotting the once-flawless skin.

"Paige?"

She didn't turn around, didn't so much as hesitate, and for a brief second, Simon entertained the fantasy that he had been wrong, that Charlie Crowley had been wrong, that this disheveled bag of bones with the rancid smell and shot voice was not his firstborn, not his Paige, not the teenager who played Hodel in the Abernathy Academy production of *Fiddler on the Roof*, the one who smelled like peaches and youth and broke the audience's heart with her "Far from the Home I Love" solo. Simon had never made it through one of her five performances without welling up, nearly breaking into sobs when Paige's Hodel turned to Tevye and said, "Papa, God alone knows when we shall see each other again," to which her stage father replied, "Then we will leave it in His hands."

He cleared his throat and got closer. "Paige?"

She slowed but did not turn around. Simon reached out with a trembling hand. Her back still faced him. He rested his hand on the shoulder, feeling nothing but dried bone covered by papery skin, and tried one more time.

"Paige?"

She stopped.

"Paige, it's Daddy."

Daddy. When was the last time she had called him Daddy? He had been Dad to her, to all three kids, for as long as he could remember, and yet the word just came out. He could hear the crack in his voice, the plea.

She still wouldn't turn toward him.

"Please, Paige—"

And then she broke into a run.

The move caught him off guard. Paige had a three-step lead when he snapped into action. Simon had recently gotten himself into pretty good shape. There was a health club next to his office and with the stress of losing his daughter—that was how he looked at it, as losing her—he had become obsessed with various cardio-boxing classes during his lunch hour.

He leapt forward and caught up to her pretty quickly. He grabbed Paige by the reedlike upper arm—he could have circled the flimsy bicep with his index finger and thumb—and yanked her back. The yank may have been too hard, but the whole thing— the leaps, the reach—had just been an automatic reaction.

Paige had tried to flee. He had done what was necessary to stop her.

"Ow!" she cried. "Let go of me!"

There were loads of people around, and some, Simon was sure, had turned at the sound of her cry. He didn't care, except it added urgency to his mission. He would have to act fast now and get her out of here before some Good Samaritan stepped in to "rescue" Paige.

"Honey, it's Dad. Just come with me, okay?"

Her back was still to him. Simon spun her so that she would have to face him, but Paige covered her eyes with the crook of her arm, as though he were shining a bright light in her face.

"Paige? Paige, please look at me."

Her body stiffened and then, suddenly, relaxed. Paige lowered her arm from her face and slowly turned her gaze up at him. Hope again took flight. Yes, her eyes were sunken deep into the sockets and the color was yellow where it should have been white, but now, for the first time, Simon thought that maybe he saw a flicker—life—there too.

For the first time, he saw a hint of the little girl he once knew.

When Paige spoke, he could finally hear the echo of his daughter: "Dad?"

He nodded. He opened his mouth, closed it because he felt too overwhelmed, tried again. "I'm here to help you, Paige."

She started to cry. "I'm so sorry."

"It's okay," he said. "It's going to be okay."

He stretched out his arms to sweep his daughter into safety, when another voice sliced through the park like a reaper's scythe.

"What the fuck...?"

Simon felt his heart drop. He looked to his right.

Aaron.

Paige cringed away from Simon at the sound of Aaron's voice. Simon tried to hold on to her, but she pulled her arm loose, the guitar case banging against her leg.

"Paige..." Simon said.

But whatever clarity he had seen in her eyes just a few seconds ago shattered into a million pieces.

"Leave me alone!" she cried.

"Paige, please—"

Paige started to backpedal away. Simon reached out for her arm again, a desperate man falling off a cliff and trying to grasp a branch, but Paige let out a piercing scream.

That turned heads. Lots of them.

Simon did not back away.

"Please, just listen—"

And then Aaron stepped between them.

The two men, Simon and Aaron, were eye to eye. Paige cowered behind Aaron. Aaron looked strung-out, wearing a denim jacket over a grungy white T-shirt—the latest in heroin chic minus the chic. He had too many chains around his neck and had that stubble that aimed for fashionable but fell way short, and work boots, which were always an ironic look on someone who wouldn't recognize a day of honest work if it kicked him in the groin.

"It's okay, Paige," Aaron said with a smooth sneer, still meeting Simon's gaze. "You just keep moving, doll."

Simon shook his head. "No, don't..."

But Paige, almost using Aaron's back for leverage, pushed off and started to sprint down the path.

"Paige?" Simon shouted. "Wait! Please just—"

She was getting away. Simon veered right to go after her, but Aaron slid with him, blocking his path.

"Paige is an adult," Aaron said. "You got no right—"

Simon cocked his fist and punched Aaron straight in the face.

He could feel the nose give way under his knuckles, heard the break like a boot stomping on a bird's nest. Blood flowed.

Aaron went down.

That was when the two tourists from Finland screamed.

Simon didn't care. He could still see Paige up ahead. She turned to the left, off the pavement and into the trees.

"Paige, wait!"

He jumped to the side of the fallen man and started toward her, but from the ground, Aaron grabbed his leg. Simon tried to pull free, but now he could see other people—well-meaning but confused people—approaching, a lot of them, some taking videos with their damn phones.

They were all shouting and telling him not to move.

Simon kicked free, stumbled, got his legs back. He started down the path, down toward where Paige had veered off.

But it was too late now. The crowd was on him.

Someone tried to tackle him up high. Simon threw an elbow. He heard the tackler make an *oof* noise and his grip slackened. Someone else wrapped their arms around Simon's waist. Simon pulled him off like a belt, still running toward his daughter, still moving like a halfback with defenders all over him toward the goal line.

But eventually there were too many of them.

"My daughter!" he screamed. "Please...just stop her..."

No one could hear over the commotion, or perhaps they simply weren't listening to the violent madman who had to be taken down.

Another tourist jumped on him. Then another.

As Simon finally began to fall, he looked up and saw his daughter back on the path. He landed with a crash. Then, because he tried to get back up, blows rained down on him. A lot of them. When it was all over, he would have three broken ribs and two broken fingers. He would have a concussion and need twenty-three stitches in total.

He didn't feel a thing, except for the ripping in his heart.

Another body landed on him. He heard shouts and screams and then the police were on him too, flipping him onto his stomach, digging a knee into his spine, cuffing him. He looked up one more time and spotted Paige staring from behind a tree.

"Paige!"

But she didn't come to him. Instead she slipped away as, once again, Simon realized that he had failed her.

CHAPTER
TWO

F or a while, the cops just left Simon facedown on the asphalt with his hands cuffed behind his back. One cop— she was female and black with a nametag that read HAYES—bent down and calmly told him that he was under arrest and then read him his rights. Simon thrashed and screamed about his daughter, begging someone, anyone, to stop her. Hayes just kept reciting the Miranda rights.

When Hayes finished, she straightened up and turned away. Simon started screaming about his daughter again. No one would listen, possibly because he sounded unhinged, so he tried to calm himself and conjure up a more polite tone.

"Officer? Ma'am? Sir?"

They all ignored him and took statements from witnesses. Several of the tourists were showing the cops videos of the incident, which, Simon imagined, did not look good for him.

"My daughter," he said again. "I was trying to save my daughter. He kidnapped her."

The last part was a quasi lie, but he hoped for a reaction. He didn't get one.

Simon turned his head left and right, looking for Aaron. There was no sign of him.

"Where is he?" he shouted, again sounding unhinged.

Hayes finally looked down at him. "Who?"

"Aaron."

Nothing.

"The guy I punched. Where is he?"

No answer.

The adrenaline rush began to taper off, allowing a nauseating level of pain to flow through his body. Eventually—Simon had no idea how much time had passed—Hayes and a tall white cop with the nametag WHITE hoisted him up and drag-walked him to a squad car. When he was in the backseat, White took the driver's side, Hayes the passenger. Hayes, who had his wallet in her hand, turned around and said, "So what happened, Mr. Greene?"

"I was talking to my daughter. Her boyfriend got in the way. I tried to move around him..."

Simon stopped talking.

"And?" she prompted.

"Do you have her boyfriend in custody? Can you please help me find my daughter?"

"And?" Hayes repeated.

Simon was crazed, but he wasn't insane. "There was an altercation."

"An altercation."

"Yes."

"Walk us through it."

"Walk you through what?"

"The altercation."

"First tell me about my daughter," Simon tried. "Her name is Paige Greene. Her boyfriend, who I believe is holding her against her will, is named Aaron Corval. I was trying to rescue her."

"Mm-hmm," Hayes said. Then: "So you punched a homeless guy?"

"I punched—" Simon stopped himself. He knew better.

"You punched?" Hayes prompted.

Simon didn't reply.

"Right, that's what I thought," Hayes said. "You got blood all over you. Even on your nice tie. That a Hermès?"

It was, but Simon didn't say anything more. His shirt was still buttoned all the way to the throat, the tie ideally Windsored.

"Where is my daughter?"

"No idea," Hayes said.

"Then I don't have anything else to say until I speak to my attorney."

"Suit yourself."

Hayes turned back around and didn't say anything else. They drove Simon to the emergency room at Mount Sinai West on Fifty-Ninth Street near Tenth Avenue, where they took him immediately to X-ray. A doctor wearing a turban and looking too young to get into R-rated films put Simon's fingers into splints and stitched up his scalp lacerations. There was nothing to be done for the broken ribs, the doctor explained, other than "restrict activity for six weeks or so."

The rest was a surreal whirlwind: the drive to Central Booking at 100 Centre Street, the mug shots, the fingerprints, the holding cell. They gave him a phone call, just like in the movies. Simon was going to call Ingrid, but he decided to go with his brother-in-law Robert, a top Manhattan litigator.

"I'll get someone over there right away," Robert said.

"You can't handle it?"

"I'm not criminal."

"You really think I need a criminal—?"

"Yeah, I do. Plus Yvonne and I are at the shore house. It'll take me too long to get in. Just sit tight."

Half an hour later, a tiny woman in her early to mid seventies with curly blonde-to-gray hair and fire in her eyes introduced herself with a firm handshake.

"Hester Crimstein," she said to Simon. "Robert sent me."

"I'm Simon Greene."

"Yeah, I'm a top-notch litigator, so I pieced that together. Now repeat after me, Simon Greene: 'Not guilty.'"

"What?"

"Just repeat what I said."

"Not guilty."

"Beautiful, well done, brings tears to my eyes." Hester Crimstein leaned closer. "Those are the only words you're allowed to say—and the only time you'll say those words is when the judge asks for a plea. You got me?"

"Got you."

"Do we need to do a dry rehearsal?"

"No, I think I got it."

"Good boy."

When they headed into the courtroom and she said, "Hester Crimstein for the defense," a buzz started humming through the court. The judge raised his head and arched an eyebrow.

"Counselor Crimstein, this is quite the honor. What brings you to my humble courtroom?"

"I'm just here to stop a grave miscarriage of justice."

"I'm sure you are." The judge folded his hands and smiled. "It's nice to see you again, Hester."

"You don't mean that."

"You're right," the judge said. "I don't."

That seemed to please Hester. "You're looking good, Your Honor. The black robe works on you."

"What, this old thing?"

"Makes you look thin."

"It does, doesn't it?" The judge sat back. "What does the defendant plead?"

Hester gave Simon a look.

"Not guilty," he said.

Hester nodded her approval. The prosecutor asked for five thousand dollars in bail. Hester did not contest the amount.

20

Once they went through the legal rigmarole of paperwork and bureaucracy and were allowed to leave, Simon started for the front entrance, but Hester stopped him with a hand on his forearm.

"Not that way."

"Why not?"

"They'll be waiting."

"Who?"

Hester pressed the elevator button, checked the lights above the doors, said, "Follow me."

They hit the steps and took them down two levels. Hester started leading him toward the back of the building. She picked up her mobile.

"You at the Eggloo on Mulberry, Tim? Good. Five minutes."

"What's going on?" Simon asked.

"Odd."

"What?"

"You keep talking," Hester said, "when I specifically told you not to."

They headed down a dark corridor. Hester led the way. She turned right, then right again. Eventually they reached an employee entrance. People were flashing badges to come in, but Hester just barreled through to exit.

"You can't do that," a guard said.

"Arrest us."

He didn't. A moment later, they were outside. They crossed Baxter Street and cut through the green of Columbus Park, passed three volleyball courts, and ended up on Mulberry Street.

"You like ice cream?" Hester asked.

Simon did not reply. He pointed to his closed mouth.

Hester sighed. "You have permission to speak."

"Yes."

"Eggloo has a Campfire S'mores ice cream sandwich that's to die for. I told my driver to grab two for the ride."

The black Mercedes was waiting in front. The driver had the ice cream sandwiches. He handed one to Hester.

"Thanks, Tim. Simon?"

Simon shook off the other. Hester shrugged. "All yours, Tim." She took a bite of her own and slipped into the backseat. Simon got in next to her.

"My daughter—" Simon began.

"The police never found her."

"How about Aaron Corval?"

"Who?"

"The guy I punched."

"Whoa whoa, don't even joke around about that. You mean the guy you allegedly punched."

"Whatever."

"Not whatever. Not even in private."

"Okay, I got it. Do you know where—?"

"He took off too."

"What do you mean, 'took off'?"

"What part of 'took off' is confusing? He ran away before the police could learn anything about him. Which is good for you. No victim, no crime." She took another bite and wiped the corner of her lips. "The case will go away soon enough, but... Look, I got a friend. Her name is Mariquita Blumberg. She's a ballbuster—not a sweetheart like me. But she's the best handler in the city. We need Mariquita to get on your PR campaign right away."

The driver started up the car. The Mercedes started north and turned right on Bayard Street.

"PR campaign? Why would I need—?"

"I'll tell you in a minute, but we don't need the distraction right now. First tell me what happened. Everything. From beginning to end."

He told her. Hester turned her small frame to face him. She was one of those people who raise the phrase "undivided attention" into an art form. She had been all energy and movement. Now that energy was more like a laser beam pointed directly at him. She was focusing on every word with an empathy so strong he could reach out and touch it.

"Oh man, I'm sorry," Hester said when he finished. "That truly sucks."

"So you understand."

"I do."

"I need to find Paige. Or Aaron."

"I'll check again with the detectives, but like I said, my understanding is that they both ran off."

Another dead end. Simon's body started to ache. Whatever defense mechanisms, whatever chemical responses that delay if not block pain were eroding in a hurry. Pain didn't so much ebb through as flow in.

"So why do I need a PR campaign?" Simon asked.

Hester took out her mobile phone and started futzing with it. "Hate these things. So much information and so many uses, but mostly it ruins your life. You have kids, right? Well obviously. How many hours a day do they spend..." Her voice drifted off. "Not the time for that particular lecture. Here."

Hester handed him the phone.

Simon saw that she'd brought up a YouTube video with 289,000 views. When he saw the screenshot preview and read the title, his heart sank:

PROSPERITY PUNCHES POVERTY

WALL STREET WALLOPS VAGABOND

DADDY WARBUCKS DESTROYS THE DESTITUTE

BROKER BOPS BUM

"HAVE" HITS "HAVE-NOT"

He flicked his eyes up at Hester, who gave him a sympathetic shrug. She reached across and tapped Play with her index finger. The video had been taken by someone with the screen name ZorraStiletto and posted two hours ago. ZorraStiletto had been panning up from three women—perhaps his wife and two daughters?—when some kind of disturbance drew his attention. The lens jerked to the right, regaining focus with ideal timing on a pompous-looking Simon—why the hell hadn't he changed out of that suit or at least loosened the goddamn tie?—just as Paige was pulling away from him and Aaron was stepping up to get between them. It looked, of course, as though a rich, privileged, suited man was accosting (and maybe worse) a much younger woman, who was then being rescued by a stand-up homeless guy.

As the scared, fragile young woman cowered behind her savior's back, the man in the suit started screaming. The young woman ran away. The man in the suit tried to push past the homeless guy and follow her. Simon knew, of course, what he was about to see. Still he watched, wide-eyed and hopeful, as though there were a chance that the suited man would not be moronic enough to actually pull back his fist and punch the brave homeless man straight in the face.

But that was exactly what happened.

There was blood as the kindly homeless Samaritan crumpled to the pavement. The uncaring rich man in the suit tried to step over the rubble of him, but the homeless Samaritan grabbed his leg. When an Asian man in a baseball cap—another Good Samaritan no doubt—entered the fray, the suited man elbowed him in the nose too.

Simon closed his eyes. "Oh man."

"Yep."

When Simon opened his eyes again, he ignored the cardinal rule for all articles and videos: <u>Never ever read the comment section.</u>

"Rich guys think they can get away with stuff like this."
"He was going to rape that girl! Lucky that hero stepped in."
"Daddy Warbucks should get life in jail. Period."
"I bet Richie Rich gets off. If he was black, he would have been shot."
"That guy who saved that girl is so brave. If the mayor lets this rich guy buy his way to freedom."

"Good news," Hester said. "You do have a few fans." She took the phone, scrolled down, pointed.

"The homeless guy is probably on food stamps. Congrats to the suit for cleaning up the trash."
"Maybe if that smelly meth bum gets a job instead of living off the dole, he won't get decked."

The profile avatars of his "supporters" had either eagles or American flags on them.

"Terrific," Simon said. "The psychos are on my side."

"Hey, don't knock it. A few might be on the jury. Not that this is going to a jury. Or even a trial. Do me a favor."

"What?"

"Hit the Refresh button," Hester said.

He wasn't sure what she meant, so Hester reached across and hit the arrow at the top. The video reloaded. Hester pointed to the viewer count. It had jumped up from 289,000 views to 453,000 in the last, what, two minutes.

"Congrats," Hester said. "You're a viral hit."

CHAPTER

THREE

S imon stared out the window, letting the familiar green of
the park blur in front of him. When the driver made the left
off Central Park West onto West Sixty-Seventh Street, he
heard Hester mutter, "Uh-oh."

Simon turned.

News vans were double-parked in front of his apartment.
Maybe two dozen protestors stayed behind blue wooden-horse
barriers that read:

POLICE LINE—DO NOT CROSS

NYPD

"Where's your wife?" Hester asked.

Ingrid. He had completely forgotten about her or what her reaction might be to all this. He also realized that he had no idea
what time it was. He checked his watch. Five thirty p.m.

"At work."

"She's a pediatrician, right?"

He nodded. "At New York–Presbyterian at 168th Street."

"What time does she finish?"

26

"Seven tonight."

"Does she drive home?"

"She takes the subway."

"Call her. Tim will pick her up. Where are your kids?"

"I don't know."

"Call them too. The firm has an apartment in midtown. You guys can stay there tonight."

"We can get a hotel."

Hester shook her head. "They'll find you if you do that. The apartment will be better, and it's not like we don't charge."

He said nothing.

"This too shall pass, Simon, if we don't feed the fire. By tomorrow, the next day at the latest, the loonies will all be on to the newest outrage. America has zero attention span."

He called Ingrid, but with her working in the emergency room today, it went directly into her voicemail. Simon left her a detailed message. Then he called Sam, who already knew all about it.

Sam said, "The video's gotten over a million hits." His son seemed both startled and impressed. "I can't believe you punched out Aaron." Then he repeated: "You."

"I was just trying to get to your sister."

"Everyone's making it sound like you're some rich bully."

"That's not what happened."

"Yeah I know."

Silence.

"So this driver, Tim, will pick you up—"

"That's okay. I'll stay with the Bernsteins."

"Are you sure?"

"Yeah."

"Is it okay with his parents?"

"Larry says it's no problem. I'll just go home with him after practice."

"Okay, if you think that's best."

"It'll just be easier."

"Yeah, that makes sense. If you change your mind though..."

"Right, got it." Then Sam said in a softer voice, "I saw...I mean, Paige in that video...she looked..."

More silence.

"Yeah," Simon said. "I know."

Simon tried his daughter Anya three times. No answer. Eventually he saw on his caller ID that she was calling him back. When he picked up though, it wasn't Anya on the line.

"Hey, Simon, it's Suzy Fiske."

Suzy lived two floors below him. Her daughter Delia had been going to the same schools as Anya since Montessori when they were both three.

"Is Anya okay?" he asked.

"Oh, she's fine. I mean, don't worry or anything. She's just really upset. You know, about that video."

"She saw it?"

"Yeah, you know Alyssa Edwards? She was showing it to all the parents during pickup, but the kids had already...you know how it is. All the tongues wagging."

He did. "Can you put Anya on, please?"

"I don't think that's a great idea, Simon."

I don't give a shit what you think, he thought, but wisely enough—learning curve after his earlier outburst?—he didn't actually say it out loud.

This wasn't Suzy's fault anyway.

He cleared his throat and aimed for his calmest tone. "Could you please ask Anya to get on the line?"

"I can try, Simon, sure." She must have turned away from the phone, because the sound was tinnier now, more distant. "Anya, your dad would like...Anya?" Now all sound was muffled. Simon waited. "She just keeps shaking her head. Look, Simon, she can stay here as long as you need. Maybe you can try later or maybe Ingrid could give her a call when she's off work."

There was indeed no reason to push it. "Thanks, Suzy."

"I'm really sorry."

"I appreciate your help."

He pressed the End button. Hester sat next to him, staring straight ahead with her ice cream sandwich.

"I bet you wish you'd taken that ice cream when I offered it to you, right?" Then: "Tim?"

"Yes, Hester."

"You have that extra ice cream in the cooler?"

"I do." He handed it back to her.

Hester took out the sandwich and showed it to him.

Simon said, "You're billing me for the ice creams, aren't you?"

"Not me personally."

"Your firm."

She shrugged. "Why do you think I push them so hard?"

Hester handed the ice cream to Simon. He took a bite, and for a few seconds, it was better.

But that didn't last.

———————

The law firm apartment was located in a business tower one floor beneath Hester's office, and it showed. The carpets were beige. The furniture was beige. The walls were beige. The accent pillows...beige.

"Great interior decorating, don't you think?" Hester said.

"Nice if you like beige."

"The politically correct term is 'earth tones.'"

"Earth tones," Simon said. "Like dirt."

Hester liked that one. "I call it Early American Generic." Her phone buzzed. She checked the text. "Your wife is on her way. I'll bring her up when she arrives."

"Thanks."

Hester left. Simon risked a peek at his phone. There were too many messages and missed phone calls. He skipped them all except the ones from Yvonne, both his partner at PPG Wealth Management and Ingrid's sister. He owed her some sort of explanation. So he texted her:

I'm fine. Long story.

He saw the little dots showing Yvonne was writing him back:

Anything we can do?

No. Might need coverage tomorrow.

No worries.

I'll fill you in when I can.

Yvonne's reply was some comforting emojis telling him that there was no pressure and that all would be good.

He scanned the rest of the messages.

None from Ingrid.

For a few minutes he paced around the apartment's beige carpeting, checked out the view from the windows, sat on a beige couch, stood again, paced some more. He let the calls go to voicemail until he saw one coming in from Anya's school. When he picked it up and said, "Hello," the caller sounded startled.

"Oh," a voice Simon recognized as belonging to Ali Karim, the principal of Abernathy Academy, said, "I didn't expect you to answer."

"Is everything okay?"

"Anya is fine. This isn't about her."

"Okay," Simon said. Ali Karim was one of those academics who wore it—tweed blazers with patches on the elbow, unruly muttonchops on the sides of his face, balding with too-long shocks of hair on the crown. "So what can I do for you, Ali?"

"This is a bit sensitive."

"Uh-huh."

"It's about the parent charity ball next month."

Simon waited.

"As you know, the committee is meeting tomorrow night."

"I do know," Simon said. "Ingrid and I are co-chairs."

"Yes. About that."

Simon felt his hand tighten around the phone. The principal wanted him to say something, to dive into the silence. Simon didn't.

"Some of the parents feel it's best you not come tomorrow."

"Which parents?"

"I'd rather not say."

"Why not?"

"Simon, don't make this harder than it has to be. They're upset about that video."

"Aww," Simon said.

"Pardon?"

"Is that all, Ali?"

"Uh, not exactly."

Again he waited for Simon to fill the silence. Again Simon didn't.

"As you know, the charity ball this year is raising funds for the Coalition for the Homeless. In light of the recent developments, we feel that perhaps you and Ingrid shouldn't continue as co-chairs."

"What recent developments?"

"Come on, Simon."

"He wasn't homeless. He's a drug dealer."

"I don't know about that—"

"I know you don't," Simon said. "It's why I'm telling you."

"—but perception is often more important than reality."

"Perception is often more important than reality," Simon repeated. "Is this what you guys teach the kids?"

"This is about doing what's best for the charity."

"The ends justify the means, eh?"

"That's not what I'm saying."

"You're some educator, Ali."

"It seems that I offended you."

"More like disappointed, but okay, whatever. Just send us back our check."

"Pardon?"

"You didn't make us co-chairs because of our winning personalities. You made us co-chairs because we donated big bucks for this ball." He and Ingrid hadn't given the money strictly because they believed in the cause. Things like this—it's rarely about the cause. The cause is a by-product. It's about sucking up to the school and the administrators like Ali Karim. If you want to support a cause, support a cause. Do you really need the enticement of some boring rubber-salmon dinner where you honor a random rich guy to get you to do the right thing? "Now that we're no longer co-chairs..."

Ali's tone was incredulous. "You want to take back your charitable donation?"

"Yep. I'd prefer if you overnighted the check, but if you want to send it two-day express, that's fine too. Have a great day, Ali."

He hung up and chucked the phone onto the beige pillow on the beige couch. He'd still give the money to the charity—he couldn't be that much of a hypocrite—just not via the school's fundraising ball.

When he turned around, Ingrid and Hester were standing there, watching him.

"Personal rather than legal advice," Hester said. "Don't engage with anyone for a few hours, okay? People have a tendency to be rash and stupid under this kind of pressure. Not you, of course. But better safe than sorry."

Simon stared at Ingrid. His wife was tall with a regal bearing, high cheekbones, short blonde-to-gray hair that always looked in vogue. In college she'd worked a bit as a model, her look described as "aloof, icy Scandinavian," and that was still probably the first impression, which made her career choice—pediatrician who needed to be warm with kids—a bit of an anomaly. But kids never saw her that way. They loved and trusted Ingrid immediately. It was uncanny, the way they saw straight to her heart.

Hester said, "I'll leave you guys to it."

She didn't specify what "it" referred to, but maybe she didn't have to. When they were alone, Ingrid shrugged a what-the-hell and Simon launched into the story.

"You knew where Paige was?" Ingrid asked.

"I told you. Charlie Crowley said something to me."

"And you followed up. Then this other homeless guy, this Dave—"

"I don't know if he's homeless. I just know he runs the schedule for the musicians."

"You really want to play semantics with me now, Simon?"

He did not.

"So this Dave . . . he told you that Paige was going to be there?"

"He thought she might, yes."

"And you didn't tell me?"

"I didn't know for sure. Why upset you if it was nothing?"

She shook her head.

"What?"

"You never lie to me, Simon. It's not what you do."

That was true. He never lied to his wife and in a sense, he wasn't lying here, not really, but he was shading the truth and that was bad enough.

"I'm sorry," Simon said.

"You didn't tell me because you were afraid I'd stop it."

"In part," Simon said.

"Why else?"

"Because I'd have to tell you the rest of it. How I'd been searching for her."

"Even though we both agreed that we wouldn't?"

Technically he hadn't agreed. Ingrid had more or less laid down the law, and Simon hadn't objected, but now didn't seem the time for that kind of nuance.

"I couldn't...I couldn't just let her go."

"And what, you think I could?"

Simon said nothing.

"You think you hurt more than I do?"

"No, of course not."

"Bullshit. You think I was being cold."

He almost said, "No, of course not" again, but didn't part of him think that?

"What was your plan, Simon? Rehab again?"

"Why not?"

Ingrid closed her eyes. "How many times did we try...?"

"One time too few. That's all. One time too few."

"You're not helping. Paige has to come to it on her own. Don't you see that? I didn't 'let her go'"—Ingrid spat out the words—"because I don't love her anymore. I let her go because she's gone—and we can't bring her back. Do you hear me? We can't. Only she can."

Simon collapsed on the couch. Ingrid sat next to him. After some time passed, she rested her head on his shoulder.

"I tried," Simon said.

"I know."

"And I messed up."

Ingrid pulled him close. "It'll be okay."

He nodded, even as he knew it wouldn't be, not ever.

CHAPTER
FOUR

Three Months Later

S imon sat across from Michelle Brady in his spacious office on the thirty-eighth floor directly across the street from where the World Trade Center towers once stood. He had seen the towers fall on that terrible day, but he never talked about it. He never watched the documentaries or news updates or anniversary specials. He simply couldn't go there. In the distance on the right, over the water, you could see the Statue of Liberty. It was small out there, dwarfed by all the closer high-rises, bobbing alone in the water, but she looked fierce, torch held high, a green beacon, and while Simon had long grown tired of most of his view—no matter how spectacular, if you see the same thing every day, it grows stale—the Statue of Liberty never failed to offer comfort.

"I'm so grateful," Michelle said with tears in her eyes. "You've been a good friend to us."

He wasn't a friend, not really. He was a financial advisor, she his client. But her words touched him. It was what he wanted to hear, how he himself viewed his job. Then again, wasn't he a friend?

Twenty-five years ago, after the birth of Rick and Michelle

Brady's first child, Elizabeth, Simon had set up a custodial account so that Rick and Michelle could start saving for college.

Twenty-three years ago, he helped them structure a mortgage for their first home.

Twenty-one years ago, he got their paperwork and affairs in order so they could adopt their daughter Mei from China.

Twenty years ago, he helped Rick finance a loan to start a specialized printing service that now served clients in all fifty states.

Eighteen years ago, he helped Michelle set up her first art studio.

Over the years, Simon and Rick talked about business expansion, about direct depositing paychecks, about whether he should become a C corporation and what retirement plan would work best, about whether he should lease or buy a car, about whether private school for the girls would be affordable or too big a stretch. They talked investments, portfolio balance, the company payroll, the cost of family vacations, the purchase of the fishing cabin by the lake, a kitchen upgrade. They had set up 529 accounts and reviewed estate plans.

Two years ago, Simon helped Rick and Michelle figure out the best way to pay for Elizabeth's wedding. Simon had gone, of course. There had been lots of tears on that day as Rick and Michelle watched their daughter walk down the aisle.

A month ago, Simon ended up sitting in the same pew in the same church for Rick's funeral.

Now Simon was helping Michelle, still reeling from losing her life partner, learn how to do the little things she'd left Rick to handle: balancing a checkbook, setting up charge cards, seeing what funds had been in joint and separate accounts, not to mention how to keep the business running or decide whether they should sell.

"I'm just glad we can help," Simon said.

"Rick prepared for this," she said.

"I know."

"Like he knew. I mean, he always seemed so healthy. Were there any health issues he hid from me? Did he know, do you think?"

Simon shook his head. "I don't, no."

Rick had died of a massive coronary at age fifty-eight. Simon wasn't an attorney or an insurance agent, but part of being someone's wealth manager was to prepare the estate for any eventuality. So he talked about it with Rick. Like most men his age, Rick had been reluctant to consider his own mortality.

Simon felt his phone buzz in his pocket. He had a strict rule: No interruption when he was with clients. Not to get highfalutin about it, but when people came to this office, they wanted to talk about something that meant a great deal to them.

Their money.

Pooh-pooh it all you want. Money may not buy happiness, but...well, nonsense. Money, pretty much more than anything else you might be able to control, can conjure up and elevate that elusive ideal we call happiness. Money eases stress. It provides better education, better food, better doctors—some level of peace of mind. Money provides comfort and freedom. Money buys you experiences and conveniences and most of all, money buys you time, which, Simon had realized, was right up there with family and health.

If you believe that—and even if you don't—the person you chose to handle your finances was up there with choosing a doctor or clergyman, though Simon would argue that your wealth manager was even more involved in your daily life. You work hard. You save. You plan. There are virtually no major life decisions you make that are not in some way based on your finances.

It was an awesome responsibility when you stepped back and thought about it.

Michelle Brady deserved his undivided attention and complete focus. So the pocket phone-buzz was a signal that something important was up.

He surreptitiously glanced at the computer screen. A message had come up from their new assistant, Khalil:

A POLICE DETECTIVE IS HERE TO SEE YOU.

He stared at the message long enough for Michelle to notice.

"You okay?" she asked him.

"I'm fine. It's just..."

"What?"

"Something has come up."

"Oh," Michelle said. "I can come back..."

"Can you just give me two seconds to...?" He gestured toward the phone on his desk.

"Of course."

Simon lifted the receiver and pressed Khalil's line.

"A Detective Isaac Fagbenle is on his way up to see you."

"He's in the elevator?"

"Yes."

"Keep him in reception until I tell you."

"Okay."

"Do you have the credit card forms filled out for Mrs. Brady?"

"Yes."

"Have her sign them. Make sure that the cards are issued for her and Mei today. Show her how the automatic payment works."

"Okay."

"I should be done by then."

Simon hung up the phone and met Michelle's eyes. "I'm really sorry about this interruption."

"It's okay," she said.

No, it wasn't. "You know about my, uh, situation from a few months ago."

She nodded. Everyone knew. Simon had joined the pantheon of viral video villains, up there with the dentist who shot the lion and the racist lawyer who had the meltdown. The morning shows

38

on ABC, NBC, and CBS had fun with it the day after it happened. Cable news too. As Hester Crimstein had predicted, the notoriety had burned hot for a few days and then quickly faded to near oblivion by the end of the month. The video shot up to 8 million views in the first week. Now, nearly three months later, it was still short of 8.5.

"What about it?" Michelle asked.

Maybe he shouldn't go there. Then again, maybe he should. "There's a cop on his way up here to see me."

If you expect your clients to open up to you, well, was it fair to make that street one-way? It wasn't Michelle's business, of course, except that now he was interrupting her time and so he felt that she had the right to know.

"Rick said the charges were dropped."

"They were."

Hester had been right about that too. There had been no sign of either Aaron or Paige in the past three months, and with no victim, there was no case. It also didn't hurt that Simon was fairly well-off or that Aaron Corval, as Simon soon found out to his chagrin if not surprise, had a fairly extensive criminal record. Hester and the Manhattan DA made a deal quietly, away from prying eyes.

Nothing signed, of course. No obvious quid pro quo. Nothing so gauche. But then again, hey, there was a fundraising campaign coming up, if Simon and Ingrid wanted to attend. Principal Karim had also reached out two weeks after the incident. He didn't directly apologize but wanted to offer his support, reminding Simon that the Greenes were part of the Abernathy Academy "family." Simon was all set to tell him to go fuck off, but Ingrid reminded him that Anya would be entering her freshman year there soon, so Simon smiled and returned the check and life continued.

The one small caveat was that the Manhattan DA wanted to wait a bit before he officially dropped the charges. The incident needed to be far enough in the rearview mirror that the media wouldn't notice or ask too many questions about privilege or any of that.

"Do you know why the police are here?" Michelle asked.

"No," Simon said.

"You should probably call your attorney."

"I was thinking the same thing."

Michelle stood. "I'll leave you to it."

"I'm really sorry about this."

"Don't worry about it."

Simon's office had a glass wall looking into the cubicles. Khalil walked by and Simon nodded for him to come in.

"Khalil will get you all set with the paperwork. When I'm done with this police officer—"

"Just take care of yourself," Michelle said.

She shook his hand across the desk. Khalil escorted her out. Simon took a deep breath. He picked up his phone and called Hester Crimstein's office. She got on the line fast.

"Articulate," Hester said.

"What?"

"That's how a friend answers his phone. Never mind. What's up?"

"A cop is here to see me."

"Where is here?"

"My office."

"Seriously?"

"No, Hester, this is a prank call."

"Great, wiseasses are my favorite clients."

"What should I do?"

"Asswipes," she said.

"What?"

"Those asswipes know I'm your attorney of record. They shouldn't approach you without calling me first."

"So what should I do?"

"I'm on my way. Don't talk to him. Or her. I don't want to be sexist here."

"It's a him," Simon said. "I thought the DA was dropping the charges—that they had no case."

"They are and they don't. Sit tight. Don't say a word."

There was a gentle knock on his door and Yvonne Previdi, Ingrid's sister, slid into his office. Yvonne, his sister-in-law, was not quite as beautiful as her model sister—or was that bias on Simon's part?—but way more fashion obsessed, Yvonne wore a pink pencil skirt with a sleeveless cream blouse and four-inch, gold-studded Valentino pumps.

He had met Yvonne before Ingrid, when they were both in the training program at Merrill Lynch. They had become instant best friends. That was twenty-six years ago. Not long after they finished their training, Yvonne's father, Bart Previdi, had taken two partners into his growing firm—his daughter Yvonne and his not-yet son-in-law Simon Greene.

PPG Wealth Management—the P's in the name stood for the two Previdis, the G stood for Greene.

Motto: We Are Honest But Not Very Creative With Names.

"What's up with the hot cop?" Yvonne asked.

Yvonne and Robert had four kids and lived in the tony New Jersey suburb of Short Hills. For a short time, Simon and Ingrid had tried the suburbs too, moving from their Upper West Side apartment to a center-hall colonial, right after Sam's birth. They did that because that's what you did. You lived in the city until you had a kid or two and then you moved out to a nice house with a picket fence and a backyard and good schools and lots of sports facilities. But Simon and Ingrid didn't like the suburbs. They missed the obvious: the stimulation, the bustle, the noise. You take a walk at night in the big city, there is always something to see. You take a walk at night in the suburbs...well, nada. All that open space—the hushed backyards, the endless soccer fields, the town pools, the Little League diamonds—it was all so damned claustrophobic. The quiet wore on them. So did the commute. After giving it two full years, they moved back into Manhattan.

A mistake in hindsight?

You could make yourself crazy with such questions, but Simon didn't think so. If anything, the bored kids out in the burbs were acting out and experimenting more than their urban counterparts. And Paige had been fine in high school. It was when she left the big city for the rural-ensconced college—that was when the problems had started.

Or maybe that was rationalization. Who knows?

"You saw him?" Simon asked.

Yvonne nodded. "He just got to reception. Why's he here?"

"I don't know."

"Did you call Hester?"

"Yes. She's on her way."

"He's awfully good-looking."

"Who?"

"The cop. Looks like he should be on the cover of *GQ*."

Simon nodded. "That's good to know, thanks."

"You want me to take care of Michelle?"

"Khalil's on it, but you might want to look in on her."

"Done."

Yvonne turned to leave, when a tall black man in a sleek gray suit suddenly blocked the doorway. "Mr. Greene?"

Yep, right out of *GQ*. The suit didn't look so much tailored as birthed, created, cultivated for him and only him. It fit like some tight superhero suit or like a second skin. His build was rock solid. He sported a shaved head and perfectly trimmed facial hair and big hands and everything about the guy just screamed "cooler than you."

Yvonne gave Simon a nod that said, "See what I mean?"

"I'm Detective Isaac Fagbenle with the NYPD."

"You shouldn't be back here," Simon said.

He flashed a smile so dazzling Yvonne took a step back. "Yeah, well, I'm not here for a standard appointment, am I?" He took out his badge. "I'd like to ask you some questions."

Yvonne didn't move.

"Hi," he said to her.

Yvonne waved, speechless for once. Simon frowned.

"I'm waiting for my attorney," Simon said.

"Would that be Hester Crimstein?"

"Yes."

Isaac Fagbenle crossed the office and sat uninvited in the chair across from Simon. "She's good."

"Uh-huh."

"One of the best, I hear."

"Right. And she wouldn't want us talking."

Fagbenle arched an eyebrow and crossed his legs. "No?"

"No."

"So you're refusing to talk to me?"

"I'm not refusing. I'm waiting for my attorney to be present."

"So you won't talk to me right now?"

"Like I said, I'm going to wait for my attorney."

"And you just expect me to do the same?"

There was an edge in his voice now. Simon glanced at Yvonne. She'd heard it too.

"Is that what you're telling me, Simon? Is that your final answer?"

"I don't know what you mean."

"I mean, are you really refusing to talk to me?"

"Only until my attorney gets here."

Isaac Fagbenle sighed, uncrossed his legs, and stood back up. "Buh-bye then."

"You can wait in reception."

"Yeah, that's not going to happen."

"She should be here soon."

"Simon? Can I call you Simon, by the way?"

"Sure."

43

"You take good care of your clients, don't you?"

Simon glanced at Yvonne, then back to Fagbenle. "We try."

"I mean, you don't waste their money, right?"

"Right."

"I'm the same. My clients, you see, are the taxpayers of the city of New York. I'm not going to waste their hard-earned dollars reading financial magazines in your reception area. Do you understand?"

Simon said nothing.

"When you and your attorney are available, you can come down to the precinct."

Fagbenle smoothed down his suit, reached into his jacket pocket, and plucked out a business card. He handed it to Simon.

"Bye now."

Simon read the card and saw something that surprised him. "The Bronx?"

"Pardon?"

"It says your precinct is in the Bronx."

"That's right. Sometimes you guys in Manhattan forget that New York has five boroughs. There's the Bronx and Queens and—"

"But the assault"—Simon stopped, hit rewind—"the *alleged* assault took place in Central Park. That's in Manhattan."

"Yep, true," Isaac Fagbenle said, flashing the dazzling smile again, "but the murder? That took place in the Bronx."

CHAPTER
FIVE

W hen Elena Ramirez limped into the ridiculously
large office with the ridiculously over-the-top views,
she braced for the inevitable. He did not disappoint.

"Wait, you're Ramirez?"

Elena was used to this skepticism bordering on shock.

"In the flesh," she said. "Perhaps too much of it, am I right?"

The client—Sebastian Thorpe III—openly studied her in a
way he would never openly study a man. That wasn't being sensitive or any of that. It was just a fact. Everything about Thorpe
stank of money—the "III" at the end of his name, the hand-
tailored pinstripe suit, the rich-boy-ruddy complexion, the
slicked-back '80s Wall Street hair, the sterling bull-and-bear cuff
links.

Thorpe kept staring at her with what someone must have told
him was his most withering glare.

Elena said, "Want to check my teeth?"

She opened her mouth wide.

"What? No, of course not."

"You sure? I can twirl for you too." She did so. "Plenty of ass
back here, am I right?"

"Stop that."

Thorpe's office was decorated in Early American Douchebag, all white and chrome with a zebra-skin throw rug in the center as if he might strike a pose on it. All show, no work. He stood across a white desk large enough to garage a Honda Odyssey. There was one framed picture on the desk—a too-posed wedding photograph of a tuxedoed Thorpe wearing a shit-eating grin standing next to a firm-bodied young blonde who probably called herself a "fitness model" on Instagram.

"It's just that you come highly recommended," Thorpe said by way of explanation.

Meaning he expected something a little more polished for his money—not a pudgy Mexican barely five feet tall in mom jeans and practical shoes. These guys heard her name and expected Penélope Cruz or a lithe flamenco dancer, not someone who resembled the summer help at their beach house.

"Gerald says you're the best," Thorpe said again.

"And the most expensive, so let's get to it, shall we? I understand your son is missing."

Thorpe lifted his cell phone, tapped it, spun the screen toward her. "This is Henry. My son. He's twenty-four years old."

In the image, Henry was dressed in a blue polo shirt and gave an awkward smile, the kind where you're trying but it's just not in you. Elena leaned forward for a closer look, but the desk separating them was too wide. They both stepped toward a window that offered a killer view of the Chicago River and downtown.

"Nice-looking boy," she said.

Thorpe nodded.

"How long has he been missing?" she asked.

"Three days."

"Did you report it to the police?"

"Yes."

"And?"

46

"They were very polite. They listened to me, took a report, put Henry in the system or whatever, just because of who I am..."

He was white, Elena thought, and with money. That was all. That was enough.

"I hear a 'but,'" Elena said.

"But he sent me a text. Henry, I mean."

"When?"

"The day he went missing."

"What did the text say?"

Thorpe tapped the phone some more and handed it to her. Elena took it and read:

Heading west with a few friends. Back in two weeks.

"You showed this to the police?" Elena asked.

"I did."

"And they still took a report?"

"Yes."

Elena tried to imagine the reaction if a black or Hispanic father came in to report a missing son and showed them a text like that. He'd get laughed out of the station.

"There's another"—Thorpe looked into the air—"'but,' if you will."

"What's that?"

"Henry has been in some trouble with the law."

"What kind of trouble?"

"Minor stuff. Drugs. Possession."

"Has he served time?"

"No. Nothing really serious. He got community service. A sealed juvie record. You understand."

Oh yeah, Elena understood.

"Has Henry disappeared before?"

Thorpe stared at the window.

"Mr. Thorpe?"

"He's run off before, if that's what you mean."

"More than once?"

"Yes. But this is different."

"Uh-huh," Elena said. "How do you and your son get along?"

A sad smile came to his face. "Used to be great. Best buds."

"And now?"

He tapped his chin with his forefinger. "Our relationship has been strained of late."

"Why's that?"

"Henry doesn't like Abby."

"Abby?"

"My new wife."

Elena picked up the framed photograph from the desk. "This Abby?"

"Yes. I know what you're thinking."

Elena nodded. "That she's smoking hot?"

He grabbed away the frame. "I don't need you to judge me."

"I'm not judging you. I'm judging Abby. And my judgment is, she's smoking hot."

Thorpe frowned. "Maybe calling you was a mistake."

"Maybe, but let's recap what we know about your son Henry. One, he sent you a text saying he was traveling west for two weeks with some friends. Two, he's disappeared before—several times, in fact. Three, he's been arrested on a variety of drugs charges. Anything I'm missing? Oh, right, four, he resents your relationship with Abby, who looks to be about his age."

"Abby is almost five years older than Henry," Thorpe snapped.

Elena said nothing.

Thorpe deflated right in front of her eyes. "I didn't think you'd take me seriously." He waved his hand dismissively. "You can go."

"Yeah, not so fast."

"Pardon me?"

"You're clearly worried about him," Elena said. "My question is: Why?"

"It doesn't matter. I'm not hiring you."

"Humor me," she said.

"The text message."

"What about it?"

"It's going to sound stupid."

"Go for it."

"The other times Henry disappeared…well, he just disap-peared."

Elena nodded. "He didn't send you a text message telling you he was disappearing. He would just run off."

"Yes."

"So texting you like this—it's out of character."

Thorpe nodded slowly.

"And that's it?"

"Yes."

"Not very convincing evidence," Elena said.

"The police didn't think so either."

Thorpe rubbed his face with his hands. She could see now that he hadn't slept in a while, that the cheeks were ruddy but the skin around the eyes was too pale, drained of color.

"Thank you for your time, Miss Ramirez. I won't be needing your services."

"Oh, I think you will," Elena said.

"Excuse me?"

"I took the liberty of doing a little digging before I arrived."

That got his attention. "What do you mean?"

"You said your son sent you a text from his phone."

"Right."

"Before I got here, I pinged that phone."

Thorpe narrowed his eyes. "What does that mean exactly? 'Pinged'?"

"Truth? I don't have a clue. But the shorthand is, I got a genius tech guy named Lou. Lou can send a ping—whatever that is—to a cell phone, and the cell phone pings back its location."

"So you could see where Henry is?"

"Theoretically, yes."

"And you did that already?"

"Lou did, yes."

"So where is he?"

"That's just it," Elena said. "There was no answer to our ping."

Thorpe blinked several times. "I don't understand. Are you saying his phone should have...pinged you back?"

"I am," Elena said.

"Maybe Henry just turned his phone off."

"No."

"No?"

"That's a common misconception. Turning your phone off does not turn off the GPS."

"So anyone can track you anytime?"

"In theory the police need a warrant and probable cause to get your service provider to do it."

"Yet you were able to do it," Thorpe said. "How?"

Elena did not reply.

Thorpe nodded slowly. "I see," he said. "So what does it mean—that you couldn't get his phone to ping?"

"Could be a lot of things. Could be something completely innocent. Maybe Henry figured you'd hire someone like me so he changed phones."

"But you doubt it?"

Elena shrugged again. "Fifty-fifty—maybe more—that there is a rational explanation for all this and Henry is fine."

"But you still think I should hire you?"

"You buy burglary insurance, even though there is maybe half of one percent chance your home will be robbed."

Thorpe nodded. "Well put."

"I figure I'm worth the peace of mind, if nothing else."

Thorpe played with his phone and brought up a picture of his younger self holding an infant in his arms. "Gretchen...that's my first wife...she and I couldn't have kids. We tried everything. Hormones, surgeries, three rounds of IVF. Then we adopted Henry."

There was a smile on his face now, albeit a wistful one.

"Where is Gretchen now?"

"She died ten years ago, when Henry had just started high school. It was hard on him. I tried my best. I really did. I could see he was slipping away. I took a sabbatical from work to spend more time with him. But the tighter I held on to him..."

"The more he pulled away," Elena said.

When Thorpe looked up, his eyes were moist. "I don't know why I'm telling you this."

"Background. I need to hear it all."

"Anyway, I know how this all sounds. That's why I asked Gerald to find me the best private investigator in Chicago. You see, Miss Ramirez, despite the drugs, despite that text, despite his issues with Abby, I know my son. And I have a bad feeling about this. Simple as that. Something feels very wrong. Does that make sense?"

"Yeah," she said softly. "It does."

"Miss Ramirez?"

"Call me Elena."

"Elena, please find my boy."

CHAPTER
SIX

S imon knew he was being played.

He knew Detective Fagbenle was trying to goad him or trip him up or whatever, but he also knew that he hadn't done anything wrong ("Famous last words of the convicted," Hester would later tell him), and there was no way, as Fagbenle obviously knew, that Simon was going to let him drop that nuclear warhead and walk out the door.

"Who was murdered?" Simon asked.

"Ah, ah." Fagbenle waved a mocking, semi-scolding finger. "You said not to talk to you until your attorney was present."

Simon's mouth felt dry. "Is it my daughter?"

"I'm sorry. Unless you waive that right to counsel—"

"Oh for God's sake," Yvonne snapped. "Be a human being."

"I waive the right to counsel or whatever," Simon said. "I'll talk to you without my attorney present."

Fagbenle turned to Yvonne. "I think you better leave."

"Paige is my niece," Yvonne said. "Is she okay?"

"I don't know if she's okay," Fagbenle said, still staring at the cubicles, "but she's not the murder victim."

Relief. Pure, sweet relief. It was like every part of him had been starving for oxygen.

"Then who?" Simon asked.

Fagbenle didn't answer right away. He waited until Yvonne was gone—Yvonne promised to wait by the elevator for Hester—and the door to the office was closed. For a moment Fagbenle stared through the glass wall into the cubicle area. It was odd to visitors, he guessed, having an office that never offered complete privacy.

"Do you mind telling me where you were last night, Simon?"

"What time?"

Fagbenle shrugged. "Let's just make it all night. Six o'clock on, say."

"I was here until six. I took the subway home."

"Which train do you take?"

"The one."

"From Chambers Street?"

"Yes. I get out at the Lincoln Center stop."

Fagbenle nodded as though this was significant. "What's that altogether? Door to door, I mean. A twenty-, thirty-minute commute?"

"Thirty minutes."

"So you get home around six thirty?"

"That's right."

"Was anyone home?"

"My wife and youngest daughter."

"You have a son too, correct?"

"Yes. Sam. But he's at college."

"Where?"

"Amherst. It's in Massachusetts."

"Yeah, I know where Amherst is," Fagbenle said. "So you get home. Your wife and daughter are there . . ."

"Yes."

"Did you go back out?"

Simon thought about it, but only for a second. "Twice."

"Where did you go?"

"The park."

"What times?"

"Seven, and then again at ten p.m. I was walking our dog."

"Oh, nice. What kind of dog do you have?"

"A Havanese. Her name is Laszlo."

"Isn't Laszlo a boy's name?"

He nodded. It was. They got Laszlo on Sam's sixth birthday. Sam had insisted on that name, no matter what the dog's gender. It was an old story, but once they got the dog home, despite the promises of Sam and his two sisters, taking care of the dog had fallen on the only family member who'd been reluctant about the adoption.

Simon.

Also not surprising: He had fallen hard for Laszlo. He loved those walks, especially the one where he'd come through the door at the end of the day and Laszlo would greet him like a re-leased POW on a tarmac—every day, without fail—and she'd drag him enthusiastically to the park as though she'd never been there before.

Laszlo was twelve now. Her step was slowing. Her hearing was gone, so that some days she didn't know that Simon was home until he was already in the house, which saddened Simon more than it should.

"So other than the dog walks, did you go out?"

"No."

"So the three of you were home all night?"

"I didn't say that."

Fagbenle sat back and opened his arms. "Do tell."

"My wife went to work."

"She's a pediatrician up at New York–Presbyterian, correct? Doing an overnight shift, I assume. So that leaves you alone all night with your daughter Anya."

That slowed Simon down. He knew where his wife worked. He knew his daughter's name. "Detective?"

"Call me Isaac."

Hard pass, as his kids would say. "Who was murdered?"

The door to his office flew open. Hester Crimstein may have been small of frame but she was large of step. She burst in and stormed over to Fagbenle.

"Are you effing kidding me?"

Fagbenle remained unruffled. He slowly stood, towering over Hester, and stuck out his hand. "Detective Isaac Fagbenle with Homicide. What a pleasure to meet you."

Hester stared at his face. "Put your hand away before you lose it—like your job." Then she turned her withering glare toward Simon. "I'm not happy with you either."

Hester carried on a bit more. She then insisted that they move to a windowless conference room. Change of venue. It had to be a psychological play, but Simon wasn't sure how. Once they entered the room though, Hester took full control. She had Fagbenle sit on one side of a long conference table. She and Simon took the other.

When they were all settled in, Hester nodded toward Fagbenle and said, "Okay, get to it."

"Simon—"

"Call him Mr. Greene," Hester snapped. "He's not your pal."

Fagbenle looked as though he were about to argue, but he smiled instead. "Mr. Greene." He reached into his pocket and took out a photograph. "Do you know this man?"

Hester kept a hand on Simon's forearm. He was not to answer or react until she said it was okay. The arm was there as a reminder.

Fagbenle slid the photograph across the table.

It was Aaron Corval. The scum was smiling that awful, smug smile, the one he'd had on his face not long before Simon punched it away. He was standing in a field somewhere, trees behind him, and he'd been standing next to someone in the photograph, someone he had his arm around, someone Fagbenle had cropped out—you could see the person's shoulder on the left—

and Simon couldn't help but wonder whether the cropped-out person was Paige.

"I know him," Simon said.

"Who is he?"

"His name is Aaron Corval."

"He's your daughter's boyfriend, is that correct?"

Hester squeezed his arm. "It's not his job to describe the relationship. Move on."

Fagbenle pointed his finger at Aaron's smug face. "How do you know Aaron Corval?"

"Seriously?" It was Hester again.

"Is there a problem, Ms. Crimstein?"

"Yes, there's a problem. You're wasting our time."

"I'm asking—"

"Stop." She held up her palm. "You're embarrassing yourself. We all know how my client knows Aaron Corval. Let's pretend you've already lulled Mr. Greene and myself into a state of relaxation with your insightful albeit obvious interrogation techniques. We are putty in your hand, Detective, so let's cut to it, okay?"

"Okay, fair enough." Fagbenle leaned forward. "Aaron Corval was murdered."

Simon had been expecting that and yet the weight of the words still sent him reeling. "And my daughter...?"

Hester squeezed his arm.

"We don't know where she is, Mr. Greene. Do you?"

"No."

"When was the last time you saw her?"

"Three months ago."

"Where?"

"In Central Park."

"Would that be the day you assaulted Aaron Corval?"

"Wow," Hester said. "It's like I'm not even sitting here."

Fagbenle said, "Again I ask: Is there a problem?"

"And again I answer: Yeah, there's a problem. I don't like your characterization."

"You mean my use of the word 'assault' to describe what happened?"

"I mean exactly that."

He sat back and put his hands on the desk. "I understand the charges in that case were dropped."

"I don't care what you understand."

"Getting off like that. With all that evidence. It's interesting."

"I also don't care what interests you, Detective. I don't like your characterization of the incident. Please reword."

"Now who's wasting time, Counselor?"

"I want the interview done right, hotshot."

"Fine. The alleged assault. The incident. Whatever. Can your client answer the question now?"

Simon said, "I haven't seen my daughter since the incident in Central Park, yes."

"How about Aaron Corval? Have you seen him?"

"No."

"So over the last three months, you've had zero contact with your daughter or Mr. Corval, is that correct?"

"Asked and answered," Hester snapped.

"Let him answer, please."

"That's correct," Simon said.

Fagbenle flashed a quick smile. "So I guess you and your daughter Paige aren't very close, huh?"

Hester wasn't having it. "What are you, a family counselor?"

"Just an observation. How about your daughter Anya?"

"What about his daughter Anya?" Hester countered.

"Earlier Mr. Greene mentioned that he and Anya were home alone all night," Fagbenle said.

"He what?"

"That's what your client told me."

Hester gave Simon another withering glare.

"Mr. Greene, you took your dog for another walk about ten p.m., am I right?"

"You are."

"Did you or Anya go out after that?"

"Whoa," Hester said, making her hands into a T. "Time-out."

Fagbenle looked annoyed. "I'd like to continue my questioning."

"And I'd like to tongue-bathe Hugh Jackman," Hester said, "so both of us are going to have to live with a little disappointment." Hester rose. "Stay here, Detective. We will be right back."

She dragged Simon out of the room and down the corridor, working her mobile phone the entire time. "I'll skip the obvious admonishments."

"And I'll skip the part where I defend myself by reminding you that I didn't know if the murder victim was my daughter."

"That was a ploy."

"As I was well aware."

"What's done is done," she said. "What did you already tell him? Everything."

Simon filled her in on their earlier conversation.

"You noticed that I just sent a text," Hester said.

"Yes."

"Before we go back in and say something stupid, I want my investigator to dig up all he can on Corval's murder—time, circumstances, method, whatever. You're not a fool, so you know what's going on here with our hunky detective."

"I'm a suspect."

She nodded. "You had a serious 'incident'"—Hester made quote marks with her fingers—"with the deceased. You hated him. You blamed him for your daughter's drug problems. So yes, you're a suspect. So is your wife. So is . . . well, Paige. My guess is, she's the biggest suspect. Do you have an alibi for last night?"

"Like I said, I was home all night."

"With?"

"Anya."

"Yeah, that's not going to hold."

"Why not?"

"Where in your apartment specifically was Anya?"

"In her room, mostly."

"Door open or shut?"

Simon saw where she was going with this. "Shut."

"She's a kid, right? Door shut, maybe blasting music on her headphones. So you could have sneaked out at any time. What time did Anya go to sleep? Let's say eleven o'clock. You could have left then. Does your building have any security cameras?"

"Yes. But it's an old building. There are ways of getting out without being seen."

Hester's phone dinged. She put it to her ear and said, "Articulate."

Someone did. And as he did, Hester's face lost color. She didn't say a word. Not for a very long time. When she finally spoke again, her voice was uncharacteristically soft. "Email me the report."

She hung up.

"What?" Simon asked.

"They don't think you did it. Correction: They *can't* think you did it."

CHAPTER

SEVEN

Ash watched the target pull up to the dilapidated two-family home.

"Is he driving a Cadillac?" Dee Dee asked him.

"Looks like it."

"Is it an Eldorado?"

Dee Dee never stopped talking.

"No."

"You sure?"

"It's an ATS. Cadillac stopped making the Eldorado in 2002."

"How do you know that?"

Ash shrugged. He just knew stuff.

"My daddy had an Eldorado," Dee Dee said.

Ash frowned. "Your 'daddy'?"

"What, you think I don't remember him?"

Dee Dee had been in foster homes from the age of six. Ash had entered his first when he was four. Over the next fourteen years he had been in over twenty. Dee had probably been in about the same. On three occasions, for a total of eight months, they had ended up in the same foster home.

"He bought it used, of course. Like, really used. The bottom was rusted out. But Daddy loved that car. He let me sit in the front seat with him. No seat belt. The leather in the seats? It was all cracked. It'd scrape my legs. Anyway, he'd play the radio loud and sometimes he'd sing along. That's what I remember best. He had a good voice, my old man. He'd smile and start singing and then he'd sort of let go of the wheel and steer with his wrists, you know what I mean?"

Ash knew. He also knew Daddy steered with one hand while jamming his other between his young daughter's legs, but now didn't seem to be the time to bring that up.

"Daddy loved that damned car," Dee Dee said with a pout. "Until..."

Ash couldn't help himself. "Until what?"

"Maybe that's where it all went wrong. When Daddy found out the truth about that car."

Ash cringed every time she used the word "Daddy."

The target got out of the car. He was a burly guy in jeans, scuffed Timberland-knockoff boots, and a flannel shirt. He sported a beard and a camouflage-colored Boston Red Sox baseball cap too small for his pumpkin head.

Ash gestured with his chin. "That our guy?"

"Looks like it. What's the plan?"

The target opened the car's back door, and two young girls wearing bright-green school backpacks got out. His daughters, Ash knew. The taller, Kelsey, was ten. The younger, Kiera, was eight.

"We wait."

Ash sat in the driver's seat. Dee Dee was in the passenger's. Ash hadn't seen her in three years. He'd figured that she was dead until their recent reunion. He'd expected it to be awkward—too much time, too many bridges—but they quickly fell into their old patterns.

"So what happened?" Ash asked.

"What?"

"With your dad's Eldorado. Where did it all go wrong? What was this truth he learned?"

The smile dropped off her face. Dee Dee shifted in her seat.

"You don't have to tell me."

"No," she said. "I want to."

They both stared out the front window at the target's home. Ash put his hand on his hip, where his gun was holstered. He had his instructions. He couldn't imagine what the burly guy had done—what any on the list had done—but sometimes the less you knew, the better.

"We went out to this fancy fish restaurant for dinner," Dee Dee began. "This was right before my grandma died. So she paid. My dad, well, he was a steak guy. Always. He hated fish. I mean, really hated it."

Ash had no idea where this was going.

"So the waiter comes over and starts reading off the daily specials. He has this blackboard with him and the specials, they're all written out in chalk. Fancy, right?"

"Right."

"So anyway, the waiter gets to the fish special and he has this weird accent and anyway, he says, 'The chef strongly recommends the'—then this waiter, he waves at the board like it's a car on *The Price Is Right*—'Grilled Dorado with walnuts and parsley pesto.'"

Ash turned to look at her. You'd think the years wouldn't have been kind to Dee Dee, all she'd been through, but she looked more beautiful than ever. Her golden-blonde hair was tied in a thick braid running down her back. Her lips were full, her skin flawless. Her green eyes were a bright emerald shade most assumed involved contact lenses or some kind of cosmetics.

"So Daddy asks the waiter to repeat that, the name of the fish, and the waiter does and Daddy—"

Man, Ash wished she'd stop calling him that.

"—and Daddy starts fuming. I mean, he just runs out of the restaurant. Knocks over his chair and everything. See, his car, his supercool car—it's named for a fish! Daddy can't handle that, you know?"

Ash just looked at her. "You're serious?"

"Of course I'm serious."

"It's not named for a fish."

"What, you never heard of a Dorado fish?"

"I've heard of it, but El Dorado is a mythical city of gold in South America."

"But it's also a fish, right?"

Ash said nothing.

"Ash?"

"Yeah." He sighed. "Yeah, it's also a fish."

The target stepped back out of his house. He started toward his garage.

"They all have to be done differently?" Ash asked.

"I don't know about differently, but they can't be connected."

Meaning it couldn't be like Chicago. Still, that gave him plenty of flexibility on this one.

"Watch the house," he said.

"I'm not coming with you this time?"

She sounded hurt by this.

"No. Take the wheel. Keep the car running. Watch the door. If anyone comes out, call me."

He didn't repeat the instructions. The target had gone into the garage. Ash started toward it.

Here is what he did know about the target. Name, Kevin Gano. Married twelve years to his high school sweetheart, Courtney. The four Ganos lived on the top floor of this two-family home on Devon Street in Revere, Massachusetts. Six months ago, Kevin had been laid off from Alston Meat Packing plant in Lynn, where he'd worked for the previous seven years. He'd been trying to find another job since, to no avail, so last month Courtney had been forced to go back to work as a receptionist at a travel agency on Constitution Avenue.

Kevin, trying to make himself useful, picked up the girls every day from school at two p.m. That was why he was home right now when the rest of this working-class neighborhood was quiet and still.

Kevin was standing by his workbench unscrewing a DVD or Blu-ray player—he earned a little money doing small repairs—when Ash approached. He looked up and gave Ash a friendly smile. Ash smiled back and then Ash pointed his gun at him.

"This will all be fine if you stay quiet."

Ash stepped all the way into the garage and pulled the door down closed behind him. He kept the gun trained on Kevin, never taking his eyes off him. Kevin still had the screwdriver in his hand.

His right hand.

"What do you want?"

"Put down the screwdriver, Kevin. Cooperate and no one gets hurt."

"Bullshit," Kevin said.

"What?"

"You're letting me see your face."

Good point.

"I'm in disguise. Don't worry about it."

"Bullshit," Kevin said again.

Kevin looked toward the side door, like he was going to make a run for it.

"Kelsey and Kiera," Ash said.

Hearing his daughters' names froze him.

"It can go one of two ways. If you make a run for it, I'll shoot you dead. Then I'll have to make it look like a bad home invasion. That means I go into your house. What are Kelsey and Kiera doing in there, Kevin? Homework? Watching TV? Having a nice snack? Whatever. I'll go in, and I'll do things so horrible you'll be glad you're dead."

Kevin shook his head, tears coming to his eyes. "Please."

"Or," Ash said, "you can drop the screwdriver right now."

Kevin did as he was asked. The screwdriver clanked on the concrete floor.

"I don't understand. I never hurt anyone. Why are you doing this?"

Ash shrugged.

"Please don't hurt my girls. I'll do whatever you want. Just don't..." He swallowed and stood a little taller. "So...so what now?"

Ash crossed the garage and placed the muzzle of the gun against the side of Kevin's temple. Kevin closed his eyes right before Ash pulled the trigger.

The echo was loud inside the garage, drawn out, but Ash doubted anyone outside of it would take notice.

Kevin was dead before he hit the floor.

Ash moved fast. He placed the gun in Kevin's right hand and pulled the trigger, firing a bullet straight into the ground. Now there would be gunpowder residue on the hand. He pulled the phone out of Kevin's back pocket and used Kevin's thumb to unlock it. Then he quickly scrolled through and found his wife's contact information.

Courtney's name was typed into the contacts with two hearts before and after her name.

Hearts. Kevin had put hearts next to his wife's name.

Ash typed up a simple text: I'm sorry. Please forgive me.

He hit Send, dropped the phone on the workbench, and headed back to the car.

Don't rush. Don't walk too quickly.

Ash figured that there was probably an 80 to 85 percent chance the suicide scenario would hold. You had a gunshot wound to the head—to the victim's right temple, the way a righty might do it if the wound was self-inflicted. That was why Ash had made note of which hand Kevin was holding the screwdriver in. You had a suicide text. You had gun residue on the hand. The extra bullet would probably look like Kevin had tried once and chickened out and then steeled himself for the real deal.

So the suicide scenario would probably be a buy. Eighty, eighty-five percent—maybe more like 90 percent when you added in that Kevin was out of work and probably depressed about it. If some cop was super aggressive or watched too much *CSI*, he might find some stuff didn't add up. For example, there hadn't been enough time to prop Kevin up before firing the second shot, so if some crime tech really spent the money to study the bullet's trajectory, he might notice the shot originated from near the floor.

Someone might even spot Ash right now, or the car, and that might raise a few eyebrows too.

But that was all doubtful.

Either way, he and Dee Dee would be long gone. The car would be wiped down and abandoned. Nothing would track back to them.

Ash was good at this.

He got into the passenger side of the car. No curtains on the block had moved. No doors had opened. No cars had driven by.

Dee Dee said, "Is he...?"

Ash nodded.

Dee Dee smiled and started the car down the road.

CHAPTER
EIGHT

Ingrid met Simon at the door when he arrived home. She threw her arms around him.

"I'd just crashed in bed," Ingrid said, "when the police arrived."

"I know."

"And suddenly the door buzzer kept going off. It took me forever to wake up. I figured it was a delivery, except they always protect me from that stuff."

By "they," she meant the doormen in the building. Ingrid worked one overnight shift in the emergency room per week. The doormen knew that meant she slept during the next day, so if there were any deliveries, they were to leave them for Simon to bring up when he got home at six thirty.

"I threw on some sweats. This cop comes up. He actually asked me for an alibi. Like I was a suspect."

Simon knew, of course. Ingrid had contacted him as soon as the doorman told her why she was being buzzed. Hester then had sent a colleague from her firm to be with Ingrid for the police questioning.

"And I just got a call from Mary in the ER. The cops actually went to the hospital to double-check I was there. Can you believe this?"

"They wanted an alibi for me too," Simon said. "Hester thinks it's just routine."

"I don't understand though. What happened exactly? Aaron was killed?"

"Murdered, yes."

"And where is Paige?"

"No one seems to know."

Laszlo the dog started pawing Simon's leg. They both looked down and into the dog's soulful eyes.

"Let's take her for a walk," Simon said.

Five minutes later, they crossed Central Park West at Sixty-Seventh Street, Laszlo pulling hard on the leash. On their left, in plain view yet somehow slightly hidden, was a tiny playground bursting with color. A lifetime ago, and yet not that long ago, they used to bring Paige, then Sam, then Anya here to play. They'd sit on a bench, able to watch the entire playground without so much as turning their heads, feeling safe and secure in the midst of this enormous park in this enormous city, less than a block from their home.

They headed past the Tavern on the Green, the famed restaurant, and turned right to head south. A group of schoolchildren in matching yellow T-shirts—easy to spot on field trips—filed past them. Simon waited until they were out of earshot.

"The murder," Simon said. "It was gruesome."

Ingrid wore a long thin coat. She dug her hands into her pockets. "Go on."

"Aaron was mutilated."

"How?"

"Do you really need the details?" he asked.

Ingrid almost smiled. "Strange."

"What?"

"You're the one who can barely stomach the violence in R-rated movies," she said.

"And you're the physician who never so much as blinks at the sight of blood," he finished for her. "But maybe I understand better now."

"How's that?"

"What Hester told me—it didn't gross me out. Maybe because it's real. So you just react. Like you with a patient in the ER. On the screen I have the luxury of looking away. In real life..."

His voice just faded away.

"You're stalling," Ingrid said.

"Which is dumb, I know. According to Hester's source, the killer slit Aaron's throat, though she said that's a tame way of putting it. The knife went deep into his neck. Almost took off his head. They sliced off three fingers. They also cut off..."

"Pre- or post-mortem?" Ingrid asked in her physician tone.

"What?"

"The amputations. Was he still alive for them?"

"I don't know," Simon said. "Does it matter?"

"It might."

"I'm not following."

Laszlo stopped and did the butt-sniff greeting with a passing collie.

"If Aaron was still alive when they cut him up," Ingrid said, "someone may have been trying to get information out of him."

"What kind of information?"

"I don't know. But now no one can find our daughter."

"You think...?"

"I don't think anything," Ingrid said.

They both stopped. Their eyes met and for a brief moment, despite all the people walking by, despite the horror of what they were going through, Simon fell back into her eyes and she fell into his. He loved her. She loved him. Simple but there you have it. You both have careers and you raise kids and there are victories and defeats and you just sort of coast along, living your life, the days long, the years short, and then every once in a while, you remember to pull up and look at your partner, your life partner, really look at the one who travels down the lonely road right by your side, and you realize how much you are in this together.

"To the police," Ingrid said, "Paige is just a worthless junkie. They won't look for her, and if they do, it will be to arrest her as an accessory or worse."

Simon nodded. "So it's up to us."

"Yes. Where was Aaron murdered?"

"In their apartment in Mott Haven."

"You know that address?"

He nodded. Hester had given it to him.

"We can start there," Ingrid said.

The Uber driver drove up to two concrete barriers, set up on the street like something you'd see in a war zone. "Can't go no further." The driver—named Achmed—turned around and frowned at Simon. "You sure this is it?"

"It is."

Achmed looked dubious. "If you're looking to make a buy, I know a safer place—"

"We're fine, thanks," Ingrid said.

"I don't mean no offense."

"None taken," Simon said.

"You're, uh, not going to give me a one-star rating because of this, are you?"

"You're pure five stars, my man," Simon said, opening the passenger door.

"We'd give you six if we could," Ingrid added.

They slipped out of the Toyota. Simon wore gray sweats and sneakers. Ingrid was in jeans and a sweater. They both wore baseball caps, hers with the classic New York Yankees NY overlap, his with a golf club logo, a giveaway at a charity outing. Everything discreet, casual, trying to blend in, which wasn't happening.

The four-level walk-up of decrepit brick wasn't so much falling apart as flaking away, fraying at the seams like an old coat. The fire escape looked ready to give at the gentlest push, far more rust than metal, posing the question if burns were worse than tetanus. On the sidewalk, a much-mistreated mattress had been thrown atop black plastic trash bags, crushing them into misshapen masses. The front stoop looked as though it shed concrete dust. The metallic-gray door had some kind of ornate graffiti lettering spray-painted on it. Car parts and old tires were strewn across the tall weeds next door, all surrounded, for some odd reason, by a fresh chain-link fence topped with razor wire—as if anyone would ever want to steal any of that stuff. The building to the right, perhaps a once-proud brownstone, had plywood covering broken glass, giving it a look of loneliness and despair that shattered Simon's heart anew.

Paige, his baby, had lived here.

Simon turned to look at Ingrid. She stared at the building too, a look of loss on her face. Her eyes gazed up, above the rooftops to the public-housing high-rises looming in the near distance.

"So now what?" Simon asked her.

Ingrid took in their surroundings. "We didn't really think this through, did we?"

She stepped toward the graffiti-laden door, turned the knob without hesitation, and pushed hard. The door ground open grudgingly. When they stepped into what one might generously dub a foyer, the stale, acrid odor, a mix of the musty and the rotting, encircled them. A bare light bulb, dangling from the ceiling with no fixture, provided a modicum of twenty-five-watt illumination.

She lived here, Simon thought. *Paige lived in this place.*

He thought about life choices, about bad decisions and forks in the road, and what moves, what sliding doors, had led Paige to this hell-spawned place. It was his fault, wasn't it? Of course it had to be in some way. The butterfly effect. Change one thing, you change everything. The constant what-ifs—if only he could go back and change something. Paige had wanted to write. Suppose he had sent one of her essays to his friend at that local literary magazine, the one that worked off donations, and had gotten it published. Would she have focused more on her writing then? Paige had been denied early decision to Columbia. Should Simon have pushed his alma mater more, gotten more of his old friends to contact Admissions? Yvonne's father-in-law had been on the board at Williams. She could have done something there, if he'd pushed it. And that was the big stuff, of course. Anything could have changed her course, right? Paige wanted a cat for her dorm room, but he didn't get it for her. She had a fight with Merilee, her best friend in seventh grade, and he as a father had done nothing to patch it up. Paige liked American cheese on her turkey sandwich, not cheddar, but sometimes Simon forgot and used the wrong one.

You could drive yourself mad.

She'd been such a good girl too. The best daughter in the world. Paige hated to get in trouble and when she did, even for something minor, her eyes would fill with tears so that Simon couldn't bear to scold her. But maybe he should have. Maybe that would have helped. It was just that she cried so damn easily, and it got under his skin because the truth, the truth he never had the courage to tell her, was that he cried easily too—too easily— pretending something was wrong with his contact lens or that he had nonexistent allergies or leaving the room altogether rather than admitting it. Maybe if he had, it would have made it easier for her and she could have found some kind of outlet or way to bond with her father who chose to keep up some kind of false machismo, some kind of idea that if her dad didn't cry, maybe she'd feel safe, more protected. Instead it just made her more vulnerable in the end.

Ingrid had already started up the warped stairs. When she re-alized Simon was not with her, she turned and said, "You okay?"

He snapped out of it, nodded, followed her. "Third floor," he said. "Apartment B."

There were broken pieces of what might have once been a sofa on the first landing. Crushed beer cans and overflowing ashtrays were piled high. Simon peered down the hall as they made the turn for the next floor. A thin black man in a wifebeater tee and threadbare denim stood at the end of the hallway. The man had a white beard so thick and curly it looked as though he were eating a sheep.

On the third floor, there was yellow tape that read CRIME SCENE DO NOT CROSS forming an X in front of a heavy metal door with the letter B on it. Ingrid did not hesitate or slow down. She reached for the knob and tried to turn it.

The knob wouldn't move.

She stepped back and gestured for Simon to give it a try. He did. He twisted the knob back and forth and pushed and pulled.

Locked.

The walls around them might very well be decaying to the point that maybe Simon could punch his fist through one and en-ter that way, but this locked door was not about to surrender.

"Hey."

The simple word, spoken in a normal tone of voice, shattered the stale air like a gunshot. Simon and Ingrid jumped at the sound and turned. It was the thin black man with the sheep beard. Simon checked for an exit route. There was none except via the way they came, and that path was blocked now.

Slowly and without conscious thought, Simon took a step to slip in front of Ingrid, putting himself between her and the man.

For a moment no one spoke. The three of them just stood in that grimy corridor and didn't move. Someone on the floor above them turned up music with a loud thumping bass and an angry vocalist.

Then the man said, "You're looking for Paige."

It wasn't a question.

"You," the man said, raising his hand and pointing a bony finger at Ingrid. "You're her mother."

"How did you know?" Ingrid asked.

"You look exactly like her. Or does she look like you?" He petted the sheep beard. "I always mix that up."

"Do you know where Paige is?" Simon asked.

"Is that why you're here? You're looking for her?"

Ingrid took a step toward him. "Yes. Do you know where she is?"

He shook his head. "Sorry."

"But you know Paige?"

"Yeah, I know her. I live right below them."

"Is there somebody else who might know?" Simon asked.

"Somebody else?"

"Like a friend."

The man smiled. "I'm her friend."

"Maybe another friend then."

"I don't think so." He gestured with the beard toward the door. "You trying to get in?"

Simon looked at Ingrid. Ingrid said, "Yeah, we were hoping to see..."

His eyes narrowed. "See what?"

"I don't know, to tell you the truth," Ingrid said.

"We're just trying to find her," Simon added.

The man stroked the sheep beard some more, pulling at the end as though to make it longer. "I can let you in," he said.

He reached into his pocket and fished out a key.

"How do you have...?"

"Like I said, I'm her friend. Don't you have a friend who has your key, just in case you get locked out or something?" He started toward them. "If the cops get mad about ripping the tape, I'm blaming it on you. Come on, let's go inside."

The apartment was a claustrophobic hovel, maybe half the size of Paige's college dorm room. There were two single mattresses, one on the floor by the right wall, one up against the wall on the left. Just mattresses. No beds. No other furniture at all.

Paige's guitar was propped up in the right-hand corner. Her clothes were on the floor in three stacks next to it. The place was a cyclone of a mess, but her clothes were neatly folded. Simon stared at them and felt Ingrid slip her hand into his and squeeze. Paige had always taken good care of her clothes.

On the left side of the room, dried blood stained the wood.

"Never did no one harm, your daughter," the black man said. "Except herself."

Ingrid turned her eyes toward him. "What's your name?"

"Cornelius."

"I'm Ingrid. This is Paige's father, Simon. But you're wrong, Cornelius."

"About?"

"She hurt more than herself."

Cornelius considered that before nodding. "Guess that's true, Ingrid. But there's a lot of good in her, you know. Still. She'd play chess with me a lot." He met Simon's eye. "She told me you taught her."

Simon nodded, afraid to speak.

"She loved to walk Chloe. That's my dog. Cocker spaniel. Said she had a dog of her own back home. Said she missed her. I get that Paige hurt you, but I'm talking here about intent. Seen it before, I'll see it again. It's the devil—he gets ahold of you. He pokes and prods until he finds your weakness and then, see, he wiggles right through your skin and gets into your bloodstream. Could be through drink. Could be through gambling. Could be through a virus, like cancer or something. Or the devil could be in the smack, the rock, the meth, whatever. It's all the devil in different forms."

75

He turned and looked down at the blood on the floor.

"The devil could even be a man," Cornelius said.

"I assume you knew Aaron too?" Simon asked.

Cornelius just kept staring at the blood. "You know all my talk about the devil getting into your bloodstream?"

Ingrid said, "Yes."

"Sometimes he don't need to do any poking or prodding. Sometimes a man does it for him." Cornelius looked up at them. "I don't like wishing someone dead, but I tell you—there were times I came up here and he'd be so wasted, Paige too, lying in their own stink, and I'd look at him, at what he done, and I'd day-dream..."

His voice faded away.

"Did you talk to the police?" Ingrid asked.

"They talked to me, but I got nothing to say to them."

"When did you last see Paige?"

Cornelius hesitated. "I kinda hoped you guys would tell me."

"What do you mean?"

There was a noise in the corridor. Cornelius stuck his head out. A young couple stumbled toward them, arms wrapped around each other, limbs so entwined it was hard to say where one began and the other ended.

"Cornelius," the young man said, a lilt in his voice. "What's happening, mah man?"

"All good, Enrique. How are you, Candy?"

"Love ya, Cornelius."

"Love you too."

"You cleaning out the place?" Enrique asked.

"Nah. Just making sure it's all okay."

"Dude was a turd."

"Enrique!" Candy said.

"What?"

"The man is dead."

"So now he's a dead turd. That better?"

Enrique peered in the door, saw Simon and Ingrid, and asked, "Who that with you?"

"Just some cops," Cornelius said.

That changed their demeanor. Suddenly their slow saunter became more purposeful.

"Uh, nice to meet you," Candy said.

They unwound their limbs and hurried their step, both disappearing into a room at the end of the hall. Cornelius kept the smile on his face until the couple was out of sight.

"Cornelius?" Ingrid said.

"Hmm."

"When did you last see Paige?"

He turned slowly, his eyes taking in the sad room. "What I'm going to tell you," he said, "well, I didn't tell the police this for obvious reasons."

They waited.

"You have to understand. Maybe I've been sugarcoating, telling you how nice Paige was to Chloe and me. But fact is, she was a mess. A junkie. When she was in my place—I mean, like when she came by to play chess or get a bite to eat—truth is, and I don't like saying it, I kept an eye on her. You know what I'm saying? I always worried she'd steal something because that's what junkies do."

Simon knew. Paige had stolen from them too. Cash went missing from Simon's wallet. When several pieces of Ingrid's jewelry disappeared, Paige claimed innocence in near Oscar-worthy performances.

That's what junkies do.

A junkie.

His daughter was a junkie. Simon had never let himself articulate that, but hearing it come from Cornelius's lips just made it land with a horrible, undeniable thud.

"Two days before Aaron got killed, I saw Paige. Down by the front door. I was coming in. She was flying down the stairs. Almost tumbling. Like someone was chasing her. She was going so fast, I thought she'd lose her step."

Cornelius looked up and off now, as though he could still see her.

"I put my hands out, like to break her fall." Cornelius lifted his arms, palms up, demonstrating. "I called out to her. But she just sprinted past me and outside. Didn't even break her stride. I mean, that's happened before."

"What's happened before?" Ingrid asked.

Cornelius turned his attention to her. "Paige just sprinting by me, like that. Like she's so out of it, she doesn't know who I am. Lots of times, she runs to that empty lot next door. You see it when you come in?"

They both nodded.

"Got that razor wire up front, but there's an opening around the side. Goes there to get her fix from Rocco."

"Rocco?"

"Local dealer. Aaron worked for him."

Ingrid said, "Aaron dealt drugs?"

Cornelius cocked an eyebrow. "That surprise you?"

Simon and Ingrid exchanged a glance. It did not.

"Point is, when a junkie needs a fix, you could put NFL defensemen in her way and she'd break through. So what I'm saying is, that part—her sprinting out like that—that isn't what made it strange."

"So what did make it strange?" Simon asked.

"Paige had bruises on her face."

Simon felt a rushing in his ears. His own voice sounded far away. "Bruises?"

"Some blood too. Like she'd taken a beating."

Simon's hands tightened into fists. The rage crawled up him, heating his entire body. Drugs, junkie, strung-out, whatever—somehow he could either deal or block on all that.

But someone had punched his little girl.

Simon could see it, a cruel hand tightening into a fist—tightening just as his was now—and then the fist cocking back, a sneer on the face, and that fist launching straight at his helpless daughter.

Anger, fury, rage consumed him.

If it was Aaron—and if Aaron could somehow be alive and standing in front of him right this very moment—Simon would kill him without a moment's hesitation or thought. No regret. No guilt.

He'd end him.

Simon felt Ingrid's hand on his arm, a warm touch, an attempt perhaps to bring him back.

"I get what you're feeling," Cornelius said, looking straight at Simon.

"So what did you do?" Simon asked.

"Who says I did anything?"

"Because you get what I'm feeling," Simon said.

"Doesn't mean I did anything. I'm not her father."

"So you just shrugged and went about your day?"

"Could be."

Simon shook his head. "You wouldn't just let something like that slide."

"I didn't kill him," Cornelius said.

"If you did," Simon said, "it would never leave this room."

Cornelius glanced toward Ingrid. She nodded as if to reassure.

"Please tell us the rest," Ingrid said.

Cornelius fiddled with the gray-white beard. He took another look around the room, making a face as though he'd just entered the room for the first time and realized the filth.

"Yeah, I came up here."

"And?"

"And I banged on the door. It was locked. So I took out my key. Just like I did today. I opened the door..."

The music upstairs stopped. The room was completely silent now.

Cornelius looked down to the mattress on the right. "Aaron was right there. Passed out. Stench so bad I could barely breathe. I just wanted to run out of there, forget the whole thing."

He stopped.

"So what did you do?" Ingrid asked.

"I checked his knuckles."

"Pardon?"

"The knuckles on Aaron's right hand, they were scraped up. Fresh scrapes too. So I knew then. No surprise, I guess. It'd been him who beat her. So I stood over him..."

Again he stopped. This time he closed his eyes.

Ingrid stepped toward him. "It's okay."

"Like I told you before, I daydreamed about it, Ingrid. Maybe...maybe I would have done more, if I got the chance. I don't know. If that punk was awake. If he was awake and tried to explain himself. Maybe then I would have just exploded. You know what I'm saying? So I'm standing there and I'm staring down at this piece of garbage. And maybe this time, after what I'd seen, maybe I thought I'd do more than just shake my head and shuffle away."

Cornelius opened his eyes.

"But I didn't."

"You left the room," Ingrid said.

He nodded. "Enrique and Candy come down the hall, just like today. I closed the door and went back downstairs."

"And that's it?"

"That's it," Cornelius said.

"You haven't seen Paige since?"

"Not Paige. Not Aaron either. When you two showed up, I figured maybe I was wrong."

"Wrong about what?"

"Maybe Paige didn't go to that empty lot and see Rocco. Maybe she ran home and told her mommy and daddy what happened. Maybe they came out here and...well, they're her kin. They're her blood. So maybe they did more than daydream."

Cornelius studied their faces.

"That's not what happened," Simon said.

"Yeah, I get that now."

"So we need to find her," Simon said.

"I get that too."

"We need to follow her steps after she ran out of here."

Cornelius nodded. "That means you got to go see Rocco."

CHAPTER

NINE

C ornelius had told them how to find Rocco: "You duck through the opening in the fence. He'll be in the abandoned building on the other side of the lot."

Simon wasn't sure what to expect.

On TV, he'd seen plenty of drug deals amongst urban blight, men with dark stares and guns and do-rags and low-slung jeans, little kids on bikes doing the deals because they were easier to get out of jail or some such thing, probably just TV nonsense. As he stood with Ingrid by the opening in the fence, there was no one visible. No lookout. No armed guard. He could hear faint voices in the distance, probably coming from the abandoned building, but the expected menace was not yet visible.

Which did not mean that this was a safe situation.

"So," Simon said to Ingrid, "yet again I ask: What's our plan?"

"Damned if I know."

They looked at the opening in the fence.

"Let me go in first," he said, "just in case it isn't safe."

"And leave me out here alone? Oh right, that sounds super-safe."

Ingrid had a point.

"I could tell you to go home," he said.

"You could," Ingrid agreed, as she pulled back the chain link and ducked into the abandoned lot.

Simon quickly followed. The weeds were up past his knees. They both walked, lifting their feet as though in deep snow, afraid of tripping over rusted axles and bearings, shredded hoses and worn tire treads, shattered windshields and cracked headlights.

They had been somewhat smart, though some might say stereotyping, before making the trek to this neighborhood. Ingrid had removed all her jewelry, including her wedding band and engagement ring. Simon wore only his wedding band, which wasn't worth that much money. Between them, they had maybe a hundred dollars in cash. Robbery—and face it, they were walking into some sort of drug den—was a possibility but it wouldn't be a profitable one.

The steel exterior cellar doors were open. Simon and Ingrid looked down into the darkness. They could see a concrete floor. Nothing else. Sounds came up from the depths, muffled voices, maybe whispers, maybe light laughter. Ingrid took the first step, but Simon wasn't having any of that. He jumped in front of her and hurried down, reaching the dank concrete before Ingrid reached the second step.

The smell hit him first—that always-awful sulfurous stench of rotten eggs mixed with something more chemical, an ammonia-like taste that stayed on his tongue.

The voices were clearer now. Simon started toward them. He didn't hide his step or try to be silent. Sneaking up on them would be the wrong move. He didn't want to startle them into doing something stupid.

Ingrid caught up to him. When they reached the center room of the basement, the voices stopped as if they'd been on a switch. Simon took in the scene, even as the stench started to get to him. He tried to breathe through his mouth. To his right, four people were sprawled as though they had no bones or were old socks someone had casually tossed there. The light was dim. Simon could make out their wide eyes more than anything else. There was a torn futon and what might have been a beanbag chair. Cardboard boxes once used for cases of cheap wine had been turned into makeshift tables. Spoons and lighters and burners and syringes lay atop them.

No one moved. Simon and Ingrid just stood there. The four people on the floor—was it four? might have been more, hard to tell in this light—stayed still, as though maybe they were camouflaged and if they didn't move, they might not be seen.

A few more seconds passed before someone in the group began to stir. A man. He got to his feet slowly, moment by moment, a huge man, rising off the floor like Godzilla wading out of the water, his entire being expanding and filling the room. When he stood all the way up, the top of his head nearly scraped the ceiling. The big man shuffled toward them like a planet with two feet.

"What can I do for you fine folks?"

The voice was pleasant, affable.

"We're looking for Rocco," Simon said.

"That's me."

The huge man stuck out a hand that belonged on a balloon in the Macy's Thanksgiving Day Parade. Simon shook it, his hand disappearing into the folds of flesh. Rocco's smile split his face in two. He wore a Yankees cap, same as Ingrid's, though his looked much too small for his head, like one of those mascots with a giant baseball on his shoulders. Rocco was dark-skinned black. He was decked out in a hemp hoodie with kangaroo pockets, denim shorts, and what looked like Birkenstock sandals.

"Is there something I can help you guys with?"

His voice stayed light, folksy, maybe a bit of the stoner. The other people in the room went back to their business, which involved the lighters and the burners and plastic bags with un-known—unknown to Simon, at least—powder or other contents.

"We're looking for our daughter," Ingrid said. "Her name is Paige."

"We understand she came here recently," Simon added.

"Oh?" Rocco folded Greco-Roman-column arms across his chest. "How do you understand that?"

Simon and Ingrid exchanged a glance. "We just heard," Simon said.

"Heard from who?"

Someone from the floor yelled, "Whom!"

"What?"

A white hipster wearing an overgrown soul patch and skinny-legged jeans tucked into faux work boots scrambled to his feet. "Heard from whom, not who. Come on, Rocco. Prepositional phrase."

"Shit, right, sorry."

"You're better than that, man."

"It was a mistake. Don't make a big thing of it." Rocco turned his attention back to Simon and Ingrid. "Where were we?"

"Paige."

"Right."

Silence.

"You know Paige, right?" Simon asked.

"I do, yes."

"She's"—Ingrid stopped, searched for the word—"a client of yours?"

"I don't really discuss clients. Whatever business you might imagine I am in, confidentiality would have to be a key component of it."

"We don't care about your business," Ingrid said. "We are just trying to find our daughter."

"You seem like a nice woman, Miss...?"

"Greene. And it's Doctor."

"You seem like a nice woman, Dr. Greene, and I hope you don't take offense, but look around you." He spread his arms wide, as though he were about to pull in the entire basement for a hug.

"Does this look like the kind of place where we tell relatives where their loved ones might be hiding?"

"Is she?" Simon asked.

"Is she what?"

"Is Paige hiding from us?"

"I'm not going to tell you that."

"Would you tell me for ten thousand dollars?" Simon asked.

That caused a hush.

Rocco rolled a little closer to them, almost like that boulder in the first Indiana Jones movie. "You might want to keep your voice down."

"The offer stands," Simon said.

Rocco rubbed his chin. "You got the ten grand on you."

Simon frowned. "Uh, no, of course not."

"How much do you have on you?"

"Maybe eighty, a hundred dollars. Why, you want to rob us?" Simon raised his voice. "But what I said goes for anyone in this room: Ten grand if you tell me where Paige is."

Ingrid looked up into Rocco's face, forcing him to make eye contact. "Please," she said. "I think Paige is in danger."

"Because of what happened to Aaron?"

That name—just hearing Rocco say it—changed the very air in the room.

"Yes," Ingrid said.

Rocco tilted his head. "What do you think happened, Dr. Greene?"

His tone remained calm, level, even, but Simon thought that perhaps he heard something else in it now. A crackle. An edge. What should have been obvious was starting to reach him. Rocco might have a friendly facade. He may come across as a great big Teddy bear come to life.

But Rocco was a drug dealer working his turf.

The brutality of Aaron's murder suggested a drug hit, didn't it? And if Aaron worked for Rocco...

"We don't care about Aaron," Ingrid said. "We don't care about this place or your business or any of that. Whatever happened to Aaron, Paige had nothing to do with it."

"How do you know?" Rocco asked.

"What?"

"Seriously. How do you know Paige had nothing to do with what happened to Aaron?"

Simon took that one. "Have you seen Paige?"

"I have."

"Then you know."

Rocco nodded slowly. "A strong wind could knock her over. I get that. But that doesn't mean she couldn't drug a man and slice him up when he's out."

"Ten thousand dollars," Simon said again. "All we want to do is bring our daughter home."

The dank basement went still. Rocco stood there, his face expressionless. He was mulling it over, Simon thought. He didn't interrupt. Neither did Ingrid.

Then a voice said, "Hey, I know you."

Simon turned toward the corner. It was Hipster Grammar guy. He pointed at Simon and then started snapping his fingers. "You're that guy."

"What are you talking about, Tom?"

"He's that guy, Rocco."

"What guy?"

Hipster Grammar Tom used his thumbs to hitch his jeans up by the belt loops. "He's the guy in that video. The guy who punched Aaron. In the park."

Rocco rested his hands in the hoodie's kangaroo pouch. "Whoa. I think you're right."

"I'm telling you, Rocco. That's the guy."

"For real." Rocco smiled at Simon. "Are you the guy in that video?"

"Yes."

Rocco put up his hands in mock surrender and stepped back. "Oh, Lordy, please don't hit me."

Hipster Grammar Tom laughed. Some of the other guys did too.

Later, Simon would claim he felt the danger before it all went wrong.

There may indeed be something primal in human beings, some survival mechanism from our caveman days of constant danger that lies dormant in modern man, some sixth sense or instinct that almost never needs to surface in our society, but it's still there, still potent yet latent in a deep part of our genetic makeup.

As the young man stumbled into the basement, the hackles on the back of Simon's neck rose.

Rocco said, "Luther?"

The rest took a second, maybe two at the most.

Luther was shirtless, his chest gleaming and completely hairless. He was early twenties, all coiled muscle, wiry, bouncing on his toes like a bantamweight boxer impatient for the bell. He stared wide-eyed at Simon and Ingrid and then without the least bit of hesitation, he whipped out a gun.

"Luther!"

Luther took aim. There was no warning, no delay, no words spoken. Luther simply took aim and pulled the trigger.

BLAM!

Simon swore that he could actually feel the bullet graze by his nose, could hear the whistling hiss as it sped past him. He remembered a time when he was golfing and his brother-in-law Robert shanked the ball and it sailed right past his nose and hit the caddy next to him, giving him a concussion. Sounded like a dumb comparison, but even though this whole experience couldn't have taken more than a second, that was where his mind traveled to—a golf outing in Paramus, New Jersey—as the bullet shrieked past him and the blood splashed onto his cheek.

Blood...

Ingrid's eyes rolled back as she dropped to the ground.

Simon watched her fall in slow motion. Gone was all that primitive survival stuff, the stuff that might tell him to flee or fight or whatever. He watched Ingrid, his entire world, crumble to the concrete, bleeding, and another instinct took over.

Protect her...

He collapsed to the ground and, without conscious thought, covered her body with his, trying to position himself in such a way as to shield as much of her as possible, while at the same time seeing if she was alive, where the wound was, whether he could stem the bleeding.

Somewhere else, in another part of his brain, he knew that Luther was still there, still armed with a gun, still in all probability preparing to fire again. But that was a secondary or even tertiary thought.

Protect her. Save her...

He risked a look. Luther stepped toward him and pointed his gun down at Simon's head. A dozen thoughts raced through his head—kick out, roll away, try to strike him in some way, any way, before he could fire again.

But there was nothing to be done. He could see that too.

There was no time to do anything to save himself, so he pulled Ingrid even more under him and curled his body inward, making sure none of Ingrid was exposed. He lowered his head toward hers and braced himself.

Simon heard the gunshot.

And Luther went down.

CHAPTER
TEN

Ash placed the cup of coffee on the table. Dee Dee bowed her head in prayer. Ash tried not to roll his eyes. Dee Dee finished the prayer in the same way she always did, "Forever be the Shining Truth."

Ash sat across from her. The target's name was Damien Gorse. He owned a tattoo parlor in a New Jersey strip mall across the highway from where they now sat. They both turned and stared at the name on the awning.

Dee Dee started giggling.

"What's so funny?"

"The name of the parlor."

"What about it?"

"Tattoos While U Wait," Dee Dee said. "Think about it. I mean, how else would you do it? 'Hey, man, here's my arm, put a skull and crossbones on it, I'll be back in two hours.'"

She covered her mouth as she giggled some more. It was all kinds of adorable.

"Good point," Ash said.

"Right? Tattoos While U Wait. I mean, what name came in second place?"

He chuckled now too, either because the joke was a little funny or more likely because her giggle was contagious. Dee Dee drove him crazy. She could be annoying as all get-out, no question about it, but mostly, he was terrified that soon these jobs would end and she'd be gone from his life again.

Dee Dee noticed him looking at her funny. "What?"

"Nothing."

"Ash..."

Then he just said it: "You don't have to go back."

Dee Dee looked up at him with those damned beautiful get-lost-forever-in green eyes. "Of course I do."

"It isn't the Shining Truth. It's a cult."

"You don't understand."

"That's what all cultists say. You have a choice here."

"The Shining Truth is the only choice."

"Come on, Dee Dee."

She sat back. "I'm not Dee Dee there. I didn't tell you that."

"What do you mean?"

"At Truth Haven. They call me Holly."

"Seriously?"

"Yes."

"They made you change your name?"

"They didn't make me change anything. Holly is my Truth."

"Name changing is Cult Indoctrination 101."

"It represents that I'm a new person. I'm not Dee Dee. I don't want to be Dee Dee."

He made a face. "So you want me to call you Holly?"

"Not you, Ash." She reached across the table and covered his hand. "You always saw Holly. You were the only one."

He felt the warmth of her hand on his. For a moment they stayed like that, and Ash wished that the moment would never move on. Stupid. He knew that it wouldn't last. Nothing lasted. But for another moment or two, he just soaked this in and let it be.

Dee Dee smiled at him as if she knew just what he was feeling. Maybe she did. She could always read him in a way no one else could.

"It's okay, Ash."

He said nothing. She patted his arm several times, disengaging slowly, so it wouldn't just be a sudden pull away.

"It's getting late," she said. "We should probably get in position."

He nodded. They headed to the stolen car with the stolen plate. They took the highway north and exited on Downing Street. The local road led to the back of a ShopRite supermarket. They parked near the exit, away from any surveillance cameras. They started through a wooded area and came up on the back of the tattoo parlor.

Ash checked his watch. Twenty minutes until closing time.

Murder was simple if you kept it simple.

Ash already had the gloves on. His outfit was black from head to toe. The ski mask was off because those things were too hot and itchy to put on prematurely. But it was at the ready.

There was a rusted green dumpster behind the tattoo parlor. A side window had a red neon sign reading PIERCINGS—ANYWHERE, EVERYWHERE. Ash could see the silhouette of someone sweeping up inside. There were two cars left in the lot—a Toyota Tundra pickup truck, hopefully belonging to the last client of the day, and in the back, near the dumpster and out of sight from the highway, a wood-paneled Ford Flex belonging to Damien Gorse.

Their intel, such as it was, had informed them that Gorse always closed up.

The plan was to let Damien Gorse lock up, walk to his car, then kill him in a "robbery gone wrong."

Ash heard the tinkling of the shopkeeper bell when the front door of the parlor opened. A man with a long red ponytail stepped out, turned back around, and shouted, "Thanks, Damien."

Damien shouted something back to the ponytailed man, but

they couldn't make out what. The ponytailed man nodded and trudged through the gravel lot toward the Toyota Tundra. His arm was completely bandaged. He stared at the arm with a big smile as he walked.

"Maybe he just came back to pick it up," Dee Dee whispered.

"What?"

"His arm. You know. Tattoos While U Wait?"

Inside the shop, the silhouette stopped with the sweeping.

She giggled as the ponytailed man got into the Toyota, started it up, and merged onto the highway.

Dee Dee moved closer to Ash. She smelled the way only a beautiful woman can, like honeysuckle and lilacs and some form of ambrosia. Her proximity was a distraction. He didn't like that.

Ash shifted a little away from her and put on the ski mask.

Inside the shop, the lights went out.

"Showtime," Dee Dee said.

"Stay here."

Staying low, Ash moved closer to the back of the lot. He squatted behind a tree and waited. He looked at the Ford Flex. The faux wood paneling made it look like a family car, though Gorse was unmarried and childless. Maybe it was his mother's car. Or his father's. If there had been more time, Ash would have known all that, would have done all his own intel. But knowing all that was often, pardon the pun, overkill.

Just do the job, move on, don't leave any tracks.

The rest was flotsam and jetsam.

It also helped to think methodically. It would take him fewer than ten seconds to make it to the car. Don't hesitate. Don't give him a chance to react. Walk up to him and shoot him in the chest twice. He'd normally go for a headshot, but one, a robber might not do that, and two, Kevin Gano had gone down with a headshot. No reason to repeat himself.

Of course, there was nothing else connecting Damien Gorse and Kevin Gano. Ash was using completely different handgun makes and models obtained in completely different ways. One death—Gano's—had been a "suicide" in the Boston area, the other—Gorse's—would be a robbery gone wrong in New Jersey.

There would be no law enforcement link.

More than that, Ash could find no other connections between Kevin Gano and Damien Gorse or any of the others. They were all between the ages of twenty-four and thirty-two. They lived in various parts of the country. They all attended different schools, held different jobs. There had to be an overlap, of course, something that linked the targets, and maybe if Ash had more information or more time he could figure out what it was.

But for now he didn't have either and that was okay.

The tattoo parlor's shopkeeper bell trilled.

Ash had the gun in his gloved hand. The ski mask was in place. Ash had learned over the years that ski masks don't offer enough peripheral vision, so he'd already made the eye holes a little bigger. He stayed in his squat and waited. To his left, he could see Dee Dee had moved closer to the periphery. He frowned. She should know better and stay back. But that was Dee Dee.

Gorse was coming at him from the right. Dee Dee was on the left. There was no chance he would spot her before the bullets hit him.

She just wanted a better view.

Still, he didn't like it.

The crunching of feet on gravel made him turn his head toward the side of the building.

It was Damien Gorse.

Perfect.

Now Ash just needed to time the strike, but really there was plenty of room for error, especially on the late side. Arrive too early and maybe Gorse could run toward the road or back into the shop, though that was unlikely. Arrive too late and it meant that Gorse was in his car, but glass doesn't stop bullets.

No matter. His timing was perfect.

Gorse stuck out a hand holding the car remote. Ash heard the familiar beep-beep as the car unlocked. He waited until Damien Gorse arrived at his back bumper. Ash stood up straight and rush-walked toward him. Don't run. Running will throw off your aim.

Gorse's hand was just reaching out for the car door handle when he spotted Ash. He turned toward him, a questioning look on his face. Ash raised the weapon and fired two shots into Gorse's chest. The sound was louder than Ash had anticipated, though that wasn't really a big deal. Gorse's body fell against the car. For a second the car seemed to hold him up before he slid down the door onto the gravel.

As Ash hurried toward the still body, he spotted Dee Dee, thanks to his peripheral vision, moving to her right so she could get a better view of the dead body. He had no time for that. He bent down, made sure Gorse was dead, and then rifled through the man's pockets. He took out the wallet. Gorse also wore a Tag Heuer watch. He took that too.

Dee Dee moved closer.

"Will you get back?" he snapped.

He started to rise, but then he saw the look on Dee Dee's face. She was staring over his shoulder. Ash felt his stomach drop.

"Ash?" she said.

Then she gestured with her chin.

Ash spun. There, next to the green dumpster, a man stood holding a garbage bag.

The man—no, more likely a teen, a freaking kid for crying out loud—must have exited out the back of the store to throw out the trash. He still held the bag up in the air, as though he'd stopped in mid-toss, frozen by what he'd witnessed.

The kid just stared at Ash, who was wearing a ski mask.

And he stared at Dee Dee, who wasn't wearing one.

Shit, Ash thought.

No choice. He aimed his gun and fired, but the kid was on the move. He ducked behind the dumpster. Ash started toward him, taking another shot. The kid scrambled on his hands and knees, the bullet flying over his head. The kid ducked back in through the exit door and slammed it shut.

Damn it!

Ash had chosen to use a revolver for this murder, a six-shooter. He'd already fired four shots, leaving him two. He couldn't waste them. But he couldn't waste time either. It would take only a few seconds for the kid to call the police or...

An alarm shattered the air.

The sound was so loud Ash stopped for a moment and started to cover his ears with his hands. He spun back toward Dee Dee.

"Go!" Ash shouted.

She nodded, understood the protocol. Take off. He was tempted to do the same—get out of here before the cops came. But the kid had seen Dee Dee's face. He could describe her.

So the kid had to die.

Ash tried the knob on the back door. It turned. Maybe five seconds had passed since he took the first shot. If there was a gun in the store, it was doubtful the kid would have had time to find it. Ash burst in and looked around.

No sign of the kid.

He'd be hiding.

So how long did Ash have? Not long enough. But.

The mind is a computer, so in the brief time it took him to make a step, a lot of probabilities and outcomes flowed through him. The first one was the most obvious and instinctive: The kid had seen Dee Dee's face. He could identify her. Leaving him alive was thus a clear and present danger to Dee Dee.

Conclusion: He had to be killed.

But as he took the next step, he began to realize that his gut reaction might be a bit too extreme. Yes, the kid had seen her and perhaps he could make an ID. But what would he say exactly? A beautiful woman with a long blonde braid and green eyes who didn't live in New Jersey, had no connection to New Jersey, who would soon be out of state and perhaps back on her commune or retreat or haven or whatever the fuck she called it...how would the police even know how to find her?

Then again, suppose Dee Dee didn't make it that far. Suppose the police caught her now, before she could get away cleanly. The kid could identify her. But again—see how the mind works?—so what?

Strip it down: Dee Dee had been standing in a parking lot when Damien Gorse was murdered. That's all. So had a man with a ski mask and a gun—why would anyone assume that the two of them were together? If she was in on the killing, wouldn't she have worn a mask too? Wouldn't Dee Dee be able to easily claim that she had nothing to do with the killing, that she'd stumbled upon the scene, even if she was somehow caught and somehow identified because of the kid's testimony?

Inside the tattoo parlor, Ash took another step.

More silence.

Really, when he thought about it, what were the odds that if this kid lived, it would bring danger to Dee Dee? When you added it all up—when you weighed all the pros and cons—wouldn't the best route, the best chance of a successful outcome, derive from Ash getting away now, before the cops came? Was it worth the time lost pursuing this scared kid and risking getting caught—versus the miniscule threat that this witness's survival could really harm Dee?

Let the kid live.

Ash heard a siren.

He didn't relish killing him either. Oh, he'd do it, sure, and with no problem. But killing the kid now seemed wasteful, and when you can, you might as well err on the side of the angels, no? He didn't believe in karma, but then again there was no reason to poke karma in the ribs.

Sirens. Getting closer.

This was the kid's lucky day.

Ash turned. He sprinted toward the back door to make his escape, because in truth his options were down to one—flee.

That was when he heard the click come from the closet door next to the exit.

Ash almost kept going.

But he didn't.

Ash opened the door. The kid was down on the floor, his shaking hands on top of his head as though readying to ward off blows.

"Please," the kid said, "I promise I won't—"

No time to hear more.

Ash used one bullet, a headshot, leaving himself one last bullet just in case.

CHAPTER

ELEVEN

Everyone fled the tenement basement.

Out of the corner of his eye, Simon saw Rocco toss Luther over his shoulder like a laundry bag as he sprinted out. For a few seconds, maybe longer, Simon stayed in position, shielding his wife. When he realized that the danger had passed, he reached for his phone to dial 911. Sirens sliced through the stale air.

Maybe someone had already called. Maybe the sirens had nothing to do with this.

Ingrid's eyes were closed. Blood poured from a wound located somewhere between her right shoulder and upper chest. Simon did all he could to stop the flow, ripping off his own shirt and pressing it hard against the wound. He didn't bother checking Ingrid for a pulse. If she was dead, then he'd find out soon enough.

Protect her. Save her.

The 911 operator told him that help was on its way. Time passed. Simon didn't know how much. They were alone in this dank, disgusting basement, he and Ingrid. They had first met in a restaurant on Sixty-Ninth Street, only two blocks from where they now lived, when Ingrid was finally back in the country and Yvonne had set them up. He had arrived first and sat nervously waiting at a table by the window, and when she entered, head high, the regal catwalk strut, he'd been blown away. Corny or not—and maybe everyone did this—but whenever Simon was on a first date, he let himself imagine a full life with the person, looking waaaaay ahead of himself, picturing him and this woman married and raising kids and sitting across the kitchen table as they aged and reading in bed, all that. How did he feel when he first saw Ingrid? He thought that she was too gorgeous. That was the first thought. She looked too put together for him, too composed and confident. He'd later learn that it was for show, that Ingrid had the same fears and insecurities that plague all of us, that part of the human condition is that all decent people think they are phonies and don't belong at some point or another.

Whatever. Their relationship had started at that bright window table on West Sixty-Ninth Street and Columbus Avenue and now it could end in this dank, dark basement in the Bronx.

"Ingrid?"

His voice came out as a pitiful plea.

"Stay with me, okay?"

The police arrived, as did the EMTs. They pulled him away and took over. He sat on the concrete, pulling his knees up to his chest. A cop started asking him questions, but he couldn't hear, could only stare at his still wife as the EMTs worked on her. An oxygen mask covered the mouth he had kissed so many times, kissed in every single way imaginable, from perfunctory to passionate. He didn't say anything now, just watched. He didn't demand to know whether she was still alive, whether they could save her. He was too terrified to disturb them, to break their concentration, as though her lifeline was so fragile that any interruption could snap it like an overused rubber band.

Simon wanted to say that the rest was a blur, but it actually crawled by in slow motion and vivid color—loading Ingrid onto the gurney, rolling her to the ambulance, hopping into the back with her, staring at the IV bag, the rigid expressions on the EMTs' faces, the paleness of Ingrid's skin, the screams of the siren, the maddeningly frustrating traffic along the Major Deegan, finally stopping, crashing through the emergency room doors, a nurse firmly but patiently pulling him away and leading him to a yellow molded plastic chair in the waiting room...

He called Yvonne and gave her the broad strokes. When he finished, Yvonne said, "I'll head straight over to your place and get Anya."

Simon's voice sounded weird in his own ears. "Okay."

"What do you want me to tell her?"

He felt a sob rise up his throat. He stuffed it back down. "Nothing specific, just stay with her."

"Did you call Sam?" Yvonne asked.

"No. He's got a biology test. He doesn't need to know."

"Simon?"

"What?"

"You're not thinking straight. Their mother has been shot. She's in surgery."

He squeezed his eyes shut.

"I'll pick up Anya," she said, "Robert will get Sam. They should be at the hospital."

Yvonne left off the "me too," maybe because the kids were more important or maybe because Yvonne and Ingrid were not very close. They were civil to each other, unfailingly polite with no obvious rancor, but Simon was the bridge between the two sisters.

Yvonne spoke again. "Okay, Simon?"

Two cops appeared, doing the room-scan thing. They spotted Simon and swaggered toward him.

"Okay," he said, and hung up.

At the scene, Simon had given the cops a description of the shooter, but now they wanted more details. He started to tell the cops everything, but it was slow going without full context, without going into Aaron and the other murder and all that. He was also distracted, staring at the door, waiting for a doctor to appear, a god really, to tell him whether his world was over or not.

Fagbenle burst into the waiting room. The two cops moved toward him. The three of them huddled in the corner. Simon took the break to once again head over to the desk and ask about his wife—and once again the receptionist politely told him that she had no new information, that the doctor would come out as soon as there was an update.

When Simon turned back around, Fagbenle was right there. "I don't understand. Why were you two in the Bronx?"

"We were trying to find our daughter."

"By visiting a drug den?"

"Our daughter is a drug addict."

"Did you find her?"

"No, Detective. In case you didn't hear, my wife was shot."

"I'm really sorry about that."

Simon closed his eyes, waved him off.

"I hear you also visited the murder scene."

"Yes."

"Why?"

"That's where we started."

"Started what?"

"Looking for our daughter."

"How did you get from that apartment to the drug house next door?"

Simon knew better than to go there. "What does that matter?"

"Why don't you want to tell me, Simon?"

"Because it doesn't matter."

"Gotta be honest," Fagbenle said. "This all doesn't look good."

"Gotta be honest," Simon said. "I don't care how it looks."

Simon moved back toward his yellow plastic molded chair.

"Occam's razor," Fagbenle said. "You know it?"

"I'm not in the mood, Detective."

"It states—"

"I know what it states—"

"—that the simplest explanation is usually the right one."

"And what's the simplest explanation, Detective?"

"You killed Aaron Corval," he said. Just like that. No emotion, no rancor, no surprise. "Or your wife did. I wouldn't blame either of you. The man was a monster. He was slowly poisoning your daughter, killing her right in front of your eyes."

Simon frowned. "Is this the part where I break down and confess?"

"Nah, you just listen. I'm talking about the old moral quandary."

"Uh-huh."

"Question: Would you kill someone? Answer: No, of course not. Question: Would you kill someone to save your child? Answer...?"

Fagbenle raised both palms and shrugged.

Simon sat back down. Fagbenle pulled up a nearby chair and sat close to him. He kept his voice low.

"You could have sneaked out of your apartment building when Anya was asleep. Or Ingrid could have run over to the Bronx during her work break."

"You don't believe that."

He made a maybe-yes, maybe-no gesture with his head. "I heard when your wife was shot, you jumped on top of her. Used your body as a shield."

"What's your point?"

"You were willing to die to save someone you love," Fagbenle said, moving in a little closer. "How much of a stretch is it to believe you'd kill?"

There was movement all around them—people in and out— but Simon and Fagbenle saw none of that.

"I have an idea, Detective."

"I'm all ears."

"My wife was shot by a man named Luther." Simon gave him

the same description he'd already given twice now. "Why don't you guys find and arrest him?"

"We already did."

"Wait, you caught him?"

"It wasn't really hard. We just followed the blood trail. We found him unconscious about two blocks away."

"The big guy, Rocco, he took him out of the basement. He was carrying him."

"Rocco Canard. Yeah, we know him. Gang affiliated. Luther Ritz—that's his last name, by the way—worked for Rocco. So did Aaron. Rocco probably tried to hide him. When he saw the blood trail, Rocco dumped him in an alley. At least that's our theory. We will need you to identify the guy to make sure he's your shooter."

"Okay," Simon said. "How bad was he hit?"

"He'll live."

"Did he say anything on the way in?"

"Yeah," Fagbenle said, flashing the smile, "he said you and Ingrid shot him."

"That's a lie."

"That much we know. But I still don't understand what happened. Why did he shoot?"

"I don't know. We were just talking to Rocco and—"

"You and your wife?"

"Yes."

"So you two, what, just waltzed into this drug den and started chatting up a gang leader?"

"Like you said, Detective: what we do to help a loved one."

Fagbenle seemed to like that answer. "Go on."

Simon told him what happened, leaving out only one key aspect.

"And then Luther just started firing at you?"

"Yes."

"No warning?"

"None."

"There you go." Another flash of teeth. "Occam's razor again."

"How so?" Simon asked.

"Rocco is a drug dealer. Luther and Aaron both worked for him. That's a world loaded with violence. Aaron ends up dead, Luther shoots at you guys—speaking of which, who shot Luther?"

A man plopped down in the molded yellow seat across from them. He was holding a bandage on his head. Blood oozed through the gauze.

"Simon?"

"What?"

"Your wife is hit with a bullet. You dive to cover her. Luther is going to finish you off. So who stopped him?"

"I didn't see anyone," he said.

Fagbenle heard something in his tone. "I didn't ask if you saw anyone. I asked who saved you from Luther."

But just then Anya came sprinting into the room. Simon stood as his daughter wrapped her arms around him, nearly knocking him over. He closed his eyes and held her close, willing the tears to stay back. Anya buried her face in his chest.

"Mom..." she muffle-cried.

He almost said, "It's going to be okay" or "She'll be fine," but he saw no reason to tell more lies. His eyes opened. Yvonne crossed the room and kissed his cheek as he still held Anya.

"Robert is on his way to get Sam," she said.

"Thank you."

Then a man in hospital scrubs came into the room. "Simon Greene?"

Anya slowly released her grip and freed her father.

"Right here."

"Follow me, please. The doctor will see you now."

CHAPTER
TWELVE

You often hear that a physician's bedside manner is more or less irrelevant. The theory seems to suggest that you just want someone who coldly, mechanically, robotically does the job, who doesn't get distracted by emotion, who lives by that old saw that you'd rather have a surgeon who cuts straight and cares less.

Ingrid, Simon knew, believed the opposite.

You want a real person—a caring, empathic person—to be your physician. You want a person who sees you as a fellow human being who is scared and hurting and in need of reassurance and comfort. It was a responsibility Ingrid took very seriously. When a parent brought their child to see her—well, step back and think about it: When are you ever more vulnerable? You're stressed, you're terrified, you're confused. Physicians who do not understand that, who act as though you are an anatomical object in need of repair like a MacBook visiting the Genius Bar are going to not only make the experience more miserable but they will miss something in the diagnosis.

Sometimes, like right now, you are scared and hurting and stressed and terrified and confused as you take a seat across from a physician who speaks words that will change your life like no others. They could be the worst words in the world or the best words or, as in this case, somewhere in between.

So Ingrid would really like Dr. Heather Grewe, who oozed both exhaustion and empathy. Grewe tried to break it down, aiming for a combination of real-world terminology and medical jargon. Simon focused on the bottom line.

Ingrid was still alive.

Barely.

She was in a coma.

The next twenty-four hours would be crucial.

Simon nodded along, but somewhere the doctor's words had untethered him. He was trying to hold on, but he was floating away. Yvonne, who sat next to him, remained firmly grounded. She asked follow-up questions, probably good ones, but they didn't change the meaning or clarify the murky diagnosis. This is another thing you learn about doctors. We may think they are gods sometimes, but the limits of what they know or can do are both astounding and humbling.

They were closely monitoring Ingrid's condition, but there was nothing to do right now but wait. Dr. Grewe rose and extended her hand. Simon rose and shook it. So did Yvonne. There were no visitors allowed yet so they stumbled back down the corridor toward the waiting room.

Fagbenle cut Simon off and pulled him aside.

"I need something from you," Fagbenle said.

Simon, still reeling, managed a nod. "Okay."

"I need you to look at something."

He handed Simon a sheet of cardboard with six photographs on it, three in the top row, three on the bottom. They were all headshots and underneath each headshot was a number.

"I want you to study this carefully and tell me if—"

"Number Five," Simon said.

"Let me finish. I want you to study this carefully and tell me if you recognize any of these men."

"I recognize Number Five."

"How do you know Number Five?"

"He's the man who shot my wife."

Fagbenle nodded. "I'd like you to make a formal ID in person."

"This"—Simon pointed to the cardboard sheet—"isn't enough?"

"I think it would also be better to do it in person."

"I don't want to leave my wife right now."

"You don't have to. The suspect is here too—recovering from the gunshot. Come on."

Fagbenle started down the corridor. Simon looked back at Yvonne, who nodded for him to go. The walk wasn't far, just to the end of the corridor.

"Did you catch Rocco too?" Simon asked.

"We brought him in, yeah."

"What did he say?"

"You and your wife came into his establishment, he had his back turned, there were gunshots, he ran. He has no idea who fired or who got shot or any of that."

"That's bullshit."

"Really? Rocco, a leading drug dealer, is lying to us? Wow, I for one am shocked."

"Did you ask him about my daughter?"

"Doesn't know her. 'White girls all look the same to me,' he said, 'especially junkies.'"

Simon didn't wince. "Can you hold him?"

"On what charge? You yourself said Rocco never attacked you, right?"

"Right."

"Luther was the one who pulled the trigger. Speaking of which."

He stopped in front of a room with a uniformed cop sitting by the door. "Hey, Tony," Fagbenle said.

Tony the guard looked at Simon.

"Who's this?"

"The vic's husband."

"Oh." Tony the guard nodded toward Simon. "Sorry."

"Thanks."

"He's here to make an ID," Fagbenle said. "Assume the perp is still out?"

"Nah, he's awake."

"Since when?"

"Five, ten minutes ago."

Fagbenle turned to Simon. "Probably not a good idea to do this now."

"Why not?"

"Protocol. Most witnesses are scared to be face-to-face with the perp."

Simon frowned. "Let's just do this."

"It doesn't bother you that he'll see you?"

"He saw me when he shot my wife. You think I care?"

Fagbenle shrugged a suit-yourself and pushed open the door. A television played something in Spanish. Luther sat up in the bed, his shoulder wrapped. He gave Simon a scowl and said, "What's he doing in here?"

"Oh, so you know this man?" Fagbenle asked.

Luther's eyes shifted left and right. "Uh . . ."

Fagbenle turned to Simon. "Mr. Greene?"

"Yes, he's the man who shot my wife."

"That's a lie!"

"You're certain?" Fagbenle asked.

"Yes," Simon said, "I'm certain."

"They shot me!" Luther shouted.

"Did they, Luther?"

"Yeah. He's a liar."

"Where did they shoot you exactly?"

"In the shoulder."

"No, Luther, I mean geographical location."

"Huh?"

Fagbenle rolled his eyes. "The place, Luther."

"Oh, in that basement. In Rocco's lot."

"So why did we find you hiding in an alley two blocks away?"

You could see the dumb stamped all over him. "Uh, I ran. From him."

"And hid in an alley even when the police came searching for you?"

"Hey, I don't like cops, that's all."

"Great, thanks for confirming that you were at the shooting scene, Luther. Really helps us wrap this all up."

"I didn't shoot nobody. You got no proof."

"Do you own a gun, Luther?"

"No."

"Never fired one?"

"A gun?" He got a cagey look. "Maybe once, like years ago."

"Man, Luther, don't you watch TV?"

"What?"

"Like every cop show."

Luther looked confused.

"There's always the part where some moronic perp says, 'I never fired the gun,' you know, like you just did, and then the cop says they ran a gunshot residue test—this ringing any bells, Luther?—and they find residue, usually in the form of gunpowder particles, on the moronic perp's hands and clothes."

Luther's face lost color.

"And, see, once they have all that, the cops—that would be me—have the guy dead to rights. We have witnesses and gun residue and scientific proof our moronic perp is a liar. It's over for him. He usually confesses and tries to cut a deal."

Luther sat back and blinked.

"You want to tell us why you did it?"

"I didn't do it."

Fagbenle sighed. "You're really boring us now."

"Why don't you ask him why?" Luther asked.

"Pardon?"

Luther tilted his chin toward Simon. "Ask him."

Simon took deep breaths. He'd been blocking since he entered the room, but now it all came crashing down on him. Ingrid, the woman he loved like no other, was nearby, in this very building, clinging to life because of this piece of shit. Without conscious thought, Simon took a step toward the bed, raising his hands to throttle the useless turd, this nothing, this worthless dung who had tried to snuff out the life of such a wonderful, vibrant being.

Fagbenle put an arm out to keep Simon in check, more a mental blockade than a physical one. He met Simon's eyes and gave an understanding but firm shake of the head.

"What should I ask him, Luther?" Fagbenle asked.

"What were they two doing at Rocco's, huh? Let's say I did do it. Not really, but like pretend, like what's the word . . . hypodermically, let's say I did it."

Fagbenle tried not to frown. "Go for it."

"Maybe Rocco needs protection."

"Why would Rocco need protection?"

"Don't know. I'm talking hypodermically."

"So Rocco told you to shoot Dr. Greene?"

"Doctor?" He sat up, wincing. "What are you talking about? I didn't shoot no doctor. You ain't pinning that on me." He pointed at Simon. "I just shot his old lady."

Simon didn't know whether he should burst out punching or laughing. Again the sheer outrage of the situation—that even this worthless slice of nothing has the power to destroy something as vital and cherished and loved as Ingrid—consumed him, making him realize that there was nothing just in this world, no control, no center force, just random chaos. He wanted to kill this punk, stomp him out like the bug that he was, except no bug could ever be this callous and harmful, so yes, stomp out this nothing for the good of mankind—much gained, nothing lost. And yet he suddenly felt exhausted by the notion, that in the end there was no point in doing even that. It was all a big fucking joke.

"I was just protecting my boss," Luther said. "Self-defense, you know what I'm saying?"

Simon felt his phone vibrate. He glanced at the screen. It was from Yvonne:

We can see Ingrid now.

When Simon first entered her room, when he first saw Ingrid on that bed, stiller than sleep, tubes everywhere, gurgling machines—when he first saw all of that, his knees buckled and his body fell toward the floor. He didn't catch himself. He probably could have, probably could have reached out and grabbed the wheelchair accessibility bar on his right. But he didn't. He let himself land and land hard and let himself have the silent scream, that moment, because he knew that he needed it.

When that was over, he rose and there were no more tears. He sat next to Ingrid and held her hand and talked to her. He didn't will her to live or tell her how much he loved her or any of that. If Ingrid could hear, she wouldn't want those words. She wasn't big on melodrama for one thing, but more than that, she wouldn't want him expressing thoughts like this when she couldn't reciprocate or at least comment. Declarations of love or loss with no response were meaningless to her. It was like playing catch with yourself. It had to go two ways.

So he talked about general stuff—his work, her work, the remodeling of the kitchen that might one day happen (or more likely, not), about politics and the past and a few favorite memories he knew she liked to bathe in. That was also Ingrid. She liked when he repeated certain stories. She was the kind who listened deeply, with her entire being, and a smile would come to her lips and he could see that she was back there with him, reliving the moment with a clarity few people could experience.

But of course, there was no smile on her face today.

At some point—Simon couldn't say how much time had passed—Yvonne put her hand on his shoulder. "Tell me what happened," she said. "Everything."

So he did.

Yvonne kept her eyes on her sister's face. She and Ingrid had taken such different paths, and maybe that explained the rift. Ingrid had chosen something of a high life to start—the modeling, the travel, some experimentation with drugs that oddly made her less sympathetic to Paige, not more—whereas Yvonne had always been more the dutiful type-A daughter who studied hard and loved her parents and stayed on the straight and narrow.

In the end, Ingrid had discovered, as she put it, that searching the whole world just makes you find home. She'd come back and done a year of what was called "post-baccalaureate" at Bryn Mawr College, so as to cram in all her pre-med requirements. With the sort of determination and single focus that Yvonne would undoubtedly admire in another person, Ingrid excelled through med school, residency, and internship.

"You can't stay here," Yvonne said when he finished.

"What are you talking about?"

"I'll sit with Ingrid. But you can't just sit here, Simon. You have to go find Paige."

"I can't leave now."

"You have to. You have no choice."

"We always promised..." Simon stopped. He wasn't going to explain to Yvonne what she already knew. He and Ingrid were like one. If one of them got sick, the other was going to be there. That was the rule. That was part of the bargain in all this.

Yvonne understood, but she still shook her head. "Ingrid is going to wake up from this. Or she's not. And if she wakes up, she's going to want to see Paige's face."

He didn't reply.

"You can't find her if you're sitting here."

"Yvonne—"

"Ingrid would tell you that if she could, Simon. You know this."

Ingrid's hand felt lifeless now, no feel of blood pumping through it. Simon stared at his wife, willing her to give him some kind of answer or sign, but she seemed to be growing smaller, fading away, right in front of his eyes. This didn't seem to be Ingrid in this bed anymore, just an empty body, as if her being had already fled the building. He wasn't naïve enough to think the sound of Paige's voice could bring Ingrid back, but he sure as shit didn't think him sitting there would do it either.

Simon let go of Ingrid's hand. "Before I go, I'll need to—"

"I got the kids. I got the business. I got Ingrid. Go."

CHAPTER
THIRTEEN

Night had passed and it was nearly daybreak when the car dropped Simon back off by those concrete blocks in the Bronx. There was no one on the street—no one awake anyway. Two guys were sleeping on the sidewalk in front of the overgrown, abandoned lot, scant feet from where he and Ingrid had entered, what, just a few hours ago. Someone had hung up police tape, but it'd been torn down the middle, flying in the predawn breeze.

Simon reached the decrepit four-floor brick tenement house that his daughter had called home. He headed back inside this time with no hesitation or fear. He started up the stairs but stopped on the second floor rather than heading up to the third. It wasn't quite six a.m. Simon hadn't slept, of course. He felt rattled and juiced up on something that he knew would ebb out of him soon.

He knocked on the door and waited. He figured that he might be waking him up, but he didn't much care. Ten seconds later, no more, the door opened. Cornelius looked as though he hadn't slept much either. The two men looked at each other for a long moment.

"How is she?" Cornelius asked.

"Critical."

"Better come inside."

Simon wasn't sure what he expected when he stepped into Cornelius's apartment—something like the dirty hovel Paige had called home—but the interior was like stepping through a magic portal into another world. The place could have been featured on one of those home TV shows Ingrid loved to watch. Built-in oak bookshelves framed the windows on the far wall. A classic Victorian tufted sofa of green sat to the right. The embroidered accent pillows had botanical themes. Prints of butterflies hung to the left. A chess set sat atop an ornate wood table and for a moment, Simon could almost see Paige sitting there with Cornelius, the way her brow would furrow and she'd play with her hair when she concentrated on a move.

A cocker spaniel burst around the corner, tail wagging so hard she could barely keep her balance. Cornelius scooped her up and held her close. "This here is Chloe."

There were photographs in front of the books on the shelves. Family photographs. Lots of them. Simon moved toward them for a better look. He stopped at the first photograph, a standard family shot in front of a rainbow backdrop—a younger Cornelius, a woman who looked to be his wife, and three smiling teenage boys, two of whom were already taller than Cornelius.

Cornelius put down the dog and joined him.

"This picture gotta be eight, ten years old. Me and Tanya, we raised three boys here in this apartment. They're grown now. Tanya . . . she passed two years ago. Breast cancer."

"I'm sorry," Simon said.

"Do you want to sit? You look exhausted, man."

"If I sit, I'm afraid I'm not going to get back up."

"Might not be a bad idea. You need some rest if you want to keep going."

"Maybe later."

Cornelius placed the family photograph down gently, as

though it were exceedingly fragile, and pointed to a portrait of a Marine in uniform.

"This here is Eldon. He's our oldest."

"A Marine."

"Yes."

"He looks like you."

"That he does."

"You serve, Cornelius?"

"A Marine corporal. First Persian Gulf War. Operation Desert Storm." Cornelius turned and faced Simon full-on. "You don't seem surprised."

"I'm not."

Cornelius rubbed his chin. "Did you see me?"

"Just a flash."

"But enough to figure it out?"

"I think I would have guessed anyway," Simon said. "I don't know how to thank you."

"Don't. I saw Luther heading in, so I followed him. Should have taken him out before he shot Ingrid."

"You saved our lives."

Cornelius glanced back over at the family photos, as though the images might impart some kind of wisdom to him. "So why are you back here?" he asked.

"You know why."

"To find Paige."

"Yes."

"She went there too. To that basement. Same as you." Cornelius moved toward the far corner. "I never saw her after that."

"And then Aaron ended up dead."

"Yes."

"Do you think they killed Paige?"

"I don't know." Cornelius squatted down. He opened a cabinet, revealing a safe. "But you should be prepared for bad news, no matter how this shakes out."

"I am," Simon said.

Cornelius pressed his thumb against the door. Simon heard the beep-beep as the safe read his prints. The door opened. "And you shouldn't go in this time without backup."

He reached inside and pulled out two handguns. He stood up and shut the cabinet. He handed one weapon to Simon and kept the other for himself.

"You don't have to do this," Simon said.

"You didn't come here just to thank me, did you?"

"No."

"Let's go find Rocco."

The Judge Lester Patterson Houses was one of the city's oldest and largest low-income housing complexes, featuring fifteen monotonous high-rises of tired brick. The complex sat on more than seventeen acres and housed more than eighteen hundred families.

Cornelius led the way. The elevators in Building 6 were out of order so they took the stairs. The hour was early, but the place was alive. The stairwells were filled with laughing kids getting ready for school. Adults began their daily treks to the nearby bus and subway stops for the work commute. Most everyone was leaving, heading down the stairs, so that Cornelius and Simon had to swim upstream, two salmon on their way to the eighth floor.

Rocco's mother and siblings lived in apartment 8C. Two children sprinted out the door, leaving it open. Simon rapped his knuckles on the door, and a woman's voice told him to come in.

Simon entered. Cornelius stayed by the door. Rocco rose from a Barcalounger and started toward him. Again Simon was taken aback by the pure size of the man. A woman came out of the kitchen.

"Who's this?" she asked.

Rocco stared daggers at Simon. "Don't worry about it, Mama."

"Don't tell me not to worry about it. This is my house."

"I got it, Mama. He's just leaving." Rocco stepped right up to Simon, spreading out to his full size. Simon was eye to eye with his pectorals. "Aren't you?"

Simon tilted so he could see past Rocco, which was no easy task. "I'm looking for my daughter," he said to Rocco's mother. "I think your son may know where she is."

"Rocco?"

"Don't listen to him, Mama."

But she wasn't having any of that. As his mother strode toward him, the big man seemed to wither. "Do you know where this man's daughter is?"

"I don't, Mama." He sounded like a ten-year-old now. "I'm telling the truth."

Now she turned on Simon. "What makes you think he knows, mister?"

"Let me talk to him a second, Mama." Rocco started moving them toward the door. "I got this."

Rocco used his bulk to shove Simon back into the corridor, followed him out, and closed the door behind him. "Not cool, man—coming to my mama's." He spotted Cornelius. "What the fuck are you doing here?"

"Just helping him out."

Rocco snapped his fingers and pointed at him. "Now I get it. You're the one who sent him to me in the first place. Get the fuck out of here, both of you."

Simon didn't move. "Rocco?"

The big man looked down at him. "What?"

"My wife is in a coma fighting to survive. She got shot in your basement by your man. My daughter is missing. The last place anyone saw her was also in your basement." Simon didn't flinch or waver or even move. "I'm not going anywhere until you tell me everything you know."

"You think I'm scared of you?"

"You should be," Cornelius said.

"Why's that?"

"Look at him, Rocco. He's a desperate man. You smart enough to know it don't pay to mess with a desperate man."

Rocco did indeed look at him. Simon held his gaze.

"I'll tell the police you ordered Luther to shoot us," Simon said.

"What? You know that isn't true."

"You called out Luther's name."

"To stop him, man. I didn't want him to shoot!"

"I don't know that. I think it was an order. I think you told him to shoot us."

"Ah, I see." Rocco spread his hands. He looked at Simon and then at Cornelius. "So that's how it is, is it?"

Cornelius shrugged.

"I just want to find my daughter," Simon said.

Rocco did a let-me-think-about-it head roll. "Okay, fine, but then I want you gone."

Simon nodded.

"Yeah, she came to me. Paige, I mean. She came to the basement. I could see right away that someone had beaten her up."

"Did she say who?"

"I didn't have to ask. I knew."

"Aaron."

Rocco didn't bother replying.

"So why did Luther shoot at us?"

"Because he's crazy."

Simon shook his head. "There's gotta be more to it than that."

"I didn't tell him to do it."

"Who did?"

"Look, man, the business I'm in—it isn't an easy one. Always someone trying to move in on us. Aaron, yeah, he was a shitbag. But he was one of us. We figure a rival, shall we say, 'enterprise' took him out. Maybe the Fidels."

"Fidels?"

Cornelius said, "Cuban gang," and even in the middle of all this, with his wife fighting for her life and his daughter God knows where, Simon laughed out loud. The sound echoed in the corridor. People turned and stared.

"You're kidding me."

"I'm not."

"A Cuban gang called the Fidels?"

Cornelius let a smile hit his lips. "The leader's name is Castro."

"You're making that up."

"Swear to God."

Simon spun back toward Rocco. "Why did Paige come to you after this beating?"

"Why do you think?"

"For a fix," Simon said. "Did you give it to her?"

"She didn't have any money."

"Is that a no?"

"I'm not a charity," Rocco said.

"So what next?"

"She left, man. Next thing I know, Aaron is dead."

"Do you think Paige did it?"

"Smart money is on the Fidels," he said. "But yeah, I think there's a chance Paige killed him. Or maybe you did it, man. Maybe that's what Luther was thinking. Luther was there when Paige came in. Think about it. Let's say I'm a father. If some dude hurt my daughter the way Aaron hurt yours, I'd get revenge. So maybe that's your play."

"What's my play?"

"Maybe you killed Aaron. And now you're looking for your daughter to complete the rescue."

"That's not my play," Simon said.

But he kind of wished that it was. Rocco was right. If someone hurts your daughter, a father has an obligation to stop him, no matter what. Simon hadn't. He'd let Paige slip away, trying to throw her useless lifelines instead of doing what a man should do.

Anything to rescue his child.

Protect her. Save her.

Some father he'd turned out to be.

"She's probably around here somewhere," Rocco said. "You can look for her, man, I can't blame you for trying. But she's a junkie. Even if you find her, this story won't have a happy ending."

———————

Cornelius led the way back to his apartment. When he closed the door behind them, Simon reached into his coat pocket and took out the gun.

"Here," Simon said, holding it out toward him.

"Keep it."

"You sure?"

"I'm sure," Cornelius said.

"Do you think Rocco will be able to find her?"

"With that reward money?"

Simon had ended up making a simple offer to Rocco: Find Paige and get $50,000.

"Yeah," Cornelius said. "If she's still down here, he'll find her."

There was a knock on Cornelius's door.

"Put that gun back in your pocket," Cornelius whispered. Then raising his voice: "Who's there?"

What sounded like a little old lady with an accent—Polish, Russian, Eastern European maybe—said, "It's Lizzy, Mr. Cornelius."

Cornelius opened the door. The woman was as voice-advertised—small and old. She wore a strange white gown of some sort, long and flowing, almost something you'd wear to bed. Her gray hair ran down her back, loose and unkempt. The hair seemed to be swaying from a breeze, even though there was none.

"Something I can do for you, Miss Sobek?" Cornelius said.

The old woman peered around Cornelius with her huge eyes and spotted Simon. "Who are you?" she asked him.

"My name is Simon Greene, ma'am."

"Paige's father," Cornelius added.

The old woman gave Simon a look so heavy he almost stepped back. "You can still save her, you know."

Her words chilled him.

"Do you know where Paige is?" Simon asked.

Miss Sobek shook her head, the long gray hair dancing across her face like a bead curtain. "But I know what she is."

Cornelius cleared his throat, trying to move this along. "Did you want something, Miss Sobek?"

"Someone is upstairs."

"Upstairs?"

"On the third floor. A woman. She just sneaked into Paige's apartment. I thought you'd want to know."

"Did you recognize her?"

"Never seen her before."

"Thank you, Miss Sobek. I'll go check right now."

Cornelius and Simon stepped back into the corridor. Miss Sobek hurried away.

"Why did she come to you with this?" Simon asked, following him down the corridor.

"I'm not just a tenant."

"You're the super?"

"I'm the owner."

They headed up the stairs and down the hall. The yellow tape on the apartment door—blocking off the murder scene, Simon reminded himself—was torn. Cornelius reached out for the knob. Simon realized that he had—intentionally? subconsciously?—put his hand on the gun in his pocket. Is that what happens when you carry? Is it always there, by your side, like some kind of pacifier that calms or gives comfort in stressful situations?

Cornelius flung the door open. A woman stood there. If she was startled by their interruption, she was doing a good job of keeping it to herself. She was short and squat, maybe Latina, with a blue blazer and jeans.

She spoke first. "Are you Simon Greene?"

"Who are you?"

"My name is Elena Ramirez. I'm a private detective. I need to talk to your daughter."

————————

Elena Ramirez showed them a fancy embossed business card, a private investigator's license of some kind, and an ID showing she was a retired FBI agent. They were all back in Cornelius's apartment now. The two men sat in leather armchairs while Elena Ramirez took the green tufted sofa.

"So where is your daughter, Mr. Greene?" she asked.

"I don't understand. Your card says you're from Chicago."

"That's correct."

"So why do you want to talk to my daughter?"

"It involves a case I'm working on," Ramirez said.

"What case?"

"That I can't say."

"Miss Ramirez?"

"Please call me Elena."

"Elena, I'm not really up for games. I don't care what your case is and I don't have any reason to be cagey, so I'm going to be forthright and I hope you will be too. I don't know where my daughter is. That's why I'm here. I'm trying to locate her. I basically have no leads other than the fact that she's probably getting high within a one-square-mile radius of where we now are. Following me so far?"

"You bet," Elena said.

"So now you come along—a private eye from Chicago no

less—and want to talk to my daughter. I'd love you to talk to her. There's nothing I'd like more, in fact. So maybe we can help each other out by cooperating?"

Simon's phone buzzed. He had it in his hand, constantly checking for any text updates, feeling that phantom vibration thing every ten seconds. This one was real.

Yvonne texted:

Stabilizing, which doctor says is good. Moved to a private room.
Still in a coma. Sam and Anya with us.

"Just to make sure I'm following," Elena Ramirez said, "your daughter is missing. Is that correct?"

Simon still had his eyes on the phone's screen. "Yes."

"Since when?"

There was nothing to gain by being coy. "Since her boyfriend was murdered."

Elena Ramirez took her time, crossed her arms, thought it over.

Simon said, "Elena?"

"I'm looking for a missing person too."

"Who?"

"A twenty-four-year-old male who disappeared from the Chicago area."

Cornelius spoke for the first time since they sat down. "How long has he been missing?"

"Since last Thursday."

Simon asked, "Who is it?"

"I can't divulge the name."

"For crying out loud, Elena, if your missing twenty-four-year-old is someone my daughter knows, maybe we can help."

Elena Ramirez considered that for a moment. "His name is Henry Thorpe."

Simon picked up his phone and started typing.

"What are you doing?" she asked.

"I don't recognize the name. I'm checking with my son and other daughter. They'd have a better handle on Paige's friends."

"I don't think Paige and Henry were friends."

"So what is the connection between them?"

Elena Ramirez shrugged. "That's part of why I'm here. To try to find out. Without going into full detail, it seems that not long before he vanished, Henry Thorpe was in touch with either your daughter or perhaps her boyfriend, Aaron Corval."

"In touch how?"

She took out a small notepad, licked her fingers, started paging through it. "There was a phone call first. From your daughter's phone to Henry's. This was two weeks ago. Then there were texts for a while, followed by emails."

"What did the texts and emails say?"

"I don't know. The texts are on their phones, I guess. We can't access them. The emails were all deleted. We can see some were sent, but nothing beyond that."

"What makes you think these communications are important?"

"I don't know that they are, Mr. Greene. This is what I do. When someone goes missing, I look for anomalies—something that doesn't fit into their normal routine."

"And these emails and texts—"

"Anomalies. Can you think of any reason Henry Thorpe, a twenty-four-year-old man from Chicago, would suddenly be in touch with your daughter or Aaron Corval?"

Simon didn't really have to think about it long. "Does Henry Thorpe have a history of drug use?"

"Some."

"It could be that."

"Could be," Elena said. "But you can buy drugs in Chicago."

"Could be something more professional in that respect."

"Could be. But I don't think so, do you?"

"No," Simon said. "And either way, my daughter and your client are both missing."

"Yes."

"So what can I do to help?" Simon asked.

"The first thing I asked myself was why the communications moved from texting by phone to emails via a computer."

"And?"

"And how into drugs were they? Your daughter and her boyfriend."

Simon saw no reason to lie. "Very."

Cornelius snapped his fingers, getting it. "Paige probably sold her phone. To raise cash for a fix." He turned to Simon. "Happens all the time down here."

"That phone is no longer active," Elena agreed, "so that would be my theory too."

Simon wasn't so sure. "So Paige moved from using a phone to using a computer?"

"Yes."

"So where is the computer now?"

"Probably sold that too," Cornelius said.

"That would be my guess," Elena said. "She could have taken it with her when she vanished, I guess. Or the killer could have stolen it. But the key question is, How did she get the computer in the first place? She couldn't have bought it, right?"

"Unlikely," Simon said. "I mean, if she was selling her phone to buy drugs, why would she spend the money on a computer?"

"Which means she probably stole it."

Simon just let that sit there. His daughter. Junkie. Selling her own stuff. Thief.

And what else?

"Are you good with computers, Mr. Greene?"

"Simon. And no."

"If you know what you're doing—like my tech guy, Lou— you can check an IP address," Elena said. "Sometimes you can

127

track the computer down to a town or a street or even an individual."

"Was Lou able to figure out who owned her computer?"

"No," Elena said, "but it came from Amherst, Massachusetts. More specifically, the campus of Amherst College. Doesn't your son go there?"

CHAPTER

FOURTEEN

Anya was asleep in one of those yellow molded chairs when Simon and Elena arrived in the hospital waiting room. Her head rested on her uncle Robert's bowling ball of a shoulder. Robert, Yvonne's husband, was a big boisterous man, thick all over, a mostly bald ex–football player with a heart-on-his-sleeve charm. He was a great litigator—juries loved his winning smile, his every-guy banter that masked a nimble legal mind, his larger-than-life pace during a cross-examination—and other than Yvonne, Robert happened to be Simon's closest friend.

Robert gently moved Anya so that he could stand without waking her. He greeted Simon with a monster bear hug. Robert was good with the bear hugs, and for a moment, Simon closed his eyes and took it in.

"You okay?"

"No."

"Didn't think so."

The two men let go. Both looked down at the sleeping Anya.

"They won't let anyone under eighteen in Ingrid's room," Robert explained.

"So Sam is...?"

"He and Yvonne are in with her, yeah. Room seven-one-seven."

Robert glanced a who's-this toward Elena Ramirez. Simon figured that she could explain, so he patted Robert's shoulder, thanked him, and headed toward room 717. Cornelius had stayed at home. There was nothing more for him to do—he had done more than enough already—and he felt as though his time might be better used if he stayed in Mott Haven as "eyes on the ground."

"But if you need me..." Cornelius had added, as they exchanged phone information.

Simon opened the door to Ingrid's room. The sounds got to him first. Those damn beeping machines and sucking sounds and whatever other goddamn clanks signal the direct opposite of warmth and care.

His son, his beautiful eighteen-year-old boy, Sam, sat in the chair next to his mother's bed. He turned toward his father, his face soaked from tears. Sam was always an emotional child, what Ingrid lovingly called "an easy cry." Like his father. When Simon's mother died three years ago, Sam had cried for hours straight, with zero letup, just sobbing and sobbing, and Simon couldn't believe that the boy could do this, just keep sobbing full throttle, without passing out from sheer exhaustion.

You couldn't comfort Sam when he was like that. As emotional as he could be, physical contact of any kind made it worse. He needed to be alone, he'd tell them. If you tried to stop him or comfort him in any way, it backfired. Even as a small child, Sam would look up through pleading eyes and say, "Just let me get it out, okay?"

Yvonne stood by the window. She gave Simon a half-hearted smile.

Simon crossed the room. He put a hand on his son's shoulder and bent down to kiss his wife's cheek. Ingrid looked worse to him, colorless, fading, like this whole thing was one of those scenes in a movie where Death is battling Life and right now Death had the upper hand.

He felt a hand reach into his chest and twist his heart.

He looked back over at Yvonne and signaled with a glance toward the door that he needed her to leave. Yvonne got the message right away. Without another word she slipped out of the room. Simon grabbed a chair and pulled it up next to Sam. Sam wore a red T-shirt with a Sriracha Hot Chili Sauce logo on it. Sam loved logo tees. Ingrid had bought it for him two weeks ago after Sam had told them that the food at college was okay but he had discovered that putting Sriracha sauce on everything made it better. Ingrid had dutifully gone online, found a Sriracha T-shirt, and shipped it up to him.

"You okay?"

Which was a dumb thing for Simon to say, but what else? Silent tears still cascaded down his son's face and when Simon said those two words, Sam's face tightened as though holding back a fresh surge. Sam was so happy up at Amherst. Where Paige had been slightly homesick at college—why the hell hadn't they paid more attention to that? why had they listened to everyone's unsolicited advice to give it time and not be so available to her?— Sam took to freshman campus life immediately. Everyone new that he encountered was the coolest person in the whole world. His roommate, Carlos, a slacker dude from Austin who sported a soul patch, was even cooler than that. Sam right away signed up for clubs and intramural sports and academic groups.

Ingrid would probably be annoyed that Simon had snatched him away from all that.

Sam kept his eyes on his mother. "What happened?"

"What did your aunt and uncle tell you?"

"Just that Mom had been shot. They said I'd have to wait for you."

Yvonne and Robert had done the right thing yet again. "You know who Aaron is, right?"

"That guy Paige..."

"Yes. He was murdered."

Sam blinked.

"And Paige has disappeared."

"I don't understand."

"They lived together in the Bronx. Your mom and I went down to see if we could find her. That's when she got shot."

He filled his son in on the details, not stopping, not taking a breath, not letting up even when Sam started to go pale and his blinking got worse.

At some point, Sam said, "Do you think Paige did it? Do you think she killed Aaron?"

That stopped Simon cold. "Why would you ask that?"

Sam just shrugged.

"I need to ask you something, Sam."

Sam's eyes wandered back to his mother's face.

"Have you seen Paige recently?"

He didn't reply.

"Sam, it's important."

"Yes," he said in a soft voice. "I saw her."

"When?"

He wouldn't take his eyes off his mother. "Sam?"

"Two weeks ago maybe."

That made no sense. Sam was at school two weeks ago. There had been one break in the school year, but he was having so much fun on campus he didn't want to leave. Unless that was a lie. Unless he really didn't love school or damned Sriracha hot sauce or Carlos or the intramural sports or any of that.

"Where?" Simon asked.

"She came to Amherst."

"Paige came to your campus?"

He nodded. "Peter Pan Bus Lines. It's twenty-four dollars from Port Authority."

"Did she come up alone?"

He nodded.

"Did you know she was coming up?"

"No. She didn't tell me. She just...showed up."

Simon tried to envision this—that catalogue-picture-ready college quad with healthy-looking students playing Frisbee or lounging with their books in the sun being infiltrated by one who would have belonged there as much as any of them a year ago but who was now a horrible warning, like that wrecked car a police station keeps around to teach kids not to drink and drive.

Unless, again unless...

"How did she look?" Simon asked.

"The same as in that video."

The words stomped out his small flame of hope.

"Did she tell you why she came up?"

"She said she needed to get away from Aaron."

"Did she tell you why?"

Sam shook his head.

"So what happened?"

"She asked if she could crash with me for a few days."

"You didn't tell us?"

His eyes stayed on Ingrid. "She asked me not to."

Simon wanted to say something more about that, about not trusting his parents, but now was not the time. "Your roommate didn't mind her staying?"

"Carlos? He thought it would be cool. Like she was some school project to help the underserved or something."

"How long did she stay?"

His voice was soft. "Not very."

"How long, Sam?"

The tears started pushing through his eyes again.

"Sam?"

"Long enough to clean us out," he said. The tears came, flowing down, but his voice remained clear. "Paige slept on Carlos's blow-up mattress on the floor. We all fell asleep. When we woke up, she was gone. So was our stuff."

"What did she take?"

"Our wallets. Our laptops. Carlos had a diamond stud."

133

"How could you not have told me?"

He hated the irritation in his voice.

"Sam?"

He didn't reply.

"Did Carlos tell his parents?"

"No. I had some money. I'm trying to make him whole."

"Tell me how much and we'll make him whole now. And what about you?"

"I called your office," Sam said. "I told Emily I lost the credit card. She sent me another."

Simon recalled that now. He hadn't thought twice about it. Visa cards were lost or stolen all the time.

"I'm using the computers in the library for now. It's not a big deal."

"How could you not tell me?"

Which again was dumb to harp on, but he couldn't stop himself.

His son's face collapsed. "It's my fault," Sam said.

"What? No."

"If I had told you—"

"Nothing, Sam. It wouldn't have changed a thing."

"Is Mom going to die?"

"No."

"You don't know that."

Which was true enough.

He didn't protest or say any more lies. No point. The lies would aggravate rather than comfort. He glanced toward the door. Yvonne watched them from the little window in the door. Simon went over and again, when you're this close to someone, when you spend as much time together as he and Yvonne, you just read their mind.

So Simon left the room, and Yvonne took over.

He found Elena Ramirez playing with her phone at the end of the corridor.

"Tell me," she said.

He did.

"So that explains Paige using the laptop," Elena said.

"So what now?" Simon asked.

Elena actually managed a smile. "You think we're a team?"

"I think we can help each other."

"I agree. I think we need to find the connections." Elena played with her phone some more. "I'm sending you the details on Aaron's family. They are having some kind of memorial service for him in the morning. Maybe you should be there. Maybe Paige will show. Look for someone hiding nearby. If not, talk to the family. See if you can figure out how Aaron might know Henry Thorpe."

"Okay," Simon said. "What will you be doing?"

"Visiting someone else Henry Thorpe contacted."

"Who?"

"Don't have a name," Elena said. "Only a location."

"Where?"

"A tattoo parlor in New Jersey."

CHAPTER

FIFTEEN

T he Corval Inn and Family Tree Farm was located in far east Connecticut, near the Rhode Island border. Simon arrived at eight thirty a.m. The memorial service for Aaron, according to Elena Ramirez, was to start at nine.

The inn was a white Federal-style farmhouse with tasteful additions on both sides. Green wicker rocking chairs lined the wraparound porch. A sign read FAMILY OWNED SINCE 1893. Pure New England postcard. On the right, a bus let out tourists for hayrides. The barn in the back was a "Rootin' Tootin' Petting Zoo" promising "petting interactions" with goats, sheep, alpacas, and chickens, though Simon wondered how specifically you went about petting a chicken.

At Christmastime, visitors chopped down their own Christmas trees. In October, they set up the place as the "Haunted Farm," complete with the "Haunted Maze," the "Haunted Silo," the "Haunted Hayride" (key word: Haunted) driven by the "Haunted Headless Horseman." There was also seasonal pumpkin and apple picking. You could make your own cider in the small cabin on the right.

Simon parked the car and headed toward the inn's front door.

An ornate sign by the door said, INN GUESTS ONLY. Simon ignored it and entered the foyer. The decor was of the period and more formal than Simon would have expected. Cherrywood chairs with fanned Windsor backs sat on either side of mahogany settees with winged paw feet. The grandfather clock stood next to the over-sized fireplace like a sentinel. One mahogany breakfront displayed fine china, the other leather-bound books. There were old oil portraits of stern-looking, hearty men—past patriarchs of the Corval family.

"May I help you?"

The woman behind the desk smiled at him. She wore a blouse checkered in the same design as those Italian restaurants that were trying too hard to be authentic. He wondered whether this woman was Aaron's mother, but then he followed the old oil portraits until he reached a framed photograph of a smiling couple circling sixty behind her head. A plaque under the photograph read:

THE CORVALS

WILEY AND ENID

Simon said, "I'm here for the memorial service."

The woman gave him suspicious, if not stink, eye. "May I ask your name?"

"Simon Greene."

"I don't know you, Mr. Greene."

He nodded. "I knew Aaron."

"You knew Aaron," she said, her voice tinged with disbelief, "and you're here to pay your respects?"

Simon didn't bother to reply. The woman took out a pamphlet and opened it carefully. Her reading glasses were dangling from a chain. She put them on the end of her nose. "You head back behind the barn. Turn right here. You'll see the corn maze. Don't go in it. Twice this week we've had to send in employees to get people out. Walk around here."

She pointed on the map.

"There's a path into the woods. Head down it. You'll see a green arrow on a tree pointing right. That's for the hikers. You instead turn left."

"Complicated," Simon said.

She handed him the pamphlet and frowned at him. "This lobby is only for guests staying at the inn."

"And subtle."

He thanked her and headed back outside. The hayride was getting under way, a tractor pulling a bunch of people at much too slow a pace. Everyone was smiling, though they looked pretty uncomfortable. A family—man, woman, daughter, son—waved at him in unison. He waved back, and boom, he dropped back in time to taking the kids apple picking in Chester, just north of the New Jersey border. It had been a glorious autumn day, and yes, he remembered putting Paige on his shoulders so that she could reach a higher branch, but what he remembered most, right now, as he stood there and tried not to stare at this happy, innocent, blissfully ignorant family, was the way Ingrid looked in her dark flannel shirt tucked into thin-legged blue jeans and high boots. He had just turned toward her, Paige giggling on his shoulders, and Ingrid had smiled back at him, tucking her hair behind her ear, and even now, just thinking about how their eyes met on that day, Simon could feel his knees give way just a little bit.

He grabbed his phone and stared at the screen for a few seconds, willing it to give him good news. It didn't.

He followed the route past the petting zoo barn. The chickens were loose. One ran up to him, stopped, looked up at him. Simon was tempted to try to pet it. A man dressed in farmer overalls was giving a demonstration involving eggs and an incubator. The corn stalks at the maze were ten feet high. There was a line to get in and a sign telling visitors that the maze's theme for this year was THE FIFTY STATES—FIND THEM ALL.

He spotted the walking path, took it as told to the green

arrow, turned left when the arrow wanted him to turn right. The woods grew thicker. He looked back to where he'd started, but he couldn't see the clearing anymore.

Simon kept going, the path sloping down now, steeper and steeper. He heard what sounded like running water in the distance. A brook maybe. The path veered right. The trees in front of him thinned until Simon found himself in a clearing. It was a perfect square, the clearing made by man rather than natural design. A low wooden picket fence, a foot high, no more, formed the perimeter around small tombstones.

A family plot.

Simon stopped.

Behind the clearing was indeed a roaring brook and a faded teakwood bench. Simon didn't think the dead cared much, but for the living, this would be a Zen place to grieve and meditate on those you lost.

A man Simon recognized as Wiley Corval, Aaron's father, stood alone, staring down at a newer tombstone. Simon waited. Wiley Corval eventually lifted his head toward him.

"Who are you?" he asked.

"My name is Simon Greene."

Wiley Corval looked a question at him.

"I'm Paige's father."

"Did she do it?"

Simon said nothing.

"Did she kill my son?"

"No."

"How do you know for sure?"

"I don't." The man was about to bury his son. It wasn't the time to lie. "I could tell you my daughter is not a killer, but that's not going to offer you much comfort, is it?"

Wiley Corval just stared at him.

"But I don't think it was Paige. The death... it was violent. Do you know the details?"

"Yes."

"I don't think she could do that."

"But you don't know, do you?"

"I don't, no."

He turned away. "Leave."

"Paige is missing."

"I don't care."

In the distance, Simon could hear the scream-laughter of children, probably coming from the corn maze. Aaron Corval had grown up here, in this Norman Rockwell painting come to life, and look how it ended up. Then again, in all fairness, hadn't Paige been raised in a slightly altered version of an idyllic childhood? And not just on paper. We all see the picket fences or the pretty facades, the two smiling parents, the healthy siblings, all that, and part of us gets that we have zero idea what's going on behind closed doors, that there is anger and abuse, shattered dreams and blown expectations.

But that hadn't been the case with Paige.

Were their lives perfect?

Of course not.

Were their lives pretty close to perfect?

As close, Simon imagined, as you get.

And yet their daughter had succumbed to the worst out there. Simon had asked himself a million questions, pondered every decision—had he shown enough interest, paid attention to her friends and studies, supported her hobbies? Were they too strict or too lax? There was that time Simon had exploded in anger and actually thrown a glass on the floor during dinner. Just once. Years ago. He remembered how Paige, only eight at the time, had started to shiver.

Was that to blame?

You go through every damn moment like that because even though his mother had warned him, "Kids don't come with instruction manuals," and you quickly learn that your child comes to you hardwired, that in the battle of nature vs nurture, nature kicks complete and total ass—still, when things go wrong, when something this dark invades your child's soul, you can only wonder where the hell you went wrong.

From behind him, a woman asked, "Who's this?"

Simon spun toward the voice. Again he recognized her from the picture in the foyer—Aaron's mother, Enid. There were people traipsing down the path with her, ten or twelve, Simon estimated, including a man with a clerical collar carrying a Bible.

"Just a nice gentleman who walked down the wrong path," Wiley Corval said.

Simon considered countering that with the truth—full-on confrontation, to hell with niceties—but he concluded that it would probably backfire. He muttered an apology and started past the family and friends and back up toward the farm. There was no one close to Aaron's age here, and Simon remembered Paige telling him something about Aaron being an only child. That meant there'd be no sibling to question—and none of these people looked the right age to be a close friend, if indeed a junkie like Aaron had any close friends.

So now what?

Let them have their service, he thought. Whatever their son had turned into, Wiley and Enid had lost him now—brutally, suddenly, unnaturally, permanently. Give them this moment.

When he got back to the clearing, a group of kids Simon estimated were around ten or eleven years old emerged from the maze breathless. They all started high-fiving each other. Simon pulled out his phone. There were a lot of messages. He went to his favorites. Ingrid was listed first. Yvonne was second, and then Paige (whose number no longer worked but he still kept it in Favorites), Sam, Anya. Age order with the kids. Only fair.

He hit Yvonne's number.

"No change," Yvonne said.

"I have to be there with her."

"No, you don't."

He looked back at the kids who'd just finished the corn maze. They all had their phones out now, some taking photos, both selfies and group shots, others doing whatever it was we all do on those screens.

"Reverse roles," Yvonne said. "You're the one shot. You're the one lying here in a coma. Do you want Ingrid sitting next to you and holding your hand? Or—"

"Yeah, okay, I get it."

"So have you found Aaron's family?"

He filled her in on what had just occurred.

"So what's your plan?"

"Hang here. Wait until the service is over. Try to talk to them again."

"The father doesn't sound amenable," Yvonne said. "A mother might be more understanding."

"Sexist," he said.

"Yep."

"How are things at work?"

"We got you covered."

Simon hung up and moved back to his car. He took out his phone again and started to listen to the messages. Word about the shooting had somehow not yet made the papers, so most of the messages were mercifully client- rather than solace-related. He returned some of the client calls, not mentioning his own situation, making it just another workday. Doing something routine was comforting.

He was blocking on Ingrid. He knew that. But he also knew that was the right way to go right now.

Half an hour later, while discussing with Dr. Daniel Brocklehurst, a neurosurgeon at Mount Sinai, the financial benefits of retiring in Florida versus Arizona, Simon spotted the mourners coming back over the gentle hill. They were led by Wiley Corval and the clergyman. Wiley's back was bent over in apparent if not melodramatic grief, and the clergyman had his arm around his shoulders, whispering what Simon assumed were words of comfort. The other mourners trailed them, some squinting up into the sun, others nodding to passing tourists.

In the back of the group—way in the back, come to think of it—was Enid Corval, Aaron's mother. For a brief flash, Simon imagined them as a pack of gazelles and him the lion, readying to take down the one farthest away from the pack. Silly image, but there you go.

But that one would be Enid, the mother.

Simon kept watching. Enid looked distracted. She glanced at her watch, slowing her walk, staying farther and farther back from the rest of the mourners. Alone.

Odd, Simon thought. She was the mother. You'd think a few of them would be with her, putting an arm around her, offering her comforting words. No one did.

She was also dressed differently. The rest of the group, including Wiley Corval, had gone with the blue-blazer, khaki, loafer-sans-socks spirit, even if that wasn't exactly what they were wearing. Poor man's yacht club. Enid wore mom jeans, Velcro white sneakers, and a stretched-out cable-knit sweater that was a yellow usually found on a Ticonderoga pencil.

Wiley and the clergyman started up the porch steps. The receptionist who'd helped Simon greeted Wiley at the door with a buss on the cheek. The rest of the mourners filed in after him.

Except Enid.

She was now trailing the group far enough that she remained outside after the door had closed. She glanced left, then right, then headed behind the inn.

Simon wasn't sure what his move was here. Get out of the car and confront? Stay where he was and see where she was going?

When Enid Corval disappeared around the back of the inn, Simon slid out of the car to get a better view. He spotted her getting into a pickup truck. She started it up and put the truck into reverse. Simon hurried back to his car and hit the ignition button.

Thirty seconds later, he was following Enid Corval's pickup down Tom Wheeler Road.

The road was lined with low stone walls offering a modicum of protection to the vast farmland on both sides. Simon didn't know enough about this area—were these real farms or for show or what?—but most looked pretty worn and dilapidated.

Fifteen minutes later, the pickup truck pulled into a dirt parking lot with like-minded vehicles. There was no sign visible advertising a name or description for this establishment. Enid got out of the pickup and headed toward a converted barn with aluminum siding, like it'd been snapped together. The color was faux bright orange, like a clown's hair.

Simon pulled in, self-conscious of his Audi, and cruised to a far corner. He looked to his left. Hidden from the road on the far side of the barn were a couple of dozen motorcycles lined up in two anally straight lines. Harley-Davidsons for the most part. Simon didn't know much about motorcycles, had never been on one, but even from this vantage point, he could spot the iconic Harley logo on a few of the bikes.

Enid was heading across the dirt lot for the saloon-style doors. Two husky men in leather chaps and black bandannas stumbled into the lot as she arrived. Their thick, somewhat flabby arms were loaded with tats. Both sported paunches and the prerequisite beard. Bikers.

They greeted Enid warmly with handshakes and hugs. She kissed one on the cheek and disappeared inside. Simon debated waiting for her to come back out—this place clearly wasn't his usual hangout—but that seemed like a waste of time. He turned off his car and started for the swinging doors.

When he pushed them open, he somehow expected that the music would stop and everyone would turn and stare at the interloper. But no one did. There was also no music playing. A television old enough for rabbit ears showed a baseball game. The bar was odd. Too wide in spots, space enough for a dance maybe, but Simon doubted that there'd been one recently. There was a jukebox in the right corner, but it was unplugged. The floor beneath him was mostly dirt, the same as the parking lot.

Enid Corval took a seat at the bar. Considering it was only eleven a.m., business seemed pretty brisk. There were maybe ten people scattered amongst the thirty or so stools, equally spaced apart, no one right next to anyone else, like men's urinals in a public bathroom. They all huddled over their drink, eyes down in protective, don't-converse-with-me mode. A group of bikers on the right played pool on a table with ugly rips in the green fabric.

There were cans of Pabst Blue Ribbon everywhere.

Simon sported a dress shirt, tie, and black loafers—he had, after all, been heading to a memorial service—while half the guys in here wore cotton gym tanks with no sleeves, a look no man over forty should ever try, no matter how well built. And these guys weren't well built.

Hats off to them, Simon thought, for not caring.

He took a stool two away from Enid. She didn't look up from her drink or glance his way. On the other side of him a guy wearing a porkpie hat was bouncing his head up and down as though to music but no music was playing and he wasn't wearing earphones. A rainbow of rusted license plates took up most of the back wall—probably plates representing all fifty states, but Simon wasn't really up for checking. There were neon signs for Miller High Life and Schlitz. An oddly ornate chandelier hung from the ceiling. This place, like the inn, was all dark wood, but that was the only similarity, like this was the poorest of poor cousins of the inn's rich dark wood.

"What'll you have?"

The barmaid's hair was the color and texture of the hay on that hayride and done in a quasi mullet that reminded Simon of an '80s hockey player. She was either a hard forty-five or a soft sixty-five, and there was little question she had seen it all at least twice.

"What kind of beer do you have?" he asked.

"We have Pabst. And Pabst."

"You choose for me."

Enid still had her eye on her drink, not so much as glancing in his direction, when she said, "You're Paige's dad."

"Wiley tell you?"

She shook her head, still not looking at him. "He didn't say a word. Why did you come today?"

"To pay my respects."

"That's a lie."

"Yeah, it is. But I am sorry for your loss."

She didn't react to or acknowledge that. "So why are you here?"

"My daughter is missing."

The barmaid opened the can and plopped it in front of him.

Enid finally turned her head toward him. "Since when?"

"Since Aaron's murder."

"That can't be a coincidence."

"I agree."

"Your daughter probably killed him and ran."

Just like that. No emotion in her voice.

"Would it matter," Simon said, "if I said I don't think that's the case?"

Enid made a maybe-yes, maybe-no gesture. "You gamble at all?"

"No."

"Yeah, but you're some big stockbroker or something, right?"

"I do financial advising."

"Yeah, whatever. You still play the odds, right? Try to figure out what's safe and what's risky, all that?"

Simon nodded.

"So you know what the two most likely possibilities are, don't you?"

"Tell me."

"One, your daughter killed Aaron and is on the run."

"And two?"

"Whoever killed Aaron took or killed her too." Enid Corval took a sip of her drink. "Come to think of it, Possibility Two is much more likely."

"What makes you say that?" Simon asked.

"Junkies aren't great at not leaving clues or eluding the police."

"So you don't think she killed him?"

"I didn't say that."

"Let's assume you're right," Simon said, trying to stay methodical here, detached. "Why would someone take Paige?"

"No clue. Hate to say this, but odds are, she's dead." She took another sip. "I'm still not sure why you're here."

"I'm hoping you know something."

"I haven't seen Aaron in months."

"Do you recognize this guy?"

Simon handed her his phone. Elena Ramirez had texted him a photograph of her client's missing son, Henry Thorpe.

"Who is he?"

"His name is Henry Thorpe. He's from Chicago."

She shook her head. "I don't know him. Why?"

"He may be connected into this."

"Into this how?"

"I don't have a clue. It's why I'm here. He's missing."

"Like Paige?"

"I guess."

"Can't help you, I'm afraid."

A scowling biker with a shaved head pulled out the stool between them so he could lean on the bar. Simon noticed the black iron-cross tattoo and maybe a half swastika sticking out from under his shirt sleeve. The biker noticed him noticing and stared him hard in the eye. Simon stared back and felt the red start to rise.

"What are you looking at?" Biker Boy said.

Simon did not blink or move.

"I asked you—"

Enid said, "He's with me."

"Hey, Enid, I didn't mean—"

"And you're interrupting a private conversation."

"I, I mean, how was I supposed to know?"

Biker Boy sounded scared.

"I was just getting some beers, Enid."

"That's fine. Gladys will bring them over to you. You wait over by the pool table."

And with that, Biker Boy was gone.

"Enid," Simon said.

"Yeah?"

"What is this place?"

"Private club."

"Yours?"

"You here to ask about your daughter or about me?"

"I'm just trying to figure this all out."

"What out?"

"Do you mind telling me about Aaron?"

"What about him?"

"I don't know. Anything. Everything."

"Can't much see the purpose."

"There are threads here," he said, the words sounding weird coming from his mouth even to him. "Connections. I don't know what they are, but I feel like I'm missing something. So I'm asking questions and plowing ahead and hoping."

She frowned. "You're going to have to do better than that."

"My wife was shot yesterday," Simon said.

Enid looked a question at him.

"She's alive but...We were looking for Paige. Where they lived. Where Aaron was killed."

He told her the story, taking chugs of the Pabst as he went

along. Simon couldn't remember the last time he drank a cold beer this early in the day, but today, in this place, it felt right. Simon glanced around the room as he spoke. Biker Boy wasn't the only one with white supremacist tattoos. A number of guys had swastikas, and yeah he was outnumbered and he had bigger fish to fry at the moment, but this was America now, his country, this crap just out in the open and accepted, and he could feel his blood boil despite it all.

"You saw where Aaron grew up," Enid said when he finished.

"On that farm."

"It's not really a farm. It's a tourist spot, but yeah. Nice, right?"

"Seems so."

"Seems so," she repeated with a nod. "When Aaron was little, he lived in the actual inn. Back then, they only rented out six rooms. The family lived in the rest. Then they grew. Started renting out all ten rooms. Five, six years ago, we built those additions, so now it's up to twenty-four rooms. We got a pretty good restaurant too. Wiley always calls it a 'bistro.' Thinks it sounds fancier. And the gift shop does a nice business. Sells souvenirs and candles, junk like that. I'm getting off topic, aren't I?"

"Not at all."

"You want to know about Aaron."

Simon didn't reply.

"Well, Aaron, even as a kid, he was always a little dark, if you know what I mean."

One of the tattoo guys met her eye by a back door. Enid nodded and the guy slipped out.

"I don't see how any of this could possibly help you," she said.

"They."

"What?"

"You said, 'They only rented out six rooms.' They."

"So?"

"I'd think you'd say 'we' instead of 'they.'"

"No 'we' yet," she said. "Wiley and I weren't married back then."

"Back when?"

"When Wiley lived in the original inn."

"But you said Aaron lived there."

"Yeah. With Wiley. I'm his stepmom. I wasn't on the scene until he was nine. Truth be told, I'm not the maternal type. Surprised, right? Aaron and me, we were never close."

"And his real mom? Where is she?"

Enid glanced at the back door. The tattoo man came back in, making sure that Enid spotted him. Her glass was empty. Gladys with the Hay Hair filled it without being told.

"Mrs. Corval?" Simon said.

"Call me Enid."

"Enid, what happened to Aaron's real mother?"

"It has nothing to do with any of this."

"It might."

"How?" Enid turned now, placing one arm on the bar, and faced him full-on. "I mean, I told Aaron from Day One in here: You don't try it. Not ever. Not a taste. He saw every day what that crap does to you. Still he ended up murdered in a junkie-infested shithole. So tell me, Mr. Greene. How could his birth mom have anything to do with Aaron ending up like that? And while you're at it: How could his birth mom have anything to do with your daughter vanishing into the wind?"

"I don't know," Simon said.

"I'd probably be more the one to blame, don't you think?"

Simon said nothing.

"His dad and I get married. When he's a teen he wants to start hanging out here. That's the problem with growing up in a quiet place. People think it's magical or some shit. Beauty bores. It traps. Someone like Aaron, he's got that edge in him. Just the way he is. Like me, even though we aren't blood."

He wanted to ask what this place was, but that would be the wrong way to go. He shifted gears and asked, "Was Aaron's birth mother at the service today?"

Enid kept her head down.

"Can't you at least tell me—"

"No," Enid said. "She wasn't there."

"Is she still alive? Did she have any kind of relationship with her son?"

"I don't know you, Mr. Greene."

"Yeah, you do. I mean, you know enough. I don't care what you do here or what's going on with the inn or any of that. I don't mean you the least bit of trouble. But at the risk of sounding one-note, my daughter is missing."

"And I don't see how that has anything to do with—"

"It probably doesn't," he interrupted. "Except that's not how it feels, does it? The police think maybe Paige killed Aaron to save herself. Or maybe I did it. Or my wife. To protect our child. Or maybe it was a drug deal gone wrong. Those are all good theories, but I'm asking for your help."

She started swirling her glass, her eyes on the liquor.

"Is Aaron's mother alive or not?"

"The truth?" Enid looked up and studied his face for a very long time. "I don't know."

"You don't know if she's alive or dead?"

"That's right." Enid turned to Gladys. "Get my friend here another beer and bring it to the corner booth. He and I need to talk for a bit."

CHAPTER
SIXTEEN

T he entrance to Tattoos While U Wait was blocked off with old-school A-frame traffic barricades, the kind with slanted reflective orange-and-white stripes running across the horizontal beam.

Elena Ramirez spotted two fully emblazoned police cars plus two other vehicles that looked to be unmarked. She pulled her rental Ford Fusion with the overbearing cherry scent into the tattoo parlor's entry between the highway and the barricades.

A cop frowned and started toward her.

"You'll need to leave."

"What's going on here?"

"Please remove your car from the premises."

Elena could wave her credentials, but they probably wouldn't get her anyplace. She also had no idea what the situation was or why the police were here, and it was never a good idea to go in blind.

Time to do a little recon.

Elena thanked the officer, put the car in reverse, and got back onto the highway. She pulled off a hundred yards down the road at a Sonic Drive-In. She took out her phone and made some calls.

It took maybe half an hour to get the details on the double murder from the day before.

The two victims were Damien Gorse, age twenty-nine, co-owner of the parlor, and eighteen-year-old Ryan Bailey, a high school senior who worked there part time. The initial report indicated that the two victims had been shot in a robbery gone wrong.

Wrong, Elena thought to herself, being the operative word.

She made a few more calls, waited, got the confirmation. Then she headed back down the highway and pulled up to those barricades. The same police officer moved one of them aside, so that she could pass. He pointed for her to park on the left. She nodded a thanks and did as requested.

Elena looked in her rearview mirror and tried on a sympathetic, we're-all-in-this-together smile. Meh. This part would be a pain in the ass. Cops and egos. Tough recipe. Add in a dollop of territorial bullshit and customary dick swinging plus the rarity of landing a single murder case let alone a double murder, and Elena expected a shitshow of epic proportions.

A man Elena figured was midthirties, maybe forty, came out of the tattoo parlor's front entrance, pulled off his crime scene gloves, and headed toward her. His stride was confident but not cocky. The guy was good-looking as hell. More lumberjack than pretty boy, what they used to call "rugged." If she still had a type—and Elena had felt dead in that area since Joel's death—this guy would be it.

The cop gave her a nod and a tight smile, an appropriate greeting under the circumstances.

"You must be Special Agent Ramirez," the man said.

"Retired."

She shook his hand. His hand was big. Like Joel's. She felt another pang.

"I'm Detective Dumas. Everyone calls me Nap."

"Nap," she repeated, "like . . . ?"

"A short sleep, yes."

"I'm Elena. I work private now."

"Yeah, my boss filled me in."

"Would that be County Prosecutor Loren Muse?"

"It would."

"I hear she's good."

"Yeah," Nap said, "she is."

No resentment in his tone at having a young woman over him. No faux virtual signaling over it either. Good signs.

Here was how it worked: Elena's firm, VMB Investigations, was one of the most prestigious in the country, with offices in Chicago, New York, Los Angeles, and Houston. Investigators like those at VMB need access, so they donate generously to political campaigns and police benevolent groups of various stripes. One of her senior partners, Manny Andrews, was a big backer of the current governor. That governor is the one who named Loren Muse county prosecutor. So Manny Andrews calls the governor, the governor calls Muse, Muse in turn calls the lead detective on the case, Nap Dumas.

The message: Cooperate.

Nothing illegal. If you gasp at this sort of favor exchanging, you are hopelessly naïve. The world had always been a place of "you scratch my back and I'll scratch yours." When that breaks down, for better or worse, so does your society.

Cops often bristled at this particular back-scratch, however, which leads to the territorial dick swinging Elena had braced for. Nap Dumas seemed okay with it. For now.

"Follow me," he said.

He began walking to the left side of the building. Elena, who still had the limp from a long-ago bullet, caught up with him.

"I just took over the case an hour ago," Nap said, "so I'm still catching up myself."

"I appreciate you letting me on the scene."

A small, knowing smile came to Dumas's lips. "No problem."

Elena didn't bother with a follow-up.

"Any chance you can tell me your interest in this?"

"I have a case," Elena said. "There may be an overlap."

"Whoa," Dumas said, "let's go easy on the specifics."

She smiled at that. Up ahead Elena spotted a wood-paneled Ford Flex. Two crime scene technicians dressed all in white worked the scene.

"Can you tell me what kind of case?" he asked.

She pondered playing hardball, reminding him that his boss had already told him to cooperate and that she couldn't talk about her case because it was work product, but that felt wrong here. This Nap guy seemed alright. More than that, actually. Good aura, Elena's mother would tell her. Elena had always been skeptical of that stuff—first impressions, gut instincts—because, let's face it, people can be complete psychos and fool you. But in truth, they rarely fooled Elena. As the years had gone on, she realized that her gut worked better than she imagined. The guys who gave her the creeps off the bat? They always ended up being creeps. The guys, the very few guys, who gave off this kind of positive aura? They ended up being trustworthy.

And Nap reminded her of Joel. Her Joel. God help her.

The pang moved to her heart and stayed there.

"Nap?"

He waited.

"I think it's better if we wait," Elena said.

"Oh?"

"I'm not going to keep anything from you," Elena said, "but right now I'd like to hear what you think without any preconceptions."

"Preconceptions," Dumas repeated.

"Yes."

"You mean like context and facts?"

"You seem like a straight shooter."

"As do you."

"Can we just play it my way for now?"

Nap hesitated but not for very long. He nodded his okay as they reached the Ford Flex and started right in: "The way we see it, the first shooting took place here, as Damien Gorse was getting in his car."

"So Gorse was shot first?"

"We're pretty sure, yeah." Nap tilted his head. "Is that important?"

She didn't reply.

He sighed. "Right. Preconceptions."

"How many shooters?" Elena asked.

"We don't know. But initial ballistics indicate the same gun killed both victims."

"So maybe there was only one."

"Hard to say, but it feels that way."

Elena took in the scene. She looked at the back of the building and then up toward the sky. "No security cameras in the parking lot?"

"None."

"How about inside?"

"Also none. Just a routine ADT alarm with a panic button and motion detector."

"I assume the business takes cash."

"Yes."

"What do they do with it?"

"One of the two owners—and Gorse was one of them—takes the cash home every night and stores it in their safe."

"Their safe?"

"Pardon?"

"You said *their* safe. The two owners share a safe?"

"They live together, yeah. And to answer your next question, Gorse was robbed. The cash, his wallet, some of his jewelry were gone."

"So you're thinking robbery?"

Nap gave her a crooked smile. Again like Joel's. Damn. "Well, I was," he said.

The implication was clear: I was—until you showed up.

"So where's the co-owner?" she asked.

"On his way from the airport. He should be here any minute."

"Airport?"

"His name is Neil Raff. He was on vacation in Miami."

"Is he a suspect?"

"A business partner taking a trip during the time of a murder?"

"Right," she said. "So of course he is."

"Like I said, it's early."

"Any idea how much cash Gorse had on him?"

"Not yet, no. Some days, we've been told, it could be as high as a few thousand dollars—some days it could be next to nothing. Depends obviously on how business was that day and how many people used plastic."

There was no chalk drawing of a body or any of that stuff, but Nap had crime scene photographs. Elena studied them for a moment.

"Do you think the perp robbed Gorse first and then shot him," Elena began, "or shot him first and then robbed him?"

"Shot him first," Nap said.

"You seem pretty certain."

"Look at Gorse's pocket in the photograph."

She did, nodding. "Turned inside out."

"Also the shirt untucked, one ring left on like it's been too difficult to get off—or someone interrupted him."

Elena saw it now. "Where was the shooter standing?"

Nap showed her. "The first cops on the scene figured that the shooter had just driven in and fired from his car or that maybe he'd parked and waited."

"You're not buying that?"

"It could be," Nap said. "But my bet is the shooter came out from the woods. Look at this angle."

Elena nodded.

"It's possible," Nap continued, "that the killer could have driven in earlier, parked, and then hidden in the woods. But I don't think so."

"Why not?"

"Because there was only one other person here at the time of the shooting—the second victim, Ryan Bailey. Bailey doesn't own a car. He takes the bus from the mall and walks."

She glanced around, subtracted out the cop cars both marked and unmarked. "So when the first responders got here, were any cars in the lot other than Gorse's?"

"None," Nap said. "The lot was empty."

Elena stood back up. "So if someone—say, the killer—drove in and parked in the lot, Gorse would have noticed it when he left."

"Agree," Nap said. "Damien Gorse is the owner. It's closing time. If a strange car is in his lot, I think he'd walk over and check it out. Unless there was a getaway driver."

Elena frowned. "Getaway driver?"

"I use all the cool cop lingo. Either way, we will go through all relevant nearby CCTV footage."

"I understand one of the two victims called nine-one-one."

"Ryan Bailey. The second victim."

"What did he say on the call?"

"Nothing."

"Nothing?"

Nap explained his working theory. The shooter kills Damien Gorse by the Ford Fusion. The shooter starts going through the dead man's pockets; takes the money, the watch, the wallet; and he is pulling off Gorse's jewelry when the door opens and Ryan Bailey comes out. Bailey sees what's happening, runs back inside, hits the alarm, and hides in the closet.

Elena frowned.

"What?" Nap asked.

"Bailey sets off an alarm inside the tattoo parlor?"

Nap nodded. "The panic button is right near the back door."

"Is it a silent alarm?" she asked.

"No."

"Loud?"

"The alarm? Yeah. Really loud."

Elena frowned again.

"What?"

"Show me," she said.

"Show you what?"

"Inside. The closet where Ryan Bailey hid."

Nap studied her for a moment. Then he handed her a pair of crime-scene gloves. She snapped them on. He did the same. They walked toward the back entrance.

"Full garbage bag," Nap said, pointing to one lying split on the ground. "We figured Bailey came out to throw it in the dumpster."

"And that was when he interrupted the robbery?"

"That's our theory."

Except it didn't make sense.

Another cop handed them each a white crime-scene suit with footies. Elena slipped hers on over her suit. All white—they both looked like giant sperms. There were more white-covered lab guys inside. The closet was adjacent to the back door.

Elena frowned again.

"What?"

"It doesn't add up."

"Why not?"

"You figure Ryan Bailey came outside to throw away the garbage."

"Right."

"He spots our killer looting Gorse's body."

"Right."

"So our perp didn't know the kid was inside. That's most likely."

"I don't know, probably. So what?"

"So Ryan Bailey goes outside. He spots the killer. He runs back in and hits the alarm. Then he hides in the closet."

"Right."

"And our killer is in hot pursuit, right?"

"Right."

"So our killer follows him inside. The killer searches for him. All the while, this alarm is blaring."

"Yeah, so?"

"Why?" she asked.

"What do you mean, why? Ryan Bailey had spotted the killer. He could identify him."

"So our killer wanted to silence him?"

"Yes."

"So that sort of rules out a professional hit job," Elena said.

"How so?"

"Do you know any pro that wouldn't have been wearing a ski mask or some kind of disguise? A pro would have run when the alarm went off. Because what could the kid tell us? A man wearing a ski mask killed his boss? That's it. The only reason the killer would follow him in and kill him is that Ryan Bailey could identify him."

Nap nodded. "Or maybe it was someone they both knew."

"Either way," Elena said, "I don't think it fits in with my case. My guy would be a pro. He'd use a mask."

"So what is your case?"

And then she spotted the computer on top of the counter. She didn't know who Henry Thorpe had been in touch with—just that the communications came from an IP address and Wi-Fi located in this building.

Elena turned to Nap. "Can I take a look at that computer?"

CHAPTER

SEVENTEEN

Enid Corval and Simon were comfortably ensconced on the ripped fabric of a corner booth in this "private club."

Simon had already put most of it together. Not about Aaron's mother. He had no idea about that. But about this club. They were selling something out back. Drugs probably. This wasn't a pub or bar. It was a private club. Different regulations. The inn was her front, her legitimacy, and probably where she laundered a lot of the money from here.

He might, of course, be way off in his assumptions. His theorizing, if you wanted to call it that, didn't even raise itself to the level of flimsy conjecture, and either way, he wasn't going to bring it up unless he absolutely needed to.

But the theory felt right to him.

"Wiley and me, our marriage is kind of old-fashioned." She stopped, shook her head. "Don't know why I'm telling you this. I'm getting older, I guess. Aaron is dead. And maybe you're right, Mr. Greene."

"Simon."

"I prefer Mr. Greene."

"Maybe I'm right about what?"

Enid spread her hands. "Maybe it's all related. That stuff in the past. And now. Who am I to say?"

Simon waited, but not long. Enid dove in.

"I'm not from around here. I grew up in Billings, Montana. You don't need to hear the tale of how I ended up in this part of Connecticut. The winds blow, as they do. That's life. But when I met Wiley he had a nine-year-old son named Aaron. A lot of women found all that attractive. The single-father thing. Raising the boy on his own. The beautiful inn and farm. Someone would ask Wiley about the boy and what happened to his mother, but he'd politely shake them off. Didn't like to talk about it. Used to get a tear in his eye. Even with me."

"But eventually?"

"Oh, I'd heard the story before he told me. Everyone around here knew parts of it. Wiley and the boy's mother met during a time in his life when he didn't want anything to do with the inn. Like everyone else who grows up here, Wiley longed to escape. So he started backpacking through Europe and met a girl in Italy. Her name was Bruna. Tuscany. That was what Wiley told me. The two worked in a vineyard for a while. He said working in the vineyard was a little like working on the inn. It reminded him of it anyway. Made him long for home a little, that's what he said." She gestured at the Pabst can with her chin. "You're not drinking your beer."

"I have to drive."

"Two beers? Come on, you're not that big a girl."

But he was. Ingrid could drink hard liquor for hours and show no signs of it. Simon had two beers and tried to French-kiss a light socket.

"So what happened?"

"They fell in love. Wiley and Bruna. Romantic, right? They had a boy. Aaron. A blissful story until, well, Bruna died."

"She died?"

Enid kept still. Too still.

"How?" he asked.

"Car accident. Head-on collision on Autostrada A11, and yeah, Wiley always added that detail. Autostrada A11. I looked it up once. Don't know why. It connects Pisa to Florence. Bruna was going to visit her family, he said. And he didn't want to go. They had a fight about it before she left. See, Wiley was supposed to have been in the car with her. That's what he said. So he blames himself. It's very hard for him to talk about. He gets all choked up."

She looked at him over her glass.

"You sound skeptical," Simon said.

"Do I?"

"Yes."

"Wiley tells the story with gusto. He's quite theatrical, my husband. You'd believe every word."

"You didn't?"

"Oh, I believed it. But see, I also wondered why Bruna would go to visit her family and not bring her infant son. You'd do that, right? You're a young mom, traveling the"—she made quote marks with her fingers—"'autostrada' to see your family. You'd take your baby."

"Did you ask Wiley about that?"

"No, I never said anything. I mean, why would I? Who'd question a story like that?"

There was a chill in the stale-beer air. Simon wanted to ask a follow-up, but more than that, he wanted Enid to tell it. He kept silent.

"Wiley came back home after the accident. Here. The inn, I mean. He was afraid that maybe Bruna's family would sue for custody or hold him up—they'd never been legally married or anything—so he flew to the States with the baby. They moved into the inn..."

Her voice faded out as she shrugged.

End of the story.

"So," Simon said, "Aaron's mother is dead."

163

"That's what Wiley says."

"But when I asked you if she was alive, you said you didn't know."

"You're a quick one, Mr. Greene." She raised her glass and smiled. "Why the hell am I telling you any of this?"

She stared at him and waited for an answer.

"Because I have an honest face?" Simon tried.

"You look like my first husband."

"Was he honest?"

"Shit no." Then: "But oh, man, he was great in bed."

"So we have something in common."

Enid snorted. "I like you, Mr. Greene. And ah, what the hell. I can't see how it will help you and yet...I've seen some strange shit. And bad stays. Bad doesn't go away. You bury bad, it digs itself out. You throw bad in the middle of the ocean, it comes back at you like a tidal wave."

Simon just waited.

"Do you keep your old passports?" she asked him. "I mean, after they're expired?"

"Yes."

In fact, Simon advised his clients to do the same, just in case they ever needed to prove they'd been someplace. He was big on saving any official paperwork, because you never knew.

"So does Wiley. Not where someone could easily find them. They're boxed up in storage in the basement. But I found them. And you know what?"

"What?"

Enid put her hand to the side of her mouth and stage-whispered, "Wiley has never been to Italy."

The office at Tattoos While U Wait was glass enclosed, so whoever sat in it could look out at the chairs and the artists and the waiting area and vice versa. The computer's monitor faced a wall, however, so that while privacy was pretty much nonexistent, you couldn't see what the person sitting at the desk may have been surfing or browsing or whatever people called it nowadays.

The desk was partner-style, so that two people could sit facing each other. The top was cluttered with scraps of paper, three pairs of drugstore reading glasses, a dozen or so assorted pens and markers. There was a bag of cherry cough drops on the left, a few paperback books, bills strewn about with no reason or guiding principle behind them.

In the center of the desk, facing the glass, was a slightly faded photograph of six men with huge smiles. Two were up front, with arms around each other's shoulders, the other four slightly behind them with folded arms. It'd been snapped in front of the parlor—opening day from the looks of the ribbons and the oversized faux scissors. The clothes, the facial hair, the poses—the whole vibe made it feel like a Doobie Brothers album cover.

Elena picked up the photograph and showed it to Nap. Nap nodded and pointed to the guy in the front on the right.

"That's the victim. Damien Gorse."

Nap slid his finger toward the guy next to him—a hefty dude in full leather motorcycle wear and a salt-'n'-pepper handlebar mustache. "That's the partner, Neil Raff."

Elena sat in the swivel chair in front of the monitor. The computer's mouse was red and in the shape of a heart. For a moment Elena just stared at it. A heart. Damien Gorse's computer mouse was in the shape of a heart. As an investigator, you keep your head down and you think analytically because that was often the best. You focus on your particular goal—in this case finding Henry Thorpe—but Joel had always told her not to forget the devastation, the lives lost or destroyed or irrevocably torn apart. Damien Gorse had sat in this chair and used this heart-shaped mouse. The heart-shaped mouse was a gift—it had to be, it was not the kind of thing you buy for yourself—and the person who gave it to him wanted Damien to know that he was in some way loved.

"Don't let those emotions cloud you," Joel would tell her. "Let them fuel you."

When Elena touched the mouse, the screen lit up. A photograph appeared of Damien Gorse and Neil Raff, with an older woman between the two. They were on a beach somewhere, all smiles.

In the center of the screen was a box asking for a password. Elena looked over at Nap as if he might know. He shrugged no-idea at her. There were Post-it notes all over the computer. She scanned them for what might be a password, but nothing jumped out at her. She opened the top drawer. Nothing.

"You have someone who can crack this?" she asked.

"Yeah, but he's not here yet."

The front door flew open, and a man she recognized from the photographs as Neil Raff burst into his own tattoo parlor. The outfit was denim now rather than leather—almost more dated than in the photograph—and the handlebar mustache was now full-on salt. But there was no mistaking him for anyone else. Dazed, he turned his head and looked about his own business, as though seeing it for the first time, through red-tinged, swollen-from-crying eyes.

Nap hurried over to the man. Elena watched. Nap put a hand on the man's shoulder and lowered his head and talked softly. Nap was good. Again, something in the way Nap carried himself brought on Joel's echo. It stirred her. God, she missed Joel. Every part of him. She missed the conversations, the company, the heart, but right now she couldn't help but think of how much she missed the sex. This may sound odd to some, but making love to Joel was the greatest thing she would ever do. She missed the weight of him on her. She missed the way he looked at her when he was inside her, as if she were the only woman on God's green earth. She missed—and this wasn't very feminist of her—the way Joel towered over her and made her feel safe.

She was thinking this because it suddenly dawned on her, as she looked at the photographs of Gorse and Raff, as she thought back to what Nap had said about the owners taking the cash home to *their* safe, and as she watched the devastation on the face of Neil Raff, that she recognized this particular grief, the gut-wrenching, all-consuming devastation of losing a life partner rather than a friend or business partner.

She could be projecting, but she didn't think so.

Nap got Raff seated on a leather couch in the waiting area. He wheeled over a chair and sat right in front of the grieving man. Nap had a notepad in his hand, but he didn't want to risk appearing anything less than completely focused and sym-pathetic, so he took no notes. Elena waited. There wasn't much else to do.

Half an hour later, after she offered her condolences, Elena moved the heart-shaped mouse again, waking up the screen. The photograph appeared.

"Oh God," Raff said. He turned to Nap. "Has anyone told Carrie?"

"Carrie?"

"Damien's mother. Oh my God, she's going to be devastated."

"How could we reach her?"

"Let me call her."

Nap didn't reply to that.

Raff said, "She lives in a condo in Scottsdale now. On her own. Damien is all she has."

Is, Elena thought. *Is all she has.* Still using present tense. Com-mon.

"Did Damien have siblings?" Nap asked.

"No siblings. Carrie couldn't have kids. Damien was adopted."

"And his father?"

"Out of the picture. His parents had a nasty divorce when he was three. His adoptive father hasn't been part of Damien's life since."

Elena pointed to the white box on the screen. "Do you know Damien's password?"

Raff blinked and looked away. "Of course I know his password."

"Could you tell me what it is?"

He blinked some more, his eyes brimming with tears. "Guanacaste."

He spelled it for her.

"It's a province in Costa Rica," Raff said.

"Oh," Elena said because she wasn't sure what else to say.

"We...we honeymooned there. It's our favorite spot."

Elena hit the Return key and waited for the icons to appear on the screen.

"What are you looking for?" Raff asked.

"This was Damien's computer?"

"It's our computer, yes."

Again with the present tense.

"Are there any other computers on your network?" she asked.

"No."

"How about clients? Could they access your network?"

"No. It's password protected."

"And this is the only computer on it?"

"Yes. Damien and I shared it, though I'm not really good with technology. Sometimes I would sit here and use it, and then Damien would sit on the other side of the desk. But most of the time, it was Damien's."

Elena was not great with technology either—that was why her firm had Lou—but she knew the basics. She brought up the browser and started checking the history. Neil Raff had been in Miami for the past five days, so all the recent surfing would have been done by Damien Gorse.

"I still don't understand what you're looking for," Raff said.

There were a lot of image searches. She clicked on a random few. They were, as one might expect, tattoos, a wide variety of them. There were roses-and-barbed-wire tattoos, skeletons with crossbones, hearts of all shades and sizes. There was one tattoo of Pennywise the Clown, from Stephen King's *It*, and several involving full-on sex acts including, uh, all fours (who actually got that as a tattoo?), and there were ones that said "Mom" and ones of tombstones for friends who'd died and full-arm sleeves and lots of wing designs for the lower back, what they used to call (maybe still do?) tramp stamps.

"We get ideas from the images," Raff said. "We show the clients what's been done so we can take it to the next level."

The rest of the browser history looked equally routine. Damien Gorse had visited Rotten Tomatoes and bought movie tickets. He'd bought socks and K-Cup coffee pods from Amazon. He visited one of those DNA sites that tell you your ancestral makeup. Elena often thought about taking one of those tests. Her mother was Mexican and swore Elena's biological father was too, but he'd died before she was born, and Mom always acted funny when Elena would ask, so who knew?

"Maybe I can help?" Raff asked. It was more of a plea than a question.

Elena kept her eyes on the screen. "Do you—or really, did Damien—know someone named Henry Thorpe?"

He thought about it. "Not that I can think of."

"He's twenty-four years old. From Chicago."

"Chicago?" Raff thought some more. "I don't think I know anyone with that name. And I never heard Damien mention him either. Why do you ask?"

Elena blew through his question. "Have you and Damien been to Chicago recently?"

"I went when I was a senior in high school. I don't think Damien's ever been."

"How about the name Aaron Corval? Does that ring any bells?"

Raff petted the handlebar mustache with his right hand. "No, I don't think so. Is he also from Chicago?"

"Connecticut. But he lives in the Bronx now."

"Sorry, no. Can I ask why you're asking?"

"It would be better right now if you could just answer my questions."

"Well, I don't recognize either name. I could search our customer database, if you'd like."

"That would be great."

Raff reached over her shoulder and started typing.

Nap said, "Can you print the full client list for us?"

"You think one of our clients...?"

"Just covering all bases," Nap said.

"How do you spell Thorpe?" Raff asked Elena.

She suggested that he try it both ways—with the *e* and without the *e*. Nothing. Same with Aaron Corval.

"Who are these men?" Raff asked. There was an edge there now. "What do they have to do with Damien?"

"You said only you and Mr. Gorse used this IP and Wi-Fi?"

"Yeah, so?"

"Don't ask me for the technical explanation," she said, "but Henry Thorpe had contact with someone using this computer's IP."

Nap just listened.

"Meaning?" Raff said. There was more edge now.

"Meaning just that. Someone who used this computer communicated with Henry Thorpe."

"So? This Thorpe guy could be an ink salesman for all I know."

"He's not."

Elena stared at him hard.

"Damien didn't keep secrets from me," Raff said.

Didn't. Finally the past tense.

"Maybe our computer was hacked or something."

"That's not what happened, Neil."

"So what are you insinuating?"

"I'm not insinuating anything. I'm asking."

"Damien wouldn't cheat on me."

She hadn't really been going there, but maybe she should. Maybe there was some kind of romantic connection here. Was Henry Thorpe gay? She hadn't bothered to ask. Then again, who in this day and age cares?

And if that was the case—if Damien and Henry were lovers— how did Aaron Corval fit into this? Wasn't Paige Greene his girl- friend? Could that be tied in somehow? Could there be some kind of romantic entanglement Elena hadn't yet considered at the cen- ter of this?

She didn't see how.

Nap tapped her on the shoulder. "Can I speak to you for a mo- ment?"

Elena got up from the chair. She put a hand on Raff's shoul- der. "Mr. Raff?"

He looked at her.

"I'm not insinuating anything. Really. I'm just trying to help find who did this."

He nodded, his eyes down.

Nap headed out the back door. She followed him.

"What's up?" she asked.

"Aaron Corval."

"What about him?"

"It isn't hard to use Google," he said. "He was murdered days ago."

"That's right."

"So you want to tell me what's going on?"

CHAPTER

EIGHTEEN

Simon's car route back to Manhattan ran past the Corval Inn and Family Tree Farm.

He almost drove straight past it—what was the point, and he wanted to get back to the hospital—but then again, nothing ventured, nothing gained. He pulled into the lot and parked in the same spot he'd left earlier.

The inn was quiet. If the mourners had all been heading to a reception when Enid peeled off for her club, the reception was over. He looked for any familiar faces at all—anyone who'd been at the memorial service down by that brook—but the only person who looked familiar was the woman behind the desk with the tablecloth-checked blouse. She had another map of the grounds flattened on the desk and was showing a color-coordinated young couple that Simon would anachronistically call yuppies the "most arduous hiking trail on the property."

The woman clearly spotted Simon waiting out of the corner of her eye, and she clearly wasn't happy about it. Simon stood, bouncing on his toes, and glanced around. There was a staircase on the right. He debated going up it, but what good would that do? There were glass doors covered with lace behind him. They would lead to another room.

Maybe the reception was in there.

As he started toward them, he heard the woman behind the desk say, "Excuse me, that room is private."

Simon didn't stop. He reached the door, turned the knob, and pushed into the room.

There had indeed been a reception of some sort in here. Debris from finger sandwiches and crudités sat on a stained white tablecloth in the center of the room. An antique rolltop desk complete with those mail slots and tiny file drawers was to Simon's right. Wiley Corval swiveled from the desk and rose.

"What are you doing here?"

The woman behind the desk came in behind Simon. "I'm so sorry, Wiley."

"It's okay, Bernadette. I got it."

"Are you sure? I can call—"

"I have it. Close the door and see to our guests, please."

She threw an eye dagger at Simon before heading back into the lobby. She closed the doors a little harder than necessary, shaking the glass.

"What do you want?" he asked Simon with a snap.

Wiley Corval now wore a brown herringbone tweed vest with pewter buttons. A gold chain hung from a middle button, attached no doubt to a pocket watch that was in the vest pocket. His crisp white shirt had puffy arms moving down to a tapered cuff.

Dressed for the role of innkeeper, Simon thought.

"My daughter is missing."

"You told me that already. I have no idea where she is. Please go away."

"I have some questions."

"And I don't have to answer them." He stood a little straighter, threw back his shoulders for effect. "I'm mourning my son today."

There was no reason to be subtle. "Are you?" Simon asked.

Surprise came to Wiley's face—Simon had expected that—but there was something deeper.

Fear.

"Am I what?"

"Aaron's father."

"What are you talking about?"

"You don't look like him at all."

Wiley's mouth dropped open. "Are you serious?"

"Tell me about Aaron's mother."

He looked as though he were about to say something, caught himself, and then a smile crossed Wiley Corval's face. The smile was creepy. Extra creepy. Simon almost took a step back.

"You've been talking to my wife."

Something occurred to Simon at that moment, something that perhaps Enid had been hinting at, or perhaps it was seeing Wiley in the flesh, dressed right now to play some part, or perhaps it had been the expression on Wiley's face when Simon first stumbled across him down in the woods.

There was no grief emanating from Wiley Corval.

Of course, all the clichés apply here—people grieve in their own way, just because you can't see a man is hurting doesn't mean he isn't, he could be putting on a brave face—but they all rang hollow. Enid had described her husband as theatrical. Simon got that now, as if everything he did was part of an act, including his feelings.

That little boy. Living alone with a man who claimed to be his father.

Simon tried to hold back his imagination, but it became a bucking horse, running wild, running toward the worst thoughts, the most awful, depraved scenarios.

They can't be true, Simon told himself.

And yet.

"I'll get a court order."

"For what?" Wiley asked, spreading his hands, the picture now of pure innocence.

"Parentage."

"Seriously?" That damned creepy smile. "Aaron was cremated."

"I can find his DNA in other ways."

"Doubtful. And even if you could somehow get his DNA and mine, it would show that I'm his father."

"You're lying."

"Am I?"

He's enjoying this, Simon thought.

"And just for the sake of a fun mental exercise, suppose you did run the test and suppose it showed I wasn't Aaron's biological father, what would that prove?"

Simon said nothing.

"Maybe his mother cheated on me. What difference could that make all these years later? The test wouldn't show that, of course—this is all a hypothetical; I was Aaron's father—but what do you think you'd be able to prove?" Wiley took two steps toward Simon. "My son was a drug dealer living with your junkie daughter in the Bronx. That's where he was murdered. Whatever gossip Enid told you, you have to see that his murder has nothing to do with his childhood."

That made sense, of course. On the surface, there was no way to argue with any of that. There was not a scintilla of evidence that linked whatever potential awfulness had occurred to a young boy in this very inn and his bloody murder decades later in that Bronx tenement.

And yet.

Simon shifted gears.

"When did Aaron start getting into drugs?"

The oily smile was back. "Maybe you should ask Enid about that."

"When did he move away?"

"When did who move away?"

"Who are we talking about? Aaron."

Another smile. Christ, he was *really* enjoying this.

"Enid didn't tell you?"

"Tell me what?"

"Aaron didn't move away."

"What are you talking about?"

"Enid has a place. It's a sort of club."

"What about it?"

"There's an apartment off the back," Wiley said. "Aaron lived there."

"Until when?"

"I wouldn't really know. Aaron and I...we were estranged."

Simon tried to follow this. "So when did he move near Lanford College?"

"What are you talking about?"

"He moved there. I think Aaron was working at a club when he met Paige."

Wiley actually laughed out loud now. "Who told you that?"

Now Simon felt the chill again.

"You think they met in Lanford?"

"They didn't?"

"No."

"Where then?"

"Here." He nodded at the look of surprise on Simon's face. "Paige came here."

"To the inn?"

"Yes."

"Did you see her?"

"I did." Now the laugh was gone, the smile falling away. His voice turned grave. "I also saw her...after."

"After what?"

"After she'd been with Aaron for a few months. The difference, what he did to her..." Wiley Corval stopped, shook his head. "If you did harm my son, I almost can't blame you. I can only tell you that I'm sorry."

Bullshit. He wasn't sorry. This was all an act.

176

"What did Paige want?" Simon asked. "When she came here."

"What do you think?"

"I have no idea."

"She wanted to meet Aaron."

———————

It made no sense.

Why would Paige, a seemingly happy college freshman, come here looking for a scumbag like Aaron Corval? How would his daughter even know who he was? Had they met earlier? Not according to Wiley Corval. Paige had specifically come to the inn seeking to meet Aaron. Did she come to him to score drugs? That also seemed a long shot. Driving this distance to score drugs—hours from Lanford College—seemed patently ridiculous.

Did Aaron and Paige meet online in some way?

This seemed most likely. They met online, and Paige drove up here to meet in person.

But how? Why? How did their paths cross? Paige didn't seem like the type for online dating or Tinder or any of that—and even if she was, even if Simon was being naïve about his own daughter, couldn't she hook up with someone closer to her school?

It made no sense.

Could Wiley be lying about Paige coming to the inn? Could he be trying to muddy the waters and distract from what Enid had told Simon about Aaron's parentage?

Simon didn't think so.

Wiley Corval was a sleazebag and untrustworthy and maybe—no, probably—worse. But his words about Paige coming here to meet Aaron had that odd yet unmistakable scent of truth.

Simon drove back to Enid's club, but she was gone. He hit Yvonne's speed dial.

Yvonne answered on the first ring. "If there's a change, I'll call you."

"No change at all?"

"None."

"And the doctors?"

"Nothing new."

Simon closed his eyes.

"I spent the day making calls," Yvonne said.

"To whom?"

"Well-connected friends. I wanted to make sure we have the absolute best doctors on this."

"And?" he asked.

"And we do. Fill me in on your visit to the inn."

He did. When he finished, Yvonne simply said, "Holy shit."

"I know."

"So where do you go next?"

"I'm not sure."

"Yeah, you are," Yvonne said.

She knew him too well.

"Something at that college changed Paige," he said.

"I agree. Simon?"

"Yes."

"Call me in three hours. I want to know you arrived at Lanford safely."

CHAPTER

NINETEEN

That weekend," Eileen Vaughan told Simon, "Paige borrowed my car."

They sat in the four-person common room with cathedral ceiling. The dorm's oversized bay window looked out over a Lanford College quad dripping so green it might as well have been a still-wet painting. Eileen Vaughan had been Paige's freshman-year roommate. On Paige's first day of college, when Simon, Ingrid, Sam, and Anya had all brought her to this campus brimming with hope, Eileen Vaughan had been the first to greet them. Eileen was smart and friendly and on the surface, at least, seemed to be the perfect roommate. Simon had taken her phone number, "just in case," for emergency purposes only, which is why he still had it now.

Simon and Ingrid had left Lanford College that day on such a high. Squinting into the campus sun, they'd held hands as they walked back to the car, even as Sam grumbled about his parents' "gross PDA" (Public Display of Affection) and Anya scoffed out an "Ugh, can you not?" Back in the car, Simon had reminisced about his own college years, how he'd lived in a four-person suite like the one he was in now—but not like this one. Simon's had been littered with empty pizza boxes and emptier beer cans, decorated in Early American Pub Crawl, while Eileen Vaughan's suite looked like something out of an Ikea catalogue, all pale woods and real furniture and freshly-vacuumed throw carpets. There was nothing ironic or college-y on the walls, no decorative bongs or Che posters or heck, posters of any kind, favoring instead handcrafted tapestries with mild Buddhist designs or geometric patterns. The whole effect was less true collegiate and more model showroom, the dorm you use to sway prospective students (and more, their parents) during campus visits.

"Had Paige ever done that before?" Simon asked Eileen.

"Borrowed my car? Never. She told me she didn't like to drive."

It was more than that, Simon thought. Paige didn't know how to drive. Not really. She'd managed to get her license after taking lessons from a driving school in Fort Lee, but because they lived in Manhattan, she never drove.

"You know how Paige was," Eileen continued, not realizing how the "was" rather than "is" struck him deep in the chest. It was appropriate, of course—Paige was a "was" in terms of this campus and probably Eileen's life, but as he looked at this lovely, healthy-looking girl—yes, he should call her a woman, but right now he only saw Eileen as a girl, a girl like his daughter—there was a deep, heavy thud in his heart reminding him that his daughter should be there, occupying one of the suite's four bedrooms with a box spring on the floor and a desk with a gooseneck lamp.

Eileen said, "Even if Paige had to get something at the supermarket or CVS, she'd ask me to drive instead."

"So it must have surprised you when Paige asked to borrow the car."

Eileen wore jeans and a dark gray cable-knit sweater with a turtle neck. Her long reddish hair was parted in the middle and hung down behind her shoulders. Her eyes were big and indigo blue and she just reeked of youth and college and possibilities, and it killed him.

Her voice was hesitant. "It did."

"You seem unsure."

"Can I ask you something, Mr. Greene?"

He was going to correct her and tell her to call him Simon, but the formality felt somehow right here. She was his daughter's friend. He was asking about his daughter.

"Of course."

"Why now?"

"Pardon?"

"This was a long time ago. What happened with Paige...I know I agreed to see you, but this wasn't really easy for me either."

"What wasn't easy?"

"What happened with Paige. Here, I mean. At Lanford. We had that small room, the two of us, and, I don't know, we connected. She was my best friend right away. I'm an only child. I don't want to make too much of this, but Paige was like a sister to me. And then..."

Eileen had been hurt and she'd recovered and now Simon was ripping open the stitches. He felt bad about that, but Eileen was young, and thirty minutes after he walked out the door, she'd go to a class or one of her roommates would get her for dinner in the Cushman Cafeteria and then they'd study at the Elders Library and probably hit a dorm party—and those "wounds" would be back sealed up tight.

"What happened?" Simon asked.

"Paige changed."

No hesitation.

"Why?"

"I don't know."

He tried to think how to approach this. "When?"

"It was toward the end of first semester."

"After this trip with your car?"

"Yes. Well, no. Something was off even before then."

Simon leaned forward a little, making sure to keep away from her personal space. "How long before?"

"I'm not sure. It's hard to remember. It's just that..."

He nodded for her to go on.

"When Paige asked to borrow the car, I remember feeling weird about it. Not just because it was out of character. But because she'd been distant lately."

"Any idea why?"

"No. I was hurt. I was maybe a little angry with her about it." Eileen looked up. "I should have reached out to her instead, you know? Instead of getting all hurt about it. Making it all about me. Maybe if I had been a good friend—"

"None of this is on you, Eileen."

She didn't seem convinced.

"Could Paige have been taking drugs?" Simon asked.

"You mean before she met Aaron?"

"One theory is that Paige was doing drugs already—so Aaron might have been a source or something."

Eileen considered that. "I don't think so. For one thing, I know this is a college campus and drugs are supposed to be rampant. But that's not really how it is here. I wouldn't even know where to buy anything stronger than weed."

"Maybe that was it," Simon said.

"What?"

"Maybe Paige wanted to buy something stronger."

"So she went to Aaron?"

"That's one theory."

Eileen wasn't buying it. "Paige didn't even smoke weed. I don't mean to make her sound like some kind of priss. She drank and stuff, but I never saw her stoned before or high or whatever you want to call it. The first time I saw her like that was after she met Aaron."

"So it comes back to the same thing," Simon said. "Why did Paige borrow your car? Why did she drive to this quiet corner of Connecticut?"

"I don't know. I'm sorry."

"You said she was different."

"Yes."

"How about her other friends?"

"I think..." Her gaze traveled up and to the left. "Yes, looking back on it, I think Paige just kind of withdrew. From all of us. One of our friends, Judy Zyskind—do you know her?"

"No."

"Judy's one of my suitemates now. She's at a lacrosse game at Bowdoin or I'd ask her to explain. Anyway, I don't think this is it, but Judy thought maybe something had happened to her at a frat party."

Simon felt a cold jolt run through him. "What do you mean, 'happened to her'?"

"We talk a lot about sexual assault on campus here. A. Lot. I'm not saying too much. We really need it. But I think Judy sort of has it on the brain now. So when someone becomes withdrawn, it's kinda all we see. I remember one night Judy confronting Paige about it. About some guy who Judy thought was bothering Paige."

"What guy?"

"I don't know. They didn't say a name."

"And this is before Aaron?"

"Yes."

"How did Paige react?"

"She said that it had nothing to do with any of that."

"Did she say what it did have to do with?"

Eileen hesitated, turned away.

"Eileen? Did she say something else?"

"Yes."

"What?"

"I think Paige was just trying to deflect. To get us off her back."

"What did she say?"

"She said"—Eileen turned back, met Simon's eyes—"that there were problems at home."

Simon blinked and leaned back, taking the blow. He hadn't been expecting that. "What kind of problems at home?"

"Paige wouldn't elaborate."

"No clue at all?"

"I thought, well, with what happened after, with Aaron and the drugs and everything, I thought maybe you and Dr. Greene were having problems."

"We weren't."

"Oh."

Simon's mind swirled.

Problems at home?

He tried to piece it together. It wasn't the marriage—he and Ingrid were good, better than ever, actually. It wasn't financial—her parents were both at the height of their careers and earning power. How about Paige's siblings? Nothing strange, nothing that he could remember. There had been a minor drama with Sam's science teacher, but no, that had been the year before, and that wouldn't warrant a "problems at home" comment.

Unless something had been going on that Simon didn't know about.

But even if that were the case—even if Paige imagined or saw some real problem with something back home with her family—how had that led her to drive to Connecticut and Aaron?

He asked Eileen that.

"I'm sorry, Mr. Greene. I don't know."

Eileen Vaughan glanced at her mobile phone the way someone older might glance at their watch. She shifted on the couch, her body language suddenly all wrong, and Simon knew that he was losing her.

"I have a class soon," she said.

"Eileen?"

"Yes?"

"Aaron's been murdered."

Her eyes widened.

"Paige has run off."

"Run off?"

"She's missing. And now I think whoever killed Aaron is after her too."

"I don't understand. Why?"

"I don't know. But I think whatever brought them together—whatever made Paige seek Aaron out—is responsible. That's why I need your help. I need to figure out what happened to her, on this campus, that made her borrow your car and go to Aaron."

"I don't know."

"I get that. And I get that you just want me to leave. But I'm asking you for your help."

"Help how?"

"Start from the beginning. Tell me everything that happened, no matter how insignificant it might seem."

————————

Paige became a "Try Hard," Eileen Vaughan told him.

"A what?"

"A Try Hard," Eileen repeated. "You know how during Orientation Week they tell you that you can be all you want to be, that this is your chance to start anew and take advantage of all the opportunities?"

Simon nodded.

"Paige took that to heart."

"Isn't that a good thing?"

"I thought she was overdoing it. She wanted to be in a play. She tried out for two a cappella groups. There's this club on campus of science nerds who build robots. She joined that. She ran for a freshman judiciary seat and won. She got obsessed with the Family Tree Club, which hooked up with our genetics class, to figure out where you're from and all that. She also wanted to write a play. Looking back on it, it was all too much. She was driving herself too hard."

"Did she have any boyfriends?"

"No one serious."

"The guy your lacrosse roommate mentioned..."

"I don't know anything about that. I'll text Judy, if you like."

"Please."

Eileen took out her phone, her fingers dancing on the screen. She nodded when it was done.

"How about her academics?" Simon asked. "What classes was she taking?"

A father should know that, of course, but before all this, Simon had prided himself on not being one of those helicopter parents. He didn't know her classes, even in high school. Some parents checked an online program called Skyward every day, to make sure their child did their homework or was keeping up with their grades. Simon didn't even know how to log on. He had smugly thought back then that that made him a better father.

Stay out of the way. Trust your child.

And it had been easy with Paige. She was self-driven. She excelled. Oh, what satisfaction Simon had felt back then, what foolish superiority over those overbearing and overinvolved parents he'd felt, bragging that he didn't even know his Skyward password like that asshole at the party who brags about not owning a television.

What arrogance before the fall.

Eileen wrote down the names of Paige's classes and the professors who taught them. She handed him the slip of paper and said, "I really have to go now."

"Do you mind if I walk with you?"

She said that would be fine, but she said it grudgingly.

Simon read the class list as they headed for the door. "Does anything jump out at you?"

"Not really. Most of the classes were pretty big. I don't think the professors will really remember her. The only exception would be Professor van de Beek."

They started across that bright, green quad.

"What did van de Beek teach?"

"That genetics class I told you about."

"Where can I find him?"

Still walking, Eileen pecked something out on her mobile phone. "Here, this is him."

She handed him the phone.

Professor Louis van de Beek was young, probably not yet thirty and—not to be that father—he looked like the kind of professor that made young co-eds swoon. His so-black-it's-blue hair was a touch too long, his skin a little too waxy. He had good teeth, a nice smile. He wore a tight black T-shirt in the picture, his toned arms folded over his chest.

What the hell happened to professors with tweed sport coats?

Under his portrait, it read "Professor of Biological Science." It also listed his office address at Clark House, his email address, his website, and finally, the classes he taught, including Introduction to Genetics and Genealogy.

"You said he was an exception."

"Yes."

"Why?" Simon asked.

"For one thing, Genetics and Genealogy was a small class," she said. "So we got to know the professor pretty well. But for Paige, he was something more."

"Like what?"

"Professor van de Beek ran that Family Tree club I told you she got obsessed with. I know she visited him during office hours. A lot."

Simon frowned again. Eileen must have spotted it.

"Oh no, nothing like that."

"Okay."

"When Paige got here, she didn't know what to major in. Like the rest of us. You knew that, right?"

He nodded. He and Ingrid had encouraged that. No need to lock yourself down, they'd told her. Explore. Try new things. You'll find your passion.

"Paige talked a lot about her mom and her job." Then she quickly added, "Not that she didn't talk about you too, Mr. Greene. I mean, I think she found your job interesting too."

"It's okay, Eileen."

"Anyway, I think she sort of hero-worshipped her mom. Professor van de Beek is also the freshman counselor for students who want to go into medicine."

Simon swallowed. "Paige wanted to be a physician?"

"Yeah, I think so."

The revelation crushed him anew. Paige had wanted to be a doctor. Like her mother.

"Anyway," Eileen continued, "I don't think this has anything to do with her meeting Aaron, but Professor van de Beek was a big part of her life here."

They crossed in front of Ratner dormitory, where Paige and Eileen had lived freshman year, walking right across the spot where Simon had hugged his daughter goodbye a lifetime ago.

The painful hits just kept coming.

When Eileen spotted some friends in front of the Isherwood building, she told Simon that her class was inside and bid him a quick goodbye. He waved as she left and then headed over to Clark House. When he entered the front foyer, an older woman with a face that had seen it all before the Eisenhower administration sat behind the desk and scowled at him.

A small nameplate read MRS. DINSMORE. No first name.

"May I help you?" Mrs. Dinsmore said in a voice that indicated any help would come very reluctantly.

"I'm looking for Professor van de Beek."

"You won't find him."

"Pardon?"

"Professor van de Beek is on sabbatical."

"Since when?"

"I'm not at liberty to answer any additional questions on the matter."

"Is he around or is he traveling?"

Mrs. Dinsmore had a pair of glasses on a chain around her neck. She put them on now and frowned with even more disapproval. "What part of 'not at liberty to answer' did you find confusing?"

Simon had Louis van de Beek's email from that web directory. That seemed the more prudent way to go. "You've been a delight, thank you."

"I aim to please," Mrs. Dinsmore replied, head down, writing something down.

Simon headed back toward his car. He called Yvonne and heard yet again how nothing with Ingrid's condition had changed. He wanted to ask a million questions, but an odd memory came to him. Early in his relationship with Ingrid, Simon worried about the overseas markets and political upheaval and upcoming earnings reports—anything that could affect his clients' portfolios. That was natural enough, part of the job on the surface, but it actually made him a less focused and less effective financial analyst.

"The serenity prayer," Ingrid had told him one night. She'd been sitting at the computer, wearing one of his dress shirts, her back to him.

"What?"

He came up behind her and rested his hands on his beautiful wife's shoulders. The printer whirred. She reached for a sheet of paper and handed it to him.

"Put this on your desk," she said.

He should have been familiar with the prayer, of course, but he wasn't. He read it, and odd as this sounds, it changed his life almost immediately:

God, grant me the SERENITY to accept the things I cannot
change,
The COURAGE to change the things I can,
The WISDOM to know the difference.

No, Simon wasn't religious in the least and the prayer was short and obvious. Yet it resonated. And more than that, it resonated with Ingrid. He couldn't change Ingrid's condition. She was comatose in a hospital, the pain of that constant and ripping, but he had to let it go because it was foolhardy to think he could change that fact now.

He couldn't.

So accept that. Let it go. Change the things that he could.

Like finding his daughter.

When Simon reached his car, he called Elena Ramirez.

"Anything?" he asked.

"You first."

"Paige came to Aaron, not the other way around. I always thought that they met near Lanford College. But she sought him out."

"So she knew him before?"

"Somehow."

"Probably met online. A dating app or something."

"Why would she have been on a dating app?"

"Why is anyone?"

"She's a college freshman, all caught up in her studies and new friends. And that's not my Dad goggles talking."

"Dad goggles?"

"You know. Bias. Seeing your kids through Dad goggles."

"Oh, right."

"This was what Paige was like, according to her roommate, not me. Did you talk to the guy at the tattoo parlor yet?"

"Damien Gorse. Stick with me first, Simon. Is there anything else you think I should know?"

"Just something really weird about Aaron's upbringing. Or his parentage anyway."

"Tell me."

So Simon filled her in on the story Enid told him about Aaron and Wiley's tale of a dead Italian mother. When he finished, there was silence on the other end of the phone. Then he heard her tapping on a keyboard.

"Elena?"

"I'm trying to Google photographs of Aaron and his father."

"Why?"

There was a pause.

"I don't see any. I see some of the father at the inn. Wiley."

"Why, what's up?"

"This is going to sound weird," she began.

"But?"

"But you've seen both Aaron and Wiley in person."

"Yes."

"Do you think they are father and son? I mean, biologically."

"No." Simon said it that fast, without really processing his response. "I mean... look, I don't know. Something is off. Why?"

"It might be nothing."

"But?"

"But Henry Thorpe was adopted," Elena said. "So was Damien Gorse."

Simon felt a chill, but he still said, "You're reaching."

"I know."

"Paige wasn't adopted."

"I know that too."

"Elena?"

"Yes?"

"What did Damien Gorse tell you?"

"Nothing, Simon. Gorse is dead. Someone murdered him too."

TWENTY

A sh always tried to be prepared.

There were fresh clothes in the car for both of them. They managed to change on the move and dumped the old clothes in a charity bin behind a Whole Foods near the New York state border. At a Rite Aid, Dee Dee, donning a baseball cap, bought ten items, but only two really mattered—hair dye and a scissors.

He didn't go in with her.

There were cameras everywhere. Let them look for a lone woman or lone man. Confuse them. Don't stay anyplace too long.

Dee Dee had thought she could just color her hair in the Rite Aid bathroom. Ash told her that would be a mistake.

Keep moving. Don't give them anything to go on.

They drove another ten miles and found an old-school gas station—poorer CCTV, Ash figured. Dee Dee headed into the bathroom wearing the baseball cap. Using the newly bought scissors, she sawed off the long blonde braid and cropped her hair close, then she flushed the cut hair down the toilet. She dyed the shorter locks a subtle auburn, nothing too striking, and put the cap back on her head.

Ash had told her: Always walk with your head tilted down. CCTV cameras shot from above. Always. So wear a cap with a bill and keep your eyes on the ground. Sometimes, depending on the weather, sunglasses were a good idea. Other times, they drew the wrong kind of attention.

"This is overkill," Dee Dee said.

"Probably."

But she didn't argue—and if Dee Dee really had an issue with his precautions, she'd argue.

Once they were back on the road, Dee Dee took off the cap and mussed her hair with her hand. "How do I look?"

He risked a look and felt the ka-boom in his heart.

Dee Dee pulled her knees up to her chest and fell asleep in the seat next to him. Ash kept sneaking glances at her. At a red light, he rolled up a shirt he'd kept in the backseat and placed it between her head and the car door, just to make sure she was comfortable and didn't hurt herself.

Three hours later, when she woke up, Dee Dee said, "I need to pee."

Ash pulled off at the next rest stop. They put on baseball caps. Ash bought some chicken fingers and fries to go. When they got back on the highway, Dee Dee asked, "Where are we headed?"

"We don't know what the cops have on you."

"That's not an answer to my question, Ash."

"You know where we're going," he said.

Dee Dee did not reply.

"I know it's near the Vermont border," Ash said. "But I don't know the exact location. You'll have to direct me."

"They won't let you in. No outsiders."

"Got it."

"Especially men."

Ash rolled his eyes. "Gee, that seems normal."

"That's the rules. No outside men in Truth Haven."

"I don't have to go in, Dee. I just need to drop you off."

"Why?"

"You know why."

"You think it's not safe for me anymore."

"Bingo."

"But it's not up to you to decide what's safe," she said. "It's not up to me either."

"Don't tell me," Ash said. "It's in God's hands."

She smiled at him. It was, as always, even with the strange hair color and new cut, beatific. The smile struck his heart with a gentle boom.

"It's not just God. It's the Truth."

"And who tells you the truth?"

"For those who can never understand, it's easiest to call him God."

"He talks to you?"

"Via his personage on earth."

Ash had studied up on the nonsense of her cult. "That would be Casper Vartage?"

"God made his choice."

"Vartage is a con man."

"The devil doesn't want the Truth to flourish. The devil dies in Truth's light."

"So Vartage's jail time?"

"That's where he was told the Truth. In solitary. After they beat him and tortured him. Now when the media and outsiders speak ill of him, it is because they are trying to silence the Truth."

Ash shook his head. Pointless.

"It's the second exit after the Vermont border," she said.

Ash flipped the station. The seventies classic "Hey, St. Peter" by Flash and the Pan came on the radio. Ash had to smile. In the song, a man arrives at the gates of heaven and pleads for St. Peter to let him in because living in New York City means he's already done his time in hell.

"Do you have music at the compound?" Ash asked.

"We call it Truth Haven."

"Dee Dee."

"Yes, we have music. Many of our members are talented musicians. They write their own songs."

"You don't have outside music?"

"That wouldn't spread the Truth, Ash."

"One of Vartage's rules?"

"Please don't use his before name."

"His before name?"

"Yes. It's forbidden."

"Before name," he said again. "You mean like you're now Holly?"

"Yes."

"Did he give you that name?"

"The Truth Council did."

"Who makes up the Truth Council?"

"The Truth, the Volunteer, the Visitor."

"Three people?"

"Yes."

"All men?"

"Yes."

"Like the Trinity."

She turned toward him. "Nothing like the Trinity."

No reason to get into that, he thought. "I assume the Truth is Casper Vartage."

"He is, yes."

"And the other two?"

"They are the offspring of the Truth. They were born and raised in the Haven."

"His sons, you mean?"

"It's not like that, but for your purposes, yes."

"My purposes?"

"You wouldn't understand, Ash."

"Another line from every cult." He held up a hand before

she could admonish him. "And what happens if you question the Truth?"

"Truth is truth. By definition. Anything else is a lie."

"Wow. So everything your leader says is gospel."

"Can the lion not be a lion? He's the Truth. How can what he says not be true?"

Ash shook his head as they crossed into Vermont. He kept sneaking glances at her.

"Dee Dee?"

She closed her eyes.

"Do you really want me to call you Holly?"

"No," she said. "It's okay. When I'm not in Truth Haven, I'm not Holly, am I?"

"Uh-huh."

She said, "Dee Dee can do things that Holly cannot."

"Nice moral out."

"Isn't it?"

Ash tried not to grin. "I think I like Dee Dee more."

"Yes, I think you do. But Holly is more complete. Holly is happy and understands the Truth."

"Dee Dee?" Then, pausing, he sighed and said: "Or should I say, 'Holly'?"

"This exit." He took it. "What, Ash?"

"Can I be blunt?"

"Yes."

"How can you believe this crap?"

He glanced at her. She tucked her legs up so that she was sitting cross-legged in the seat. "I really do love you, Ash."

"I love you too."

"You did some Googling, Ash? On the Shining Truth?"

He had. Their leader, Casper Vartage, was born of a mysterious birth in 1944. His mother claimed to have woken up one day seven months pregnant—the very moment her husband died leading the charge on Normandy Beach. There is no proof of any of this, of course. But this is the story. As a youngster in Nebraska, Casper was considered a "grain healer" and farmers sought him out during droughts and the like. Again no one backs up this claim. Vartage rebelled against his powers—something about the Truth being so potent he tried to fight it off—and ended up in prison sometime around 1970 for fraud. That part—the fraud—there is evidence of and plenty of it.

After losing an eye in a prison fight and being thrown into a hellhole described as the "heat box," ol' Casper was visited by an angel. Hard to say if Vartage just made this part up out of whole cloth or if the sun caused delusions. Either way, the angel who visited him is known in the cult's clever folklore as the Visitor. The Visitor told him about the Truth and the symbol he had to find behind a rock in the Arizona desert when he was free, which supposedly he did.

There was more crap like that, typical nonsense mythology, and now "The Shining Truth" had a compound where they brainwashed disciples, mostly women, or beat or drugged or raped them.

"I don't expect you to see the Truth," Dee Dee said.

"I just don't get how you don't see this is a crazy-ass cult."

She angled her body toward him. "Do you remember Mrs. Kensington?"

Mrs. Kensington, a foster mother they'd had in common, took those in her care to church twice a week—Tuesday afternoons for Bible studies and Sunday mornings for mass. Always. She never missed them.

"Of course you do."

"She was good to us," he agreed.

"Yes, she was. Do you still go to church, Ash?"

"Rarely," he said.

"You liked it though. When we were kids."

"It was quiet. I liked the quiet."

"Do you remember the stories that we heard back then?"

"Sure."

"Mrs. Kensington believed every one of them."

"I know."

"So remind me: How old was Noah when he built the ark?"

"Dee Dee."

"Somewhere around five hundred years old, if I recall. Do you really think Noah put two of every creature on that ark? There are a million types of insects alone. Think he managed to get them all on board? That all makes sense to you and all the Mrs. Kensingtons out there—but the Truth doesn't?"

"It's not the same thing."

"Sure it is. We sat in that church and Mrs. Kensington had tears in her eyes and nodded when they told us about salvation. Do you remember the stories?"

Ash frowned.

"Let me see if I can recap: A celestial baby boy, who was his own father, was born to a married virgin. Then the baby's father—who was also him—tortured and killed him. Oh, but then he came back from the dead like a zombie, but if you eat his flesh, which is a wafer, and drink his wine blood and promise to kiss his ass, he will suck all the evil out of you—"

"Dee Dee—"

"Wait, I'm getting to the best part. The reason why there is evil at all in the world—do you remember this part, Ash?"

He did, but he kept quiet.

"No? Oh, you'll love this. Evil exists because an airheaded bimbo, who started life as a man's rib, got tricked into eating a piece of bad fruit by a talking reptile." Dee Dee clapped her hands together and fell back on the car seat, laughing. "Do I need to go into the other stuff? The parting of seas, the prophets ascending on animals up to the sky, Abraham pimping out his wife to the pharaoh? How about even now, all these 'holy' men who live in Roman compounds with homoerotic art and wear costumes that would make a drag queen blush?"

He just kept on driving.

"Ash?"

"What?"

"It may sound like I'm mocking these beliefs," she said, "or that I'm mocking Mrs. Kensington."

"That it does."

"I'm not. My point is, maybe before you dismiss other beliefs as wacko, you should take a closer look at the stories that 'normal'"—Dee Dee air-quoted—"people find credible. We think all religions are crazy—except our own."

He didn't want to admit it, but she had a point. And yet something in her tone . . .

"The Truth is more than a religion. It's a living, breathing entity. The Truth has always existed. It will always exist. Most people's God lives in the past—thousands of years ago, stuck in old books. Why? Do they think God gave up on them? Mine is here. Today. In the real world. When this Truth dies, his offspring will continue. Because the Truth lives. The Truth, if you could be objective, Ash, if you hadn't been brainwashed by the big religions since childbirth, makes more sense than talking snakes or elephant gods, doesn't it?"

Ash said nothing.

"Ash?"

"What?"

"Talk to me."

"I don't know what to say."

"Maybe that's because you're hearing the Truth."

"Uh no, that's not it."

"Take your next right," she said. "We're getting close."

The road was one lane now, with forest on either side.

"You don't have to go back," Ash said.

Dee Dee turned and stared out her window.

"I have some money saved," Ash continued. "We could go somewhere. Just you and me. Buy a place. You could be Holly with me."

She didn't reply.

"Dee?"

"Yes."

"Did you hear me?"

"I did."

"You don't have to go back."

"Shh. We're getting close now."

CHAPTER

TWENTY-ONE

S imon called the phone number on Professor van de Beek's bio page. After two rings, it went to voicemail. Simon left a message asking van de Beek to call him back about his daughter, Paige Greene. Simon doubled up then, sending an email to the professor with the same request.

He called both Sam and Anya, but the calls went right into voicemail, which was no surprise. Kids never talked on the phone, only texted. He should have known better. He sent them both the same text:

You okay? Wanna call me?

Sam answered right away.

All good. Nah no need.

Again, no surprise.

He started back toward New York City. He and Ingrid shared a stream or cloud or whatever, so that all his photos and documents and all her photos and documents were in the same place. Music too. They shared a service, so he told Siri to play Ingrid's most recent playlist and sat back and listened.

The first song Ingrid had put on her playlist made him smile: "The Girl from Ipanema," the 1964 version sung by Astrud Gilberto.

Sublime.

Simon shook his head, still in awe of the woman who had somehow, out of all the options, chosen him. Him. Whatever life had thrown at him, whatever turns he'd made or bizarre forks he'd seen in the road, that fact—that Ingrid had chosen him—always kept him balanced, made him thankful, guided him home.

The phone rang. The caller ID appeared on the car's navigation screen.

Yvonne.

He quickly answered it.

"It's not about Ingrid," Yvonne said right away. "No change there."

"What then?"

"And nothing is wrong."

"Okay."

"Today is the second Tuesday of the month," she said.

He'd forgotten about Sadie Lowenstein.

"Not a big deal," Yvonne continued. "I can call Sadie for you and postpone or I can head out myself or—"

"No, I'll go."

"Simon..."

"No, I want to. It's on my way anyhow."

"Are you sure?"

"Yeah. If something changes with Ingrid—"

"I'll call you. Or Robert will. He's taking over for me soon."

"How are the kids?"

"Anya is with your neighbor. Sam is on his phone all the time, texting or whatever. He started dating a girl two weeks ago. Did you know that?"

Another pang, though a small one this time. "No."

"The girlfriend wants to come down from Amherst and sit here with him, which is making him smile in spite of himself, but Sam's told her not to yet."

"I'll be back soon."

"They miss you, but they don't need you, if you know what I mean. They get what you're doing."

———————

Sadie Lowenstein lived in a brick colonial in Yonkers, New York, just north of the Bronx. The neighborhood was no-frills and working class. Sadie had lived here for fifty-seven of her eighty-three years. She could afford better. As her financial advisor, Simon knew that better than anyone. She could get a place down in Florida for the rough winters too, a condo maybe, but she scoffed. No interest. She took two trips per year to Vegas. That was it. Other than that, she liked her old home.

Sadie still smoked and had the raspy voice to prove it. She wore an old-school housedress/muumuu. They sat in her kitchen, at the round Formica table where Sadie once sat with her husband Frank and their twin boys, Barry and Greg. They were gone from here now. Barry died of AIDS in 1992. Frank succumbed to cancer in 2004. Greg, the only one still living, had moved out to Phoenix and rarely came home to visit.

The floor was filmy linoleum. A clock above the sink had the numbers displayed with red dice, a souvenir from one of her early Vegas trips with Frank, maybe twenty years ago.

"Sit," Sadie said. "I'll make you some of that tea you like so much."

The tea was a store-brand chamomile with lemon and honey. He didn't drink tea. For Simon, tea was weak, a "coffee wannabe," and much as he wanted tea to be something more, tea always ended up being little more than brown water.

But a decade ago—maybe more, he couldn't remember

anymore—Sadie had made him tea with this particular flavor bought at this particular store, and she'd asked him if he liked it, and he said, "Very much," and now that tea was here, waiting for him, every time he visited.

"It's hot, so be careful."

A monthly calendar, the kind with generic photographs of mountains and rivers, hung on the ivory-to-yellow refrigerator. Banks used to hand out calendars like these for free. Maybe banks still did that. Sadie was getting them somewhere.

Simon stared at the calendar, that simple, old-world scheduler and to-do list.

He did that pretty much every time he came. Just stared at the thirty or thirty-one boxes (yes, twenty-eight or twenty-nine in February for the anal). Most—almost all—of those boxes had no writing in them. Just white. A blue ballpoint had scratched out the words "Dentist, 2PM" for the sixth of the month. Recycling day was circled every other Monday. And there, on the second Tuesday of every month, written with a purple marker in big, bold letters, was one word:

SIMON!

Yes, his name. With the exclamation point. And an exclamation point was really not Sadie Lowenstein.

That was it.

He had first seen that calendar entry—his name in purple with an exclamation point—on this same refrigerator eight years ago, when he was debating cutting down his visits because really, at this stage, with her investments and costs pretty much fixed, there was no reason to come out monthly. It could be handled by phone or by a junior colleague or at the most, they could wrap it up in quarterly visits.

But then Simon looked at the refrigerator and saw his name on the calendar.

He told Ingrid about the entry. He told Yvonne about it. Sadie had no family nearby anymore. Her friends had either moved or passed away. So this meant something to her, his visits, sitting at the old kitchen table where she once raised a family, Simon going over the portfolio as they both sipped tea.

And so it meant something to him too.

Simon had never missed an appointment with Sadie. Not once.

Ingrid would be angry if he'd canceled today. So here he was.

He was able to access her portfolio from his laptop. He went over a few of the holdings, but really that was all beside the point.

"Simon, do you remember our old store?"

Sadie and Frank had owned a small office-supply store in town, the kind of place that sold pens and paper and made photocopies and business cards.

"Sure," he said.

"Have you driven by it lately?"

"No. It's a clothing store now, right?"

"Used to be. All those tight teen clothes. I used to call it Sluts R Us, remember?"

"I remember."

"Which I know isn't nice. I mean, you should have seen me in my prime. I was a looker, Simon."

"You still are."

She waved a dismissive hand at him. "Stop with the patronizing. Back then though, boy I knew how to use my curves, if you know what I'm saying. My dad would throw a fit with what I wore." A wistful smile came to her lips. "Got Frank's attention, that I can tell you. The poor kid. Saw me at Rockaway Beach in a two-piece—he never had a chance."

She turned the smile toward him. He smiled back.

"Anyway," Sadie said, the smile and the memory vanishing, "that whore costume place closed down. Now it's a restaurant. Guess what kind of food?"

"What kind?"

She took a drag from her cigarette and made a face like a dog had left a dropping on her linoleum. "Asian fusion," she spat out.

"Oh."

"What the hell does that even mean? Is fusion a country now?"

"I'm not sure."

"Asian fusion. And it's called Meshugas."

"Yeah? I don't think that's the name."

"Something like that. Trying to appeal to us tribe members, right?" She shook her head. "Asian fusion. I mean, come on, Simon." She sighed and toyed with her cigarette. "So what's wrong?"

"Pardon?"

"With you. What's wrong?"

"Nothing."

"You think I'm *meshuga*?"

"Are you speaking fusion to me?"

"Very funny. I could tell the moment you walked in. What's wrong?"

"It's a long story."

She leaned back, looked left, looked right, looked back at him. "You think I got a lot going on right now?"

He almost told her. Sadie looked at him with wisdom and sympathy, and she clearly welcomed it, would probably even enjoy, if that was the word, listening with a learned ear and offering, at the very least, moral support.

But he didn't.

It wasn't about his own privacy. It was about the line. Simon was her financial advisor. He could exchange niceties about his family. But not something like this. His issues were his issues, not his client's.

"Something with one of your children," Sadie said.

"What makes you say that?"

"When you lose a child..." Sadie said. She stopped, shrugged.

"One of the side effects is this kind of sixth sense. Plus, I mean, what else would it be? Okay, so which kid?"

Easier to just say it: "My oldest."

"Paige. I won't pry."

"You're not prying."

"May I give you a little advice, Simon?"

"Sure."

"I mean, that's what you do, right? Give advice. You come here and you give me financial advice. Because you're an expert in money. My expertise is...anyway, I always knew Barry was gay. It was strange. Identical twins. Raised in the same house. Barry used to sit right where you are. That was his seat. Greg sat next to him. But from as young as I can remember, they were different. It gets everyone mad when I say that Barry from Day One was, I don't know, more flamboyant. That doesn't mean you're gay, people tell me. But I know my truth. My boys were identical—and different. If you knew them both, even as little children, and had to guess which was gay—go ahead, say I'm stereotyping—you'd know. Barry was into fashion and the-ater. Greg was into baseball and cars. I mean, I was practically raising clichés."

She tried to smile at that. Simon folded his hands and put them on the kitchen table. He had heard some of this before, but this wasn't a place Sadie went to very often.

And that was when it began to dawn on him.

The twins, genetics.

The story of Barry and Greg had fascinated him the first time he'd heard it because he'd wondered how identical twins, who had the exact same DNA and were raised in the same home, ended up with different sexual preferences.

"When Barry got sick," Sadie continued, "we didn't see what it was doing to Greg. We ignored him. We had to deal with all the immediate horror. Meanwhile Greg is seeing his identical twin wither away. There's no reason to go into the details. But

Greg never recovered from Barry's illness. He was scared, so he just...ran away. I didn't see that in time."

Greg was the only beneficiary of his mother's estate, so Simon still kept somewhat in touch with him. Greg was now thrice divorced and currently engaged to a twenty-eight-year-old dancer he'd met in Reno.

"I lost him. Because I didn't pay attention. But also..."

She stopped.

"Also what?"

"Because I couldn't save Barry. That was really it, Simon. For all the problems, all Greg's fears of maybe being gay too, all that, if I could have saved Barry, Greg would have been okay." She tilted her head. "Can you still save Paige?"

"I don't know."

"But there's a chance?"

"Yeah, there is."

Genetics. Paige had been studying genetics.

"Then go save her, Simon."

TWENTY-TWO

There were no signs for Truth Haven, which was hardly a surprise.

"Take a left," Dee Dee said, "by that old mailbox."

Old was an understatement. The mailbox looked as if passing teenagers had started whacking it daily with a baseball bat during the Carter administration.

Dee Dee looked at his face.

"What?"

"Something else I read," Ash said.

"What?"

"Are you forced to have sex with them?"

"With . . . ?"

"You know what I mean. Your truth or your visitor or whatever the leaders call themselves?"

She said nothing.

"I read that they force you."

Her voice was soft. "The Truth can't be forced."

"Sounds like a yes."

"Genesis 19:32," she said.

"What?"

"Do you remember the story of Lot in the Bible?"

"Seriously?"

"Do you remember the story or not?"

This sounded to him like a deflection, but he answered, "Vaguely."

"So in Genesis chapter 19, God allows Lot and his wife and their two daughters to escape the destruction of Sodom and Gomorrah."

He nodded. "But Lot's wife turns around when she's not supposed to."

"Right, and God turns her into a pillar of salt. Which is, well, seriously messed up. But that's not my point. It's Lot's daughters."

"What about them?"

"When they get to Zoar, Lot's daughters complain there are no men. So they come up with a plan. Do you remember what it is?"

"No."

"The older daughter tells her younger sister—I'm quoting Genesis 19:32—'Come on, let's get our father drunk, so that we can sleep with him and have children by him.'"

Ash said nothing.

"And they do. Yep, incest. Right there in Genesis. The two daughters get their father drunk, sleep with him, and become pregnant."

"I thought the Truth had nothing to do with the Old or New Testament."

"We don't."

"So why are you using Lot as an excuse?"

"I don't need an excuse, Ash. And I don't need your permission. I just need the Truth."

He kept staring out the front windshield.

"That still sounds like a 'yes, I have sex with them.'"

"Do you like sex, Ash?"

"Yes."

"So if you were in a group where you got to have sex with a lot of women, would it be an issue?"

He didn't reply.

The car tires kicked up dirt from the road as he headed into the woods. No Trespassing signs—a wide variety of them in various colors and sizes and even wording—hung from trees. As they approached the gate, Dee Dee rolled down her window and made a complicated hand gesture, like a third-base coach signaling a runner to steal second.

The car glided to a stop before the gate. Dee Dee opened her car door. When Ash did the same, she stopped him with a hand on his shoulder and a shake of her head.

"Stay here. Keep both hands on the steering wheel at all times. Don't take them off, even to scratch your nose."

Two men in gray uniforms that reminded Ash of a Civil War reenactment appeared from the small guardhouse. They were both armed with AR-15s. They both had huge beards and scowled at Ash. Ash tried to look nonthreatening. He had his own handguns within reach and was probably a better shot than either of these posers, but not even the best marksman is a match for two AR-15s.

That was the part people didn't get.

It isn't about talent or skill. You could be LeBron James, but if you're using a basketball with no air, you're not going to be able to dribble as well as someone whose ball got plenty.

Dee Dee approached the guards and did something with her right hand that looked a bit like someone crossing themselves, but the shape she made was more triangular. The two men returned the gesture/salute.

Ritual, Ash guessed. Like all religions.

Dee Dee spoke to the two men for a minute or two. The men never took their eyes off Ash, which took considerable self-discipline when you consider what Dee Dee looked like. Ash would have had to look.

Perhaps this was why the religious life had never called to him.

The Truth. What bullshit.

She came back to the car. "Just pull over there to the right."

"Why can't I just turn around and go?"

"What happened to you taking me away from all this?"

His heart leapt into his throat when she said that, but her just-kidding smile brought it back down again. He tried to keep the disappointment off his face.

"You're back," he said. "You're safe. There's no need for me to hang around."

"Just wait, okay? I need to check with the council."

"Check what?"

"Please, Ash. Just wait."

One guard handed her folded clothes. Gray. Like theirs. She slipped them over the clothing she was wearing. The other guard handed her headgear that looked like something you'd find in a convent. Also gray. She put it on top of her head and tied it like a bonnet under her chin.

Dee Dee always strode with her head high, her shoulders back, the definition of confidence. Now she was bent over, eyes lowered, her whole persona subservient. The transformation startled him. And pissed him off.

Dee Dee has left the building, Ash said to himself. *Holly is here now.*

He watched her walk through the gate. He tilted his torso to the right, so his eyes could follow her up a path. There were other women milling about, all dressed in the same drab-gray uniform. No men. Maybe they were in a different area.

The two guards saw that he was watching Dee Dee and the compound. They didn't like it. So they stood in front of his car to block his view. He debated shifting the car into drive, hitting the gas, and mowing the fuckers down. Instead he chose to turn the car off and get out. The guards didn't like that, but then again they didn't like much that he did.

The first thing that hit Ash as he got out of the car was the silence. It was pure, heavy, almost suffocating but in a good way.

There were normally sounds everywhere, even in the deepest part of the woods, but there was only quiet here. Ash didn't move for a moment, didn't even want to risk shattering the silence by shutting his car door. He stood and closed his eyes and let the quiet consume him. For a second or two, he got it. Or thought he got it. The appeal. He could surrender to this, this quiet, this tranquility. It would be so easy to turn over control and reason and thoughts. Just be.

Surrender.

Yes, that was that applicable word. Let someone else do the heavy mental work. Just toil or live in the moment. Get sucked into the stillness. Hear your heart beating in your chest.

But this wasn't a life.

It was a vacation, a break, a cocoon. It was the Matrix or virtual reality or something like that. And maybe when you grow up like he did—or more, like Dee Dee did—a comforting delusion beats harsh reality.

But not in the long run.

He took out a cigarette.

"Smoking is forbidden," one of the guards said.

Ash lit up.

"I said—"

"Shh. Don't spoil the quiet."

Guard One took a step toward Ash, but Guard Two put a hand out to block him. Ash leaned against the car, took a deep inhale, made a production out of blowing the smoke out. Guard One was not pleased. Ash heard the crackle of a walkie-talkie. Guard Two leaned in and whispered into it.

Ash made a face. Who uses walkie-talkies anymore? Don't they have mobile phones?

A few seconds later, Guard Two whispered something in the ear of Guard One. Guard One grinned.

"Hey, tough guy," Guard One said.

Ash let loose another long trail of smoke.

"You're wanted up in the sanctuary."

Ash started toward them.

"No smoking inside Truth Haven."

Ash was going to argue, but what was the point? He threw the cigarette onto the road and crushed it under his foot. Guard Two had opened the gate with a remote control. Ash took in the setup now—the fencing, the security cameras, the remote. Pretty high tech.

He started toward the opening, but Guard One stopped him with his AR-15.

"You armed, tough guy?"

"Yes."

"Maybe hand the weapon over to me then."

"Aw, can't I keep my gun?"

Both guards pointed their weapons at him.

"Holster on my right side," Ash said.

Guard One reached for it, felt nothing.

Ash sighed. "That's your right, not mine."

Guard One slid his hand to the other side of Ash's body and removed the .38.

"Nice piece," the guard said.

"Put it in my glove compartment," Ash said.

"Excuse me?"

"I won't bring it in, but I'm leaving here with it. Put it in my car. The door is open."

Guard One didn't like it, but Guard Two nodded that he should listen. So he did. When the task was completed, Guard One made a big deal of slamming the door really hard.

"Any other weapons?" Guard One asked.

"No."

Guard Two gave him a cursory search anyway. When he was done, Guard One gestured with his head for him to proceed through the gate. They flanked Ash as they entered the compound—Guard One on his right, Guard Two on his left.

Ash wasn't overly concerned. He figured that Dee Dee had spoken to the Truth or the Volunteer or whoever and that they wanted to see him. Dee Dee hadn't made it clear, but it seemed pretty obvious that someone in the cult was paying for these hits. Dee Dee wasn't coming up with the cash or the names on her own.

Someone in this cult wanted these guys dead.

They started up the hill. Ash wasn't sure what he expected to find inside Truth Haven, but the overriding word to describe the compound was..."generic." In a clearing, Ash could make out a building painted the same drab gray as the uniform, maybe three stories high. The architecture was rectangular and functional and had all the personality of a roadside chain motel. Or maybe military barracks. Or maybe, and perhaps most accurately, it looked like a prison.

There were no breaks from the drab gray—no splashes of color, no texture, no warmth.

But maybe that was the point. There were no distractions.

There was nature, pushed to the side, and of course there was beauty in that. There was calm and quiet and solitude. If you are troubled, if you feel out of place amongst normal society, if you are desperately trying to escape modernity and its noises and constant stimulation, what locale could be better? That was how cults worked, wasn't it? Find the disillusioned outcasts. Offer them easy answers. Isolate. Induce dependency. Control. Allow only one voice, one that cannot be questioned or doubted.

Succumb.

Several three-story drab-gray structures formed a courtyard. They led him across it. All windows and doors faced the courtyard, so you couldn't even view the trees from your room. The courtyard had green grass and wooden benches, again painted in drab gray, and the benches, like the windows, all faced a large statue sitting high atop a pedestal with the word TRUTH written on all sides. The statue was maybe fifteen feet high. It was of a beatific Casper Vartage, his hands raised, half exaltation, half embrace of his flock. That was what you saw from every window—"The Truth" staring you in the face.

There were more women in the courtyard, all uniformed, all wearing headgear of some kind. None spoke. None made a sound. None so much as glanced at this stranger in their midst.

Ash was getting a bad feeling about this.

Guard One unlocked a door and signaled for Ash to enter. The room had polished hardwood floors. On the wall were portraits of three men. The portraits formed a triangle. The Truth aka Casper Vartage was at the top. His two sons—you could see the resemblance—were below him on either side. The Volunteer and the Visitor, Ash assumed. Some folding chairs were stacked in the corner. That was it in terms of decor. If one of the walls was mirrored, you might mistake this for an exercise studio.

Guards One and Two came and stood by the door.

Ash didn't like this.

"What's going on?"

They didn't speak. Guard Two left. He was alone now with a heavily armed Guard One. Guard One grinned at him.

The bad feeling grew.

Ash started mentally prepping. Suppose, as he had already, that the cult had been the ones who hired him. Perhaps the people he killed were all former members of the cult, though on the surface that didn't seem to add up. Gorse, for example, was a gay tattoo-parlor owner who lived in New Jersey. Gano was married with kids outside Boston. But still, it could be that. Maybe they were Truthers in their youth, and for some reason they needed now to be silenced.

Or maybe there was another motive. It didn't matter.

What did matter was that Ash had done the job. The money had come through. Ash knew how to get funds and transfer them around so they wouldn't be found. He'd been paid in full—half on taking each job, half on completion.

But now the cult was done with him. Perhaps. That was one of the things Dee Dee didn't know yet—why she wanted him to wait. Whoever was hiring him was communicating through her. So perhaps she had come to the Truth Council when he dropped her off. Perhaps the Truth or one of his advisors had said, "No, we are done."

And suppose they wanted to completely tie up any loose ends.

Ash was professional. He would never talk. That was part of what you got for your money.

But maybe the cult leaders didn't know that about him.

Maybe they figured that under normal circumstances, they'd be more trusting, but because Ash and Dee Dee knew each other—had a special connection even—the Vartages felt more exposed.

The simplest solution to the problem? The smart play for Vartage and his sons?

Kill Ash. Bury him in the woods. Get rid of his car.

If Ash was the cult leader, that was what he would do.

A door on the other side of the room opened. Guard One lowered his gaze as a woman Ash guessed was in her early fifties entered the room. She was tall and imposing and unlike everyone else he'd seen in the compound, she held her head high, chest out, shoulders back. She wore the gray uniform, but there were red stripes on her sleeves, like something in the military. Against all the drab gray, the stripes stood out like neon lights in the dark.

"Why are you here?" she asked him.

"Just dropping off a friend."

She glanced over his shoulder at the guard. As if he felt her gaze, he looked up, semi-wincing. This woman wasn't the Truth or part of their trinity, but whoever she was, she clearly outranked this guy.

Guard One stood at attention. "As I informed you, Mother Adiona."

"Adiona?"

She turned to Ash. "You recognize the reference?"

He nodded. "Adiona was a Roman goddess."

"That's correct."

He'd loved mythology as a kid. He tried to remember the details. "Adiona was the goddess of returning children home safely or something. She was paired with another goddess."

"Abeona," she said. "I'm surprised you know this."

"Yeah, I'm full of surprises. So you're named after a myth?"

"Exactly." She smiled widely. "Do you know why?"

"I bet you'll tell me."

"All gods are myths. Norse, Roman, Greek, Indian, Judeo-Christian, pagan, whatever. For centuries people bowed to them, sacrificed for them, spent their lives following them. And it was all lies. How sad, don't you think? How pathetic. To spend your life deluded like that."

"Maybe," Ash said.

"Maybe?"

"If you don't know any better, maybe it's okay."

"You don't really believe that, do you?"

He said nothing.

"Gods are lies. Only the Truth prevails. Do you know why all religions eventually crash and burn? Because they aren't the Truth. Unlike these myths, the Truth has always been there."

Ash tried not to roll his eyes.

"What's your name?" she asked him.

"Ash."

"Ash what?"

"Just Ash."

"How do you know Holly?"

He said nothing.

"You may know her as Dee Dee."

He still said nothing.

"You pulled up with her, Ash. You dropped her off."

"Okay."

"Where were you two?"

"Why don't you ask her?"

"I already have. I need to see if she is telling the truth."

Ash stood there. Mother Adiona moved closer to him. She gave him a mischievous smile and said, "Do you know what your Dee Dee is doing right now?"

"No."

"She's naked. On all fours. One man behind her. One man in front of her."

She smiled some more. She wanted him to react. He wouldn't.

"Well? What do you think of that, Ash?"

"I'm wondering about the third man."

"Pardon?"

"You know. Truth, Volunteer, Visitor. So if one is having her from behind and the other one is in the front, where is the third?"

She still smiled. "You've been played for a fool, Ash."

"Wouldn't be the first time."

"She offers her favors to many men. But not you, Ash."

He made a face. "Did you really just call them 'favors'?"

"This is wounding you deeply, I know. You love her."

"Very insightful. Can I go back to my car now?"

"Where were you two?"

"I'm not going to tell you."

Her nod was barely discernible. But it was enough. Guard One stepped forward. There was a baton in his hand. Two things happened simultaneously. One, Ash recognized that the baton was a cattle prod or stun baton of some kind. Two, the prod touched down on his back.

Then all thought closed down in a tsunami of pain.

Ash collapsed to that hardwood floor, writhing like a fish on a dock. The electricity shooting through him hit everything. It paralyzed the circuitry from his brain. It singed his nerve endings. It made his muscles spasm.

He started foaming at the mouth.

He couldn't move. He couldn't even really think.

There was panic in the woman's voice. "I...What setting did you have that on?"

"Highest."

"Are you serious? That will kill him."

"Then we might as well get it over with."

Ash saw the end of the baton heading for him again. He wanted to move, needed to move, but the electricity coursing through him had short-circuited any commands involving muscle control.

When the baton touched down again, this time on his chest, Ash felt his heart explode.

Then there was only darkness.

TWENTY-THREE

N o change.

Simon was so tired of hearing that. His chair was pulled up right next to Ingrid's bed. He held her hand. He stared at her face, watching her breathe. Ingrid always slept on her back, just like this, so that coma looked amazingly like sleep, which may seem obvious or perhaps not. You expect a coma to look different, don't you? Sure there were tubes and noises and Ingrid liked wearing spaghetti-strap silk negligees to bed, which of course he loved too. He loved the coil of her body, the broad shoulders, the prominent collarbone.

No change.

This was purgatory, neither heaven nor hell. There were some who argued that purgatory was the worst—the suspended, the unknown, the wear and tear of the endless wait. Simon understood that sentiment, but for now he was okay with purgatory. If Ingrid's condition darkened in even the slightest way, he'd lose it completely. He was self-aware enough to realize that he was hanging on by a fraying thread now. If he got bad news, if something more went wrong with Ingrid...

No change.

So block.

Right, pretend she was asleep. He kept staring at her face, the cheekbones so sharp the surgeons down the hall could use them as scalpels, the lips he'd gently kissed before he sat down, hoping to get some kind of reaction out of them because even when Ingrid was deep in sleep, her lips would react instinctively, in some small way at the very least, to his kiss.

But not now.

He flashed back to the last time he'd watched her as she slept—on their honeymoon in Antigua, days after they'd officially tied the knot. Simon had woken up before sunrise, Ingrid sprawled next to him on her back, like right now, like always. Her eyes were closed, of course, her breathing even, and so Simon just stared, marveling at the fact that this was how he'd wake up every day from now—next to this wondrous woman who was now his life partner.

He had watched her like this for only ten, maybe fifteen seconds, when without opening her eyes or moving at all, Ingrid said, "Cut that out, it's creepy."

He smiled at the memory, sitting now at her bedside with her still yet warm hand in his. Yes, warm. Alive. Blood flowing through. Ingrid didn't feel shrunken or sick or dying. She was just asleep and soon she'd wake up.

And the first thing she'd do is ask about Paige.

He had some questions about that too.

Simon had called Elena after leaving Sadie Lowenstein's and filled her in on Paige's interest in genetics and ancestry. Elena usually played it close to the vest, but this meant something to her. She'd peppered him with follow-up questions, only some of which he could answer.

When Elena ran out of questions, she asked for Eileen Vaughan's phone number. Simon gave it to her.

"What's going on?" he asked.

"Maybe nothing. But not long before he was killed, Damien Gorse also visited one of those DNA sites."

"So what does that mean?"

"Let me run down a few things before we get into that. Are you going to the hospital?"

"Yes."

Elena promised to meet him there and then she hung up.

The children seemed okay. Anya was home with Suzy Fiske, and Simon thought that was probably best for now. Sam had befriended some medical residents who were working the floor—Sam was good at that, always able to make friends quickly—and he was in their lounge right now, trying to study for his upcoming physics exam. He'd always been not only a smart kid but an industrious one. Simon, who'd been a do-enough-to-get-by student, was constantly amazed by his son's work ethic—up early in the morning, exercising before breakfast, getting his homework done days ahead of time—and unlike most fathers, Simon sometimes worried that he should encourage his son to ease off the gas pedal a bit and smell the roses. Sam was almost too driven.

Not now, of course. Now it would hopefully be a nice distraction.

No change.

So block—though right now, he was blocking on more than Ingrid's condition.

Simon didn't consider himself to be an overly imaginative guy, but whatever imagination he had, it had shifted into overdrive after hearing about the DNA test, careening him down this dark, ugly road, one with barbed wire and land mines, one he'd never wanted to travel, but there seemed to be no other choice at the moment.

Eileen Vaughan's words kept echoing: *"Problems at home."*

Yvonne slipped into the room. "Hey," she said.

"Is there any chance Paige isn't my child?"

Boom. Just like that.

"What?"

"You heard me."

223

Simon turned toward her. Yvonne was pale, shaking.

"Is there any chance I'm not Paige's biological father?"

"My God, no."

"I just need to know the truth."

"What the hell, Simon?"

"Could she have slept with someone else?"

"Ingrid?"

"Who else would I be talking about?"

"I don't know. This is all such crazy talk."

"So there's zero chance."

"Zero."

He turned back toward his wife.

"Simon, what's going on?"

"You can't say for sure," he said.

"Simon."

"No one can say for sure."

"No, of course no one can say for sure." A hint of impatience had crept into Yvonne's voice. "I can't say for sure you haven't fathered any other children either."

"You know how much I love her."

"I do, yes. And she loves you just as much."

"But I don't know the whole story, do I?"

"I don't know what you mean."

"Yeah, you do. There's a part of her that's hidden. Even from me."

"There's part of everybody that's hidden."

"That's not what I mean."

"Then I don't get what you do mean."

"Yeah, Yvonne, you do."

"Where is this coming from?"

"It's coming from my search for Paige."

"And now you think, what, that you're not her father?"

Simon swung his body now, faced her full. "I know everything about you, Yvonne."

"You really think so?"

"Yes."

Yvonne said nothing. Simon looked back at Ingrid in the bed.

"I love her. I love her with all my heart. But there are parts of her I don't know."

She still said nothing.

"Yvonne?"

"What do you want me to say? Ingrid has an air of mystery, I'll grant you that. Guys went gaga over it. And hey, let's be honest. It's one of the things that drew you to her."

He nodded. "At first."

"You love her deeply."

"I do."

"And yet you're wondering if she betrayed you in the worst way possible."

"Did she?"

"No."

"But there's something."

"It has nothing to do with Paige—"

"What does it have to do with?"

"—or her getting shot."

"But there are secrets?"

"There's a past, sure." Yvonne raised her hands, more in frustration now than confusion. "Everyone has one."

"I don't. You don't."

"Stop it."

"What kind of past does she have?"

"A past, Simon." Her tone was impatient. "Just that. She had a life way before you—school, travel, relationships, jobs."

"But that's not what you mean. You mean something out of the ordinary."

She frowned, shook her head. "It isn't my place to say."

"Too late for that, Yvonne."

"No, it's not. You have to trust me."

"I do trust you."

"Good. We're talking about ancient history."

Simon shook his head. "Whatever's happening here—whatever changed Paige and led to all this destruction—I think it started a long time ago."

"How can that be?"

"I don't know."

Yvonne moved closer to the bed. "Let me ask you this, Simon."

"Go ahead."

"Best-case scenario: Ingrid comes out of this okay. You find Paige. Paige is okay. She gets clean. I mean, totally clean. Puts this whole ugly chapter behind her."

"Okay."

"Then Paige decides to move away. Get a fresh start. She meets a guy. A wonderful guy. A guy who puts her up on a pedestal, who loves her beyond anything she can imagine. They build a great life together, this guy and Paige, and Paige never wants this wonderful guy to know that at one time, she was a junkie and maybe worse, living in some crack den, doing God knows what with God knows who to get a fix."

"Are you serious?"

"Yes, I'm serious. Paige loves this guy. She doesn't want to see the light in his eyes dim. Can't you understand that?"

Simon's voice, when he finally found it, was barely a whisper. "My God, what is she hiding?"

"It doesn't matter—"

"Like hell it doesn't."

"—just like Paige's drug past wouldn't matter."

"Yvonne?"

"What?"

"Do you really think this secret would change how I feel about Ingrid?"

She didn't reply.

"Because if that's the case, then our love is pretty weak."

"It's not."

226

"But?"

"But it would change the way you see her."

"The dim in the eyes?"

"Yes."

"You're wrong. I'd still love her just as much."

Yvonne nodded slowly. "I believe you would."

"So?"

"So her distant past has nothing to do with this." Yvonne held up her hand to stop his protest. "And no matter what you say, I promised. It's not my secret to tell. You have to let it go."

Simon wasn't going to do that—he needed to know—but just then he felt Ingrid's hand tighten over his like a vise. His heart leapt. He spun his head back toward his wife, hoping maybe to see her eyes open or a smile break out on her face. But her entire body convulsed, went rigid, began to spasm. Her eyes didn't open—they fluttered uncontrollably so that he could only see their whites.

Machines began to beep. An alarm sounded.

Someone rushed into the room. Then someone else. A third person pushed him aside. More people flooded the room, surrounding Ingrid's bed. The movement was constant. They were calling out urgent instructions, using unintelligible medical jargon in borderline-panic tones, as someone else, the sixth person to enter the room, gently but firmly pushed him and Yvonne out.

———

They rushed Ingrid into surgery.

No one would tell Simon anything of relevance. There was a "setback," one of the nurses told him, followed closely by the old chestnut: "The doctor will be with you as soon as she can."

He wanted to ask more, but he also didn't want to distract anyone. *Just work on Ingrid,* he thought. *Get her better. Then fill me in.*

He paced a crowded waiting room. He started biting the nail on his pointer finger, something he'd done a lot when he was young, though he'd quit for good his senior year of college. Or so he thought. He paced from one corner to the other, pausing in each corner, leaning his back for a second or two against them because what he most wanted to do was collapse to the floor there and just curl up.

He looked for Yvonne, hoping to shake the damn answer out of her about his wife's past, but she was nowhere to be found all of a sudden. Why? Did she want to avoid him, or was she just needed—especially with her partner out of commission—at work? Yvonne had said something about that, about taking care of the office, about pacing themselves for the "long haul," about not needing both of them here at the same time.

Simon was somewhere between annoyed and angry with Yvonne, but he also recognized that her argument for keeping her promise to Ingrid had merit and even nobility. Simon had known Ingrid for twenty-four years—three years before Paige was born. How could anything from before Paige was born or even before Simon and Ingrid met, no matter how bizarre or sordid or just plain awful, factor into this?

It made zero sense.

"Simon?"

Elena Ramirez was suddenly next to him. She asked whether there was any update on Ingrid's condition. Simon told her that Ingrid was in surgery and said, "So fill me in on what's going on."

They moved to one of those corners he'd been leaning against, the one farthest away from the entrance and general population.

"I haven't put it all together yet," Elena said in a low voice.

"But?"

Elena hesitated.

"You found something, right?"

"Yes. But I still don't know how it connects to you. Or your daughter."

"I'm listening."

"Let's start with Paige and this family tree club."

"Okay."

"We know that Damien Gorse visited an ancestry DNA site called DNAYourStory dot com." She looked around as though she feared someone would overhear her. "So I asked my client to check his son Henry's charge cards too."

"And?"

"There was a charge to DNAYourStory. In fact, Henry Thorpe signed up for several DNA ancestry sites."

"Wow."

"Right."

"So I guess I need to check Paige's credit cards," he said. "See if she signed up too."

"Yes."

"How about Aaron? Was he on the site?"

"There is no way to know, unless we find it on a charge card. Do you think you could ask the mother?"

"I could ask, sure, but I doubt she'll help."

"Worth a shot," Elena said. "But for the sake of argument, let's assume that they all sent in their samples to the same DNA site and got tested. Do you know how these tests work at all?"

"Not really."

"You spit into a test tube and they analyze your DNA. Different sites do different things. Some claim they can look at your DNA and give you a genetic health workup—do you possess certain variants that make you more likely to get Alzheimer's or Parkinson's?...Stuff like that."

"Is that accurate?"

"The science seems questionable, but that's not really important right now. At least, I don't think it is. The basic package is probably what you'd know about if you've read anything about these DNA sites. It gives you an ancestry composition—like you're, say, fifteen percent Italian and twenty-two percent Spanish, that kind of thing. It can map your ancestral migration too, like where your people first started and where they settled over time. It's pretty wild."

"Yeah, that might be interesting, but how does that play into this?"

"I doubt it does."

"These tests," Simon said. "They also tell you about your parents, right?"

"And other relatives, yes. I assume that's why both Henry Thorpe and Damien Gorse took the test."

"Because they were adopted," Simon said.

"And didn't know anything about their birth parents. That's the key. It's very common for adoptees to sign up for these services, so they can find their parents or learn about siblings or really, any blood relative."

Simon rubbed his face. "And Aaron Corval might have done something like that too. To learn about his mother."

"Yes. Or maybe to prove his father wasn't his father."

"You mean like maybe Aaron was adopted too?"

"It could be, I don't know yet. One of the problems is that these DNA sites are highly controversial. I mean, millions of people have done them, maybe tens of millions. More than twelve million last year alone."

Simon nodded. "I know a lot of people who sent in their samples."

"Me too. Yet everyone is naturally squeamish about sending their DNA in to an internet company. So these ancestry sites are absolutists about security and privacy. Which I get. I tried every contact I know. DNAYourStory won't tell me a thing without a warrant—and they've promised to fight any warrant to the Supreme Court."

"But the connections you found—"

"—are right now tenuous at best. Two otherwise unconnected murders—different means, different states, different weapons—

we can only link marginally to someone in Chicago via a few internet messages. It's less than nothing in a court of law."

Simon tried to absorb what she was saying. "So you think Aaron and your client and this Gorse guy—all three of these guys—could all be related?"

"I don't know. But maybe."

"Two of them have been murdered," Simon said. "And the third—your client—is missing."

"Yes."

"Which leads to the obvious question."

Elena nodded. "Paige."

"Right. How would my daughter fit into your hypothesis?"

"I've been thinking about this a lot," Elena said.

"And?"

"There have been cases where law enforcement has used these DNA tests to solve crimes. So maybe, don't ask me how, Paige stumbled across a crime."

"What kind of crime?"

Elena shrugged. "I don't know."

"And why would she track down Aaron Corval?"

"We don't know that she did. We only know Paige drove to see him in Connecticut."

Simon nodded. "So maybe Aaron Corval reached out to her first."

"Maybe. The thing is, it's hard to figure out the connections. My tech guy, Lou, is working on it. He figures Henry was using an encrypted messaging app like WhatsApp or Viber, so he can't see it all. But now Lou's thinking that maybe Henry was messaging through the ancestry site—they have their own messaging capabilities—and it just looked like a messaging app."

Simon gave her a blank look.

"Yeah, I don't get it either," Elena said, waving it away. "The important thing is, Lou is still searching for names. I also have my office looking into Aaron Corval's background—his birth certificate, anything—so we can get a handle on that. Which brings me to the big thing."

Elena stopped and let loose a deep breath.

"What?" he said.

"I found another connection."

There was something odd in her voice. "Between all of them?"

"No. Between Henry Thorpe and Damien Gorse."

"What's that?"

"They were both adopted."

"That we know."

"They were both adopted from the same agency."

Boom.

"The agency is called Hope Faith."

"Where's it located?"

"Maine. A small town called Windham."

"I don't get it. Your client lives in Chicago. Damien Gorse lived in New Jersey. Yet they were both adopted out of Maine?"

"Yes."

Simon shook his head in amazement. "So what do we do next?"

"You stay here with your wife," she said. "I'm flying up to Maine."

TWENTY-FOUR

T he last time Elena had landed at the Portland International Jetport in Maine, she'd been traveling with Joel. Joel's niece/goddaughter was having a weekend "theme wedding" at a rustic kids' sleepaway camp with a native American name—Camp Manu-something, Elena couldn't remember now—and Elena had not been looking forward to it.

For one thing, Joel's ex-wife Marlene, a gorgeous, lithe beauty, would be there, so Elena would have to deal with the odd looks from a family who could never understand what six-two, handsome, and charismatic Joel saw in the maybe-five-foot, squat-built, and seemingly charmless Elena.

Elena didn't quite get it either.

"It'll be fun," Joel had assured her.

"It'll suck."

"We have our own private cabin by the water."

"We do?"

"Okay, it's not private," he admitted. "Or by the water. And we are in bunk beds."

"Wow, sounds great."

Even under the best of circumstances, the trip sounded like

a nightmare. Elena didn't like camping or nature or insects or archery or kayaking or any of the activities listed on "Jack and Nancy's Wedding Itinerary." It was early June. Summer camps in Maine rent themselves out for retreats and events to make a little extra cash before school is out and the children descend upon them for the summer.

But to her surprise, the weekend had been fun, after all. Elena's side had won something called Color Wars, and her law enforcement background came in handy for her team during the day-long Capture the Flag battle. At night—and this was the memory that still haunted her, would always haunt her—Joel would procure a bottle of wine and two glasses from whatever festivities were on the agenda. He would wrap the glasses and bottle in one extra-large sleeping bag. When lights went out—again, like a real camp, someone actually blew taps on a trumpet—Joel would slip down from the top bunk, take Elena by the hand to the soccer field, and make love to her under a crisp-blue, star-filled Maine sky.

Why was sex so good with Joel?

Why was he able to reach a place deep within her body and soul no other man had ever come close to finding? She had tried to analyze it a thousand times, and realized that sex, great sex, is about trust and vulnerability. She trusted Joel completely. She let herself open up and be completely vulnerable with him. There was never any judgment, any hesitation, any doubt. She wanted to please him, and he wanted to please her, and she wanted to be selfish and he wanted to be selfish. There was never any agenda other than that.

You don't get that often in life. Maybe once or twice. Most likely, never.

Elena knew, despite what well-meaning friends told her, she would never get it again. There was no reason to try. She didn't date—not that she got a lot of offers anyway—and she had no interest in another relationship. She wasn't being a martyr or self-pitying or any of that. She just knew that when Joel died, that part of her died too. There was no one else out there who could give her that trust and vulnerability. That was a fact, a sad one perhaps, but as she kept hearing in this pathetic political climate, facts don't care about your feelings. She'd had that wonderful connection, it had been awesome, now it was gone.

Her room at the nearby Howard Johnson's had a view of not one but two gas stations plus a 7-Eleven. She had chosen HoJo's over the relatively swankier—she should maybe put that word in air quotes—Embassy Suites and Comfort Inn, based purely on nostalgia. When she was a little girl in Texas, the big family night out was dinner and ice cream at a Howard Johnson's Motor Lodge, one with that distinct orange roof and cupola topped with a weather vane. Elena and her father always ordered the fried clam strips, always, and right now, with her mind wandering more than usual, a bite of nostalgia sounded and would taste awfully good.

When she asked at the front desk about the restaurant, the receptionist looked at her as though she was speaking Swahili. "We don't have a restaurant."

"You're a Howard Johnson's without a restaurant?"

"That's right. The Portland Pie Company isn't far. And Dock's Seafood is about a mile and a half down the road."

Elena stepped back and, right there in the generic lobby, did some quick Googling. How had she missed that Howard Johnson's restaurants had been slowly going out of business for years? By 2005, there were only eight left and now there was only one, in Lake George, New York. She actually checked out how long the ride to Lake George would be—nearly five hours.

Too far. And the reviews were less than stellar.

She headed instead to one of those brewery-style bars, watched the game, drank too much. She thought about the two most important men in her life, her father and Joel, and how both had been taken from her far too soon. A ride share drove her back to the Howard Johnson's—the lack of an orange roof or even a weather vane should have tipped her off that times had changed—and she fell asleep.

In the morning, she put on a blue blazer and jeans and checked the app ride to Hope Faith in Windham. Half hour, no traffic. Elena's home office had already arranged to get her powers of attorney to speak on behalf of the families of both Henry Thorpe as well as recent murder victim Damien Gorse.

This was all a tremendous long shot.

The Hope Faith Adoption Agency was located in a small office complex behind an Applebee's on Roosevelt Trail. The owner, a man covered in untamed gray hair and named Maish Isaacson, greeted her with a nervous smile and a dead-fish handshake. He wore stylish tortoise-frame glasses and an unruly beard.

"I don't see how I can help," Isaacson said for the third time.

Beads of perspiration dotted his forehead. She handed him the powers of attorney as they sat down. Isaacson read them carefully and then asked, "How long ago were these adoptions?"

"Henry Thorpe would have been twenty-four years ago. Damien Gorse closer to thirty."

"So again I say: I don't see how I can help."

"I'd like to see anything you have on the adoptions."

"From all these years ago?"

"Yes."

Isaacson folded his hands. "Ms. Ramirez, you're aware, are you not, that these were closed adoptions?"

"I am."

"So even if I had this information, you know that legally I cannot unseal an adoption record."

He licked a manicured finger, plucked out a sheet of paper from the credenza, and slid it across the desk so Elena could follow along. "While the laws are somewhat looser now than they've ever been—adoptees' rights and all that—you still have to follow a certain protocol."

Elena looked down at the paper.

"So step one is to go to the county clerk—I can give you directions—and fill out a petition with the county court. Once that is done, they'll set up a date to meet with a judge—"

"I don't have time for that."

"My hands are tied here, Ms. Ramirez."

"The families filed here. In this office. They used your services and they want me to see all paperwork."

He scratched at his head, his eyes lowered. "In all due deference, the families don't really have a say here. Both adoptees are of age, so it would be up to them to petition the court or this office. Mr. Gorse is recently deceased, as I understand it. Is that correct?"

"He was murdered, yes."

"Oh God, that's awful."

"That's why I'm here, by the way."

"I'm sorry about this tragedy, but legally speaking, it probably means some other kind of legal form would need to be filled out. I don't know of a case where an adoptee died—"

"Was murdered."

"—and then one of his parents...his mother from the looks of this document...wanted information on the birth parents. I'm not sure she has any standing. As for Henry Thorpe, he's alive, correct?"

"He's missing under suspicious circumstances."

"Still," Isaacson said, "I don't see how anyone—parent, guardian, whomever—can petition on his behalf."

"They were both adopted here, Mr. Isaacson."

"I'm aware of that."

"The two men—both children adopted via your agency—have recently been in touch with one another. Are you aware of that?"

Isaacson said nothing.

"Now one is dead, and one is missing under mysterious circumstances."

"I'm going to have to ask you to leave."

"You can ask," Elena said.

She folded her arms. She didn't move. She just stared at him.

"My hands are tied here," he tried. "I'd like to help."

"Did you do these adoptions yourself?"

"We've done many adoptions over the years."

"Do you know the name Aaron Corval? Perhaps you remember his father, Wiley. The family owns a tree farm and inn in Connecticut."

He said nothing. But he knew.

"Was Mr. Corval a client?" she asked.

"I wouldn't know."

"He's dead too. Aaron Corval, I mean."

His face lost whatever color was left.

"Was he adopted here?"

"I wouldn't know," he said again.

"Check the files."

"I'm going to have to ask you to leave."

"Yeah, I'm not going to do that. You worked here back then—when these adoptions took place."

"I started this place."

"Yes, I know. It's a lovely backstory, yours, all about how you wanted to save children and unite them with loving families because of your own paternity issues. I know all about it. I know all about you. You seem like a decent guy, a guy who has tried his best, but if there is anything amiss in any of your adoption paperwork—"

"There's not."

"But if there is, I'm going to find it. I'm going to dig into everything you've ever done and if I find one mistake, honest or not, I'm going to use it as leverage. Look at me, Mr. Isaacson."

He raised his eyes and tried to hold hers.

"You know something."

"I don't."

"Yeah, you do."

"Every adoption here is above board. If one of my employees committed a fraud on us..."

Now they were getting somewhere. Elena leaned forward. "If that's the case, Mr. Isaacson, I'm your best friend. I'm here to help. Let me see the files. Your files. Not the legal ones. Let me track down the fraud and put it right."

He said nothing.

"Mr. Isaacson?"

"I can't show you the files."

"Why not?"

"They're gone."

She waited.

"Five years ago, there was a fire. All of our records were lost. That wasn't really an issue. Everything of relevance is kept with the county clerk's office. Like I said. But even if I wanted to show you the files—which I can't do legally anyway—they only exist at the county clerk's office. That's where you have to go."

She stared at him.

"You're not telling me something, Mr. Isaacson."

"Nothing illegal was done."

"Okay."

"And I think whatever was, well, it was best for the children. That's always been my concern. The children."

"I'm sure that's true. But now those children are being targeted and even killed."

"I can't see how it involves us."

"Maybe it doesn't," she said, not reminding him that the only link so far was the Hope Faith Adoption Agency. "Maybe I'll be able to clear you. Do you remember these cases at all?"

"In a way, yes. In a way, no."

"What do you mean?"

"These cases required a little extra privacy."

"In what way?"

"They were unwed mothers."

"Aren't a lot of your mothers unwed? I mean, even back then."

"Yes," he said, a little too slowly. He stroked his beard. "But these girls came from a fairly orthodox branch of Christianity."

"What brand?"

"I never knew. But I also think... they didn't like men."

"What does that mean?"

"I don't know. I really don't. But I wasn't allowed to know the mothers' names."

"You're the owner here."

"Yes."

"So you had to sign off."

"I did. That was the only time I saw the mothers' names. But I don't remember any."

He did. Of course he did.

"What about the fathers' names?"

"They were always listed as unknown."

He was stroking his beard so hard, hairs were coming off in his hand.

"You mentioned an employee before," she said.

"What?"

"You said, 'If one of my employees committed a fraud on us.'" Elena tried hard to meet his eye, but he was having none of it. "Did someone work on these cases?"

He moved his head. It may have been a nod, she wasn't sure, but she treated it as though it was.

"Who?"

"Her name," he said, "is Alison Mayflower."

"She was a case worker?"

"Yes." Then thinking more about it, he added, "Sort of."

"And this Alison Mayflower, she was the one who brought in these cases?"

His voice was low, far off. "Alison came to me in the strictest confidence. She said there were children in need. I offered my help, and it was accepted under conditions."

"What kind of conditions?"

"For one thing, I had to be kept in the dark. I couldn't ask any questions."

Elena took her time, thought it over. When she was with the FBI, her team had busted several seemingly above-board churches and agencies for illegal adoptions. In some cases, white babies were in such demand that macroeconomic reality in a capitalist society took over—supply and demand—and so they commanded a higher price. In other cases, one of the potential adoptive parents had something in their history that made legally adopting difficult. So again, money changed hands.

Big money sometimes.

Elena had to be careful here. She wasn't here to bust Isaacson for selling babies or whatever he'd maybe done twenty or thirty years ago. She wanted information.

As if reading her mind, he said, "I really don't know anything that can help you."

"But this Alison Mayflower. She might?"

Isaacson nodded slowly.

"Do you know where she is now?"

"She hasn't worked with me for twenty years. Moved away."

"To where?"

He shrugged. "I hadn't seen her in years. Lost touch."

"Hadn't."

"What?"

"You said 'hadn't,' not 'haven't.'"

"Yeah, I guess I did." He ran his hand through his hair and let loose a deep breath. "She must have moved back, I don't know. But I saw her last year working at a café in Portland. One of those weird vegan places. But when she saw me..." He stopped.

Elena prompted him. "But when she saw you?"

"She slipped out the back. I went out to follow her, just to say hi, but by the time I got there..." He shrugged it off. "Anyway, it might not have been Alison. I mean, she looked different—her hair used to be long and black as night. This woman's was super short and totally white, so..." He thought about it some more. "No, it was Alison. I'm sure of it."

"Mr. Isaacson?"

He looked up at her.

"Where is this café?"

TWENTY-FIVE

T he first thing Ash saw when he opened his eyes was Dee
Dee's beautiful face.

He might have thought that he'd died or he was hal-
lucinating or something like that, except if that was the case, Dee
Dee would have had her normal blonde braid back, not the short
auburn-dyed locks she'd been forced to adopt.

Or maybe not. Maybe in death you saw the last vision, not
your favorite one.

"It's okay," Dee Dee said in the soothing voice of something
still confusingly celestial. "Just stay still."

He glanced past her as he swam back to full consciousness.
Yep, he was still in the cult compound. The decor in the room was
closer to nonexistent than austere. Nothing on the walls, no furniture in view. The walls were that same inescapable gray.

There were other people in the room. Dee Dee tried to stop
him from sitting up, but he was having none of it. In the far corner, Ash saw Mother Adiona, her eyes on the floor, her hands
clasped in front of her. Closer to him, on either end of the bed,
stood two men he recognized from the triangle of portraits he'd
seen in that other room—the Visitor and the Volunteer.

One of Carter Vartage's sons—the Visitor maybe?—spun and walked out the door without a word. The other turned to Mother Adiona and snapped, "You're lucky."

"I'm sorry."

"What were you thinking?"

"He was an outsider and an intruder," Mother Adiona said, her eyes still on the ground. "I was defending the Truth."

"That's a lie," Dee Dee said.

The son silenced Dee Dee with a wave of his hand, his eyes still boring into the older woman.

"It isn't your place, Mother."

The woman kept her eyes on the ground.

"If you had concerns, you should have come to the council."

Mother Adiona nodded meekly. "You're right, of course."

Vartage's son spun away. "You may go."

"Before I do"—the older woman headed toward Ash—"I want to offer my sincere apologies."

Mother Adiona reached the bed and took Ash's left hand in both of hers. She met his eye and held his gaze. "I cannot express my sorrow for hurting you. Forever be the Truth."

The other two muttered, "Forever be the Truth."

Mother Adiona gripped Ash's hand tighter.

That was when she pressed a slip of paper into his palm.

Ash looked up at her. Mother Adiona gave him the smallest nod, folded his hand into a fist around the slip of paper, and left the room.

"How are you feeling?" Dee Dee asked him.

"Fine."

"Get dressed then, babe. The Truth wants to meet you."

———

The Green-N-Leen Vegan Café, Elena noticed, advertised all its products on a blackboard that used a rainbow assortment of colored chalk. Besides the obvious "vegan," the board was chock full of buzz jargon-like "organic," "fair trade," "meatless," "tempeh," "falafel," "tofu," "raw," "100% natural," "eco," "fresh," "gluten-free," "locally grown," "earth-friendly," "farm-to-table." A sign read OH KALE YEAH! Another spelled EAT PEAS NOT PIGS in a green vegetable mosaic. To the right was a corkboard with push-pins advertising all kinds of environmental fairs (was it okay to use paper for that?) as well as yoga classes and vegan cooking lessons. The whole building should have been clothed in hemp and sporting several of those rubber bracelets supporting a cause.

Alison Mayflower was behind the counter.

She looked straight out of central casting for an older, healthy vegan—tall, toned, a little too thin maybe, prominent cheek-bones, glowing skin with, per Isaacson's description, close-cropped hair so blindingly white you wondered whether it was natural. Her teeth were blindingly white too, though her smile was hesitant, shaky, unsure. She blinked a lot as Elena approached, as though she were expecting bad news or worse.

"May I help you?"

A tip jar read, FEAR CHANGE—LEAVE IT WITH US. Elena liked that. She handed the woman her business card with her private numbers on it. The woman picked it up and started reading it.

"Alison Mayflower," Elena said.

The woman—Elena guessed her age to be early sixties, though she could pass for younger—blinked more and took a step back. "I don't know that name."

"Yeah, you do. It's yours. You changed it."

"I think you have me mistaken—"

"Two choices here, Alison. One, we go somewhere right now and have a private talk and then I go away forever."

"Or?"

"Or two, I blow your life completely apart."

Five minutes later, Elena and Alison made their way to the back corner of the café. A bearded man with a real live man bun whom Alison had called Raoul had taken over behind the counter. Raoul kept glaring at Elena as he cleaned coffee mugs with a dishrag. Elena tried not to roll her eyes.

As soon as they were seated, Elena dove right into her reason for being here. She didn't sugarcoat it or take a side route. Straight ahead.

Murders, disappearance, adoptions, the whole story.

First came denial: "I don't know anything about any of this."

"Sure you do. You did adoptions at Faith Hope. You asked Maish Isaacson to keep them quiet. I could drag him in here to confirm—"

"There's no need for that."

"So let's skip the part where you pretend you don't know what I'm talking about. I don't care if you were selling babies or any of that."

The truth was, Elena did care. When this was over, if other crimes had been committed, she'd report them to the correct law enforcement agency and cooperate in any way to see that Mayflower and Isaacson were punished. But today, right now, her priority was finding Henry Thorpe, and if she involved the authorities, everyone would clam up.

It could wait.

"I gave you the names," Elena continued. "Do you remember any of them?"

"I did a lot of adoptions."

The blinking was back. She cringed into the chair, her chin on her chest, her arms crossed in front of her. Elena had studied body language when she'd been with the FBI. Somewhere along the way, Alison Mayflower had been abused, probably physically. The abuse had been at the hands of a parental figure or a spouse-type situation or both. The blinking was preparing for an assault. The cringing was acquiescing, begging for mercy.

Raoul did some more glaring at Elena. He was twenty-five, maybe thirty, too young to be the source of Alison's abuse. Maybe

Raoul knew her story and didn't want to see her suffer more. Maybe he just sensed it. You didn't have to be any kind of expert in deciphering nonverbal clues to figure it out.

Elena tried again. "You did this to help the children, didn't you?"

Her face tilted up, her eyes still doing the rapid blinks, but there was something akin to hope there now. "Yes. Of course."

"You were saving them from something?"

"Yes."

"What?" Elena moved closer. "What were you saving them from, Alison?"

"I just wanted them to have good homes. That's all."

"But there was something unique about these adoptions, right?" Elena tried to up the pressure. "You had to keep it quiet about them. So you went through a small agency in Maine. Money was exchanged, whatever, that doesn't matter."

"What I did," she said through the blinks, "I did to help the boys."

Elena was nodding, trying to coax her to say more, but one word made her pull up:

Boys.

Alison Mayflower just said she did it to help *boys*. Not kids, not babies, not children.

"Were they all boys?" Elena asked.

Alison didn't reply.

"Does the name Paige—?"

"Only boys," Alison whispered, shaking her head. "Don't you see? I did it to help those boys."

"But they're dying now."

A single tear rolled down Alison's cheek.

Elena gave another push. "Are you going to sit by and let that happen?"

"My God, what have I done?"

"Talk to me, Alison."

"I can't. I have to go."

She started to rise. Elena put a hand on her forearm. A firm hand. "I want to help."

Alison Mayflower shut her eyes. "It's a coincidence."

"No, it's not."

"Yes, it is. If you do enough adoptions, of course some of the children are going to face tragedy in their lives."

"Where did these boys come from? Who were their fathers, their mothers?"

"You don't understand," Alison said.

"So tell me."

Alison snatched her arm away and rubbed it where Elena had been holding it. Her expression was different now. She was still blinking, still scared, but there was defiance there too.

"I saved them," Alison said.

"No, you didn't. Whatever you did, whatever you've been keeping secret all the years? It's back."

"Impossible."

"Maybe you thought it was all buried—"

"More than buried. It's burned. I destroyed all the evidence. I don't even know the names anymore." Her eyes blazed now as she leaned across the table. "Listen to me. There is no way anyone can hurt those children. I made sure of that."

"What did you do, Alison?"

She said nothing.

"Alison?"

"Is this lady bothering you, Allie?"

Elena tried not to sigh as she looked up at Raoul. Raoul scowled at her, his fists on his hips like a hipster Superman.

"This is a private conversation," Elena snapped. "If you and your man bun would just scoot back behind the counter—"

"I wasn't talking to you, lady. I was talking to—"

And then without warning, Alison Mayflower took off.

Elena was caught off guard. One moment Alison was there,

meekly sitting across from her—the next she moved as though propelled from a slingshot. Alison was into the hallway, heading toward the back.

Damn.

Elena was several things, but speedy, especially with her limp, was not one of them. She tried to follow, but even as she started to stand, grunting as she did so, Elena could see the lithe vegan was pulling too far ahead.

When Elena started to follow, Raoul and his man bun stepped in her way. Elena didn't slow. He put out his hands to stop her. The second he touched her, Elena grabbed him by the shoulders, bucked up, and kneed him hard in the balls.

Raoul dropped first to both knees. His man bun followed. Then he toppled onto the floor like an axed tree. Elena almost yelled, "Timber!"

She didn't, of course. She started down the back, past bathrooms with hippie-bead curtains instead of doors, and slammed her body against the back door. It flew open into an alley. Elena looked left and then right.

But Alison Mayflower was gone.

CHAPTER
TWENTY-SIX

Still waiting for news from the doctor, Simon paced the waiting room and got down to following up on what he and Elena Ramirez had discussed. He didn't have a number for Aaron's stepmom, Enid, so he called the Corval Inn, where a woman who sounded a lot like the receptionist he'd personally encountered took a message.

That would go nowhere.

Next up: Check Paige's charge card. Simon had set up an autopay for the Visa card Paige used at Lanford College, and even though he'd been forced to cancel it when Paige started to abuse it to secure drugs for her and Aaron, he was still able to access the old records. He downloaded the charges and started going through them.

It was a painful exercise. His daughter's early expenses had been typically collegiate-innocent—local eateries for small meals, the Lanford College store for school supplies and logo-emblazoned sweatshirts, toiletries from a CVS. There were two charges to a Rita's Italian Ice in Poughkeepsie and a sixty-five-dollar charge, probably for a summer dress, from a place called Elizabeth's Boutique.

There was no charge to DNAYourStory.

But Simon did find a seventy-nine-dollar charge to something called Ance-Story. He Googled the company and yep, it was a genealogy website that concentrated on "filling the branches on your family tree" via DNA testing. He was just reading through the site when a tired female voice called his name.

"Simon Greene?"

Dr. Heather Grewe was still dressed in her classic blue surgical scrubs. Classic blue. Simon liked that. He found the color properly somber and therefore comforting. Too many of the nurses and staff members had funky or fun scrubs, bright pinks or floral patterns or ones with SpongeBob or Cookie Monster, and fine, Simon got it—if you work here all day, maybe you wanted to change it up or do something different, and sure, the contrast of wearing something bright in this grim environment made sense, but no, unless you were in the pediatric wing, Simon wanted the somber, serious scrubs, and he was glad to see Ingrid's surgeon wearing them.

"Your wife is out of surgery. She's stabilized."

"Is she still in a coma?"

"I'm afraid she is, but we alleviated the immediate problem."

Dr. Grewe began to explain in some detail, but it was hard for Simon to focus on the medical minutiae. The big picture—the words in caps, if you will—seemed to be the same:

NO CHANGE.

After Dr. Grewe finished, Simon thanked her and asked, "Can I see my wife?"

"Yes, of course."

She led him down to the recovery area. He had no idea how a body in a coma could appear more exhausted, but Ingrid's ferocious battle with whatever had dragged her back into surgery had clearly left her drained. She lay completely still, like before, but now the stillness seemed somehow worse, more sunken, fragile. He was almost afraid to take her hand, as though it might somehow break off in his.

But he did take the hand.

He tried to picture Ingrid upright and healthy and beautiful and vibrant. He tried to flash back to other times in this hospital, happier times, Ingrid holding one of her newborn children, but the vision would not hold. All he could see right now was this Ingrid, weak, pale, drawn, more gone than here. He stared at her and thought about what Yvonne had told him about the past and secrets.

"I don't care."

He said the words out loud to his comatose wife.

Whatever she had done in the past—he tried to imagine the worst: crime, drugs, prostitution, even murder—he'd forgive. Didn't matter what. No questions asked.

He stood and put his lips to his wife's ear.

"I just need you back, babe."

It was the truth. But it also wasn't. He didn't care about her past. But there were some questions that still needed to be asked. At six a.m., he checked in with the duty nurse, made sure they had his mobile phone number, and headed out of the cloying hospital air and into the city street. Normally he'd take the subway to his apartment, but he wanted to be above ground in case a call came in. At this hour, the ride from the hospital to his place on the Upper West Side should be fifteen minutes tops. As long as he had his phone with him, he could come back immediately if there were any changes.

He didn't want to leave her, but there was something he needed to do.

Simon called a ride share with his app and had the driver stop in front of a twenty-four-hour Duane Reade pharmacy on Columbus Avenue near Seventy-Fifth Street. He ran in, bought a six-pack of toothbrushes, hopped back into the car. When he got home—man, how long had it been since he'd been in his own home?—the apartment was silent. He tiptoed down the corridor and looked into the bedroom on the right.

Sam was asleep on his side, fetal position, legs pulled up tight. That was how his son always slept. Simon didn't want to wake Sam yet. He headed into the kitchen and opened the drawer with the Ziploc plastic bags. He grabbed some out and quietly made his way to what they'd dubbed "the girls' bathroom," the one Paige had shared with her little sister Anya.

It had become something of a running joke in the house that the kids never changed their toothbrushes until the bristles were not only frayed but pretty much nonexistent—so years ago, Simon took it upon himself to buy a package of new toothbrushes every two months and switch them out on his own. He was going to do that today too, so no one would notice what he was up to, even though, well, who really would?

Paige's toothbrush was still here from her last visit...sheesh, how long ago?

He took her toothbrush carefully by the handle and placed it in the plastic bag. He hoped that there would be enough DNA on it to get a sample. He started to leave the bathroom but pulled up short.

He trusted Ingrid. He really did.

But working under a better-safe-than-sorry personal philosophy, Simon put Anya's toothbrush in a second Ziploc bag. He moved to the other bathroom and put Sam's in one too.

It all felt like a sick, terrible betrayal.

When he was done, Simon headed into his own room and packed the plastic bags in his work backpack. He checked his phone. Nothing. It was still early, but he texted Suzy Fiske anyway:

Hey I'm home for a bit. If you're awake, can you wake up
Anya and send her home for breakfast?

He wasn't sure how long he'd have to wait for a response, but right away he saw the flashing dots indicating Suzy was typing him back:

I'll wake her up now.
Anything new on
Ingrid?

He told Suzy no, nothing new, and thanked her profusely for looking after Anya. She typed back that Anya was a pleasure, that having Anya around actually made it easier, and while Simon knew that she was being nice, he also knew that there was truth there. Suzy had two daughters and like most sisters that age, they fought. If you add a third element into a mix like that, it changes the chemical makeup just enough to make everything a tad more pleasant.

Simon texted back: Still I'm super grateful.

He moved back into the kitchen. All of his male New York City friends suddenly liked to cook. Or claimed they did. They waxed eloquent about some complicated risotto dish they recently made or a recipe from the *New York Times* weekly email or some such thing. When, he wondered, did cooking become the new poser claim, replacing all the amateur sommeliers? Wasn't cooking, for the most part, a chore? When you read history books or heck, watch old movies, wasn't being a person's cook one of the worst jobs in the house? What would be the next chore turned into great art? Vacuuming maybe? Would his friends start debating the wonders of Dyson over Hoover?

The mind likes to wander under stress.

The thing was, Simon did have one meal, one specialty if you will, that he prepared with great aplomb on those weekend mornings when the family were together and he, the father, was in the mood: pancakes with chocolate chips.

The secret behind Simon's beloved family breakfast recipe?

You can't have enough chocolate chips.

"It's more like chocolate with pancake chips," Ingrid had joked.

The chocolate chips were in the upper cabinet. Ingrid always made sure they had them, just in case, even though it had been a long time since Simon prepared his celebrated dish. That depressed him. He missed having his children home. Forgetting Paige's tragic descent for a moment (as if he ever could), having his oldest daughter go off to college had been more traumatic than Simon would have expected. When Sam left, the trauma doubled. They were leaving, his children. They weren't really growing up anymore—they were grown. They were abandoning him. Yes, it was natural and right and it would be a lot worse if they weren't. But it bothered him anyway. The home was too quiet. He hated that.

When Sam graduated high school, his class president posted a well-meaning meme on the school's social media. The photo was the classic self-help image of a lovely beach at sunset with the prerequisite gentle waves, and the text read:

LOVE YOUR PARENTS.

WE ARE SO BUSY GROWING UP, WE OFTEN FORGET THEY ARE

GROWING OLD.

He and Ingrid had read the meme together in this very kitchen, and then Ingrid said, "Let's print that out, roll it into a tube, and shove it up a pretentious ass."

God, he loved her.

He'd been seated as they read that meme, Ingrid leaning over his shoulder. She threw her arms around his neck, bent close so he felt her breath in his ear, and whispered, "Once the kids are all out of the house, we can travel more."

"And run around the house naked," Simon had added.

"Er, okay."

"And have a lot more sex."

"Hope springs eternal."

He fake-pouted.

"Would having more sex make you happier?" she asked.

255

"Me? No. I was thinking of you."

"You're all self-sacrifice."

Simon was still smiling at the memory when Sam said, "Whoa, Dad's pancakes."

"Yep."

His face lit up. "Does that mean Mom's gotten better?"

"No, not really."

Damn. He should have thought of that—that his son would see him making pancakes and jump to that conclusion.

"It means," Simon continued, "that she'd want us to do something normal and not just wallow."

He could hear his own "Dad voice" falling way short of the mark.

"It isn't normal when you make pancakes anymore," Sam said. "It's special."

He had a point. He also ended up being both right and wrong. The breakfast did end up being normal—and special. Anya came up from the Fiske apartment and threw her arms around her father as though he were a life preserver. Simon hugged her back, closed his eyes, rode the wave for as long as his daughter needed.

The three of them sat around the circular table—Ingrid had insisted on round for the kitchen, even though rectangular fit better, because it "promotes conversation"—and even though two chairs were glaringly empty, it felt somehow, well, normal and special. Anya soon had chocolate all over her face and Sam teased her for it, and then Anya recalled how her mother called his breakfast concoction "chocolate with pancake chips."

At some point, Sam broke down and cried, but that felt normal and special too. Anya slid off her seat and wrapped her arms around her older brother, and Sam let her, was even comforted by his little sister, and Simon felt the pang deep in his heart of Ingrid missing this moment between her children. He'd remember it though. As soon as Ingrid woke up, Simon would tell her about this moment, when her son looked for comfort from his little sister—his little sister of all people!—and she was able to give it, and one day, when Simon and Ingrid were old or gone, they'd still always have each other.

It would make Ingrid so happy.

While Sam and Anya did the dishes—family rule: whoever prepares the food doesn't do the cleanup—Simon headed back to his bedroom. He closed the door. There was a lock on it, the kind of flimsy thing you install so your kids don't walk in on you during an inopportune moment. He turned it and then opened Ingrid's closet. Toward the back, there were six hanging bags with various dresses. He unzipped the fourth one, the one with a conservative blue dress, and slid his hand down to the bottom of the bag's interior.

That was where they hid the cash.

He took out ten thousand dollars in wrapped bills and stuffed them in the backpack with the toothbrushes. Then he checked his phone to make sure that there was nothing important and headed back into the kitchen. Anya got changed for school. She gave her father another hug goodbye and left with Suzy Fiske. When he closed the door behind them, Simon had yet another of his imaginary conversations with Ingrid, this time asking her what gift they should get Suzy when this was over—a gift certificate to that dumpling place or a spa day at the Mandarin Oriental or something more personal like a piece of jewelry?

Ingrid would know.

He realized now that he was having these imaginary conversations with Ingrid all the time, running what he'd learned by her and seeing the reaction, even holding back the obvious question he wanted to ask her, the one that he and Elena danced around, the one that had been gnawing on him since this whole genealogy angle raised its ugly head.

He threw the backpack over one shoulder. "Sam? You ready?"

They headed down the elevator and grabbed a passing taxi. The driver, like pretty much every taxi driver in New York City, talked quietly into an earpiece in a foreign language Simon could not detect. That was old news, of course, everyone was used to that, but Simon wondered about the ridiculously strong family bonds of such people. As much as he loved Ingrid (and even had imaginary conversations with her), he couldn't imagine a situation in which he could stay on the phone and talk to her or anyone else for hours on end. Who were these drivers talking to all day? How much must they be loved to have someone (or "someones" plural) who wanted to share that much news with them?

"Mom had a setback," Simon said to his son, "but she's better now."

He explained. Sam bit down on his lip and listened. When they arrived at the hospital, Simon said, "Go up and sit with your mom. I'll meet you up there in a bit."

"Where are you going?"

"I have to run an errand."

Sam stared at him.

"What?"

"You let Mom get shot."

Simon opened his mouth to defend himself, but then he stopped.

"You should have protected her."

"I know," Simon said. "I'm sorry."

Simon moved away from his son then, leaving him alone on the sidewalk. He flashed back to that moment. He saw Luther aiming the gun. He saw himself ducking out of the way so that the bullet hit Ingrid instead of him.

What a chickenshit.

But was that what happened?

Had he really ducked out of the way? He didn't know. He didn't think that "memory" was real, but... Stepping back, trying to be objective, he realized that he hadn't seen any of that, that guilt and time were replacing real memories with ones that would forever wound him.

Could he have done more? Could he have stepped in the way of the bullet?

Maybe.

Part of him recognized that this thought was unfair. It had all happened so fast. There was no time to react. But that didn't change the reality. He should have done more. He should have pushed Ingrid away. He should have jumped in front of her.

"You should have protected her . . ."

He headed into Shovlin Pavilion and took the elevator to the eleventh floor. The receptionist led him down the corridor to the lab. A lab technician named Randy Spratt greeted him with a latex-gloved handshake.

"I don't know why we couldn't do this through proper channels," Spratt bristled.

Simon opened up the backpack and handed him the three plastic bags of toothbrushes. He had originally planned on bringing just Paige's toothbrush, but somewhere along the way he decided that if he was going to travel down this dark, dank road, he might as well travel all the way.

"I need to know if I'm their father." Simon pointed to the yellow toothbrush that had been Paige's. "This one is the priority."

Simon didn't like doing this, of course. It wasn't a question of trust, Simon told himself. It was a question of reassurance.

Then again, Simon also realized that was a big fat rationalization.

Didn't matter.

"You said you could rush the results," Simon said.

Spratt nodded. "Give me three days."

"No good."

"Pardon?"

Simon reached into the backpack and pulled out the wad of cash.

"I don't understand."

"This is ten thousand dollars in cash. Get me the results by the end of the day, and I'll give you ten more."

259

CHAPTER
TWENTY-SEVEN

The Truth was dying.

At least it looked that way to Ash from the foot of his bed.

Casper Vartage's sons stood on either side of the bed, two devastated sentinels guarding their father in his final days. Sorrow emanated from them. You could feel the grief. Ash didn't know the brothers' real names—he wasn't sure anyone did—nor did he remember or care which one was the Visitor and which the Volunteer.

Dee Dee stood next to Ash, hands clasped, eyes lowered as though in prayer. The two brothers did the same. In the corner, two gray-uniformed women quietly sobbed in unison, almost as if they'd been ordered to provide a soundtrack for the scene.

Only the Truth kept his eyes open and up. He lay in the middle of the bed adorned in some kind of white tunic. His gray beard was long, so too his hair. He looked like a Renaissance depiction of God, like the creation panel in the Sistine Chapel that Ash had first seen in a book in the school library. That image always fascinated him, the idea of God touching Adam, as though hitting the On switch for mankind.

God in that mural had been muscular and strong. The Truth was not. He was decaying almost in real time. But his smile was still radiant, his eyes otherworldly as they met Ash's. For a moment, maybe longer, Ash understood what was happening in this place. The Truth was tweaking him with just his gaze. The old man's charisma, even as he lay sick in this bed, was almost supernatural.

The Truth lifted a hand and beckoned for Ash to come closer. Ash turned toward Dee Dee, who nodded that he should go ahead. The Truth's head didn't move, but his eyes followed Ash, again like some sort of Renaissance painting. He took Ash's hand in his. His grip was surprisingly strong.

"Thank you, Ash."

Ash could feel the pull of the man, his magnetism. He would have never bought fully into it, of course, but that didn't mean Ash couldn't see what was happening and even be moved by it. We all have our talents. Some run faster or are stronger or better at math than others. We watch athletes because they awe us with what they can do with a ball or puck or whatever. This man, Casper Vartage, likewise had skills. Mad skills. You could get lost in those skills, hypnotized by them, especially if you were the kind who didn't focus or were of a certain mind frame.

Ash was not one of those kind.

Ash was focused, and right now he was curious and upset. He worked by anonymity. There were passwords and anonymous communications via secure websites and apps. He never came face-to-face with those who employed him. Never.

Dee Dee knew that. She knew the dangers too.

He let go of the old man's hand and glared at Dee Dee. The glare was asking why she brought him here, and her response, a rather serene smile, seemed to indicate that he should have patience.

The two sobbing women left the room, and the two guards, including the bastard who had hit him with the baton, entered.

Once again, Ash didn't like it. He especially didn't like the smug look on Guard One's face.

The old man struggled to speak, but he managed to say, "Forever be the Shining Truth."

The others in the room chimed back, "Forever be the Shining Truth."

Ritual. Ash hated mindless ritual.

"Go," the old man said to Ash. "The Truth will always prevail."

The rest of the room's inhabitants intoned, "The Truth will always prevail."

The guard smirked at Ash, then he let his eyes crawl all over Dee Dee, then he wiggled his eyebrows at Ash. Ash showed nothing. He glanced at Dee Dee. She knew.

It was starting to make some sense now.

One of the brothers handed Ash a key fob. "A new car is waiting for you. Untraceable."

Ash took the key. First chance he got, he'd stop on the road and switch the license plate with a similar car, just to be on the safe side. When they crossed state lines, he'd probably switch it yet again.

"We trust you can take care of this," the other brother said.

Ash said nothing and started toward the door. The guard smirked at him the whole time. The guard was still smirking when Ash reached him, turned, and faced him. The guard was still smirking when Ash, who had palmed the knife, slashed the blade across the guard's throat.

Ash didn't step back. He let the blood from the carotid artery spray his face. He didn't flinch. He waited for the surprised gasps. They came quickly.

Ash stepped to the other guard, still looking on in shock, and snatched his weapon away from him.

The first guard, the one with the sliced carotid artery, fell to the floor, trying in vain to keep the blood from gushing out of him. It looked as though he were strangling himself. The sounds coming from him were primitive, guttural.

No one moved. No one spoke. They all just watched the guard writhe and kick out until his convulsions slowed and then stopped.

The two Vartage brothers looked stunned. So too the surviving guard. Dee Dee had that same smile on her face. That didn't surprise him. What did surprise him was the knowing look on the Truth's face.

Had he known what Ash was about to do?

The Truth gave Ash a half nod as though to say, *Message received.*

For Ash, this was simple. The guard had hurt him, ergo the guard paid a price. You punch me, I punch you back way harder. Massive retaliation. Massive deterrent.

This was also a message to those remaining in the room. If you mess with me, I'll mess with you even worse. Ash would do the job he was hired to do. He would get paid for it, and then it would be over. There would be no benefit in trying to cross him.

In fact, crossing him would be a big mistake.

Ash looked toward the brothers. "I assume you have people who can clean this up?"

They both nodded.

Dee Dee handed him a towel to wipe the blood off his face. He did so quickly.

"We can show ourselves out," Ash said.

Ash and Dee Dee walked down the back path toward the entrance gate. An Acura RDX was waiting for them. He opened the passenger door for Dee Dee. As he did, he looked up into the distance and saw Mother Adiona on the top of the hill. She gazed down at him, and even from this distance, he could see the pleading in her eyes.

She shook her head in an ominous fashion.

He did nothing.

Ash circled around and got behind the wheel. He drove them back down the tree-lined road, watching the gates of Truth Haven grow smaller in the rearview mirror. He turned onto the main road and when they hit the first traffic light, he took out the note from Mother Adiona, opened it, and read it for the first time:

DON'T KILL HIM. PLEASE.

All in caps and block letters. Then in cursive underneath:

Don't show this message to anyone, not even her. You have no idea what's really going on.

"What's that?" Dee Dee asked.

He handed her the note. "Mother Adiona slipped this to me before she left my room."

Dee Dee read it.

"What does she mean by 'You have no idea what's really going on'?" Ash asked.

"No clue," Dee Dee said. "But I'm glad you trust me."

"I trust you more than I trust her."

"My sneaking you that knife probably helped."

"It didn't hurt," Ash said. "Did you know I'd kill him?"

"Massive retaliation. Massive deterrent."

"Were you worried about how your leaders would react?"

"The Truth will always provide."

"And killing that guard was the truth?"

She looked out the window. "He's dying. You know that, right?"

"The Truth, you mean?"

Dee Dee smiled. "The Truth cannot die. But yes, the current embodiment."

"Does his death have anything to do with why I was hired?"

"Does it matter?"

Ash thought about it. "No, not really."

She sat back and hugged her knees to her chest.

"What do you make of Mother Adiona's note?" he asked.

Dee Dee started playing with a too-long strand of hair she'd missed during her bathroom cut. "I'm not sure."

"Are you going to tell the Truth?" He heard the funny way it sounded—the play on words that is the man's moniker—even as he said it. "I mean, are you going to tell—?"

"Yeah, I know what you meant."

"Well? Are you going to tell?"

Dee Dee thought about it. "Not right now. Right now, I want us to concentrate on doing our job."

CHAPTER

TWENTY-EIGHT

W hen Simon got back to the ICU, he was surprised to
see Detective Isaac Fagbenle waiting for him. For a
second, maybe two, hope filled his chest—had he
found Paige?—but the expression on Fagbenle's face indicated
that this wasn't going to be good news. The hope fled even faster
than it came, replaced by whatever the opposite is.

Despair? Worry?

"It's not about Paige," Fagbenle said.

"What then?"

Simon glanced over the detective's shoulder to where Sam sat
bedside of Ingrid. Nothing new there, so he turned his attention
back to Fagbenle.

"It's about Luther Ritz."

The man who shot his wife. "What about him?"

"He's out."

"What?"

"On bail. Rocco posted a bond for him."

"Luther wasn't remanded to trial?"

"Presumption of innocence, Eighth Amendment. You know,
like we still do in America?"

"He's free?" Simon let loose a breath. "You think that puts Ingrid in any danger?"

"Not really. The hospital has pretty good security."

A nurse pushed past them, giving them an annoyed glance because they were somewhat blocking the entrance. The two men moved to the side.

"The thing is," Fagbenle said, "the case against Luther isn't a slam dunk."

"How's that?"

"He claims you shot him first."

"Me?"

"You, your wife, one of you two."

"Didn't you do a residue test on him?"

"Yes. He claims two things. One, he was shooting practice shots, nothing to do with you. And two, if you don't buy that, he fired back because you shot him first."

Simon scoffed. "Who's going to believe that?"

"You'd be surprised. Look, I don't know all the details, but Luther Ritz is claiming self-defense. That's going to lead to some tough questions."

"Like what?"

"Like why you and Ingrid were down there in the first place."

"To find our daughter."

"Right. So you were agitated and worried, right? You went to a drug den that your daughter frequented. No one would tell you where she was. So maybe you got more than agitated and worried. Maybe you were desperate, so desperate you or your wife pulled a gun—"

"You can't be serious."

"—and he ended up shot. Luther, I mean. So he fired back."

Simon made a face.

"Luther is back home how, convalescing from a serious wound—"

"And my wife is"—Simon felt his face redden—"lying in a coma ten yards from us."

"I know that. But you see, someone shot Luther."

Fagbenle moved in closer. Now Simon got it. Now he understood what was happening here.

"And as long as we don't know who shot him, Luther's claim of self-defense will lead to reasonable doubt. The witnesses, if there are any who come forward, won't be backing your recounting of the events. They'll back Luther's." Fagbenle smiled. "You didn't have any friends in that drug den, did you, Simon?"

"No," Simon said, the lie coming quick and easy. Cornelius had shot Luther and saved them, but there was no way Simon would ever admit that. "Of course not."

"Exactly. So there are no other suspects. Ergo, his attorney will claim, you took it upon yourself to shoot Luther Ritz. You had time after that with everyone scattering. You hid the gun. If you wore gloves, you got rid of them. Whatever."

"Detective?"

"What?"

"Are you arresting me?"

"No."

"So this can all wait, right?"

"I guess it can. I don't buy Luther's story. Just so we're clear. But I do find one thing odd."

"What's that?"

"Do you remember when we went into his hospital room so you could make a positive ID?"

"Yes."

"And Luther, well, let's just say his driveway doesn't quite reach the road, if you know what I mean. He was dumb enough to admit being shot at the scene, remember?"

"Yes."

"So he isn't fast on his feet."

"Right."

"And yet when I asked Luther why he did it, do you remember the first thing he said?"

Simon said nothing.

"He gestured toward you, Simon, and he said, 'Why don't you ask him why?'"

Simon remembered. He remembered the feeling of anger that came over him then, looking at Luther, that waste of humanity who'd made the decision to try to end Ingrid's life. The gall of it all, that someone as low as that could hold such power, had enraged him.

"He was grasping at straws, Detective."

"Was he?"

"Yes."

"I don't think he's that smart, Simon. I think Luther knows something he hasn't yet told us."

Simon considered that for a moment. "Like what?"

"You tell me," Fagbenle said. Then: "Who shot Luther, Simon? Who saved you guys?"

"I don't know."

"That's a lie."

Simon said nothing.

"And there's the rub, my friend," Fagbenle continued. "Once one lie is let in the room, even for the best of reasons, a whole bunch more will ride in on its back. Then those lies will gang up and slaughter the truth. So I'll ask you one more time: Who shot Luther?"

They were eye to eye now, inches apart.

"I told you," Simon said through gritted teeth. "I don't know. Is there anything else?"

"No, I don't think so."

"Then I'd like to go sit with my wife."

Fagbenle slapped Simon's shoulder in a gesture that was trying to be both friendly and intimidating. "I'll be in touch."

As Fagbenle headed down the corridor, Simon's mobile rang. He didn't recognize the number and debated letting it go to voicemail—too many solicitations nowadays, even on mobile phones—

but the area code was the same as Lanford College's. He moved to the side and answered.

"Hello?"

"Mr. Greene?"

"Speaking."

"I got your email and phone message, so I'm calling you back. This is Louis van de Beek. I'm a professor at Lanford College."

He had almost forgotten about leaving those messages. "Thanks for getting back to me."

"No problem."

"I'm calling about my daughter Paige."

There was silence on the other end.

"You remember her? Paige Greene."

"Yes." His voice sounded very far away. "Of course."

"Do you know what happened to her?"

"I know she dropped out."

"She's missing, Professor."

"I'm so sorry to hear that."

"I think something happened to her at school. I think something at Lanford started all this."

"Mr. Greene?"

"Yes?"

"If I recall correctly, your family lives in Manhattan."

"That's right."

"Are you there now?"

"In the city? Yes."

"I'm teaching this semester at Columbia University."

Simon's alma mater.

"Perhaps," van de Beek continued, "we should have this discussion in person."

"I can be there in twenty minutes."

"I'll need a little more time. Do you know the campus?"

"Yes."

"There's a big statue on the steps in front of the main building."

The main building was called Low Memorial Library. The bronze statue, oddly enough called *Alma Mater*, depicted the Greek goddess Athena.

"I know it."

"Let's meet there in an hour."

The cops showed up at the Green-N-Leen Vegan Café because someone called 911 when Raoul and his man bun went down from Elena's knee kick. At first, Raoul, who was still cupping his wounded nuts, wanted to press charges.

"She assaulted my family jewels!" Raoul kept shouting.

The cops rolled their eyes, but they also knew they had to take a statement. Elena pulled Raoul and the man bun into the corner and said simply, "If you press charges, I press charges."

"But you—"

"—got the better of you, yes I know."

Raoul was still cradling his crotch as if he'd found a wounded bird.

"But you assaulted me first," Elena said.

"What? How do you figure?"

"Raoul, you're new at this. I'm not. The surveillance tape will show that you reached out and touched me first."

"You were running after my friend!"

"And you assaulted me to stop that, so I defended myself. That's how this will play. And worse. I mean, look at me, Raoul." Elena spread her arms. "I'm short, I'm chubby, and even though I'm sure you're very in touch with your feminine side and all kum-baya on feminism, that tape of a small albeit round middle-aged woman kneeing you in the balls will go viral."

Raoul's eyes widened. He hadn't considered that, though maybe his man bun had.

"Do you want to roll those dice, Raoul?"

He crossed his arms over his chest.

"Raoul?"

"Fine," he said in the most petulant tone imaginable. "I won't press charges."

"Yeah, but now that I start thinking about it, I might."

"What?"

Elena made the trade. Alison Mayflower's "real" name—Allie Mason—and current address in exchange for letting bygones be bygones. Alison lived on a farm outside of Buxton. Elena made the drive up. No one was home. She debated sitting outside the house for a bit, but it didn't look as though anyone had been home in a long time.

Back at the Howard Johnson's, Elena sat in a room that couldn't be more motel generic and tried to plot her next move. Lou from her home office had discovered that Allie Mason lived in that farmhouse with another woman named Stephanie Mars.

Was Stephanie Mars a friend? A relative? A partner? Did it matter?

Should Elena drive the half hour to Buxton and try again?

There was no reason to think Alison Mayflower would be more cooperative this time, but then again, trying doggedly was why Elena made the big bucks. Literally. And it wasn't as though the first meeting hadn't borne fruit. It had. There was clearly something shady going on with those adoptions. Elena had strongly suspected that before, but after her encounter with Alison Mayflower, she knew for sure. She also knew that at least in Alison Mayflower's mind, the children had needed saving. And the big new piece of this cockamamy puzzle, though Elena had zero idea how it fit:

All the adopted babies were boys.

Why? Why not girls?

Elena took out a pad and pen and charted out the ages. Damien Gorse was the oldest, Henry Thorpe the youngest. Still, they were almost ten years apart in age. Ten years. That was a long time for Alison Mayflower to be involved in all this.

That meant her involvement was deep. Super deep.

Her phone rang. It was Lou from the home office on some special app he'd installed on her phone. The app made all calls untraceable or something like that. "The leakers in the White House use it," Lou had told her. "That's why they never get caught."

Lou didn't use it very often.

"You alone?" he asked when she picked up.

"You didn't call for phone sex, did you?"

"Uh, yeah no. Open up your laptop, wiseass."

She could hear the excitement in his voice. "Okay."

"I emailed you a link. Click on it."

Elena opened her browser and started to sign into her email. "You click it yet?"

"Give me a second, will you? I'm typing in my password."

"Seriously? You don't have it saved?"

"How do you save it?"

"Ugh, never mind. Tell me when you have the link up."

Elena found Lou's email and clicked the link. A website called Ance-Story came up.

"Bingo," she said.

"What, why?"

"Let me just double-check something."

Elena grabbed her phone and checked her texts. There was one from Simon Greene, who'd informed her that his daughter Paige had no charges on her credit card for DNAYourStory, but that he had found one for $79 to:

Ance-Story.

She filled Lou in on Simon's text. "Okay," Lou said, "so this is going to be even bigger news than I thought."

Elena's eyes traveled down the home page. No doubt about it—this was definitely one of those DNA genealogy sites. There were all kinds of photographs of people embracing and cute catchphrases like "Discover Who You Really Are" or "Only You Are You—Uncover Your Unique Ethnic Origins." There were other links that could help the potential customer—like the thrilled people in the embracing photographs—"find new relatives."

Below that, the packages the potential customer could purchase were displayed. The first option, priced at $79, offered you a breakdown of your ancestry and the chance to connect with DNA relatives. The second option was called "For Your Health Too." It offered the same as package one, but for an extra eighty dollars, you'd receive a "full medical report that could make you healthier."

The word RECOMMENDED was stamped in flashing letters above the more expensive package. What a surprise. The company itself was suggesting you spend more money on their products. Gasp.

"You on the home page?" Lou asked.

"Yes."

"Click Sign in."

"Okay."

"You'll see two fields. User name and Password."

"Right."

"Okay, this is the part where I get legal on you. I called on the secure app because I figured out how to get into Henry Thorpe's DNA account."

"How did you do that?"

"You really want to know?"

"No."

"I know we could get permission from his father—"

"But he has no standing. I already heard this today."

"So what we would be doing by signing in . . . well, I'm not sure it's completely legal. This could be viewed technically as hacking. I want to caution you."

"Lou?"

"Yeah?"

"Give me the user name and password."

He did so. She typed them in. A page came up that read: "Welcome back, Henry. Here's your ethnic composition."

Henry was 98 percent European. Under that, he was listed as 58 percent from Great Britain, 20 percent from Ireland, 14 percent Ashkenazi Jew, 5 percent Scandinavian, and then everything else was negligible.

"Scan down to the bottom of the page," Lou said.

She traveled past something called Your Chromosomes.

"You see the link that says 'Your DNA Relatives'?"

She said that she did.

"Click it."

A new page came up. On the top, it read "Sorted Strength of Relationship." Next to that, it noted that "You have 898 relatives."

"Eight hundred and ninety-eight relatives?" Elena said.

"Henry Thorpe better get a bigger Thanksgiving table, right? That's normal, maybe even on the low side. The vast majority are distant cousins who share very little of your unique DNA. But click Page One."

She could hear the excitement in his voice.

Elena clicked. The page took its time loading now.

"You see it?"

"Calm down, I'm using a Howard Johnson's Wi-Fi."

And then she did indeed see it. The whole case started to come together. That was how it felt. Like a whole bunch of those big puzzle pieces suddenly started to fit.

Four people were listed as: Half-Sibling(s) of Henry.

"Holy crap," she said.

"Yep."

Damien Gorse of Maplewood, New Jersey, was listed first. His full name. Just like that. The murdered owner of the tattoo parlor was a half brother of Elena's client.

Under that, also listed as a "half-sibling male," were just initials.

"AC from the Northeast," Elena said. It didn't take much to guess. "Aaron Corval."

"Probably."

"Any way to confirm?"

"I'm working on it. See, the site doesn't let people just list themselves anonymously. It gives you two options. Full name. Or initials. But they have to be real. I'd say half the people do full name, half do initials."

Next, also listed as a half-sibling male, were the initials NB of Tallahassee, Florida.

"Any way to trace down NB?"

"None that are legal."

"How about illegal?"

"Not really. I could send him a message as Henry Thorpe, see if he'll tell me his name."

"Do it," she said.

"That violates—"

"Can it be traced back to us?"

"Don't insult me."

"Then do it," Elena said.

"It turns me on when you bend the rules."

"Super, great. We also need to contact the authorities. Maybe they can get a warrant off what we have, I don't know."

"We can't give them what we have, remember?"

"Right, okay. But NB, if we find his identity, needs to be warned. He could be next."

"There might be more."

"What do you mean, 'more'? More what?"

"Siblings."

"How do you figure that?" she asked.

"Henry Thorpe put his DNA into at least three of these sites."

"Why would he do that?"

276

"Lot of people do. The more databases you're in, the better your odds of finding blood relatives. My point is, he found four half siblings in Ance-Story alone. He may have found more elsewhere, I don't know."

"These are all half siblings, right?"

"Right. On the father's side."

She glanced down the page. "What about this last guy, the fourth half sibling?"

"What about him?"

"He's listed as a Kevin Gano from Boston. Did you check him out?"

"Yeah. And—drumroll—this is big. You ready?"

"Lou."

"Gano is dead."

She'd expected that reply, and yet it still landed with a wallop. "Murdered?"

"Suicide. I talked to the local cops. Nothing suspicious about the case. He lost his job, seemed depressed. He went into his garage and shot himself in the head."

"But they weren't looking for anything suspicious," she said. "He was probably..."

She stopped. Her heart fell.

"Elena?"

She didn't say it out loud, but suddenly the answer seemed obvious. A suicide. Two murders.

And a disappearance.

Henry Thorpe was probably dead. If the killer wanted to make sure he didn't link to the others—if he didn't want a cop to start looking at any links between murder victims on, say, a DNA site—you'd just make one of the victims look like a runaway.

Damn.

Was Elena searching for a dead man?

"Elena?"

"Yeah, I'm here. Something else we need to look at."

"What's that?"

"We know Paige Greene signed up with Ance-Story too."

"Yeah, well, she's not a half sibling. That's the total list there. All male."

"Maybe some other way."

"There's a search engine. Use it."

She typed in "Paige Greene." Nothing. She typed in "Greene" and her initials and a few other ways that Lou suggested. Nothing. She looked through the relatives list. There was one first cousin, also male, listed and then several third cousins.

No Paige. No PG.

"Paige Greene is not a relative," Lou said.

"Then how does she fit into this?"

CHAPTER
TWENTY-NINE

A commuter app told Simon that taking the 1 train south to get to Columbia University would take eleven minutes total, which was considerably faster than a taxi or car. Simon stood waiting for the elevator that plummets you into the bowels of Washington Heights when his mobile rang.

The number was blocked.

"Hello?"

"I'll have the paternity results in two hours."

It was Randy Spratt from the genetics lab.

"Great," Simon said.

"I'll meet you in the courtyard behind the pediatric wing."

"Okay."

"Mr. Greene, are you familiar with the expression 'payment on delivery'?"

Man, it was amazing how easily people fell into small forms of corruption. "I'll have the cash."

Spratt hung up. Simon stepped back and called Yvonne's mobile.

Yvonne answered with a tentative "Hey."

"Don't worry," he said, "I'm not calling to ask about Ingrid's big secret. I need a favor."

"What's up?"

"I need to make a cash withdrawal of nine thousand nine hundred dollars from our branch near the hospital."

The amount had to be under ten thousand dollars. For any amount over that, you had to fill out a CTR—currency transaction report—with FinCEN. In short, it would be reported to the IRS or law enforcement, and Simon didn't want to deal with that right now.

"Will you arrange it, please?"

"On it." Then: "What's the cash for?"

"Maybe you and Ingrid aren't the only ones with secrets."

It was an immature thing to say, but there you go.

As soon as he hung up, the elevator doors opened revealing a dingy and poorly lit car. Commuters piled in until an alarm of some kind started to beep. Subway elevators plunging down into the earth's core are probably the closest urbanites get to what a coal miner goes through, which, of course, wasn't close at all.

The 1 train was pretty much at capacity, though not sardine-can packed. Simon chose to stand. He held on to a pole. He used to check his phone or read a newspaper, anything to escape the claustrophobic feeling of being locked in with strangers, but lately, Simon liked to look around at the faces of his fellow passengers. A subway car is a microcosm of our planet. You saw all nationalities, creeds, genders, persuasions. You saw public displays of affection and arguments. You heard music and voices, laughter and tears. There were rich people in business suits (often Simon himself) and there were panhandlers. You were all equals on the train. You all paid the same fare. You all had the same right to the same seats.

For some reason, over the last year or two, the subway hadn't been something to avoid. It had become, when there weren't issues with construction and delays, something of a refuge.

Simon entered the Columbia University campus at the center gates on Broadway and 116th Street. This was the same entranceway he had first crossed as a high school junior visiting for a prospective tour with his father. His father, the greatest man Simon would ever know, was an electrician with the IBEW union, Local 102. The idea that a child of his could one day go to an Ivy League school stunned and intimidated him.

Dad had always made Simon feel safe.

That was the thing. Two weeks before Simon graduated, Dad died of a massive coronary while he was driving to a job in Millburn, New Jersey. It had been a devastating blow to Simon's family—the beginning of the end, in many ways. When Simon started to have children of his own, he would try to remember how his own father had done it, like an apprentice trying to study the master, but he always felt as though he was falling short.

Did Simon's children love their father as much as Simon had loved his?

Did they respect him like that?

Did Simon make them feel that kind of safe?

And mostly: Would his father have taken his eye off the ball and let his daughter become a junkie? Would he have stood by idly while his wife got shot?

Those were the thoughts that haunted Simon as he stepped on the campus where he'd spent four years.

Students hurried by him, mostly with their heads down. He could make the standard whining observation about how the youngsters were all staring at their little screen or had headphones jammed into their ears, how they all wanted to shut out the world so that they could be surrounded by people and yet completely alone, but his generation was just as bad, so what was the point?

Simon spotted the bronze statue of Athena, the Greek goddess of wisdom, sitting on her throne. If you looked closely, Simon knew, you could find a tiny owl hidden in her cloak by her left leg. Legend had it that the first member of an incoming class to find the owl became the valedictorian. Athena's left arm is outstretched, purportedly to welcome visitors, but Simon sometimes saw it as more like his grandmother's shrug gesture when she'd say, "Eh, what can you do about it?"

His mobile rang again. The caller ID told him it was Elena Ramirez.

"Anything new?" he asked.

"Yeah, a lot."

Elena hit only briefly on the actual reasons she'd gone to Maine, just to say that something was clearly fishy with the adoptions. She concentrated instead on what her tech guy had helped her discover about the DNA genealogy. Simon moved up the steps of Low Library. He half sat, half collapsed on the cool marble and listened as Elena ran through what she had learned—the adoptions, the half brothers on the DNA website, the sudden deaths.

"Someone is killing them off," Simon said at one point.

"It seems so, yes."

He wasn't sure what he felt when she told him that Paige, who had signed up for the same DNA genealogy test, was not a blood relative. It should have been a comfort—didn't it mean that he was indeed the father?—but then a thought occurred to him.

"We don't know for sure," he said.

"Don't know what for sure, Simon?"

"That Paige isn't a half sibling too."

"How so?"

"Maybe Paige didn't list her real name. I read about a few cases where people put in other people's DNA or fake names or whatever. So maybe she's that other sibling, the one with initials."

"NB?"

"Right."

"No, Simon, that can't be."

"Why not?"

"He's listed as a male. If Paige put her own DNA in here, even if she used a fake name, they'd know if the DNA sample came from a male or a female. This was from a male. So NB can't be Paige."

"So maybe she used another pseudonym."

"Maybe. But we now control Henry Thorpe's page. It lists all his relatives. There are no female relatives who are closer than a third cousin."

"So I still don't get it. How is Paige involved?"

"Through Aaron somehow, but I don't know. Maybe we've been looking at it the wrong way."

"How so?"

"Maybe your daughter put someone else's DNA in instead of her own."

"I thought about that, but why?"

"I don't know. We need to track down her movements. Maybe Paige discovered something. A crime or something that made no sense. Something that led her to Aaron."

Simon thought about it. "Let's take a step back and see what we know for sure."

"Yeah, okay."

"First off, all of these men came from the same biological father."

"Right."

"They were all probably adopted out of the same small agency in Maine."

"Right."

"And there was some kind of cover-up. The father's name isn't listed on the adoption reports."

"As far as we know right now, yeah," Elena said.

Simon switched the phone from his right hand to his left. "Have you read about those cases where an infertility doctor ends up using his own semen to impregnate his patients? There was one case in Indiana, I think, where a woman found eight unknown siblings on one of these DNA sites, sort of like what you're saying here, and then the siblings all got together and figured out the infertility doctor had been using his own sperm and pretending it came from a bank or something."

"Yeah, I remember," Elena said. "There are a number of cases like that. A big one in Utah, Canada too."

"You sound skeptical."

"I just don't see how it would work here. The women in those cases weren't giving up the babies for adoption. They wanted them more than anything."

She had a point.

"We're still missing something," he said.

"Agree. So I'm going to take another run at Alison Mayflower because she's the one who set up the adoptions. I'm going to threaten her with prison, whatever it takes. I also want to try to get the FBI interested, but I'll have to do that through a backdoor channel."

"Why?"

"All the info I just gave you, you can't tell anyone. Someone could claim that it was obtained illegally—the fruits of a bad act or some such thing. Either way, even if we go to the feds today, it won't be a priority. It'll take days, probably weeks, just to get it assigned to someone. We don't have . . ." There was a pause. "Simon, hold on, I have another call."

Simon's eyes drifted across the campus. He remembered something that had impressed his father during the tour. The main campus—where Simon now sat on these steps, across College Walk where he'd entered, then past the South Fields—was bookended by Low Library and Butler Library.

"Two libraries, Simon," his father had said with a shake of his head. "What better symbol of learning?"

Odd thought to conjure up right now, but it was keeping Simon from allowing a bigger, uglier one to consume him: Even if he could figure out what was going on with these half brothers and adoptions, how could that help him find Paige?

Elena came back on the line. "Simon?"

A man hurried past him on the steps on his way, no doubt, to the *Alma Mater* statue. Simon recognized the face from his online profile—Professor Louis van de Beek. With the phone still against his ear, Simon stood to follow.

"Yeah, what's up?" he said.

"Gotta go. Alison Mayflower wants to meet."

CHAPTER

THIRTY

A sh parked the car behind the house. You couldn't see the car from the road, but Dee Dee still stood guard, just in case someone made the turn into the long driveway. Ash checked the back of the car. The bags were all there. He unzipped them and laid the weapons across the backseat.

All present and accounted for.

He grabbed what he needed, put the other weapons back in the bag, and whistled with two fingers. When Dee Dee came back, he handed her an FN 5.7.

"You had time to think," he said.

"About?"

"Mother Adiona's note. First off, who is she?"

"She serves in the chamber. That's as high up as any woman can go."

"Do you think she's loyal to your cult?"

"Don't call it a cult," Dee Dee said. "And yes. There is only one other mother, who is known as Mother Abeona. They both were of such pure Truth that they were the ones he chose to create the Visitor and the Volunteer."

"So Vartage's kids," he said, "they're only half brothers?"

"Yes."

"And which one is Mother Adiona's son?"

"The Volunteer."

"So Mother Adiona is the Volunteer's mother. And Mother Abeona is the Visitor's mother."

"Yes." They started toward the back of the house. "Why do you care, Ash?"

"I don't. But I don't like having someone on the inside working against us, do you?"

"I didn't really think of it that way."

"Mother Adiona had someone torture me to find out what we were up to. Then she slipped me a note telling me not to do it. That doesn't worry you at all?"

"Oh, it worries me," she said.

Ash checked the surroundings. "Dee Dee?"

"Yes."

"Why do I think you're not telling me everything?"

She smiled and faced him full-on. Ash felt his heart pick up the pace. "You felt it, didn't you? When you were with him."

"Vartage is charismatic. I'll give you that."

"And Truth Haven?"

"It's peaceful and quiet," he agreed.

"It's more than that. It's serene."

"So?"

"You remember what I was like before?"

He did. A mess. But it hadn't been her fault. Too many foster fathers and teachers and guidance counselors and spiritual advisors, especially the most sanctimonious of them, could not keep their hands and impure thoughts away from her.

"I remember," he said.

"Don't I seem better, Ash?"

"You do." The sun was in his eyes, and he wanted to keep looking at her, so he placed his hand on his forehead, half salute, half visor. "But it doesn't have to be either-or."

"For me it does."

"We can run away." He heard something unfamiliar in his voice now. Desperation. Longing. "I can find us a place. A peaceful place like your haven. Quiet. Serene."

"We could do that," she said. "But it wouldn't stick."

He started to say more, but she put a silencing finger to his lips. "The real world holds too many temptations for me, Ash. Even being out here now, with you, I need to focus, be disciplined, or I'll get hooked again. I'll fall. And I need more."

"More?"

"Yes."

"And blindly believing in this truth nonsense gives you more?"

"Oh, I don't believe in it."

"Wait, what?"

"Most religious people don't believe the dogma, Ash. We take from it what we want, we discard what we don't. We form whatever narrative we like—kind God, vengeful God, active God, laid-back God, whatever. We just make sure we get something out of it. Maybe we get life everlasting while people we resent burn for eternity. Maybe we get something more concrete—money, a job, friends. You just change the narrative."

"I'm surprised to hear that," Ash said.

"Really?"

He cupped both hands around the back window so he could peer into the kitchen. Empty. Lights out. More than that, the kitchen table was covered in a long white cloth, the kind of thing you put on when you're closing up for the season.

Dee Dee said, "When the Truth traveled to Arizona to find that hidden symbol in the desert—the symbol that is the entire basis for our belief in one Truth—do you know what future it foretold?"

Ash turned away from the window.

"When the current embodiment of the Truth dies and ascends to the second level, he would be replaced not by men, but the Truth would be unified and strengthened by two people representing all of humanity. A man. And joining him, a woman. A special woman."

Dee Dee grinned.

Ash looked at her. "You."

She spread her arms to indicate that he was correct.

"And the symbol really foretold this, the stuff about a man and now a woman?"

"No, of course not, Ash."

He made a face indicating he didn't understand.

"This is a recent"—Dee Dee made quote marks with her hand—'interpretation.'"

"So you know," Ash said.

"Know what?"

"You know it's all nonsense."

"No, Ash, you don't get it. Like everyone else, I get what I need to out of it. It nourishes me. Knowing it isn't literal doesn't make my beliefs a less potent force. It makes them stronger. It puts me in control."

"Or in other words," Ash said, "you figured an angle to become ruler."

"That's your perspective. You're entitled to it." Dee Dee checked the time. "Come on. It's almost time."

She started up the hill. Ash followed.

"These jobs of ours," he said. "They encouraged the Truth to form his new, uh, interpretation in your favor, didn't they?"

Dee Dee kept walking. "God isn't the only one who works in mysterious ways."

Simon said, "Professor van de Beek?"

"Please call me Louis."

Van de Beek looked like his bio page—young, pretty-boyish, waxy, toned. He wore the tight black T-shirt too, just as he had in the online photograph. His gaze flitted away as they shook hands, but he flashed a smile anyway, one—Simon couldn't help but think uncharitably—that worked on wooing your co-eds. Like his daughter maybe. Or was such a thought sexist?

"I'm really sorry about Paige," van de Beek said.

"In what way?"

"Pardon?"

"You said you were sorry. Sorry about what?"

"Didn't you say on the phone she was missing?"

"And that's what you're sorry about, Louis?"

The man cringed at the tone, and Simon cursed himself for being too aggressive.

"My apologies," Simon said in a far more genteel voice. "It's just... my wife's been shot. Paige's mother."

"What? Oh, that's awful. Is she...?"

"In a coma."

The color ebbed from his face.

"Hi, Louis!"

Two students—both male, for the record—had spotted him on their way up the Low Library steps. They stopped to be acknowledged, but their greeting hadn't registered.

The other student said, "Louis?"

Simon hated when people called professors by their first name.

Van de Beek snapped out of whatever trance he'd put him into. "Oh hi, Jeremy, hi, Darryl."

He smiled at them, but the bright bulb behind it was seriously flickering. The students sheepishly continued on their way.

"You wanted to tell me something?" Simon prompted.

"What? No, you left me messages."

"Yes, and when you called back, it was clear you had something you wanted to say."

Van de Beek started gnawing on his lower lip.

Simon added, "You were Paige's favorite professor. She trusted you."

290

This was, at best, third-hand information, but it was probably accurate and at the very least, flattering.

"Paige was a wonderful student," he said. "The kind that we professors think about when we grow up wanting to teach."

It felt like a line he'd said plenty of times in the past, but it also sounded like he meant it.

"So what happened?" Simon asked.

"I don't know."

"I sent you a bright, inquisitive young woman. It was her first time on her own, away from the only home and family she'd ever known." Simon felt something rise in him, something he couldn't quite describe—a blend of rage, sadness, regret, paternal love. "I trusted you to watch out for her."

"We try, Mr. Greene."

"And failed."

"You don't know that. But if you're here to spread blame—"

"I'm not. I'm here because I need to find her. Please."

"I don't know where she is."

"Tell me what you remember."

He looked down from their perch above the commons.

"Let's walk," van de Beek said. "It's too weird just standing on these steps like this."

He started down them. Simon stayed by his side.

"Like I said, Paige was a good student," he began. "Super engaged. A lot of kids come in that way, of course. They're almost too fired up. They want to take advantage of every opportunity, and they start burning the candle at both ends. Do you remember your undergraduate years?"

Simon nodded. "I do."

"Where did you go, if I can ask?"

"Here."

"Columbia?" They crossed over College Walk toward Butler Library. "Did you know what you wanted to be when you arrived?"

"Not a clue. I started off in engineering."

"People say college opens the world to you. In some ways, of course, that's true. But for the most part, it does the opposite. You come in thinking you can do anything when you leave. Your options are endless. Point of fact though, your options dwindle every day you're here. By the time you graduate, again, reality has splash-landed."

"What does this have to do with Paige?" he asked.

He stared off, a smile on his lips. "She did all that quickly. But in the best way. She found her calling. Genetics. She wanted to be a doctor. A healer like her mother. She knew that within weeks. She started coming to office hours as often as I'd let her. She wanted to know what track to take to become my TA. I thought she was doing really well. And then something changed."

"What?"

He kept walking. "There are rules, Mr. Greene. I need you to understand that. About what we can tell parents of students. If a student asks for confidentiality, we have to give it to them—up to a limit. Are you familiar with the campus rules on Title IX?"

Simon's blood froze. Eileen Vaughan had said something when he'd visited her at Lanford, something about how Paige and Eileen's mutual friend Judy Zyskind suspected Paige had been the victim of a sexual assault at a frat party. Simon had sort of blocked on that because one, it was too awful to even consider, but two, more importantly, Paige had dismissed it when Judy confronted her about it. That was the part that had stuck with Simon. Judy had pushed Paige, and according to Eileen, Paige had not only denied it but finally ended the conversation:

"She said there were problems at home . . ."

They veered off the path and reached the glass-enclosed structure called Lerner Hall. There was a café on the bottom floor. Van de Beek reached for the door, but Simon grabbed hold of his elbow.

"Was my daughter sexually assaulted?" he asked.

"I think so."

"Think so?"

"Paige came to me in confidence. She was distraught. There had been an incident at a campus party."

Simon felt his hands tighten into fists. "She told you about it?"

"She started to, yes."

"What does that mean, 'started to'?"

"The first thing I did, before I let her go into details, was to inform her that I'd have to follow the Title IX guidelines."

"What guidelines?"

"Mandatory reporting," he said.

"Meaning?"

"If a student tells me about an incident of sexual assault, no matter what that student wants, I have to report it to the Title IX coordinator."

"Even if the victim doesn't want you to?"

"Even if, that's right. Frankly I don't love this rule. I get it. I understand the reasoning. But I think it makes some students less likely to confide in a teacher because they know, like it or not, that the teacher will have to report it. So they clam up. And that was what happened here."

"Paige wouldn't talk to you?"

"She more or less stormed out. I tried to follow, but she ran away. I called. I texted. I emailed. I stopped by her room once. She wouldn't talk to me."

Simon felt his fingers tighten up a little more. "And you didn't think to tell her parents?"

"I thought about it, sure. But again there are rules about such things. I also checked with the Title IX coordinator."

"What did she say?"

"It was a he."

For real? "What did *he* say?"

"He talked to Paige. She denied anything happened."

"And you still didn't think to call her parents?"

"That's right, Mr. Greene."

"So instead my daughter, who was possibly raped, just suffered in silence."

"There are guidelines. We have to follow them."

That was crap and when this was all over, Simon would do what he could to get payback, but right now he had to focus on the task at hand. He didn't want to. He wanted to collapse and cry for his daughter.

"So is that when Paige started to spiral?"

Van de Beek thought it over. His answer surprised him. "No, not really. I know how that sounds, but the next time I saw her—"

"Which was when?"

"A few days later. Paige showed up in class. She seemed better. I remember standing behind the lectern and looking at her, a little surprised to see her, and she gave me this nod like 'I'm okay, don't worry about it.' A few days later, she started coming to office hours again. I can't tell you how thrilled I was to see her. I tried to raise the topic, but she said it was no big deal, that she overreacted. I'm not saying she was totally fine. I could see that she was trying to block. I urged her to get help, to talk to someone. One of the hardest parts is that the girls are still on the same campus as their alleged attacker."

"Rapist."

"What?"

"Don't call him an alleged attacker. Call him a rapist."

"I don't know what he was."

"But you do know who, right?"

He stood there.

"You do, don't you?"

"She didn't tell me."

"But you know the name of the boy."

He looked off. "I have a guess. At least I do now."

"What does that mean?"

Van de Beek put his hand through his thick hair and let loose

294

a long breath. "This is where the story takes a bizarre turn, Mr. Greene."

Like it hasn't already? Simon thought.

"I don't know the order," van de Beek continued. "I'm not sure what came first—Paige's deterioration or..." He stopped.

"Or what?"

"There was another"—he paused, looked up as though search-ing for the right word—"incident on campus."

"Incident," Simon repeated.

"Yes."

"Do you mean rape?"

Van de Beek winced. "Paige didn't use the word 'rape.' Never. Just for the record."

Now, Simon knew, was not the time to get into a semantics debate. "Was there another assault?"

"Yes."

"Was it done by the same boy?"

He shook his head. "Just the opposite."

"Meaning?"

"The boy I believe may have assaulted Paige," van de Beek said, his words coming more measured now. "He was the victim this time."

He met Simon's gaze. Simon did not blink.

"His name is Doug Mulzer, a sophomore econ major from Pitts-burgh. He was beaten with a baseball bat after a frat party on cam-pus. Broken legs. And then, the smaller end of the bat, it was..." He started to stammer. "Well, that part of the attack was never made public. The family didn't want it known, but the rumors spread around campus. He's still convalescing in Pittsburgh."

Simon could feel the chill work its way up his spine. "And you think Paige had something to do with this?"

He opened his mouth, closed it, tried again. Simon could see that he was straining to be careful with his words. "I can't say for sure."

295

"But?"

"But in class the next day, Paige just kept smiling. Everyone else was upset over what had happened. But Paige kept staring at me and grinning in this weird way, and I could see for the first time that she was glassy eyed. Like she was on something. Like she was high."

"So your evidence is that she got high and smiled?" Simon asked. "Maybe she got high to numb the pain."

Van de Beek said nothing.

"I don't care what she was on," Simon said, picturing the sickening assault in his head. "Paige wouldn't do something like that."

"I agree." Another student walked by and shouted out a "Hi, Louis!" and van de Beek gave him an absentminded nod. "She wouldn't do something like that. At least, not on her own."

Simon froze.

"But when Paige left class that day, I noticed that there was a man waiting for her. Not a kid. Not a student. A man I'd guess was about ten years older."

Aaron, Simon thought. *It was Aaron.*

THIRTY-ONE

A ll the info I just gave you, you can't tell anyone," Elena had said. "Someone could claim that it was obtained illegally—the fruits of a bad act or some such thing. Either way, even if we go to the feds today, it won't be a priority. It'll take days, probably weeks, just to get it assigned to someone. We don't have..."

Elena heard a click on her line. Another call was coming in. The caller ID was blocked. Most people would suspect that it was some kind of spam call, but Lou had arranged something on the phones to prevent that. If she got a call, it was usually something relevant.

And the last person she had given her card to was Alison Mayflower.

"Simon, hold on, I have another call."

She clicked over. "Hello?"

"Uh, hi." A woman's whisper. Not Alison Mayflower. This woman sounded young—twenties, maybe thirties. "Is this Miss Ramirez?"

"This is she. Who is this?"

"Oh, my name isn't important."

"Could you speak up?"

"Sorry, I'm a little nervous. I'm calling…I'm calling for a friend of mine. You met her today at a certain café."

"Go on."

"She needs to see you—boy, does she need to see you—but she's afraid."

Alison Mayflower, Elena recalled, lived with another woman named Stephanie Mars. Could be her on the line.

"I understand," Elena said in her gentlest voice. "Maybe we can meet someplace where she'd feel comfortable."

"Yes. Alison really wants that."

"Can you hold on just one split second?"

"Okay."

Elena moved fast. "Simon?"

"Yeah, what's up?"

"Gotta go. Alison Mayflower wants to meet."

Elena clicked back over. "I know where you two live. I can drive—"

"No!" the young-sounding woman said in a panicked hush. "They'll follow you! Don't you see?"

Elena actually put up a calming hand, which of course made no sense when you're on the phone. "Okay, sure, I see."

"They're watching you. They're watching us."

The woman sounded more than a little paranoid, but then again, at least three people were dead.

"No worries," Elena said, keeping her tone even and casual. "Let's make a plan. Something you two are both comfortable with."

It took about ten minutes for them to come up with something that seemed to pacify the caller. Elena would take an Uber to the Cracker Barrel Old Country Store near Route 95. She would stand out front. Stephanie—she finally said her name out loud—would flash her lights twice and drive up.

"What kind of car will you be driving?" Elena had asked.

298

"I'd rather not say. Just in case."

Elena would then get in the car and be taken to see Alison at a "secret location." Yes, Stephanie actually used the phrase "secret location."

"Come alone," Stephanie said.

"I will. I promise."

"If we see someone is following you, we're calling it off."

They agreed that Stephanie would "call and ring once" as a signal that she was "set up" at the Cracker Barrel. When they were off the phone, Elena sat on the bed and Googled Stephanie Mars. Nothing much came up. Elena changed into her other blue blazer, the one with a little more space for a holster and gun. She thought about calling Simon back but chose instead to send a text letting him know that she hoped to meet with Alison Mayflower soon. Her phone was charging. She let Lou know that she'd be going out for a meet. Lou had put a high-end tracker on her phone, so the home office could know her location if need be 24/7.

An hour passed before the blocked number called again. Elena waited. One ring and a hang up. The signal. Elena had been constantly checking her ride-share apps. One showed a car eight minutes away. It arrived in fifteen.

The Cracker Barrel in South Portland had the same faux rustic exterior that they all did. The front porch held a plethora of rocking chairs, all empty. Elena stood and waited. It didn't take long. A vehicle flashed its beams at her. Elena surreptitiously took a photo of the car, making sure she got the license plate, and sent it to Lou.

Just in case. You never know.

When the car pulled up, Elena opened the passenger door and looked inside. The driver was an attractive young woman wearing a Red Sox baseball cap.

"Stephanie?"

"Please get in. Quickly."

Elena wasn't the most agile, so it took a little time. As soon as she was seated, even before the door was fully closed, Stephanie Mars hit the accelerator.

"Do you have a phone?" Stephanie asked.

"Yes."

"Put it in the glove compartment."

"Why?"

"This is just between you and Alison. No recordings, no calls, no texts."

"I'm not sure I'm comfortable with giving up my phone."

Stephanie hit the brake. "Then we call this off right now. You're carrying a gun, right?"

Elena didn't answer.

"Put your gun in the glove compartment too. I don't know if you work for them or not."

"Who is them?"

"Now please."

"One of the adopted boys is missing. I work for his father."

"And we're just supposed to take your word on that?" The young woman shook her head in disbelief. "Please put your phone and gun in the glove compartment. You can have them back after you talk to Alison."

No choice. Elena took out her phone and gun. She popped open the glove compartment in front of her, dropped them inside, and closed it again. It wouldn't take long to retrieve them if there was an emergency.

Elena studied Stephanie Mars's profile. She had red-to-auburn hair, probably cut short—hard to say for sure with that baseball cap on—and was, in a word, beautiful. High cheekbones. Flawless skin. She kept both hands on the wheel at ten and two, focusing hard on the road as though she were new to driving.

"Before I let you see Alison, I need to ask you a few questions."

"Okay," Elena said.

"Who exactly hired you?"

Elena was going to say that she was not at liberty to divulge, but her client had already told her that it would be okay, that he didn't care who knew. "Sebastian Thorpe. He adopted a boy he named Henry."

"And Henry is missing?"

"That's right."

"Any clue where he is?"

"That's what I'm working on."

"I don't understand."

"Don't understand what?"

"How old is Henry Thorpe?"

"Twenty-four."

"How could his adoption have anything to do with his life now?"

"It might not."

"She's a good person, you know. Alison, I mean. She'd never hurt anyone."

"And I don't want to hurt her," Elena said. "I only want to find my client's son. But that's the thing. If Alison did do something illegal—"

"She'd never."

"I know. But if something about these adoptions was not completely by the book, and if she doesn't cooperate, well, then it's on her. All the walls come crashing down."

"That sounds like a threat."

"It's not meant to. It's meant to convey the severity of the situation. I'm Alison's best chance to do the right thing—and stay out of legal trouble."

Stephanie Mars regripped the steering wheel, her hands shaking. "I don't know what's best."

"I don't want to hurt either one of you."

"Do you promise you won't tell anyone about this?"

Elena couldn't really make that promise. It depended on what Alison Mayflower said. Still, a small deception at this stage was the least of her worries right now. "Yes, I promise."

The car veered to the right.

"Where is she?" Elena asked.

"My aunt Sally has a summer cabin." The younger woman actually managed a smile. "It's where Alison and I first met. They're friends, Aunt Sally and Alison. So, see, my aunt has a barbecue to open the season every year, and six years ago, Alison and I were both invited. I know she's older than I am, but, well, you've seen her. She's young in so many ways. We met by the grill in the backyard—she makes the best skirt steak...Alison, I mean—and we started talking and..." She shrugged, smiled, sneaked a glance at Elena. "That was it."

"Sounds nice," Elena said.

"You have someone?"

The pang. Always the pang.

"No," Elena said. Then she added, "I used to, but he died."

Elena couldn't say why she told her that. Could be a subconscious ploy to bond. Could be that she just felt it needed to be said.

"His name was Joel."

"I'm sorry."

"Thank you."

"We're almost there."

They pulled into the drive. At the end of it, there was a log cabin, the genuine article, not the snap-together look or faux-Cracker-Barrel-type situation. Elena couldn't help but smile.

"Aunt Sally has good taste."

"Yeah, she does."

"Is she here?"

"Sally? No. She's still in Philly, won't be up for months. I come here on my own once a week, kinda like a caretaker. No one really knows about the place, and you can see cars coming a mile away, so Alison thought it'd be safe." She put the car into park and looked at Elena with her big eyes.

"We're putting our trust in you. Come on."

As they got out of the car, two words came to mind: "green" and "quiet." Elena took in a deep breath of seriously fresh air. Nice. Her leg ached. That old wound, her constant companion. Stephanie Mars had told her about her initial chance encounter with Alison at a barbecue here. Fate, destiny, chaos, however two souls get thrown together. Joel loved to tease that he and Elena had the best "meet cute" in history, and while she'd wave him off, maybe Joel was right.

During a raid on a white-supremacist militia compound outside Billings, Montana, Elena had been shot in the "high upper leg"—a nicer way of saying "ass." The shot didn't hurt as much as you might think, at least not right away. It was more embarrassing than painful, and Elena, being one of the rare Hispanic women on the job, had felt as though she'd let down herself and her people.

It was at the nearby hospital, while she was recovering, her butt propped up on one of those inflatable tire-like devices so there was no undue pressure on her wound, that Special Agent Joel Marcus first came into her room—and boom, into her life.

"Little did I know," Joel often joked, "how much I'd enjoy seeing that ass up in the air in the future."

She half smiled at the memory as Stephanie pushed open the door and called out, "Alison? Honey?"

No answer.

Without conscious thought, Elena started reaching for her piece, but of course, it was back in the car. Stephanie Mars hurried inside the house. Elena came through the door right behind her. Stephanie veered left and moved faster. Elena turned her head in that direction and was about to follow.

But the younger woman had stopped moving. She slowly turned back toward Elena.

The younger woman's beautiful face broke into a smile, just

as Elena felt something cold press against the back of her skull.

Their eyes met—Elena's sad brown and the young woman's wild green.

And Elena knew.

She thought of Joel when she heard the click and hoped, in the moment before the gun exploded, that she'd be with him again.

CHAPTER
THIRTY-TWO

Ash stood over Elena's dead body.

She'd landed facedown, head turned to the side at an unnatural angle, eyes open. Blood flowed out of the back of her head, but Ash had already put down a tarp to make cleanup easier. Dee Dee put a hand on his arm and squeezed. He looked up at her and saw that smile. A man knows his great love's various smiles. That was what they said—the smile when she was happy or the smile when she was genuinely laughing or the smile when she peered into the eyes of the man she loved, all that.

Ash knew this smile—the smile she saved for extreme violence—and he didn't like it.

"Is it different for you?" Dee Dee asked him. "Killing a woman instead of a man."

Ash was not in the mood. "Where's her phone?"

"It's still in the glove compartment."

Ash had put a battery-operated jamming device in the glove compartment, so if someone was tracking her whereabouts—and he suspected that they might be—they'd be getting a no-signal. "Pull the car around back and bring me the phone."

Dee Dee put her hands on either side of his face. "You okay, Ash?"

"I'm fine, but we have to move fast."

She gave him a quick kiss on the cheek and hurried outside. Ash started to wrap the body in the tarp. They'd already dug a hole, so that no one would find her. When Dee Dee brought him Elena's phone, he would send out a few "I'm fine" texts to anyone looking for her. It would take a few days, probably more, before someone started seriously investigating Elena Ramirez's disappearance.

By then, Ash and Dee Dee would be done with the jobs. There'd be no clues.

"Ironic," Dee Dee had said when Ash told her the plan. And while the actual meaning of the word "ironic" seemed elusive to Ash—he remembered people saying that Alanis Morissette had gotten it wrong in that song—it seemed to fit here. Elena Ramirez had been hired to find a "missing" Henry Thorpe. But Thorpe had been dead the whole time. And now, Elena Ramirez would be "missing" too.

Dee Dee came back into the house with the phone and jammer. "Here you go."

"Finish wrapping her up."

She mock-saluted him. "You're in a mood."

Ash bent down next to the body and picked up Elena's hand. There should still be enough electrical impulse traveling through her body, so that her thumb could still unlock her phone. He pressed the phone against the pad.

Bingo.

The phone's wallpaper was a photograph of Elena smiling widely, her arms wrapped around a far taller man who was smiling just as wide.

Dee Dee looked over his shoulder. "Do you think that's her Joel?"

"I'd suspect so, yes." Ash had listened to the whole conversation in the car because Dee Dee kept her phone on. "Do you even have an Aunt Sally?" he asked her.

"No."

He shook his head in amazement. "You're good."

"Do you remember our middle school production of *West Side Story*?"

Ash had worked building the sets. She'd been one of the Sharks girls.

"I should have been Maria—I killed the audition—but Mr. Orloff gave it to Julia Ford because her father owned that Lexus dealership."

Dee Dee didn't say this with anger or pity. She was being accurate. Ash was enamored, no doubt about it, but Dee Dee had real star quality. You could just see it. Everyone in the auditorium, even though she'd just been in the chorus, couldn't take their eyes off her.

Dee Dee could have been a great actress, a big star, but what kind of break was she, a foster beauty constantly fending off male adults, going to get?

His tone was tender. "You were great in that play, Dee Dee."

She worked on the tarp now, wrapping it around the body.

"I mean it."

"Thank you, Ash."

He clicked on the Settings key and then found the Privacy icon. From there, he tapped Location Services and scrolled all the way to the bottom to where it said System Services. He scrolled again and found Significant Locations. When he pressed to see it, the screen asked for the thumb again. He grabbed Elena's and used it. Then he changed the password so he could get in without the thumb next time.

People don't realize how much of their privacy they casually give away. On any iPhone at any time, you could do what Ash was now doing: see the complete history of where the phone's owner—in this case, Elena Ramirez—had recently visited.

"Damn," he said.

"What?"

"She's been to the tattoo parlor."

"We had to figure that was a possibility, Ash. That's why we had to act fast."

He checked through the list of locations and saw several spots in New York City. Most recently, Elena Ramirez had been at Columbia Medical Center near 168th Street. Ash wondered why. Then he noticed something more troubling.

"She's been to the Bronx."

Dee Dee finished tying the rope around the tarp. "Same location?"

He clicked it and nodded.

"Oh, that's not good," Dee Dee said.

"We have to hurry."

He scanned through her phone log and texts. The most recent text, coming in eight minutes ago, read:

Have you met with Alison yet? Please fill me in when you can.

Dee Dee saw the look on his face. "What is it?"

"Someone else is getting close."

"Who?"

Ash flipped the phone around, so Dee Dee could read the screen. "We're going to have to do something about a guy named Simon Greene."

CHAPTER

THIRTY-THREE

S imon collapsed into a seat on the subway. He stared out the window across the car without focusing, letting the underground whiz by in a hazy blur. He tried to comprehend what he'd just learned. Nothing made sense. He'd gotten more pieces to the puzzle, important pieces, perhaps even an explanation of what had started his daughter's spiral into drug addiction. But the more pieces he got, the less clear the final image was becoming.

When he got back up onto the street, a text came in from Yvonne.

Money is ready. You'll need to sign for it. Ask for Todd
Raisch.

The bank was located between a Wendy's and a high-end bakery. There was no line and just one teller. He gave his name and asked to speak to Todd Raisch. Raisch was all professional. He showed Simon into a back room.

"Are hundreds okay?" he asked.

Simon said that they were. Raisch counted out the money.

"Would you like a bag for that?"

Simon had his own, a plastic bag Ingrid had saved from a recent trip to Zabar's. He put the cash in that and then jammed the bag into his backpack. He thanked Raisch and started on his way.

As he headed up Broadway toward the hospital, Simon called Randy Spratt, the genetics tech. When he answered, Simon said, "I have the money."

"Ten minutes."

He hung up. Simon checked to see if there were any messages yet from Elena Ramirez. Nothing. It was probably too soon, but he sent a quick text anyway:

Have you met with Alison yet? Please fill me in when you can.

No immediate reply. No dancing dots indicating an answer was forthcoming.

Simon kept staring at his phone as he walked, mostly to distract himself from this upcoming rendezvous. He'd rushed himself on the paternity test, panicked even, without really considering the repercussions. But now that he had a second or two—now that the answer was about to, like it or not, slap him in the face—he wondered what he would do if he learned the worst.

Suppose he wasn't Paige's biological father?

Suppose he wasn't Sam's or Anya's father either?

Slow down, he told himself.

But there really was no time to slow down, was there? The truth, one way or the other, was barreling toward him like a freight train. He still really couldn't fathom it. For one thing, Sam looked just like him, everyone said so, and though he couldn't see it himself—could any parents?—he knew...

He knew what?

It simply wasn't possible. Ingrid would never do that to him. And yet that small niggling voice taunted him. He remembered reading some statistic that 10 percent of fathers are unknowingly raising another man's child. Or was it really 2 percent? Or was that all nonsense?

When Simon reached the clearing behind the pediatric wing, Randy Spratt was already on a bench in the corner. Spratt sat upright with his hands jammed deep in the pockets of his trench coat, his gaze darting about like a scared rodent.

Simon sat next to him. The two men stared straight ahead.

"You got the money?" Spratt whispered.

"This isn't a ransom drop, you know."

"Do you have it or not?"

Simon reached into his backpack for the plastic bag. He hesitated. He didn't have to go through with opening this particular Pandora's box. Maybe ignorance was bliss in some cases, no? He'd lived happily without knowing Ingrid's "secret past."

Right, and look where that had brought them.

Simon handed over the cash. For a second, he feared that Spratt would count it right there and then, but the plastic bag quickly disappeared into the trench coat.

"Well?" Simon asked.

"The one you said was a priority. The yellow toothbrush."

Simon felt his mouth go dry. "Yes."

"I rushed that one, so it's the only result I have with a scientifically definitive conclusion."

Interesting that Spratt hadn't told him that before he got paid, but maybe that didn't matter.

"And what's the conclusion?" Simon asked.

"It's positive."

"Wait, does that mean ...?"

"You're the biological father."

Relief, sweet relief, flooded Simon's lungs and veins.

"And for what it's worth, even though the results are only preliminary, all indications are that you're the biological father for all three."

Without another word, Randy Spratt rose and walked away. Simon just sat there, unable to move. He watched an old woman wearing the standard-issue hospital smock and leaning on a walker make her way to a flower bed. She bent down and smelled the flowers, both literally and metaphorically. Simon did the latter by just sitting there and watching. A group of young medical residents sat on the grass and ate gyros from a nearby food truck. They all looked both frayed and happy, like Ingrid did during her residency, when she worked ridiculous hours but knew that she was one of the lucky few who found her calling.

Being a physician, Simon knew, was indeed a calling.

Weird thought, but there you go. Or maybe not so weird. Simon had recently learned that Paige had shared her mother's calling. Under normal circumstances, it would mean the world to him. In some ways, it still did.

He had to find her.

He checked his phone, hoping to see something from Elena Ramirez. No new message. He typed her another one:

DNA test shows I'm Paige's father. Still don't know how she hooked up with Aaron, but I think it's about the illegal adoptions. Call me when you finish with Alison Mayflower.

It was time to head back to Ingrid's room. He stood up, tilted his face to the sky, closed his eyes. He just needed another moment or two. He and Ingrid had taken a few yoga classes as a marital bonding thing, and the instructor had been all about the importance of breathing. So he took a deep inhale, held it, let it out slowly.

Didn't help.

He felt his phone vibrate. Elena was replying:

Heading over the border to Canada for this

> meet, so I might be out
> of touch for a few days.
> Where will you be?

Canada? He wasn't sure what to make of that.

He typed: At hospital for now, but that could change.

He hit Send and waited. The dancing dots started up, showing that Elena was typing.

> Let me know of any
> new developments.
> It's vital to keep me in
> the loop, even if I
> can't reply.

Simon wrote back that he would as he checked in with hospital security and took the elevator up to the ICU. He was tempted to ask Elena why Canada or why she might not be able to reply, but he figured that she'd tell him what he needed to know. As the elevator doors opened, the terrible ache from what van de Beek had told him returned tenfold.

What had happened to Paige on that campus?

Block, he told himself. *Block or you won't be able to take another step.*

The nurses were in with Ingrid, bathing her and changing her clothes, so Sam paced the corridor. He spotted his father and gave him a quick, hard hug.

"Sorry," Sam said.

"It's okay."

"I didn't mean it. About you getting Mom shot."

"I know."

Sam gave his father a weary smile. "You know what Mom would say if she heard me blame you?"

"What?"

313

"She'd say I was being sexist. She'd say I would never have blamed her if you got shot."

Simon liked that. "You know what? I think you're right."

"Where were you?" Sam asked.

Simon wanted to protect his son, only natural, but he also didn't want to coddle him. "I just talked to one of Paige's professors."

Sam looked at him.

He used the vaguest terms possible to let Sam know about the sexual assault—he may not want to coddle, but he didn't want to just chuck his son in the deep end either. Sam listened without interrupting. He fought to remain stoic, but Simon recognized the telltale quiver of his lower lip.

"When was this exactly?" Sam asked when his father had finished.

"I'm not sure. Toward the end of first semester."

"She called me one night. Paige. Out of the blue. I mean, I don't think we'd exchanged more than a few texts, and we never called each other."

"What did she say?"

"She just said she wanted to talk."

"About?"

"I don't know." Sam gave a too-big shrug. "It was late on a Friday night. There was a party at Martin's. I didn't really listen. I just wanted to get her off the line. So yeah, that's what I did."

Simon put his hand on his son's shoulder. "It might not have been the same night, Sam."

"Right," Sam said in the most unconvincing voice he could muster. "Might not have been."

Simon was about to follow up more, but he heard someone clear his throat. He turned and was surprised to see the man who saved Ingrid's life standing behind him.

"Cornelius?"

He still wore the ripped jeans and the unruly white-gray beard.

"How's Ingrid doing?" Cornelius asked.

"Hard to say." Simon brought Sam into the fold. "Sam, this is Cornelius. He..." Simon couldn't tell him that Cornelius had shot Luther and thus saved not just Ingrid but Simon as well. "Cornelius owns the building where Paige lived in the Bronx. He's been a big help to us."

Sam stuck out his hand. "Nice to meet you."

"You too, young man." Cornelius faced Simon. "Can I talk to you a second?"

"Sure."

"I need to use the bathroom anyway," Sam said before moving down the corridor.

Simon turned to Cornelius. "What's up?"

"I need you to come with me," Cornelius said.

"Where?"

"Back to my apartment. Rocco is going to be there. With Luther. They got something you need to hear."

CHAPTER
THIRTY-FOUR

A sh and Dee Dee had prepared, so they moved fast.

They tossed Elena's body in a wheelbarrow by the back door. Ash maneuvered the wheelbarrow into the woods while Dee Dee stayed at the cabin and finished the cleanup.

Digging a hole takes a while. Filling it in, not so much.

As they drove south, Dee Dee kept going through Elena's phone.

"Not much here," she told Ash. "Elena Ramirez is a bigwig at VMB Investigations. We already knew that. Her client was Henry Thorpe's father. We already knew that." She looked up. "It's approved, by the way."

"What's approved?"

"Simon Greene. You'll be given the same payment as the others."

"Google him," Ash said. "I want to see what we can learn."

She started typing. It didn't take long. The PPG Wealth Management group website came up, complete with Simon Greene's biography. There were two photos of him—a headshot and a group picture with the entire PPG team.

They passed the state line.

"Twelve percent battery left," Dee Dee said. "Do we have a charger for this kind of phone?"

"Check the pocket behind my seat."

Dee Dee was just stretching to do that when Elena's phone vibrated. A new message came in from Simon Greene. She read it out loud to Ash:

DNA test shows I'm Paige's father. Still don't know how she hooked up with Aaron, but I think it's about the illegal adoptions. Call me when you finish with Alison Mayflower.

Ash asked her to read it again. Then he said, "If we don't answer him, he may start to worry about Elena Ramirez and make calls."

"How about...?" She started typing:

Heading over the border to Canada for this meet, so I might be out of touch for a few days. Where will you be?

Ash nodded.

Dee Dee stared at the screen as Ash hit the accelerator. "He's typing a reply," she said.

"We should probably get off the messaging app when you're done with this."

"Why?"

"There might be a way to trace it, I don't know."

The phone vibrated again:

At hospital for now, but that could change.

"Hospital," Dee Dee repeated. "Should I ask which one?"

"No, he'll get suspicious. Besides, we know already. Elena's history had recent visits to one in upper Manhattan."

"Good point. How about...?"

She typed it up and then read it out loud to him: "Let me know of any new developments. It's vital to keep me in the loop, even if I can't reply."

Ash nodded and told her to hit Send. She did.

"Now shut it down."

They drove in silence for a few more minutes before Dee Dee said, "What?"

"You know what."

"I really don't."

"Simon Greene's text," Ash said.

"What about it?"

"I assume the Aaron is Aaron Corval?"

"I assume the same."

"So who is Paige?"

"Aaron's girlfriend, right?"

"Why would her father be involved?"

"I don't know." Dee Dee turned toward him, tucking her feet under her butt. "I thought you didn't care about the whys, Ash."

"I normally don't."

"You didn't like killing that woman," Dee Dee said. "Men are fine to kill, but a woman?"

"Will you stop? It's not that."

"Then what?"

"Someone connected the dots. That makes the motives and details my business now."

Dee Dee turned and looked out the window.

"Unless you don't trust me," he said.

"You know I trust you. I trust you more than anyone in the world."

Ash felt a small ping in his chest. "So?"

"As it was written in the Symbols, the Visitor and the Volunteer must be the first two male children born from the Truth," she began. "Being male is, of course, paramount. Daughters—and the Truth has at least twenty—don't really matter in terms of leadership. But male blood is the purest bond because it is the only one with a physical component. A spouse doesn't share your blood. Neither does the closest friend. So in terms of scientific proof—"

"Dee?"

"Yes?"

"Skip the jargon. I get it. Vartage's two sons inherit the leadership."

"They inherit everything. That's the point. That is how it is written in the Symbols: 'The two sons will rise.'"

"So what does that have to do with all this?"

"It is also written," she said, "that Truth Haven and all of the Truth's possessions will be equally divided amongst his male heirs."

"Okay, so?"

"It didn't specify 'just the oldest two.' Do you get what I'm saying?"

Ash was starting to see it. "Vartage had more than these two sons?"

"Yes."

"And the other sons—"

"—were put up for adoption, yes," Dee Dee said. "Sold really. Daughters were kept. They'd be useful. But the sons could inherit and ruin the prophesies. This was all years ago—before my time."

"So Vartage just sold his other sons off?"

"It was win-win, Ash. We keep the two-son prophesy—and we make a great deal of money for the Haven."

"Wow."

"Yes."

"And the mothers would just agree with this?"

"Some would," Dee Dee said, "and some wouldn't."

"So how did that work?"

"The Truth slept with a lot of women. Obviously, some got pregnant. They were told that if their babies were male, they would be destined for better things. That meant going to the Greater Haven in Arkansas. It would be best for the male child."

"There's another haven in—?"

"No, Ash, there's not."

He just shook his head. "And the mothers just bought this?"

"Some did, some didn't. It was an internal struggle for these mothers between the way of the Truth and their maternal instincts. The Truth usually won."

"And when the maternal instincts won?"

"The mothers were told that their babies died in childbirth."

Ash wasn't stunned often. He was now. "Seriously?"

"Yes. There was a big funeral and everything. Some of the mothers believed that the stillbirths were their fault, that if they had just agreed to send their child to the Greater Haven..."

"My God."

Dee Dee nodded. "The male babies were sold. Do you have any idea how much a healthy white male baby could fetch? Beaucoup bucks. Alison Mayflower, who is still loyal to the Truth, worked as the go-between."

"How many babies did the Truth sell?"

"All male."

"Got it. How many?"

"Fourteen."

He kept his hand on the wheel. "And now the Truth is dying."

"Yes."

"And the Vartage boys—the Visitor and the Volunteer or whatever—are afraid these biological sons are going to claim a share of the inheritance."

"For years, the Truth, the Volunteer, and the Visitor—all of us, really—had nothing to fear. There was no way to connect the adopted boys to Truth Haven at all. They were scattered about the country, and just to be on the safe side, Alison Mayflower destroyed all the records. So the Truth could never find his sons—and more important, of course, the sons could never find the Truth."

"So what went wrong?" Ash asked.

"Have you heard about these new DNA websites like 23andMe or Ance-Story?"

He had.

"Tons of adopted people put their DNA in the bank and hope for a hit," Dee Dee said.

"So I assume some of the Truth's sons—"

"Found out about each other, yes."

"And then somehow linked it back to Vartage?"

"Yes."

"So two sons go on the same site, for example. They realize that they are half brothers."

"Right. Then a third. Then a fourth. All fairly recent."

"And someone in your cult decides that the best way to eliminate the problem is to, uh, eliminate the problem." Ash looked at her. Dee Dee smiled again. "In exchange for a leadership position?"

"Something like that."

He had to shake his head in awe. "How much is Truth Haven worth, Dee?"

"Hard to estimate," she said, "but probably close to forty million dollars."

That opened his eyes. "Whoa."

"But this isn't just about the money."

"Yeah, okay."

"Stop being cynical for a second. Just imagine what would happen to Truth Haven if fourteen more sons come forward with claims. It will, in effect, destroy the Truth."

"Come on, Dee."

"What?"

"Will you stop with the Truth? You know that's all a lot of non-sense. You just admitted that to me."

Dee Dee shook her head. "You're so blind, Ash. I love the Truth."

"And you're using it to get what you want."

"Yes, of course. Those two things aren't contradictory. No one believes every passage of a holy book—they pick and choose. And every pastor who makes money from his religion—if he believes in what he preaches or not—is getting something out of it. That's life, my love."

That was wild rationalization, but on some level, it was also absolute truth.

It was getting hot in the car. Ash turned up the AC. "So we only have two more sons to eliminate."

"Yes. One in the Bronx, one in Tallahassee." Then Dee Dee added: "Oh, and now we also have to get rid of Simon Greene."

CHAPTER
THIRTY-FIVE

S imon and Cornelius stood outside the same bank branch where a few hours earlier Simon had withdrawn the money for the DNA test. Rocco had sent Cornelius to make sure Simon understood that he wasn't getting this information for free. So here Simon was, back at the bank, looking to take out more cash.

Because he'd already withdrawn a somewhat large amount of money and didn't want to draw more attention to himself, he'd called Yvonne for help. He spotted her now, walking toward him.

"Any issues?" he asked.

"No." Yvonne glanced over at Cornelius, this black man with the threadbare T-shirt and the thick white beard, then back at Simon. "Who is this?"

"Cornelius," Simon said.

Yvonne turned to him. "And who are you, Cornelius?"

"Just a friend," Cornelius said.

She looked him up and down and then asked, "And what do you need this money for?"

"It's not for him," Simon said. "He's helping me."

"Helping you what?"

Simon quickly explained about Rocco and Luther. He naturally left off the fact that Cornelius had been the one who saved his and Ingrid's lives. When he finished, he braced for Yvonne's counterarguments. None came.

"Stay out of sight," Yvonne said. "I'll get the cash from my account."

Simon wanted to tell Yvonne that he'd pay her back, but Yvonne was Ingrid's sister and would get pissed off if he made the offer, so he just nodded. When Yvonne entered, Simon and Cornelius walked down the block so they weren't loitering directly in front of the bank.

"Good time to fill me in," Cornelius said.

So he did.

"That's messed up," Cornelius said when he finished.

"Yup." Then: "Why did you help us, Cornelius?"

"Why not?"

"I'm serious."

"So am I. Not a lot of chances to be a hero in real life. You got to step up when the opportunity presents itself."

Cornelius shrugged as if to emphasize it was a no-brainer and that simple, and Simon believed that maybe it was.

"Thank you."

"Also Ingrid, she was nice to me."

"When she wakes up, I'm going to tell her what you did, if that's okay."

"Yeah, that's okay," Cornelius said. "You still got the gun I gave you?"

"Yes. You think we'll need it?"

"Never know. But no, I don't think you'll need it. Still, we will make provisions."

"Meaning?"

"Meaning we don't just walk in with thousands of dollars unarmed."

"Got it."

"And one other thing," Cornelius said.

"What's that?"

"Don't let me be the black friend who gets killed. I hate that in movies."

Simon laughed for the first time in what felt like months.

Cornelius's phone buzzed so he stepped aside. Yvonne came out of the bank and handed him the cash. "I asked for nine thousand six hundred and five dollars."

"Why that amount?"

"So it's not the exact same as yours and trips up a computer somewhere. Six hundred and five, six five. June fifth. You know the date?"

He did. Simon's godson Drew, Yvonne's oldest kid, was born on that day.

"I thought maybe it would bring you luck," she said.

Cornelius came back. "That was Rocco."

"What's up?" Simon asked.

"He'll be at my place in a couple of hours. He needs to locate Luther."

Cornelius waited outside the hospital while Simon and Yvonne headed back up to Ingrid's room. They greeted Sam. The three of them sat near the bed for over an hour and waited for Rocco to give Cornelius the okay. When the nurses changed shifts, the new nurse, a stickler for the rules, came in the room and said, "Only two people are supposed to be in the room at any one time. Do you mind rotating? One of you can stay in the waiting area down the corridor?"

Sam stood. "I need to do some studying anyway."

"You should head back to school," Simon said. "Your mother would want that."

"Maybe so," Sam said, "but I don't want that. I want to be here."

He turned and left.

Yvonne said, "He's special."

"Yes." Then: "I spoke to one of Paige's professors today."

"Oh?"

"He thinks Paige might have been raped on campus."

Yvonne said nothing. She just stared at her sister in the bed.

"Did you hear me?"

"Yeah, I heard you, Simon."

He watched her face for a tell. "Wait, you knew?"

"I'm her godmother. She...she used to confide in me."

He could feel the red rush to his face. "And you didn't think to tell me?"

"She made me promise not to."

"So if Drew came to me with a huge problem and told me not to tell you—"

"I would expect you to keep your promise," Yvonne said. "I'd trust that I picked you to be his godfather so Drew would have someone to talk to when he didn't want to go to Robert or me."

It was pointless to argue about it right now. "So what happened?" Simon asked.

"I helped Paige get private counseling."

"No, I mean, what exactly happened with this rapist?"

"It's a long story."

"Seriously, Yvonne?"

"Paige was having trouble remembering the details. He may have slipped her something, I don't know. She didn't report it for days, so the rape kit didn't help very much. The therapy was helping her, I think. She was trying to remember, work through it slowly."

"How about charging the bastard?"

"I encouraged that. But she wasn't ready. She had no memory of it. She couldn't even say for certain if she consented or not." Yvonne held up her hand to stop his next question. "It was messy, Simon."

He shook his head. "You should have told me."

"I begged Paige to. I did. Even after she shut me out. But yeah, at some point she stopped talking to me too. She said she was fine now, that it was taken care of. I don't know what happened. Paige stopped taking my calls, she started up with that Aaron guy..."

"And you just kept this from us? She's spiraling like this, and you still never said a word."

"I never said a word. To you."

He couldn't believe what she was saying. "Ingrid?"

There was a knock on the door behind them. Simon spun toward it. Cornelius opened the door and leaned his head inside.

"Come on," he said. "Rocco's waiting."

CHAPTER

THIRTY-SIX

Ash took the Major Deegan Expressway south off the Cross Bronx.

"You have to assume," Ash said to Dee, "that more of the fourteen sons are going to send their DNA to those genealogy sites."

Dee Dee nodded, flipping the phone back on to check for messages.

"So what then?"

"The Truth won't survive the week. I don't understand all the legal stuff, but once his estate goes into probate, it's harder to make a claim."

"Still," Ash said. "Someone is bound to put this together."

"How so?"

"Another one of the Truth's sons puts his DNA into the system."

"Okay."

"He sees he has three or four other brothers—and they're all dead."

"Right. One was shot in a robbery. One committed suicide. One is just missing, probably a runaway. One should be, I don't know, stabbed, maybe by a drug-addled homeless nut. Horrible set of coincidences. And that's if he's able to track them down. Which isn't easy. Their accounts stay active after their deaths. So first any new son would email his dead half brothers. They wouldn't write back. He'd probably just drop it there, but even if he somehow tracks them all down and figures out the connection and somehow gets law enforcement from various states to cooperate on these old crimes, what will they find?"

Dee Dee had thought this through.

"Ash?"

"They'd find nothing," he said.

"Right, so— Oh, hold up."

"What?"

"A text came from Simon Greene." She read it aloud:

Heading to Cornelius's apartment where we first met. May find a lead. How's it by you?

"Any thoughts on who Cornelius is?" Ash asked.

"None."

"This isn't good."

"It'll be fine."

"And what's the deal with Mother Adiona?" he asked.

"That I don't know."

"She told me not to trust you."

"But you do, Ash."

"I do, Dee Dee."

She smiled at him. "We can worry about her later, okay?"

They found a spot in front of some concrete barriers in the Mott Haven section of the Bronx. They both had guns on them. They also both had knives. This one was to look like a stabbing— something, Ash thought, that probably occurred a lot amongst the various drug factions on these streets.

He was about to open his door when he heard her say, "Ash?"

Her tone stopped him. He looked toward her. She gestured with her chin up ahead. She took out her phone and held up the image she'd screenshot from the PPG Wealth Management website.

"That's him, right?" she asked.

Ash took a look. No question. Simon Greene was walking into the building.

"Who is that with him?"

"My guess? Cornelius."

Dee Dee nodded. "I'm thinking this isn't going to be a stabbing, Ash."

"Yep."

She glanced toward the weapons bag in the backseat. "I'm thinking it's going to be more like a gun massacre."

Rocco was the kind of gigantic it was hard to fathom, so that each time you saw him, you were struck anew by the sheer size of him. When he strolled around Cornelius's apartment, Simon half expected to hear *fee-fie-fo-fum* à la "Jack and the Beanstalk."

Rocco squinted at the books on the shelves. "You read all these, Cornelius?"

"I have. You should try it. Reading gives you empathy."

"Is that a fact?" Rocco grabbed a book off the shelf, paged through it. "Do you have the fifty grand, Mr. Greene?"

"Do you have my daughter?" Simon countered.

"No."

"Then I don't have fifty grand."

"Where's Luther?" Cornelius asked.

"Stay cool, Cornelius. He's close by." Rocco lifted his mobile phone. "Luther?"

A voice came through the phone's tinny speaker. "I'm here, Rocco."

"Just stay put," Rocco said. "Our friend here doesn't have the money."

"I have money," Simon said. "It's not fifty grand, but if whatever you tell me helps me find my daughter, you get the full amount. You have my word."

"Your word?" Rocco was a big man and had a laugh to match. "And what, I'm just supposed to trust you because you white guys are so trustworthy?"

"No, none of that," Simon said.

"Then why?"

"Because I'm a father."

"Oooo." Rocco wiggled his fingers. "You think that impresses me?"

Simon said nothing.

"Only thing that impresses me right now is cash money."

Simon dropped the cash on the coffee table. "Almost ten thousand."

"That's not enough."

"It's all I could get on this short of notice."

"Then buh-bye."

Cornelius said, "Come on, Rocco."

"I want more."

"You'll get more," Simon said.

Rocco hemmed and hawed a bit, but the cash on the coffee table was calling to him. "So here's how it is: I got something to tell you first. It's pretty big. But then my boy Luther... Luther, you still there?"

From the phone: "Yeah."

"Okay, you stay there. Just in case they try something. A little insurance." Rocco flashed his teeth. "So when I'm done, I'm going to tell Luther to come in here, because he's got something way bigger to say."

Cornelius said, "We're listening."

Rocco picked up the cash. "I got a confirmed sighting of Paige."

Simon felt his pulse quicken. "When?"

Rocco started counting out the bills. "Two days after her old man got murdered. Seems your daughter stayed around here for a while. Hid maybe, I don't know. Then she got on the six."

The six train, Simon thought. Closest subway stop.

"Someone was pretty sure of that," Rocco said, still counting. "Not definite. But pretty sure. My other boy though, he's convinced he saw her. No doubt at all."

"Where?" Simon asked.

Rocco finished counting, frowned. "This is less than ten grand."

"I'll get you another ten tomorrow. Where did he see Paige?"

Rocco looked at Cornelius. Cornelius nodded.

"Port Authority."

"The bus terminal?"

"Yeah."

"Any idea where she was going?"

Rocco coughed into his fist. "Tell you what, Mr. Greene. I'm going to answer that question. Then Luther—Luther, get ready, okay?—is going to tell you the rest. For fifty K. I'm not going to negotiate either. You know why?"

Cornelius said, "Rocco, come on."

Rocco spread those huge hands wide. "Because when you hear what Luther has to say, you'll give us the money to keep our mouths shut."

Simon's eyes locked on Rocco's. Neither man blinked. But Simon could see. Rocco meant it. Whatever Luther had to say would be huge.

"But first, let me answer your question. Buffalo. Your daughter—and this is confirmed by a reliable source—got on a bus for Buffalo."

Simon scoured his brain for anyone he or his daughter knew in the Buffalo area. Nothing came to him. Of course, she could have gotten off earlier, really any place in upstate New York, but he still couldn't come up with anybody.

"Luther?"

"Yeah, Rocco."

"Come up, okay?"

Rocco disconnected the phone. Then he smiled at Cornelius. "It was you, wasn't it, Cornelius?"

Cornelius said nothing.

"You the one who shot Luther."

Cornelius just stared him down. Rocco laughed and held up his hands.

"Whoa, whoa, don't worry, I ain't going to tell him. But here's the thing you're about to find out. He had his reasons."

"What reasons?" Simon asked.

Rocco moved toward the door. "Self-defense."

"What are you talking about? I wasn't going to—"

"Not you, man."

Simon just looked at him.

"Think about it. Luther didn't shoot *you*. He shot your wife."

Rocco smiled and reached for the doorknob.

Several things happened at once.

From the corridor, Luther screamed, "Rocco, look out!"

Rocco, working on instinct, flung open the door.

And then the bullets started to fly.

CHAPTER

THIRTY-SEVEN

Five minutes earlier, Ash pushed open the door loaded with graffiti.

He entered the poorly lit foyer first. Dee Dee followed. They didn't have their weapons out. Not yet. But their hands were poised near them just in case.

"Why would Simon Greene be here?" Ash whispered.

"Visiting his daughter, I imagine."

"So why not say that in his text to Elena Ramirez? Why talk about this Cornelius guy?"

Dee put her foot on the rickety step. "I don't know."

"We should step back," Ash said. "Do more research."

"You step back then."

"Dee."

"No, Ash, listen to me. Elena Ramirez and Simon Greene are cancers. We need to get them now or they'll spread. You want to be more cautious? Fine. Go back to the car. I have enough firepower to handle this."

"That's not going to happen," Ash said. "And you know that."

A small smile toyed with her lips. "Are you being sexist again?"

"You wouldn't leave me either."

"That's true."

"This place," he said. "You know what it reminds me of?"

Dee Dee nodded. "Mr. Marshall's brewery. The smell of stale beer."

He was amazed that she'd remember. JoJo Marshall had been one of Ash's foster fathers, not hers. He made Ash work the fermenters. Dee Dee had visited him there a few times and clearly, like him, had never gotten over that stink.

She started up the stairs. Ash did a little hop-step, so he could take the lead, but she blocked him off with her body and disapproving glare. So he stayed one step back. No one passed them on the stairs. In the distance they could hear the faint hum of someone playing a television too loudly.

Other than that, not a sound.

Ash glanced down the corridor of the second floor as Dee Dee continued to ascend.

No one. That was good.

When they reached the third floor, Dee Dee looked back at him. Ash nodded. They both took out their guns. They kept them low, by their sides, and maybe if someone opened a door right now, what with the crappy lighting in this place, maybe that person wouldn't see that they were both carrying FN 5.7s with twenty-round mags.

They made their way to apartment B. Ash knocked on the heavy metal door.

They were ready.

No answer.

He knocked again. Nothing.

"Someone has to be home," Dee Dee whispered. "We saw Greene come in."

Ash took a look at the heavy metal door, put on, no doubt, to fortify against break-ins, but it had been done stupidly. The door was made of steel, but the doorframe was wood.

Not strong wood based on what Ash had seen of this place.

Ash took out his gun and nodded for Dee Dee to get ready. He raised his foot and kicked in the spot where the bolt slid into the wood.

The wood gave way as if it were made of dried twigs.

The door flew open. Ash and Dee Dee rushed inside.

No one.

Two single mattresses lay on either side of the floor. There were dried bloodstains on the floor. Ash took it all in, took it in fast, and knew something was seriously wrong. He looked on the floor. He bent down.

"What?" Dee Dee whispered.

"Yellow tape."

"What?"

"This was a crime scene."

"That doesn't make any sense."

They heard a door nearby open.

Dee Dee moved fast. She dropped her weapon onto the mattress, stepped outside, and closed what was left of the door behind her. A man had exited his apartment. He wore earbuds with music turned up so loud, Dee Dee could hear it from fifteen feet away.

He was near the stairs, almost ready to start heading down, and he hadn't seen her yet. She stayed frozen, hoping that he wouldn't turn toward her.

But he did.

When the man saw her, he pulled out his earbuds.

Dee Dee rewarded him with her full-wattage smile.

"Hello," she said, almost making this simple greeting a double entendre. "I'm looking for Cornelius."

"Wrong floor."

"Oh?"

"Cornelius is on the second floor. Apartment B."

"Silly me."

"Yeah."

He looked as though he was going to come toward her. That wouldn't be good. She slipped her hand into her back pocket and readied the switchblade.

She'd have to slice this guy's throat. Do it quickly and quietly.

Dee Dee waved at him. "Thanks for the help. Take care now."

The man looked as though he might keep walking back toward her, but it was almost as though something primitive told him it was best to move on.

"Yeah," he said, pulling up. "You too."

They looked at each other another long moment before the man turned and hurried down the stairs. Dee Dee listened for a second, wondering whether he might stop on the second floor and warn Cornelius. But she could hear him reach the ground floor and push open that graffiti-filled door.

When he was gone, Ash exited the apartment door and handed Dee Dee her gun. He'd heard it all. They moved silently to the stairwell and made their way to the second-floor apartment B. Ash put his ear near the door.

Voices. Several of them.

Ash gave the signal. They got the guns ready. The plan was simple. Burst in with guns a-blazing. Kill any and all inhabitants.

He pointed the gun at the lock so as to shoot it—no need for any kind of subtlety—but suddenly two things happened at once.

The doorknob started to turn.

And from down the corridor, a man shouted, "Rocco, look out!"

———————

"Rocco, look out!"

Simon heard the first burst of gunfire as Rocco pulled open the door.

They say time slows down at times of great danger, almost like Neo being able to see and dodge bullets in *The Matrix*. That was just an illusion, of course. Time is constant. But Simon remembered reading that this particular time illusion was caused by how we store memory. The richer and denser the memory of an event—for example, during moments when you are terrified—the longer you perceive that event lasted.

This phenomenon also explains why time seems to go faster as you age. When you're a child, experiences are new and so your memories are fresh and intense—so again time seems to slow down. As you grow older, especially when you are stuck in a routine, very few new or vibrant memories are being laid and so time flies by. That's why when a child looks back on summer, it seemed to last forever. For adults, it's barely a blink.

So now, as Simon heard a man—Luther—scream through the bullet blasts—time seemed to be knee-deep in molasses.

Rocco pulled the door all the way open.

Simon stood a few feet behind Rocco, so the big man's broad back and shoulders blocked his view. He could see nothing.

But he could hear the bullets.

Rocco's body convulsed. He hitched and jerked, almost as if he were doing some kind of macabre dance. His feet started backpedaling.

More bullets landed.

When the big man finally dropped on his back, the building shook. Rocco's eyes were open and stared unseeing at the ceiling. Blood blanketed his chest.

Now Simon could see the doorway.

Two people.

A man approximately thirty was turned to his left, firing his weapon down the corridor, probably in the direction of the now-silent Luther. A woman with short red hair, maybe a few years younger than the man, aimed down and fired two more bullets into Rocco's head.

Then she raised the gun toward Cornelius.

Simon yelled, "No!"

Cornelius was already moving, already reacting, but it wasn't going to be enough. The woman was too close, the shot too easy.

She would not miss.

Simon launched himself toward her, trying to get to the woman before she could shoot. He screamed, hoping to distract her, hoping to buy Cornelius tenths of a second.

Just as the woman began to pull the trigger, Simon reached the door and shoved hard. The edge of the door slammed against her forearm, throwing off the woman's aim just enough.

No time to hesitate.

When Simon landed on his feet, he reached around the door for the woman's wrist. His fingers found skin—some part of the arm maybe—and his hand started to encircle it. He almost had a grip on her, a good grip, but then someone, maybe the man, crashed his body against the other side of the door.

The door smashed into Simon's face, sending him spiraling.

Simon tumbled onto Rocco's dead body.

The young woman stepped into the room and aimed the gun at Cornelius, who was trying to get his gun out of his pocket while running for the fire-escape window.

But Cornelius was too late.

He had no chance.

Simon didn't know if time was slowing down or if the calculations running through his brain had sped up. But he could see the truth now.

There was no way both he and Cornelius could survive.

No way.

Which left Simon with no choice.

From his spot on the ground, he kicked the door, so that it would close on the woman. Almost casually, the woman stopped it with her foot. It had seemed a weak effort on Simon's part, a poor attempt to stop her entry.

But it had bought Simon time.

Not enough time to stop the carnage.

But enough time for Simon to scramble-jump toward Cornelius.

The move had surprised the woman. She had expected Simon to come at her. But he'd gone the other direction. It wouldn't save Simon. Just the opposite, in fact. It put him in the path of the gunfire.

His body was all that stood between the woman's bullets and Cornelius.

She fired anyway.

Simon felt the searing pain as a bullet smacked his lower back on the left.

He didn't stop.

He felt another hit him in the right shoulder.

Simon flung himself toward Cornelius like a defensive end on a blindside blitz, wrapping his arms around his friend's waist.

He tackled Cornelius into the window.

Time must have slowed down for Cornelius too. Cornelius didn't fight his natural instincts. He went with the tackle, letting his body fall back, using the time to pull his gun all the way out.

The two men both fell backward. The window shattered upon impact.

Cornelius had his gun out now. He reached over Simon's shoulder and fired as they started to fall.

Somewhere in the hail of gunfire, Simon heard a man grunt and a woman scream, "Ash!"

Cornelius and Simon, still entwined, landed hard on the fire-escape grate—Cornelius on his back, Simon, his grip slackening, on top of him.

The impact knocked the gun from Cornelius's hand. Simon watched the gun plummet toward hard asphalt.

The woman again, her cry pained: "Ash! No!"

Simon's eyes started to flutter. His mouth filled with something coppery, and he realized that it was blood. He managed then to roll off Cornelius. Simon tried to speak. He wanted to tell Cor-

nelius to run, that the redheaded woman wasn't hit and that she'd
be on them soon.

But the words wouldn't come out.

He looked at Cornelius. Cornelius shook his head.

He wouldn't leave.

This whole thing—from Rocco turning the knob to now—took
fewer than five seconds.

From inside the room, the woman let loose a primitive, guttural scream.

And now, even in this state, even as he could feel some sort of
life force leaving his body, Simon realized that the young woman
was coming toward them.

Go, Simon tried to tell Cornelius.

He wouldn't.

Simon could see the redheaded woman reaching the window.
The gun was in her hand.

Again: no choice.

Using whatever strength he had left—and perhaps the element of surprise—Simon pushed Cornelius down the fire-escape
steps.

Cornelius started tumbling down them, head feet, head feet,
like a somersault.

It might hurt, Simon thought. It might break a few bones.

But it probably wouldn't kill him.

There was nothing left now. Simon knew that. He could hear
the sirens nearing, but they'd be too late. He dropped onto his
back and looked up into the young woman's green eyes. He'd
maybe held out a glimmer of hope that there would be some
mercy in them, some hesitation, but once he saw them, once his
gaze met hers, he knew that whatever last hope he had was gone.

She would kill him. And she would enjoy it.

She leaned her body out the window. She pointed the gun at
his head.

And then she was gone.

From behind her, someone had pushed her out the window. Simon heard the scream and then a sick splat as she landed on the asphalt.

Simon looked up and saw another woman—an old woman wearing an odd gray uniform with red stripes—appear. She looked at him with concern, hurried out to the fire escape, and tried to stem the bleeding.

"It's over," the woman said to him.

He wanted to ask her who she was, if she knew Paige, anything, but his mouth had too much blood in it. He felt his body weakening and slackening, his eyes rolling back. As the darkness descended, he could still hear the sirens.

"Our children will be safe now."

And then there was nothing.

THIRTY-EIGHT

One month passed.

Simon's injuries required three operations, eighteen days in the same hospital as Ingrid, several morphine drips, and two weeks (thus far) of physical therapy. There was pain and damage and perhaps, in an odd reminder of Elena Ramirez, he would walk with a limp or even a cane for the remainder of his days, but his injuries ended up not being life-threatening.

Cornelius came out of it all with a sprained ankle and minor bruises. Rocco and Luther had both been killed by gunfire. Same with a hired hit man named Ashley "Ash" Davis. His partner, a young cult member named Diane "Dee Dee" Lahoy, had landed headfirst, cracking her skull. She had not yet regained consciousness and all indications were that she never would.

Detective Isaac Fagbenle tried to explain it to him, though it was taking some time for various law enforcement authorities to put it all together. There was something about a cult called Truth Haven and secret adoptions and hired hits.

But details were beyond sketchy.

To complicate matters, Casper Vartage, the leader of Truth

Haven, had died of natural causes. His two sons claimed complete innocence and had top-notch lawyers protecting them. Maybe, the lawyers claimed, Casper Vartage had done something—that they couldn't say—but he was dead now and his sons knew nothing.

"We'll get them," Fagbenle had told Simon.

But Simon wasn't so sure. The two killers who could best testify as to what the Vartage sons may have done were both out of commission. The police's best hope seemed to be the woman who had saved Simon's life, a woman who identified herself as Mother Adiona. They couldn't find a real name for her. That was how long she'd been in the cult. And they really couldn't hold her. She had committed no crime other than maybe saving Simon's life.

There was other stuff, of course. When Elena Ramirez learned about the illegal adoptions, Ash and Dee Dee, the police concluded, had killed her. There was CCTV of her at a Cracker Barrel Old Country Store getting in a car driven by Dee Dee Lahoy. It was believed that she was then taken to an empty cabin and murdered there, but her body had not yet been found. When the killers then looked at the texts on Elena's mobile phone and saw her communications with Simon, they knew that he had to be silenced too. There was more—how the half brothers, including Aaron Corval, had discovered each other, how they swore to keep their relationship a secret until they found their father, how one named Henry Thorpe discovered his mother too and that she had been a former cult member who ended up confronting and thus tipping off the Vartages.

But there had been nothing new about Paige.

During Simon's fifth night in the hospital, when the pain was pretty bad and he'd hit the morphine pump for all he was worth, he woke up in a semi-daze to see Mother Adiona sitting by his bedside.

"They were slaughtering all the sons," Mother Adiona said to him.

Simon knew this, though the motive remained murky. Maybe

the cult was trying to cover up their past crime of selling babies. Or maybe the murders of these men were part of some weird ritual or prophesy. No one seemed to know.

"I believe in the Truth, Mr. Greene. It sustains me. I have been its servant for almost my entire life. I birthed a son, and the Truth told me that he would be one of our next leaders. I raised him as such. I birthed another son and when the Truth told me that this son would not be able to stay with us, I let him go, even though that meant I would never see my own boy again."

Simon watched her through the hazy gauze of his painkillers.

"But last year, I used a DNA site because I wanted to know what became of my son. Harmless enough. Just a little knowledge. A little"—she almost smiled—"truth. Do you know what I found?"

Simon shook his head.

"My son's name is Nathan Brannon. He was raised by Hugh and Maria Brannon, two schoolteachers, in Tallahassee, Florida. He graduated with honors from Florida State. He married his high school sweetheart and has three boys—the oldest is ten, and then six-year-old twins. He's now a schoolteacher too—fifth grade—and by all accounts is a good man."

Simon tried to sit up, but the drugs had left him too exhausted.

"He wanted to meet me. My son, I mean. But I turned him down. Can you imagine how hard that was, Mr. Greene?"

Simon shook his head and managed to say, "No, I can't."

"But you see, it was enough for me to know that my son was happy. It had to be. It was what the Truth wanted."

Simon moved his hand closer to hers. The older woman took it. They sat there for a moment, in the dark, the rustle of the hospital distant background music.

"But then I found out that they wanted to murder my boy." She finally looked down and met his eye. "I spent my whole life bending for my beliefs. But this...you bend too far, you break. Do you understand?"

"Of course."

"So I had to stop them. I didn't want to hurt anyone. But I had no choice."

"Thank you," Simon said.

"I have to go back now."

"Back where?"

"Truth Haven. It's still my home."

Mother Adiona rose and moved toward the door.

"Please." Simon swallowed. "My daughter. She was dating one of these sons."

"So I heard."

"She's missing."

"I heard that too."

"Please help me," Simon said. "You're a parent. You understand."

"I do." Mother Adiona opened the door. "But I don't know anything more."

And then she was gone.

A week later, Simon begged Fagbenle to let him study the files. Fagbenle, perhaps pitying him, acquiesced.

Ingrid seemed to be improving, so there was some glimmer of light there. Despite what you see on television, you don't just come out of a coma. The process is more two steps up, one step back. Ingrid had regained consciousness and spoken to him twice in short spurts. In both cases, Ingrid had been encouragingly lucid. But the last one was over a week ago. There had been no improvement since then.

From the day he was shot, Simon kept digging because the biggest question remained unanswered.

Where was Paige?

He didn't get the answer for days, then weeks.

It took, in fact, a month.

A month after he had been shot, when Simon was finally well enough, he headed to Port Authority and took a bus trip to Buffalo. He stared out the window all seven hours, hoping against hope that something he'd see would spark a thought.

Nothing did.

When he arrived, he walked around the bus terminal for two hours. Simon was sure that if he just circled the block a few times, he'd find a clue.

He didn't.

With his body aching—the trip was probably too much too fast—Simon climbed back on the bus, squeezed into his seat, and took the seven-hour trip back.

Again he stared out the window.

And again nothing.

It was almost two in the morning when the bus pulled back into Port Authority. Simon took the A train north to the hospital. Ingrid was out of intensive care now and in a private room, though she remained unconscious. There was a cot in the room, so that he could sleep with his wife. Some nights, Simon felt that Sam and Anya needed him home. But most nights, like this one, he made his way up to Washington Heights and kissed his wife on the forehead and slept on the cot next to her.

Tonight though, one month after he was shot, there was someone else in Ingrid's room when he arrived.

The lights were off, so he could only see her sitting in silhouette next to Ingrid's bed.

He froze in the doorway. His eyes opened wide. Simon put his hand on his mouth, but his muffled cries were still audible. He felt his knees start to buckle.

That was when Paige turned around and said, "Dad?"

And Simon burst into tears.

CHAPTER
THIRTY-NINE

P aige helped her father up and into a chair.

"I can't stay," Paige said, "but it's been a month."

Simon was still putting himself back together. "A month?"

"Clean."

And she was. He could see it. His heart leapt. His baby looked drawn and pale and harried, but she also looked clear-eyed and sober and...He felt the tears come again, this time for joy, but he bit them back.

"I'm not there yet," she warned. "I may never be. But I'm better."

"So this whole time—"

"I didn't know any of this. We aren't allowed electronics. No access to family or friends or the outside world at all. That's the rules. Nothing for a full month. It was my best chance, Dad. My only chance really."

Simon was just numb.

"I have to go back to the retreat. You need to understand that. I'm not ready for the real world. We agreed on a twenty-

four-hour pass, and that's just because of this emergency. I need
to go back. Even being here this short of a time, I can feel the
pull stronger—"

"You'll go back," Simon said. "I'll drive you."

Paige turned toward her mother's bed. "This is because of me."

"No," Simon said. "You can't think that way."

Simon moved closer to her. She still looked so fragile, so damn
fragile, and now he worried that if Paige blamed herself, if she
took on that guilt, maybe that would make her want to slip back
into the world of oblivion.

"It's not your fault," he said. "No one blames you, least of all
your mother and me. Okay?"

She nodded a little too hesitantly.

"Paige?"

"Yes, Daddy."

"Do you want to tell me what happened?"

"When I came back to the room and saw Aaron dead...I hid.
I thought...I thought the police would think I killed him. It was
awful, seeing what was done to him, but part of me, I don't know,
Aaron was gone. Finally gone. Part of me felt free. Do you know
what I mean?"

Simon nodded.

"So I came to the retreat."

"How did you know about the place?" he asked.

She blinked and looked away.

"Paige?"

"I'd been there before," she said.

"When?"

"Do you remember when you saw me in Central Park?"

"Of course."

"I had been at the retreat before that."

"Wait, when?"

"Right before. To get clean. And it'd been working. That's what
I thought. But then Aaron found me. He sneaked into my room

one night. Shot me up while I was asleep. I disappeared with him the next day."

Simon's head spun. "Hold up, you were in rehab right before I saw you in the park?"

"Yes."

"I don't understand. How did you find this retreat?"

Paige looked toward the bed.

Simon couldn't believe it. "Your mother?"

"She took me."

Simon looked toward Ingrid too, as if maybe she would wake up right now and explain.

"I came to her," Paige said. "My one last hope. She knew this place. She'd been there before, years ago. They do things differently, she told me. So I tried it. And it was working. Or maybe it wasn't. It's easy to blame someone else, but maybe..."

Simon took the blows from these new revelations, trying to focus on what was important.

His daughter was back. His daughter was back, and she was clean.

He asked the next question as gently as possible. "Why didn't Mom tell me she was helping you?"

"I told her not to. That was part of the deal."

"Why didn't you want me to know?"

Paige turned to him. He looked into his baby's pained eyes and wondered how long it had been since he looked at her, really looked at her, like this. "Your face," she said.

"What?"

"When I failed before, when I let you down, your face, the look of disappointment..." She stopped, shook her head as though to clear it. "If I failed again and saw your face, I thought maybe I'd kill myself."

Simon put his hand back to his mouth. "Oh, honey."

"I'm sorry."

"Don't be. Please? I'm sorry if I ever made you feel that way."

Paige started nervously scratching at her arms. Simon could see the needle marks, though they seemed to be fading.

"Dad?"

"Yes?"

"I need to get back now."

"I'll drive you."

———

They stopped by the apartment on the way. Paige woke up her two siblings. Simon used his iPhone and filmed the ecstatic tears as his three children briefly but intensely reunited. He'd play the video for Ingrid. It didn't matter whether she heard it through the coma or not. He would play it for her and himself over and over.

The drive back up north was a long one. He didn't mind. For the first hours, Paige slept.

That left Simon alone with his own thoughts.

So many emotions ricocheted through him. He felt joy and relief at seeing Paige—clean Paige!—again. That was the overriding emotion. He rode that wave and tried to ignore the others—the worry about what would come next, the sorrow that he'd made Paige feel such dread about his reaction, the confusion about why Ingrid kept this huge secret from him.

How could she?

How could Ingrid have not told him about taking Paige to rehab? How could she have not said anything about it after he'd seen her in the park and had that confrontation with Aaron? It was one thing to keep your promise to your child. He got that. But that wasn't how they operated as a couple.

They told each other everything.

Or so he thought.

Simon was just remembering what Rocco said, about how Luther shot Ingrid, when Paige woke up and reached for the water bottle.

"How are you feeling?" he asked her.

"Okay. This is such a long ride, Dad. I could have just taken the bus back."

"Yeah, that wasn't going to happen."

Simon shot her a weary smile. She didn't return it.

"You can't visit me at the retreat," Paige said. "Not for another month. No visitors."

"Okay."

"They let me come down because I didn't want you to worry."

"Thank you."

He drove some more.

"So how did it work?" he asked her.

"How did what work?"

"When your first month was up, this retreat let you contact us?"

"Yes."

"You read about what happened?"

Paige nodded. "My counselor at the clinic had seen a news report. She told me about it."

"When?"

"Last night."

"So your counselor knew and kept it from you?"

"Yes. It was my only chance, Dad. Total isolation. Please understand."

"I do." Simon changed lanes. "You know we became friends with your old landlord Cornelius."

Paige turned toward him.

"He saved your mother's life."

"How?"

He filled her in on their visit to the Bronx—the whole story of how they'd gone to her apartment and met Cornelius and gone to Rocco's place in that basement.

"Cornelius was really nice to me," Paige said when he finished.

"He also told us you ran out with blood on your face two days before Aaron was killed."

Paige turned away from him and looked out her side window. "Did Aaron beat you?"

"Just that once."

"Badly?"

"Yes."

"So you ran away. And then, according to the police, that hit man killed him."

Paige's tone was off when she said, "I guess."

And he could hear the lie in his daughter's voice.

Simon knew there was something wrong with the police's theory on Aaron Corval's murder. On the one hand, it made perfect sense, it was simple, it fit. Sort of. The cult was killing the boys who were illegally adopted. Aaron Corval was one of those babies, ergo he'd been one of their targets. Ash and Dee Dee had returned to the scene because they needed to kill Simon.

But how could they have known Simon would be there?

Simon had scoured through all the information. He'd seen the E-ZPass records and noted that Ash and Dee Dee's car had never gone near the hospital. So they couldn't have followed him.

Then something else caught Simon's eye.

A witness, Cornelius's tenant Enrique Boaz, claimed to have seen Dee Dee on the third floor right before the shooting on the second floor in Cornelius's apartment.

Why? Why would she be on the third floor?

To the police this had been a small anomaly, no big deal: Every case has inconsistencies like this. But it niggled at the back of Simon's brain. So Simon went back. With Cornelius by his side, he questioned Enrique and uncovered a possible clue:

Dee Dee had been standing right in front of Aaron and Paige's room.

Again: Why? If you already killed Aaron, why would you go back to his room? Why would you, as Cornelius had noticed after the cops left, kick down the door to get in?

It didn't add up.

Unless you hadn't been there before.

"Paige?"

"Yes?"

"What did you do after Aaron beat you?"

"I ran."

"Where?"

"I . . . I went to get a fix."

Then he just asked it. "You didn't call Mom?"

Silence.

"Paige?"

"Please let this go."

"Did you call Mom?"

"Yes."

"And what did she say?"

"I . . ." She squeezed her eyes shut. "I told her what I did. I told her I had to run away."

"What else did you say, Paige?"

"Dad. Please. Please let this go."

"Not until we both tell the truth. And Paige? The truth never leaves this car. Never. Aaron was scum. His death wasn't murder—it was self-defense. He was killing you every day. Poisoning you. And when you tried to break free, he went back and poisoned you again. Do you understand?"

His daughter nodded.

"So what happened?"

"Aaron beat me that day, Dad. With his fists."

Simon felt that rage engulf him again.

"I couldn't take it anymore. But I knew I could pull out of it—I could be free—if he was just . . ."

"Gone," Simon said, finishing the thought for her.

"Remember what you saw in the park? The way I looked?"

He nodded.

"I had to break his hold on me."

Simon waited. Paige stared straight out the windshield in front of them.

"So yeah, Dad, I killed him. I killed him and made it all bloody. Then I ran away."

Simon just kept on driving. He gripped the wheel so tightly he feared he might rip it right out of the dashboard.

"Dad?"

"You're my daughter. I'll always protect you. Always. And I'm proud of you. You're trying to do the right thing."

She moved in next to him. Simon put his arm around her, kept the other hand on the wheel.

"But you didn't kill Aaron."

He could feel her stiffen under his arm.

"The beating was two days before he was murdered."

"Dad, please let it go."

How Simon wished that he could. "You called your mother. Just like you said. You asked for help."

Paige huddled closer. He could feel her quivering. It worried him, pushing her like this, but they had to get there.

"Did Mom tell you to stay away that night?"

Her voice was weak. "Dad, please."

"Because I know your mom, and I would have seen the situation the same way. We'd pick you up again and take you to this great rehab place—but as long as Aaron was alive, whatever twisted bond you two shared, well, he'd find you again. You two were entangled in some way I'll never understand. Aaron was like a parasite who had to be killed."

"So that's what I did," Paige said. She tried to say it with bravado and confidence, but it just fell flat.

"No, sweetheart, you didn't. That was why Luther shot Mom. He saw her that night. That was what he was going to tell me before he got killed. Luther saw her leave your apartment or maybe he saw the actual killing, I don't know. So then a few days later, when he sees your mother near Rocco, he figures maybe she's going to kill him too. Aaron worked for Rocco, right? That's why Luther pulled out his gun. That's why he shot Mom first, not me. That's why he kept insisting it was self-defense."

Fagbenle had been right from the beginning.

"*Occam's razor. You know it?*"

"*I'm not in the mood, Detective.*"

"*It states—*"

"*I know what it states—*"

"*—that the simplest explanation is usually the right one.*"

"And what's the simplest explanation, Detective?"

"*You killed Aaron Corval. Or your wife did. I wouldn't blame either of you. The man was a monster. He was slowly poisoning your daughter, killing her right in front of your eyes.*"

Fagbenle had even noted that Ingrid could have sneaked over to the Bronx during a work break. They had her on CCTV leaving. Ingrid knew the timing. She made sure that Aaron was alone.

"Paige?"

"I didn't know Mom was going to kill him."

She pulled away from him now and sat all the way up.

"I came back to the apartment early and saw...Mom wore hospital scrubs. They were covered in blood. I guess she dumped them later. But when I saw her, I freaked out. I ran."

"Where?"

"Another basement. Like Rocco's. I got two fixes. Laid down there for hours, I didn't even know how long. And when I woke up, I finally saw the truth."

"What truth?"

"My mom had killed someone. Think about that for a second. They say you need to hit bottom before you can get better. When you realize that you made your mother kill a man, that's rock bottom."

They were silent for a while.

Then Simon asked, "How come Mom didn't call the retreat and see if that's where you'd gone?"

"Maybe she did. But I wasn't there yet. It took me days to make my way up."

And by then she was in a coma.

"Dad?"

"What, sweetheart?"

"Can we please let this go now?"

Simon thought about it. "I think so."

"And it never leaves this car?"

"Never."

"That means Mom too."

"What?"

"Don't tell her you know. Okay? Just let it go."

CHAPTER
FORTY

I n the weeks that passed, as Ingrid started to recover and life got better, Simon wondered about his daughter's request.

Should what they said never leave the car? Was it really best not to tell his wife he knew that she had killed a man?

Was it best to live with that secret?

On the surface, the answer seemed to be yes.

Simon watched his wife come back to him and his family.

Eventually Ingrid regained enough strength to come home.

Weeks turned into months.

Good months.

Paige continued to improve too. Eventually the retreat let her come home.

Sam headed back to Amherst with the start of a new semester. Anya was doing well in school. Simon was back at work. Soon too, Ingrid returned to her patients.

Life was more than returning to normal.

Life was good. Really good. And when life is good, maybe it's best to let sleeping dogs lie.

There was laughter and joy in their lives. There were gorgeous walks through Central Park. There were dinners with friends and nights at the theater. There was love and light and family.

Ingrid and Simon both embraced Paige's return. They gave her all the support they could, while worrying that whatever demon Aaron had placed in her body may be weak or dormant, but it was still there, still waiting to pounce.

Because demons never die.

But neither do secrets.

That was the problem. All of those good things were in the room. But so too was that secret.

One night, during their walk through Central Park, Ingrid and Simon stopped in Strawberry Fields. Simon normally avoided this route. This had been where he'd seen Paige strangling out that Beatles tune. Which song was it again? He didn't remember. Strike that. He didn't want to remember.

But Ingrid wanted to sit on the bench. Out of habit he read the inscription:

> This is for Jersey, the good dog, who would be happy to
> share this bench with you

Ingrid took his hand and stared out and said, "You know."

"Yes."

"You understand why I did it."

He nodded. "I do."

"It was like she was drowning. And every time she came to the surface he would drag her back under again."

"You don't have to justify it to me."

Ingrid took his hand. He squeezed hers and held on.

"You planned it," he said.

"As soon as she called."

"And you made it violent and bloody—"

"—so the police would think it was a drug hit," she said.

He looked off, then back at her. "Why didn't you ask me to help?"

"Three reasons," she said.

"I'm listening."

"One, my job is to protect you too. Because I love you."

"I love you too."

"Two, if I got caught, I wanted one of us to be free to raise the children."

Simon had to smile at that. "Practical."

"Yes."

"And three?"

"I thought maybe you'd talk me out of it."

He said nothing. Would he have really gone along with a plan to murder Aaron Corval?

He didn't know.

"Some adventure," he said.

"Yes."

He stared at his wife and got the "overwhelms" again.

"I love our family," Ingrid said.

"I do too."

She put her head on his shoulder as she had done a million times before.

There are few moments of pure bliss in this life. Most of the time, you don't realize that you are having one of those moments until they are over. But that wasn't the case right now. Right now, as Simon sat with the woman he loved, he knew.

And she knew.

This was bliss.

And it wouldn't last.

EPILOGUE

T he state police found Elena Ramirez's body almost a year
after her murder.

There was a funeral for her in Chicago. Simon and
Cornelius decided to attend. They chose to drive rather than fly.
Cornelius planned the route, finding weird museums and road-
side sites so they could make stops.

Elena was laid to rest next to a man named Joel Marcus.

They overnighted at a hotel outside Chicago. On the drive
home the next morning, Simon asked, "Do you mind if we stop in
Pittsburgh?"

"Not at all," Cornelius said. Then, noticing the look on Simon's
face, he added, "What's up?"

"I just need to visit someone."

When Simon knocked on the door, a young man opened it and
peered out. "Doug Mulzer?"

"Yes."

Mulzer had not been able physically or emotionally to return
to Lanford College after his ordeal. Simon didn't care. Or maybe
he did. Maybe there had been enough vigilante justice.

"My name is Simon Greene. I'm Paige's father."

———

When they got back to New York City, Simon dropped off Cornelius and headed to PPG Wealth Management's office. It was late in the day, but Yvonne was still there. He pulled her aside and said, "I think I know what Ingrid's secret is."

———

That night, when he reached his apartment building, Suzy Fiske was holding the elevator door for him. She greeted him with a big smile and a kiss on the cheek.

"Hey," she said, "I see Sam is home from Amherst."

"Yeah, he came back tonight for break."

"So you got all three home?"

"Yup."

"That must be great."

Simon smiled. "It is."

"And I hear Paige enrolled at NYU."

"Yes. But she's still going to live at home."

"I'm really happy for you guys."

"Thank you, Suzy. I know I've already thanked you a million times—"

"And gave us that gift card for RedFarm. Which was too generous. We've eaten there like four times already."

The elevator stopped at Simon's floor. He got out and opened the door with his key. Bad Wolves' version of "Zombie" was playing over a Bluetooth speaker in the kitchen. Ingrid was singing the chorus:

"What's in your head, in your head, zombie..."

Simon leaned against the kitchen doorframe. Ingrid turned and smiled at him.

"Hi," Ingrid said.

"Hi."

"How was the trip?"

"Good," he said. "Sad."

"Your son is home."

"So I heard. What are you cooking?"

"My famous Asian salmon recipe. His favorite."

"I love you," he said.

"I love you too."

"Where's Paige?"

"She's in her room. Five minutes to dinner, okay?"

"Okay."

He headed down the corridor and knocked on her bedroom door. Paige said, "Come in."

His daughter still looked pale and drawn and harried, even after all this time, and he wondered whether that would ever leave her. There had been bad nights and sweats and nightmares and tears. It was a struggle and he wasn't sure that Paige would ever win it—he knew the odds—but maybe she would. He had wondered about Aaron's influence on Paige, their bizarre and twisted bond. Maybe again it was all simple. Like Fagbenle had said.

You kill a man to protect your child.

You kill a man, you save an addict.

"I never understood how you first connected with Aaron," he said. "That was the part I couldn't shake. Elena Ramirez saw Henry Thorpe's DNA test. It showed all the half brothers, including Aaron. But you took that DNA test too, Paige, didn't you?"

"Yes."

"So I never understood—what was your connection to Aaron? What would make you so attached to someone so awful?"

Paige had been pulling a hoodie out of her drawer. Now she stopped and waited.

"You know what struck me as weird about your apartment in the Bronx?" he continued. "There were two single mattresses— one on either side of the room." He spread his hands. "What kind of young couple doesn't share a bed?"

"Dad."

"Let me just finish this, okay? I went to see Doug Mulzer today in Pittsburgh. We need to talk about that at some point, about what he did to you, or maybe you have in your therapy sessions."

"I have."

"Okay, but see, he was attacked. Viciously."

"That was wrong," Paige said.

"Maybe, maybe not. That's not my point. But Doug told me that a man with a ski mask assaulted him. It was Aaron, right?"

"Yes. I should have never told him what Doug did to me."

"Why did you?"

Paige said nothing.

"I couldn't figure that out. But then Mulzer told me what Aaron kept screaming at him during the beating."

Tears came to Paige's eyes. They came to Simon's too.

"'No one hurts my sister.'"

Paige's shoulders slumped.

"When you took the DNA test, you did indeed find out that Aaron was your half brother, but not on your father's side." Simon could feel himself shaking. "You both had the same mother."

It took a few seconds, but Paige managed to raise her chin and look at him. "Yes."

"I checked with your aunt Yvonne. Your mom's big secret? She didn't model overseas when she was seventeen. She fell in with a cult. She got pregnant by the leader. But they told her...they told her that the baby was stillborn. She thought maybe they intentionally killed the baby. She became suicidal. Her family, your grandparents, they grabbed her and got her deprogrammed. At a retreat. The same one she took you to."

His daughter crossed the room and sat on her bed. Simon joined her.

"He was so damaged," Paige said. "His father abused him from a very young age."

"Aaron, you mean?"

She nodded. "And you have to remember where I was. I'd been assaulted by Doug Mulzer at school and then I take this DNA test and it was like my whole life had been a big lie. I felt lost, scared, confused. And now I had this new brother. We talked for hours. I told him about the assault. So he took care of that. It was awful, but I also felt, I don't know, protected maybe. Then Aaron got me high and it was like...I liked it. No, I loved it. It let me escape from everything. Aaron made sure I got high again and again, and..." She stopped, wiped her eyes. "I think he knew what he was doing."

"What do you mean?"

"I think Aaron loved the idea of a sister. He didn't want to lose me. He needed to keep me hooked so I didn't abandon him—and maybe, maybe he also wanted to get revenge on his birth mother. He was the child she threw away—why not destroy the one she kept?"

"And you never confronted your mother?"

"No, I did." She took a deep breath. "I came home and asked Mom if she ever had a child. She said no. I begged her to tell me the truth. She finally broke down. She told me about the cult. She said she'd been impregnated by an awful man, but the baby died."

Based on what Yvonne had just told him, Ingrid still believed that.

"I thought she was still lying to me. But you see, I didn't care anymore. I was a junkie by then. I only cared about my next fix. So I stole her jewelry—and went back to my brother."

That sick, twisted bond—it was forged in blood.

"You talked about hitting rock bottom," Simon said, feeling something harden in his chest, something that made it nearly impossible to breathe, "the fact that you'd forced your mother to kill someone..."

Paige squeezed her eyes shut tightly, so tightly, as though trying to wish this all away.

"...but she didn't just kill 'someone'..."

They both knew what was coming. Paige kept her eyes closed, bracing for the blow.

"...she killed her own son."

"We can't tell her, Dad."

Simon shook his head, remembered what he and Ingrid said on that bench in Central Park. "No more secrets, Paige."

"Dad—"

"Your mother even told me the truth about killing Aaron."

Paige slowly turned to face him, and Simon thought that she had never looked so clear-eyed. "This secret isn't like that. This secret will destroy her."

Through the door, they heard Ingrid call out in a happy singsong voice, "Dinner's ready! Wash up, everyone."

"We can't tell her, Dad."

"It might come out anyway. She may even already know."

"She doesn't know," Paige said. "The adoption agency doesn't have the records. Only we know the truth."

They headed to the table. The five of them—Simon, Ingrid, Paige, Sam, and Anya—took their seats. Sam started telling them about this goofy new lab partner he had in psych. It was a funny story. Ingrid laughed so hard, her eyes glistening. Ingrid caught Simon's eye and gave him that look, that look that said how lucky and blessed they were, that look that said hey, remember that moment in the park? This is one of those moments of bliss too. This one is even better because we are with our children. We are in that moment now, that pure bliss, and we are fortunate enough to realize it.

Simon looked across the table at Paige. Paige looked back at him.

The secret was at the table too.

If Simon kept quiet, the secret would always be with them.

He wondered what would be worse—having to live forever haunted by this secret or letting the woman he loved find out that she had murdered her own son.

The answer seemed clear. It may change tomorrow. But for tonight he knew what he had to do.

Simon might not have stepped in front of the bullet when Luther shot Ingrid. But he would step in front of the bullet now—no matter how much it hurt. He listened to his wife's beautiful laugh, and he knew that he would pay any price to keep hearing it.

So he made a solemn vow. There would be no more secrets.

Except this one.

ACKNOWLEDGMENTS

The author (who every once in a while likes to refer to himself in the third person) would like to thank the following people in no particular order: Ben Sevier, David Eagleman, Rick Friedman, Diane Discepolo, Selina Walker, Anne Armstrong-Coben, and, of course, the boys at the BMV Group—Pieter van der Heide, Daniel Madonia, and John Byren—for helping me understand Simon's occupation.

The author (still me) also wants to acknowledge Manny Andrews, Mariquita Blumberg, Louis van de Beek, Heather Grewe, Maish Isaacson, Robert and Yvonne Previdi, Randy Spratt, Eileen Vaughan, and Judy Zyskind. These people (or their loved ones) made generous contributions to charities of my choosing in return for having their names appear in the novel. If you would like to participate in the future, please visit HarlanCoben .com or email giving@harlancoben.com for details.

ABOUT THE AUTHOR

With more than seventy million books in print worldwide, Harlan Coben is the #1 *New York Times* bestselling author of numerous suspense novels, including *Don't Let Go*, *Home*, and *Fool Me Once*, as well as the multiaward-winning Myron Bolitar series. His books are published in forty-three languages around the globe and have been number one bestsellers in more than a dozen countries. He lives in New Jersey.

FIND OUT MORE ABOUT
ARLAN AND HIS BOOKS ONLINE AT

www.HarlanCoben.com

 @harlancobenbooks

 @HarlanCoben

 @HarlanCoben